TATHEA

Anne Perry

HEADLINE
FEATURE

First published in 1999 by
HEADLINE BOOK PUBLISHING

A HEADLINE FEATURE hardback

10 9 8 7 6 5 4 3 2 1

British Library Cataloguing in Publication Data

Perry, Anne, 1938-
1.Fantastic fiction
I.Title
823.9'14[F]

ISBN 0 7472 2260 6

Typeset by
Letterpart Limited, Reigate, Surrey

Printed and bound in Great Britain by
Mackays of Chatham PLC, Chatham, Kent

HEADLINE BOOK PUBLISHING
A division of Hodder Headline PLC
338 Euston Road
London NW1 3BH

TATHEA

TATHEA

Chapter One

The scream tore the night apart. Ta-Thea sat upright, the sweat cold on her skin. Moonlight poured through the long windows on to the marble floor. The screaming came again, then a man shouting and a clash of metal. But it was impossible, here in the palace!

Habi would be terrified, he was only four. She scrambled out of bed and ran to the door of his room. She put her hand on the latch and pushed, but there was a weight against it on the other side. She could hear more shouting somewhere in the main rooms, coming closer.

She threw herself against the door. She could not hear him crying. He must still be asleep, but he would waken any minute. The door yielded about a foot. She squeezed through, bruising herself, then nearly fell. Blocking the door was the body of the nurse, her neck and chest dark with blood.

Ta-Thea felt a wave of shock overtake her, suffocating her breath in the desert night and making her heart pound so that for a moment she could hear nothing else.

'Habi!' She lunged towards the small bed. He was lying there curled sideways, still asleep. She bent over and touched him. 'Habi,' she whispered. She felt the warmth of his shoulder, then something wet and sticky. His whole chest was covered with it. She stared without believing. It was black in the moonlight, but half her mind told her it would be scarlet if the torches were lit. 'Habi?' Her voice choked.

She was still bent over him, frozen and refusing to believe, when the outer door burst open, and light from the torches beyond fell across her. She turned slowly, too numb to be afraid.

It was Kol-Shamisha, captain of the Household Guard. His robes were torn and stained and there was blood on his sword.

She stared at him.

He closed the door and came towards her. 'Majesty! You must come, now! You cannot help them. They are all dead – even the Isarch.'

'Come?' she said foolishly. 'Where to? I can't leave!' She was still holding Habi as if he were alive. She did not lift him, some deep horror inside knowing his throat was severed.

'The desert,' Kol-Shamisha answered, his voice hoarse. 'The whole

1

city is in revolt. The palace is taken, but there may be people in the oases who will protect you. But you must come now.'

'I can't!' How could she leave? There were things to do – she could not leave Habi . . . for some stranger to wash, to mourn and to bury. Only she could do that . . .

Kol-Shamisha moved swiftly closer and gripped her arms.

'No!' She tried to push him away.

He pulled her and she fought. Beyond the door the sound of shouting and the clash of swords grew louder. She heard the slap of sandals on stone.

He hit her hard, a single blow, and the darkness closed over her.

When she regained her senses they were in the palace stable yard and Kol-Shamisha was shaking her. For a moment she did not remember, then it came back like a torrent of sickness. She struggled to sit up and he lifted her in his arms. It passed through her mind with amazement how gentle he was, as if he were cradling a child.

'We must ride, Majesty.' His voice was low and urgent. 'There are horses ready, one loyal groom, and the gatekeeper will let us out. We still have to get through the city. You must put on the groom's clothes. And bind your trousers for riding.'

'What?'

'Clothes, quickly.'

She did as she was told, her fingers fumbling to undo the muslin of her embroidered tunic and change it for the rough cotton. Some part of her brain understood. Urgency and fear drove her even while a part of her still knew she could not leave.

'Why?' she asked, looking over his shoulder towards the towering walls of the palace against the moonlit sky and its blaze of stars.

'I don't know,' he answered. 'We had no suspicion, but it's the whole Guard, much of the aristocracy and the army.'

'Everyone?' She was bewildered. How could it be that thousands of people she saw every day could have been feeling such a hatred concealed behind their smiling faces, their ordinary words, that they could rise and commit murder in the night? How could she not have seen it in their eyes, caught a thread of it in their voices? And Mon-Allat, her husband the Isarch . . . he saw ministers and generals every day, how could he have been so blind?

'Hurry!' Kol-Shamisha urged, pulling her towards the waiting horses. The noise of fighting was growing closer. There was little time. She climbed up into the saddle as one of the great gates swung open just wide enough for them to pass. Then she heard the clang as the keeper jammed the chains. It would buy them an hour, perhaps.

They rode close together through the wide streets of the city, its buildings tall and dark on either side of them. In the daylight one would have been able to see the squared pillars and the low relief carvings of battle and triumphant scenes on the rose and yellow sandstone walls. Now they were merely familiar masses against the sky.

They did not speak. Both knew that if they did not reach the western desert gate before news of the uprising closed it, they would be prisoners in Thoth-Moara, to be hunted down through the alleys, cornered, and their throats cut, like the others.

It seemed miles, street after street, their horses' hooves loud on the stones, shattering the silence in the squares with their pools and quiet gardens. They passed covered markets and theatres and a hundred different kinds of business and trade houses. Shinabar was the oldest civilisation in the world, the greatest empire. Even the rising power of Camassia did not yet equal it.

Ta-Thea saw the desert gate ahead of them at last. Kol-Shamisha put out his hand to take her horse's rein and slow her. Then he went ahead and spoke to the gatekeeper. After a moment he passed something over, and the small door inset in the main gate swung open. She spurred her horse forward, suddenly filled with panic that the door would close and trap her.

Outside, the ribbon of road unwound across the desert as far as the eye could see, barely discernible from the sand that stretched to the horizon, its pale expanse broken only by the occasional dark shadow from a ridge or escarpment.

'Ride!' Kol-Shamisha ordered, urging his own animal into a gallop, his long tabard flying as he gathered speed. She obeyed with thudding heart. The wind was cool on her skin, smelling of sand and stone and the vast emptiness of the moonlit night.

She did not know how long they rode, or how far. Thoth-Moara receded behind them and was lost as they followed the dips and hollows of the old trade route west. There was no hint of dawn. The wheel of stars was still bright above but the moon was lower, the shadows longer, when at last they saw the first oasis, black against the sand.

Kol-Shamisha slowed his pace. 'We'll change horses here.' He put his hand into the pocket of his tabard and pulled out a small leather pouch. He passed it across to her.

'What is it?' she asked.

'All I could salvage,' he replied. 'Take it. You'll need it.'

'Money?'

'The Isarch's jewels,' he answered. 'Something anonymous from the Treasury would have been better, but there was no time. It was one of the first places they seized.'

'You . . . you took . . .' She stopped. Her marriage to Mon-Allat had been political, an alliance of two great families. He had had a mistress. But he was still her husband, they were bound by shared duty and

3

honour, and friendship. 'You took them from his body?'

His face was unreadable, half turned away from her, watching and listening. 'Your family is dead,' he said, his voice harsh as the wind across the rock face. 'These belong to you. Come.' He urged his horse forward again.

She followed because there was nothing else she could do. Mon-Allat would have wanted her to have the jewels. She did not doubt that, whatever he felt for his mistress. She had not asked if Arimaspis had been with him, and if she were dead too.

They entered the shadow of the oasis and threaded their way through the palms towards the pool of water at its centre. The surface of the water gleamed like polished steel in the moonlight. Four figures stood at the water's edge, and behind them a string of a dozen horses.

Ta-Thea stopped. Kol-Shamisha approached the men and spoke for several minutes. He handed something to them then one of the men brought forward two horses. They were beautiful, slender-legged creatures, bred for speed and intelligence. Kol-Shamisha, a desert man before he had joined the Guard, had the love of them in his blood. He needed only a moment to know the worth of an animal. He nodded and led two of them towards Ta-Thea. She dismounted, waiting.

He was halfway across the strip of sand when shadows detached themselves from the trees and moved forward swiftly, soundlessly, and fell on the horse traders, daggers flashing bright.

Kol-Shamisha whirled round, one hand to his sword, the other slapping one of the horses so it moved towards Ta-Thea.

'Run!' he shouted. 'Run!' And the next moment the attackers were on him.

The horse loomed over Ta-Thea. She snatched at the rein and scrambled up into the saddle. Her first instinct was to turn and attack, but she had no weapon. Kol-Shamisha had told her to run. He was offering his life so she could survive.

She turned and spurred the horse away, feeling its strength beneath her, and its fear. They would pursue her, but perhaps they would be wounded, delayed long enough – for what? Where was she going?

She must rally resistance in one of the other cities. It was inconceivable that all Shinabar could have fallen. There were a hundred other cities, a thousand towns, and villages and oases beyond counting. She urged the horse still faster.

She had no idea how long she rode. Not once did she turn and look back towards the oasis. The constellations turned in the heavens, low and bright. The cold, clean smell of the sand filled her lungs and its sharp grit stung her skin as the tears stung her eyes. It was still dark. The moon was low but no pale wing of light marked the east.

4

The ground was rising a little. There was an escarpment of rock ahead of her. She slowed her horse to a walk and at the crest of the rise stopped altogether. She would be easily seen here. But then her dark figure would be seen against the moonlit ocean of sand anywhere. She made herself turn and look.

The road was as empty as the sky above. But there were a score of ridges like this one, with hollows where ancient rivers had scoured the rock. Even the great wind-driven billows of sand could momentarily hide a group of horsemen.

She turned and rode down the other side of the ridge towards an oasis dark in the hollow about four miles ahead. She was exhausted. Every muscle ached, but far greater was the void inside her, the blind, consuming loss. No physical terror or pain could dim the sight of Habi's body on the white sheets and remove the smell of his blood in her nose and throat.

At last it was dawn. It came suddenly, as it always did in the desert: a pale light high up, then a radiance across the sky. In minutes the sun would tip above the horizon and the bleached colours of the night would vanish in blue and silver. Within half an hour the sand would be warm. In an hour it would burn.

She saw the figure when she was still a hundred yards from the trees, a woman alone beside a rough grave. She was motionless as the rising sun lit her, seeming unmindful of the sand whispering across her feet in the dawn wind. There was grief in her bent head and an agony of loss in her shoulders and the leaning of her body. It was as if Ta-Thea could see herself, so perfectly did the woman mirror her own desolation.

She dismounted, leading her horse, and walked to stand beside her. There were no words to touch such bereavement. An answering silence was all that was possible.

The minutes passed. The sun rose above the horizon and poured a splendour of light across the desert floor.

At last the woman raised her face. She was not young. There was wisdom and experience in her eyes and an unanswerable sorrow.

'You must have loved him very much,' Ta-Thea said softly.

'No,' the woman replied. 'No. I wish I could say that I had, but I did not.' A smile like a ghost crossed her mouth and vanished. 'Heaven forgive me, I did not even like him.'

Ta-Thea was confounded. 'Then why . . .?'

The woman stared across the grave at the endless desert beyond. 'I came because no one else did,' she said, her voice very low. 'He was shallow, grubby, and unkind, but no one should be buried without somebody to know his passing, and to care.'

Ta-Thea stared at the woman's face, uncomprehending. 'But why do you grieve so much if you did not love him?' Surely only love could

5

hurt this much? The pain of her own love for the lost was almost too much to bear, and there was no one else left who would mourn.

There were hollows under the woman's eyes, lines around her mouth. 'Because he had life,' she answered. 'He had a chance to be brave and to seek the truth, to honour and defend it. He had time in which he could have faced fear and overcome it; to know himself without deceit, excuse or self-pity; to bear pain without bitterness. He had days in which to laugh, to see beauty, to fill his heart with gratitude. He could have been kind and brave and generous.' Her voice was very soft and she spoke slowly, as if even the words hurt. 'Above all, there were people he could have loved, and learned to forgive. He is gone, and who is there in the world that is poorer?' She looked at the grave, the dry surface already smoothing over in the wind. 'Now all his chances are finished. Of course I weep for him!'

For a moment Ta-Thea glimpsed an untrodden region of the soul which dwarfed all she knew. The woman pitied the dead man not for anything that had happened to him, great or small, but for what he was, and even more profoundly for what he was not.

'Then what was the purpose of his life?' she said aloud. 'Or anyone's?'

'I don't know.' The woman turned to face her again. 'I wish I understood, but I do not. I can only care. Perhaps if I care enough . . .' She left the rest unsaid.

Ta-Thea stretched out her hand and touched the woman's arm, as if she would be closer to her. They stood together for several minutes, heads bent, looking beyond the grave at the restless grains of sand for ever moving in the sun. Then at last they turned to walk towards the edges of the oasis where the grass was rustling in the wind, already warm.

Ta-Thea took her horse's rein and led it to the shade. She must care for it before thinking of herself; every Shinabari, Empress or slave, knew that. The knowledge ran through two thousand years of history.

She unsaddled the horse, rubbed its sweating body with a handful of grass, and was leading it back and forth to cool when she saw riders top the escarpment in the distance. They were her pursuers. She knew it as surely as if she had seen their faces. There was nowhere to run, and her horse was exhausted.

Now she, too, was going to die. The woman's words burned in her mind. The ultimate tragedy was not to die, but to have had life and let it slip through your hands, day by day, unused, until in the end it was gone, and you had learned nothing, given nothing, left no portion of grace or love in any soul. What would she leave behind her greater than she had found or been given by fate? Whom had she loved, beyond the child of her own flesh, which any woman loves? What had

6

she ever forgiven greater than the small things which came easily? What truth did she ever know with a white-hot passion of the soul, let alone defend?

The woman emerged from a mud brick house at the edge of the trees and began to walk towards Ta-Thea. In her hands were a flask of water and some food.

Ta-Thea ran towards her, waving her arms towards the riders now clear against the shimmering sand, about three miles away and moving swiftly. 'Get back inside!' she called. 'Quickly! It is only me those men are after.'

'Who are they?' the woman asked.

'I don't know, but they killed my companion and are pursuing me. Don't give your life for nothing. You can't save me.'

The woman remained motionless. 'Why do they want to kill you?'

'There has been a rebellion in Thoth-Moara. The Isarch is murdered, and all his family, except me.'

'Go inside,' the woman commanded. 'There is water in the jar. Wash, braid your hair back and put on my clothes which are there. Do not speak, whatever happens! Do it!'

'You will be killed with me!' Ta-Thea protested.

The woman's eyes blazed curiously blue for a Shinabari. 'Then so be it! Do not make my choices for me. Now do as I tell you.'

Obediently Ta-Thea went into the small mud brick house and immediately saw the jar of water. She stripped off her groom's clothes and her own shift under it, and washed the dust from her body. She did it mechanically, without thinking. She had no strength left to struggle, and perhaps no desire.

She was standing in the room, clothed in the woman's plain white robe, when the men burst in, throwing the palm-wood door wide. There were five of them and they held the woman by both arms. Their faces were streaked with dust. The first of them glared at Ta-Thea.

She met his eyes and looked into the blackness of them and saw his rage.

'Who are you?' he demanded.

'She is Mita, my servant,' the woman answered for her. 'She doesn't speak.'

'Can she hear?'

'Yes.'

The man turned to Ta-Thea, looking at her closely. 'Did you see anyone ride past here, or stop? Did you give water to anyone? A groom or a woman dressed like one? Answer me truthfully, or I'll cut your throat.' He ran a broad thumb across the blade of his knife meaningfully.

Ta-Thea shook her head.

'She saw no one,' the woman said coldly. 'She was about her duties.

She only came outside once, concerning the food.'

The man on the other side of her shook her roughly. 'Tell us again what you saw! What are you doing here, anyway? Why do you live here?'

'I live here because I choose to,' she answered him. 'I am a widow. I provide for travellers when they pass. My husband was a traveller on these routes. You are not desert men, or you would understand.'

'Which way did the rider go?'

She raised her eyebrows. 'Along the road towards the town, of course. There is nowhere else to go, unless you know the secret trade routes and how to find the hidden oases. Otherwise you could die in the heat.'

He pushed her and she stumbled against the table, then he swung round and left the hut, followed by the others.

The woman looked at Ta-Thea and held a finger to her lips, commanding silence until the men had been gone several minutes.

'There are your clothes. Go and wash them in the pool,' she said at last.

Ta-Thea understood. The men might well not have believed the woman's tale. One or more might remain.

Slowly, with an aching body and a numb mind, she washed her clothes and then worked steadily at simple, manual jobs in the small house. At noon the woman ministered to her, gently and in silence. She prepared some simple food of fruit, cheese and bread for her, and water from the spring. Then, still without speaking, she poured oil and a sharp-smelling unguent into a shallow dish and anointed Ta-Thea's blisters and abrasions, and bound them in linen.

'Now sleep,' she said gently. 'I will wake you when it is dark. Your horse will be rested.' She smiled. 'Fortunately you had rubbed it clean and walked it before those men came. They did not realise how hard it had been ridden. I told them it was mine, and they believed me. That is when I knew they were not desert men.' She looked at Ta-Thea. 'How did an Empress learn about beasts? Don't you have a score of grooms to do such things for you?'

'Five score,' Ta-Thea said blankly. 'But my father was of the desert, and my mother of the sea. That is why I was chosen.' She did not add that her mother was from the Lost Lands, those shores beyond the Maelstrom to the south of the Island at the Edge of the World, where not even the bravest Shinabari mariner dared sail.

'Sleep,' the woman repeated. 'You will need your strength. Trust in tomorrow, and the years of tomorrow.'

Ta-Thea had thought she could never sleep again, but physical exhaustion covered her over like a drowning wave, deep as oblivion.

When she awoke the fire of sunset coloured the walls of the small

8

room and the suffocating heat of the day was already touched with a breath of the dusk wind. She stared around her, sitting up slowly. For a strange, calm moment she could not think where she was. She was used to silence. The palace walls were thick and servants wore soft shoes. But the close smell of mud brick and sand was different.

Then she moved her legs and felt the ache of muscles, and it all came back in a suffocating sickness, a pain that took her breath away – the shouting, the blood, Habi's small body curled over, limp and still warm. She bent her head and wept for him with terrible, rending sobs until she had no strength left.

When the sunset was over and the desert sky was purple, the woman came in carrying a lamp and set it on the bench.

'Now you must leave,' she said firmly. 'I cannot come with you, but I can set you on the right path to find the sea by morning if you do not slow down.'

Ta-Thea had not thought where she was going, only where she must leave. Her flight had been blind. There was no future, only the need to know. Why? Was there any purpose to her life? Her child was dead when he had barely realised the gift of being alive. The man who lay in the desert grave here in this oasis had wasted himself. Was all life as futile, a moment of consciousness between one oblivion and another?

She could not believe it! There was too much passion and will in even the smallest of living things, too much caring. Surely someone she loved as much as Habi could not pass into nothingness? There had to be something more, something that lasted.

A memory flashed across her mind, as vivid as if it had been real only a moment before: her mother sitting in the evening light with the wind coming in off the desert with this same bitter-clean tang she could smell now. Her mother had a piece of embroidery in her hand, but it was forgotten as she spoke of life and love, and a sage she had heard of on the shores of the Lost Lands, who was said to know the meaning and purpose of all things.

Perhaps there was such a man, and he could tell her what she needed to know. Perhaps he could answer the greatest question of all – why?

Ta-Thea stood up. 'Thank you,' she said. 'I owe you my life. I cannot pay you for that, but—'

'No,' the woman said quickly, her curious face half ugly, half beautiful. 'You owe me nothing.' A fleeting smile touched her mouth, unreadable in the lamplight. 'My family has served the Isarch for years, for little reward. My husband died for him, and Mon-Allat never knew his name. That I would do this for you has taken my bitterness from me. Perhaps you have given me my life as well. Here is a chart of the way to the sea. Follow the stars, as the desert ships do. If you are truly your father's daughter, you will be there by sunrise.'

★ ★ ★

Ta-Thea rode as the map directed, studying the sky rather than the ground. The woman's face lingered in her mind. She had seemed full of peace as she had bidden farewell, as if the grief that had so torn her and bowed her spirit only a few hours before had been eased from her. The meaninglessness of the man's life who now lay in the hasty grave had somehow been resolved in her compassion for a woman to whom she owed only servitude.

Ta-Thea moved steadily north, disregarding the marked track and crossing the sand and shale, finding the way along gullies long dried out, and up ridges and escarpments rather than round them. The moonlight painted the desert floor with pale brilliance, blackening the shadows.

Towards dawn she saw a caravan moving slowly along the trail ahead of her, camels' feet silent on the sand, lurching like tall ships, heads silhouetted against the paling stars. There was no sound but the wind stirring the sand, and the tinkle of camel bells. They were following a known track from the inland cities towards the great seaport of Tarra-Ghum.

Without thinking, Ta-Thea spurred her horse forward so she would reach the trail as they came level with her. She breasted the last shallow ridge and picked her way down the other side.

The leader of the caravan held up his hand and the score of camels behind him came to a halt. He turned towards her, his bearded face darkened by sun and wind till in the shadow it seemed ebony.

She rode towards him and stopped. 'I travel to the sea,' she said quietly. 'May I journey with you?'

'Why do you travel alone, woman?' he asked, not harshly, but he would not be denied an answer.

'My husband is dead.' She found the words strange and hard to say. It was difficult to accept that the statement was true. She felt as if it must be a lie, an invention. 'He was killed . . . yesterday.'

'Then why are you here, and not at home mourning him?' he pressed.

There was no evading an answer. The truth was best. 'Because those who killed him would kill me also.'

'Then ride with us,' he replied. 'We shall protect you.' His answer was immediate and unequivocal, as was the way of the desert. With a jolt of familiarity and loss, it reminded her of her father.

'Thank you.' She bowed her head in acknowledgement, and moved to the rear, to follow with the last camel.

Within an hour they stopped, just after dawn, to rest the beasts and to eat. As she was drinking, the leader came to her again. She could see his face more clearly now in the first light, hawk-like, high-browed. He squatted beside her.

10

'We travel to Tarra-Ghum,' he said so quietly she could barely catch his words. The others a dozen yards away could not have heard.

'I know.'

'You cannot come with us.' His voice was final.

'Why not? I ask nothing of you but to journey behind.'

He looked at her steadily, recognition in his eyes. 'I will not give my men's lives for you, Majesty. If we were found with you, we should all be forfeit. Eat with us. Take water. Then go your way.'

She looked at him steadily. He might pity her, old loyalties might tug, but today she was not Empress, simply a liability he could not afford. If they were found with her it would be a sentence of death to those who had trusted him.

So fleeting was the crown, the power, even the identity.

She knew that what he said was true. There could be no argument. It would be futile, and shaming, to try.

He looked at her in silence for several seconds, then turned and pointed to the horizon. 'Follow the five ridges and you will come to the sea where you will find a small harbour. The mariners of the Lost Lands use it sometimes. They will not be afraid to take you. May your household gods guide you from yesterday to tomorrow.' And he rose and turned away, walking with easy strides across the sand without looking back, his pale tabard fluttering.

She rode through the sunrise streaming azure and silver across the sky, and smelled the salt in the wind. When she saw the shimmering blue of the sea, it was full daylight and the sun was already sharp and hot, stinging the bare skin of her face and so brilliant on the water it hurt her eyes to look.

She found a Lost Lander ship and paid for her passage with Mon-Allat's gold finger ring. It was the least recognisable of his jewels, a personal possession, not part of the royal regalia. The captain did not ask any questions. If he knew or guessed who she was, there was no shadow of it in his face. She told him her mother was a Lost Lander and that her husband was dead, so she was returning to her people.

They set sail on the afternoon tide and by dusk Shinabar was below the horizon. Ta-Thea stood on the gently heaving deck of the narrow barque with its single sail, and was overwhelmed with an exhaustion of the soul so deep, she could imagine no end to it. Her aching body and blistered feet were irrelevant. She was as lost as this tiny ship on the ocean, with no land and no stars in sight.

On the second day, the numbness in her mind began to lift. Grief was a dull, constant pain within her and anger was returning. Who had done this thing? Why? Who had caused this unbearable hurt?

She stood on the forward deck, the salt wind pulling her hair, tightening her skin, and watched the ever changing surface of the water seething dark blue beneath her. Above, the blue cavern of the sky shimmered with light.

The ocean was an immensity she had never seen before. There was an unimaginably savage strength to it. Never for an instant was it still. In other circumstances she would have been afraid. Now her heart was too full of rage and loss.

Someone had let in the assassins. At night the great doors to the household were closed and locked, they had been ever since a jealous prince had attacked Dar-Somet II five hundred years ago. Who knew Mon-Allat's habits well enough and was so trusted they could have caught him by surprise so he died without a cry? His mistress, Arimaspis? One of his body servants? Again the question – why?

Fury filled Ta-Thea but she was helpless. There was nothing she could do. She stared ahead, gripping the railing with white hands, waiting for the Maelstrom she knew lay somewhere beyond, a vortex in the ocean so terrible that no stranger ever tried to sail through it. It had kept the Lost Lands safe since the dawn of time, a place of mystery at the heart of old dreams and fables.

On the twelfth day she felt a change in the air, a sudden drop in temperature, and she shivered in the sun. White crests curled on the waves and spume whipped from the tops of them. There was a clean, bitter scent in the wind.

'Is that the Maelstrom?' she asked, pointing to a thin veil of grey on the horizon.

The man nearest her straightened up, narrowing his eyes against the light. 'Aye, that's it,' he agreed, shading his face with a gnarled hand, scarred by rope burns. 'Reckon we'll be there by tomorrow.'

'Tomorrow? Not tonight?'

He smiled at the impatience in her voice. 'It'll come soon enough, missy. You'll smell the fear of it tonight. You'll feel the sharper pitch of the boat beneath you and the prickle of terror in the pit of your stomach. It'll be nought but a cold whisper in the dark night, but you'll know what it means, and you'll be in no hurry then.'

She did not answer. The sun dropped and the sky burned a dull red, angry and brilliant like the embers of a fire. The mariners stood double watch, sails reefed tight. They told wilder jokes than before and laughed too quickly, stood with bodies tense, eyes always to the westward as the wind grew colder.

At dawn Ta-Thea was on deck again while they reefed the sails still tighter and swung round into the wind. The ship strained and came alive, hitting the wave crests and plunging forward.

The captain advised her to go below, where at least she would remain dry, but she declined. She would be lashed to the stanchions, as the crew were, and see the Maelstrom, not hide in a cabin to be tossed around, blind, bruised and unknowing, as her soul had become.

He told her it would be unlike anything she could imagine, he had no words to describe it. He could not see in her face that she already understood. They were closing on the Maelstrom and he had no more time to argue. He turned away to his duties.

The mist grew heavier, clinging to her skin in droplets, catching in her throat. She was bound at the waist, as were the mariners, and tied with double ropes to the deck stanchions. Even the mast might be carried overboard. She had seen two extra spars below decks and wondered what they were for. Now she understood. A shiver of fear passed over her, but it was physical only. In her mind and heart she welcomed the violence of the elements; it matched the agony of spirit within her.

They were heading into the veil of mist before them, the sun creating bright prisms of colour on its face. The water became choppy, but underneath it was a strengthening current, carrying the boat forward with increasing speed.

Ta-Thea could feel the power of the sea in the straining of the timbers beneath her, the tight canvas pulled to whipping, the high-pitched wail of the wind in the ropes. It was exhilarating. Her blood beat faster. She saw the men staring with wide, fixed eyes, their knuckles white where they clung to the rails.

Minutes passed, and she became aware of a roar, deeper-throated than the wind or the hiss and crash of water. It was a vast background thunder growing steadily louder as they were drawn towards it. The waves became steeper, the white tops brilliant in shafts of light, sheer sides translucent.

Then suddenly with a great kick the boat leaped and was caught in seething, swirling water. They were in the hollow of a howling tunnel as the ocean hurled itself from the depths in shining, pellucid towers of every shade of blue and green. It was the most beautiful and fearful thing Ta-Thea had ever seen. It was a primeval fury of nature, creation itself in the grasp of an unendurable passion. Light was caught glittering in dazzling mountains of glass, toppling, overbalancing, and spewing out sheets of smothering foam, blinding white. The noise was indescribable. It crashed and roared and screamed, obliterating every other sound.

She was drenched to the skin. Her clothes were ripped by the almost living power of the water. She was stung raw and bruised. The wet ropes tore at her skin till her wrists bled. She gasped for breath between the deluging waves, her lungs bursting, fighting, thinking it would never end. But even the withering shock of the cold could not blind her to the Maelstrom's awful beauty, nor could the fear of it make her look away.

For an hour that seemed like a lifetime they were sucked through the heart of the Maelstrom, then hurled out the far side into bright

13

sunlight, terrified and exhausted. Only a sullen roar was audible behind them, like an unforgettable beat in the blood.

The captain himself came to unlash Ta-Thea. His face was lined with weariness, his clothes were stuck to his skin, as were hers, frayed by the repeated drenching and battering of the sea.

He met her fierce black eyes and saw pride in them, and also vulnerability, and perhaps he guessed the fear and the grief. He smiled and said nothing, but there was respect in his manner, and he untied the ropes gently.

'Thank you,' she said simply, biting her lips against the pain.

He nodded.

She went below to her small cabin and dried herself. Then she crept into the bunk, pulled the rough blankets up to her neck and sank into a sleep as deep as the dark ocean floor.

The piercing cry of seabirds woke her. It was late afternoon and the boat was barely moving. Ripples whispered against the hull. She sat up slowly, seeing the patterns of light on the walls through the thick glass porthole. Her body ached in every muscle. She was bruised and her waist and her wrists were raw from the rubbing of wet ropes. Even the touch of cloth against them shot pain through her.

She rose and dressed in the robe the woman at the oasis had given her, and climbed up to the desk, her hands shaking as she gripped the rail of the ladder. She had reached the end of her journey, her mother's land which she had heard of a hundred times in childhood tales but never seen. All the past, her own life and love in Shinabar, had been torn away as one pulls up and burns a weed, destroying the future. This was a bright link with the past. It was somewhere she might make a place for herself where she could belong.

She stared around her. They were anchored in a small harbour amid ships of rich, dark colours, hulls of russet and chestnut wood, some dark as sable. The colours of the furled sails were as soft and hot as the desert sands at sundown: ochres and golds, burning browns, here and there daubs of vermilion.

Beyond the blue water she saw the town of Orimiasse, built of stone, bleached or lime-washed white. Narrow streets sloped up the hill. There were flights of steps, arches covered in vines with bright purple flowers as thick as leaves, and across them from window to window fishing nets hung to dry. All around her was the smell of salt, the cry of gulls and the shifting, moving reflection of sunlight on water.

She thanked the captain and bade him farewell, then she boarded a small boat and was rowed ashore. She set foot on the wooden pier with an almost dizzy sensation. Imagination and reality blended in damp wind cool to the skin and the firm feel of land beneath her feet. There was nothing of the stillness of the desert here, the place was

14

noisy and bursting, and the brilliance of the sun brought none of the hard, searing heat she was used to.

She walked slowly along the quay and into the narrow seafront street. Men and women passed her going about their tasks, carrying nets and bales of cotton, strings of vegetables, baskets of fish. Ships were being loaded and unloaded, rigging mended, merchandise argued over. She looked at them curiously. They were a fairer people than the black-haired, black-eyed Shinabari. Their faces were softer. Some of them had grey or sea-blue eyes. Memories of her mother awoke with a sweetness that overwhelmed her. She stood still, the pale buildings swimming around her, the filigree patterns of the nets on the stone merging until she could no longer see their edges.

She had lost her own child. This was the home of half her ancestry. The cry of the blood should be here.

'Are you looking for someone?' It was a woman's voice.

'What?'

'Are you looking for someone?' the woman repeated, concern puckering her brow.

No Shinabari assassin would be pursuing her here. 'Yes,' Ta-Thea said eagerly. 'I seek my mother's family. She came from Orimiasse.'

The woman looked at her doubtfully but without suspicion. Ta-Thea's foreign, desert face was clear for anyone to see.

'Her name?' she asked quietly.

'Tamar of Orwen.'

'Oh . . .' The woman's face softened. Her dark blue eyes smiled. 'Ah, yes. A prince of Shinabar came here nearly forty years ago. They fell in love, and he would not leave without her. He was your father?'

'Yes.' In spite of herself, Ta-Thea's heart was racing. Her fingers were stiff and the blood was pounding in her head. 'Can you tell me where I can find those of my mother's people who still live here?'

The woman guided her willingly, and within an hour Ta-Thea was being made welcome in a high-towered house whose walls were a pale peach colour in the reflected sunset.

It was the house of her mother's elder brother. His hair was streaked with white and his eyes as grey as the clouded sea. He spoke softly, but there was a sudden laughter in him, and he masked his opinions for no one. His wife was less open. What was hidden in her nature was too deep to be learned in days, or even weeks. Neither of them pressed Ta-Thea for an account of her journey. They did not even ask her why she had come to the Lost Lands. Perhaps her presence in their house was answer enough.

She was grateful for their kindness, but for days she felt a loneliness so great it was all she could do not to weep. She wished to be alone to give way to the torrent of emotion inside her, and yet she also sought company to keep her thoughts at bay.

15

She walked where her mother had walked before her, saw and touched the things she had, feeling her presence close, the only tie left with love. She wandered along the shore and knelt at the tidal pools where marvellous creatures of every imaginable shape swam, all so small she could have held them in her cupped hands. Later she climbed the cliff tops and stood in the hollows where the sea pinks blew in the wind. She drew in great breaths of air so sweet she thought that as long as she lived the cry of gulls would bring it back to her mind.

She stared at the horizon. It was the edge of the world. No man knew what lay beyond it. It was like the rim between life and eternity. She looked down a thousand feet to where the waves broke with a force that sent white spume fifty feet up into the air, dazzling in the sun, then fell back again into the cauldron of the blue-green water seething below.

Other days she walked along the pale sand on the lea shore amid the sweet, clinging scents of yellow sea lupins and wild asphodel and watched the light shimmering through the clear, shallow water.

Eventually she was ready to seek the priest and perform the ceremony to honour the dead. She could not do it in the Shinabari way. There was no one here who understood it. But then Shinabar had betrayed the dead.

She found the priest in a headland overlooking the town. He was an elderly man, with a broad forehead and thin white hair which was tousled by the sea wind. There was a mildness in his features as he listened to her, the look of a man who was not placid by nature but who has learned patience and conquered self-will.

'I will take you to the Garden of Shells,' he said gently, grief and compassion in his eyes after she had told him her purpose. He turned and walked up the long path that climbed the western cliffs overlooking the last sea. His twilight blue-grey cloak fluttered as the wind caught it and his sandalled feet were silent on the warm earth.

She followed him steadily higher and higher in the sun and the wide sky. The grasses caught at her ankles. The air smelled unlike anything she had known before. It was at once bitter and fragrant.

At last they came to the crest of a hill whose face had been sheered away by the tides of eternity, falling in a giant wall down to the sea that bounded the world. She looked down in amazement. In a shallow dip, a few steps below, nestled a garden not of flowers but of pieces of ancient wood bleached by sun and scoured by salt into bone-pale beauty and subtle shape, and smooth as ivory. Between them lay a myriad shells, each one perfect, in every shade of the sky from the pearl of dawn through the fire of sunrise to the violet of night. Each was half of a bivalve; not a single pair was complete.

The gulls wheeled and cried above, soaring in the currents of air,

16

wings white against the burning blue of the sky. Far below them the surf boomed and echoed on the rocks, half lost in the singing of the wind. From the folds of his robes the priest took a linen bag and thrust his hand into it. He brought out eight perfect bivalves, spread wide like frozen butterflies.

'Tell me of those you loved,' he invited her. 'What in them was most beautiful to you, and most precious?'

She began with her mother. This was her place. A hundred things came to mind, both of joy and of sorrow, her delight in the loveliness of the tiny things of the world, the light in the dewdrop, the petals of a flower. Her laughter at the absurd rang like a paean of belief in life. But one virtue outshone all others: courage.

'She taught me,' said Ta-Thea, 'that if you do not have courage, all other virtues may be lost, because you cannot keep even love if you are not prepared to fight for it, to endure the hurt it brings, and hold on, no matter the cost.'

'Then tell me what gift you will give to mankind in her name.'

Her mind reeled. It was utterly beyond what she had imagined. No Shinabari priest would have asked such a thing. He would have spoken of rituals, orisons. But there was a purity in this that was intensely satisfying. Gradually a slow, sweet peace spread inside her.

He saw her silence and understood it.

'Then give your time to the weary, the sick, the maimed in mind or body,' he said gently. 'Serve them one day for each new moon, in your mother's memory. Mourn with those who mourn, keep watch with those who are alone, and listen to their tale. Covenant with me here in this place that you will do so.'

'I do!' she answered without hesitation.

He held out a handful of shells, delicate, perfectly formed and polished clean. 'Choose one.'

Her eyes moved swiftly over them all. There was one, cold, clean pink, and translucent at the edges. She touched it. 'That one.'

'Take it,' he instructed. He produced a metal instrument like a stylus. 'Write your mother's name on one half, and your own on the other.'

She was reluctant to mark the smooth surface, but she did as she was commanded, then looked up, waiting.

'Break it in half,' he told her. 'Cast the half with your mother's name into the eternity of the sea, and place the half with your own name in this garden, where it will remain, and your covenant with it.'

She held the shell for a moment in the palm of her hand, then obediently she broke it. She drew her arm back and launched the half bearing her mother's name as high and as wide as she could. Its tiny gleam of white flashed up in a brief arc against the blue void of the

17

sky, then was lost. She placed her half in the shell garden, close to a piece of driftwood like the flying mane of a horse.

She repeated the act for Mon-Allat, then for Habi, placing his small, golden shell beside the pink one, for him promising to nurture everything new and young, to be tender to the innocence of all beginnings. Then she and the priest turned and walked back over the headland and down towards Orimiasse.

The days passed more and more easily. The narrow streets of the town became familiar with their sudden flights of steps, the nets strung across to dry casting intricate shadows on the soft coloured walls, and the sharp smell of salt. The pain of grief did not go, but it became less sharp. She found companionship and much to learn. There was a deep comfort in growing close to the other half of her heritage. With every passing day she felt a deepening of the bond between her mother and herself.

At an evening gathering a month after she had arrived, a Lost Lander man, about ten years older than herself, with wind-burned skin and a high, arrogant face, interrupted something she was saying and made a patronising joke, very much at her expense.

There was a moment's discomfort at his rudeness before conversation resumed. With violence as sudden as lightning she remembered who she was. As Empress of Shinabar no one alive would have dared argue with her, let alone contradict her in public, and laugh about it. How had she so far forgotten herself, her identity, as to allow this to happen? Had she become so numbed by comfort she had abandoned her dreams, her need to know? The kindness of the Lost Landers had almost smothered her.

The following morning she began her search for the sage of her mother's tales. It was mid-afternoon when an old woman told her to go over the headland along the bay to the leeward. She would find a lone house among the dunes.

As the sun turned gold and the shadows softened, Ta-Thea climbed high up the steep face of the hillside beyond Orimiasse. The wind-swept grass was dry, salt-whipped and starred with small, scentless flowers. Ahead of her was the gentle curve of the bay with its blue-green water paling limpid to the long reaches of the sand, and over the northern horizon lay the Island at the Edge of the World.

She was wearing a cloak of Lost Lands silk, indigo as the twilight sky over the desert. She wrapped it closer about her; up here the air was cool and the soft silk was warm on her shivering arms.

She walked steadily past many houses, then for a space through the dunes and the sea lupins, petals luminous in the fading light. The last house, far beyond the others, was low down by the shore, too close to the water for vines to grow. There were only sea pinks, tide-washed stones and driftwood scrubbed white.

She hesitated before knocking on the door, afraid now that she was on the brink of committing herself. What would she have left if the sage had no answers? What if he was an ordinary man with nothing but dreams and questions, like everyone else? It would almost be better to stay here in the wind and the sun's afterglow, hearing the water hiss on the wet sand and in the distance the high, harsh cry of the gulls as they rode the currents of the air.

This was her mother's land. She could hear her voice in the murmur of the sea.

Now that the cup was at her lip, it was the coward's way not to taste the answer, bitter or sweet. She rapped on the weathered board, bruising her knuckles.

It swung open and an old man, the dome of his skull walnut brown, peered up at her with eyes as blue as the sea, and as blind. His face was seamed with wrinkles, but they formed an expression of gentleness so intense it had a beauty beyond that of youth, or shape, or colouring. His was a soul that had suffered and not lost the power of love, a spirit that had travelled far, endured, and found peace. Ta-Thea knew her journey had not been in vain.

Wordlessly he invited her in, and she followed him to a small room that opened on to the sand and the sea. It was decorated with a single fishing net hung over the inner wall, but of a finer mesh than those of Orimiasse. In its folds were caught the weeds and flowers and shells of the ocean, their forms as varied as the imagination could conceive.

'What is it you seek?' he asked in a voice little more than a whisper, so cracked was it with age and disuse.

'Everyone I loved is gone, everything I thought I knew,' she replied simply. 'I want to know if there is any meaning in life. Why do I exist? Who am I?'

'So you want to know all things?' His head was a little to one side, as if he strained to hear what he could not see.

'Yes.'

'How much do you want it?' he asked. 'More than anything else, more than everything?'

She was startled, but she answered after only seconds of thought. 'What use is anything without it? Everything built on a lie must perish. Who am I?'

'Oh, child.' He shook his head slowly, but there was a smile on his lips. 'Truth does not come without cost – terrible cost. Are you willing to pay the price of it? The war in heaven is as old as time and the great enemy himself will strive with all his power against you. But God will hold you in His hand, and your name will be written in His heart.'

She gulped. Fear touched her soul. Why was it of such tremendous price? What was this enormity she sought? To know the mind of God!

19

Her words were barely a whisper in her throat. 'Yes . . . I am.'

His smile was like love itself. 'Then go to the shore, there.' He pointed out to the pale stretch of sand where it stretched down to the water. 'Go there and wait, past sunset and moonrise, all night while the stars wheel round the world, and out of the dawn will come the first step towards truth. Now go, and prepare your soul.'

'Thank you,' she whispered, then did as she was bidden. She stood on the shore while the last gold faded from the air and the sky deepened from brilliant blue to indigo over the arch of heaven, leaving the sea pellucid green in the afterglow. The air cooled and smelled salt and sharp. For a moment the foam at her feet was pearl, then the colour ebbed and the first stars glittered far above her.

She shivered in the chill breath of the ocean and held the blue cloak close round her body. The moon rose and sailed calm and silver across the heavens till it, too, set. The tide retreated leaving wave-ribbed sand where shallow pools shone pale. All night there was no sound but the hiss and ripple of water, but always she looked to the horizon.

Dawn came as a high arc of light like a bird's wing over the east, then suddenly a silver bar, brilliant, hurting the eyes, and outlined black against it the mast and single sail of a skiff.

She watched it, standing rigid, uncaring of the cold sea foam licking around her feet. The east burned with luminous colour, broadening until the whole face of the sea was spread with cold blue before the white fire of sunrise. All the time the skiff came closer until at last it grounded on the sand and a lone mariner stepped out and walked towards her. He was slender and dark. At first, from the ease of his step, the beauty of his hands, she thought he was young. Then as she gazed at him she saw the wisdom in his face, the understanding, and in his eyes the knowledge of a man who has seen heaven and hell, and will bear them both.

'Are you sure?' he said softly.

'Yes,' she answered. 'I am sure.'

He held out his hand to her. 'Then come . . .'

20

Chapter Two

Ta-Thea watched the mariner without speaking. The purple sails billowed in the wind and he stood in the stern of the boat, feet astride, balancing, the fine ropes held hard in his hands. The hull lifted and cut the water, gathering speed. His face was intent, his dark eyes watching the canvas, the swing and shift of the yards. There was a joy inside him as though he rode the wings of a bird and was at one with it.

She did not ask him where they were going. Words would be a clumsiness in the luminous stillness of the dawn where the sea was shot with silver as the sunlight fell in brilliant bars between the darkness of cloud shadows. The sky arched above them in a measureless dome, luminous, wind-scoured, as the last vestiges of night fled westward.

She was content to wait. She sat low in the boat, staring ahead of her as the sun rose. The sky and the sea became a burning, cobalt blue and the warmth gradually eased the chill from her. She let go of her silk cloak. The motion of the boat was slight, no more than a rocking, and without intending to she sank lower and lower until she slipped down on to the boards and fell asleep in the sun.

She awoke with a start. Her cloak had been tucked gently round her and something placed under her head for a pillow. She sat up, embarrassed. The mariner was seated in the stern, the ropes still in his hands. The sun was low in the west behind him.

'I'm sorry!' she said hastily.

He smiled. 'Why?'

'I fell asleep . . .'

'It doesn't matter.' His smile widened. 'My name is Ishrafeli.'

She pushed her hair back from her brow, thick and black as night. 'I am Tathea.' She robbed it of its Shinabari accent. For a little while longer she wanted that anonymity. Should she tell him more, that only a short while ago she had been an Empress? That assassins had slaughtered her family, her child, and she had been driven out of her land? It was part of who she was, of all her needs and reasons. But it was too painful to say. Words made it real, and here in this shining silence she could forget.

'I know,' he said.

She did not ask how, but an awe settled over her and she said no more.

Eventually land appeared ahead of them, a high headland crowned with ancient silver-grey trees. They sailed wide round it and past the long breakwater into a harbour scattered with ships. Beyond the harbour a city lay spread out in the fading light, pale-pillared, clean-lined façades, flights of wide steps. It was smaller than the Shinabari equivalent, built on a more intimate and human scale, as if it was to be loved rather than feared.

They passed a broad-bellied cargo ship lumbering out on the evening tide, mariners heaving on the yards to catch every breath of wind. Fishing skiffs plied back and forth, dark nets trailing. A trimaran swept past them, oars dripping three tiers of liquid gold in the setting sun.

Ishrafeli was busy hauling down the sail and reefing it to the boom. She would have helped, but she had no idea how. She knew horses and the desert, something of law and judgement, certainly of political wisdom, but nothing of the sea.

When the skiff was made fast, he stepped ashore, offering her his hand, and she followed him along the quay past merchants and fishermen into the busy streets. The city was as beautiful as it had seemed from afar. There was a grace in it unlike anything she had seen before, a simplicity of proportion that gave every aspect a unique value. Private and public buildings seemed to have been created with equal care. In open squares and colonnaded streets there were places for people to gather at ease, with fountains for the thirsty to drink at. One or two seemed in need of repair, worn by long use. Here and there with sudden sadness she saw cracks and missing stones.

Through archways she glimpsed gardens of such loveliness she longed to stop and go into them. Only fear that Ishrafeli might leave her behind prevented her. Flowers of golds and pinks spilled over walls and trailed in pale profusion from carved urns of exquisite grace. Their perfume drifted out into the street, waylaying the passer-by. In the shadow, ancient stones were covered with jewel-like moss. Vines spiralled over arches and fell in scarlet blossom.

She had to hurry to keep up with Ishrafeli as he strode up the street. It was crowded at the corners, not with men trading, or women gossiping, but with small knots of people in anxious conversation, their faces pinched, eyes wary. She saw to the left the wide circle of a theatre, but it had an empty air, as if no performances had been held there for months. The frieze of dancing figures above the entrance, a static moment of joy, was chipped at the edges and no one had repaired it.

As they drew level with a group of young men, without warning a quarrel became violent, and in a moment they were caught in the fighting. Ishrafeli clasped Tathea and pulled her away from them, shielding her with his body. But he was unarmed and the struggle was

22

ugly, no trivial difference. The youths were shouting at each other as they fought, their blows sending each other sprawling. Blood stained their white tunics.

There was a shout of command, and an instant's hesitation. One young man scrambled to his feet, but his assailant seized the opportunity to renew his attack.

The man who had spoken was tall and broad-chested. The last of the sun caught his high cheekbones and the fair brown of his hair. He wore breastplate and greaves over his white tunic, as if he were a soldier.

'Come!' he said quickly to Ishrafeli and Tathea. 'It is not safe to be abroad in the streets unarmed. Are you strangers here?'

'Yes,' Ishrafeli acknowledged. 'We just landed. My name is Ishrafeli.' He touched Tathea gently. 'This is Tathea.'

'Phraxus,' the man responded. 'Have you friends in Parfyrion?' He increased his pace and they were obliged to hasten to keep up with him. He was moving with urgency, his body bent forward. 'If you haven't, you are welcome in my home. The city is full – for the trial tomorrow. The unrest you see will become worse.' All around them were signs of disquiet. Groups of soldiers moved aimlessly, hands close to their swords. Civilians hurried about their business. There were hardly any women to be seen, and no children at all.

'Who is to be tried?' Ishrafeli asked as Phraxus started across an open square, guiding them between groups of youths and half a dozen elderly men who were arguing heatedly.

They had climbed a wide, shallow flight of steps and emerged into the golden light of the evening and saw a dazzling view of the harbour below when Phraxus finally answered them. He did so as he led them into the rose-coloured stone tower of his own house.

'Cassiodorus,' he replied when they were inside. A sadness crossed his face, and unconsciously he straightened his wide shoulders, turning away. 'He was our leader against our age-old enemy in the last war.'

They were inside the first hallway. Tathea stared around her at the walls painted in warm earth and sunset shades. Ahead of them lay another room opening on to a courtyard, and to the left stairs curved upward to a room which must overlook the sea.

'When did the war end?' Ishrafeli asked.

Phraxus glanced at him quickly. 'Ten days ago. Cassiodorus signed the treaty. That is why he is to be tried.' He watched Ishrafeli, attempting to read his face.

Tathea listened with interest. She understood diplomacy. The end of long wars between nations who had hated each other for decades, even centuries, only came with compromises. All too often the different factions would not bend. She had seen enmity become a pattern of life, the justification for a multitude of otherwise inexcusable acts, the love

23

of war an end in itself. There was a kind of hero who could not survive without it.

Ishrafeli's eyes widened. 'He is being tried for ending war?' he asked. 'Did he surrender?'

A flash of bitter humour tugged at Phraxus's mouth. 'No!' It was an honourable peace.' He went up the curved stairs and they followed him to the upper room, off which were several doors, but Tathea had eyes only for the panorama of the twilit city. The stone roofs were bathed in rose and shadowed in violet. Beyond the harbour wall, the sea was green as far as the eye could see.

Phraxus bade them sit and offered them wine and bread and a sharp, savoury butter flavoured with herbs. On the table was a bowl of golden fruit, some blushed with a tawny ripeness, and green and purple grapes. Another bowl held almonds and crystallised peel.

'It is not the terms which are wrong,' Phraxus explained, the fine lines around his eyes visible in the evening light. 'It is the fact that Cassiodorus negotiated and agreed it without reference to the city fathers. We are a democracy. For two hundred years we have made no public decisions without giving every man the right to hear and judge for himself.'

'And before that?' Tathea asked curiously. She could not imagine such a system being anything but chaotic. But she had come to learn.

Phraxus turned to her and smiled. He was a soldier, like many she had known. He would be courteous. He might like her, even find her interesting or attractive, but he would never forget the difference between the physical power of men and that of women. She could see it now in his grey-blue eyes. And here she was not an Empress to command obedience.

'Before that we had a tyranny,' he explained to her. 'At first it was wise, even benevolent. But absolute power corrupts. Care became oppression. We ceased to know how to make our own decisions. We developed a ruling class, and one that was ruled. The few governed the many.'

'Unwisely?' she asked. 'Unjustly?'

His voice was patient. 'Both, at times. But that was not the issue, nor is it now.' He turned a little in his chair to face her fully. Beyond him in the great window the light had almost gone over the city and the sea. They could see each other by the light of the lamps which burned on the walls. 'The question is not the justice of this treaty, but the assumption of the power to make it. Cassiodorus signed the treaty, and then returned home and informed Parfyrion that it was accomplished. It tore the city apart.' There was pain in his voice as if the signing of the treaty had not only divided his people but wrenched his own judgement and loyalties.

Tathea looked at Ishrafeli. A lamp shone on the wall above him and

24

another on the table beside him. The shadows threw his features into sharp relief, the plane of his cheek, the ink-black brows, the curve and shadow of his eyes. Was he searching, as she was, or did he already know? She could read nothing in him but that he was listening.

'The young men were full of hope for a new order,' Phraxus went on ruefully. 'The soldiers came home loaded with booty for everyone. There were three days and nights of celebration.'

'What kind of a new order?' Tathea asked.

'More liberal,' Phraxus answered with a flicker of bleak laughter. 'Young men always think they can change things for the better. Perhaps we would perish if they didn't. We need growth, invention. Without thought we die.' His wide mouth pinched at the corners. 'But they also hunger for power for its own sake. They would take by force what they are denied by the common voice.'

'And the old men?' Ishrafeli asked.

'They remember tyranny, the fear and the cruelty of it, and they are afraid it is coming again. And they are reluctant to let go of their own power. They feel their wisdom has earned them their place of honour. Let youth wait.'

'Then it is between age and youth,' said Tathea.

'No,' Phraxus denied it quickly. 'At least, those are only two of the factions. There are also the merchants who want peace, and the women who fear for their husbands and their sons. And there are those who have already lost much in the battles of the past, and cannot forgive. For them any concession is a betrayal of the dead. They had paid their price and will yield nothing. The past lies too heavily upon them, the future cannot pay that debt.'

'But what is Cassiodorus's crime?' Tathea asked. 'You said he is to be tried tomorrow?'

'Yes, he is.'

'Treason?' It seemed obvious to her. 'He has usurped a power to which he has no right, even if his decision was the same one the people might have reached – surely would have, if they had any wisdom?'

'No, not treason, no one could prove he has harmed the state.' Phraxus seemed puzzled even as he spoke. There was a furrow between his brows. 'Blasphemy.'

Ishrafeli stiffened. His hand on the table was perfectly still. 'Blasphemy? Against which god?'

Phraxus also sat motionless. His face was like a warrior's mask. 'We don't know. The gods gave us our laws of moderation, justice and liberty so long ago we no longer have any record of their nature.' He watched Ishrafeli as he spoke. 'There are philosophers who say they never existed, that they were created by wise men in the beginning to lend weight to the laws to govern a simpler people. They would obey gods where they would question men.'

25

Ishrafeli's lips tightened but he did not interrupt.

'Gradually, down the ages, we learned to stand on our own, to value the laws for themselves,' Phraxus continued. 'We no longer needed magic or mystery to teach us to obey. To understand was better.' There was a ring of certainty, even pride in his voice now. 'Wisdom and humanity, mastery of self, love of beauty are the measure of a man. In Parfyrion we have served these ends for a thousand years, and they have repaid us with abundance beyond measure, in peace and in war. We have gained a wealth of the spirit through the creation of loveliness which has never been surpassed.' His face softened for a moment. 'I would say it has never been equalled.'

'How can one blaspheme gods who do not exist?' Tathea asked.

He looked at her steadily. 'It is perhaps a convention. Blasphemy is an easier word for hubris, that pride of a man who when he over-reaches fate and aspires to tower above his fellows and grasp at the stars . . . when he defies that respect for the universe, that awe which the splendour of creation and the knowledge of his own frailty would forbid. It is an immodesty which offends the soul, and cries a warning within the minds of those who know the destructive power of arrogance. Do you understand?'

She was uncertain. She had a troubling vision of her own reign in Shinabar. She had always taken the Isarch's power for granted, as she had assumed every Shinabari did. But clearly that was not so . . .

Before she could struggle for an answer they were interrupted by a swift rapping on the door below and a voice calling out for Phraxus.

He excused himself to answer, and a few moments later returned followed by a small, dark man with a crooked nose and eyebrows that grew close together above burning eyes.

'This is Allomir,' Phraxus announced. 'He is to prosecute Cassiodorus tomorrow.'

Allomir was startled to see strangers. He bowed stiffly. His body was too tense to move with grace and every line of his narrow face spoke his urgency.

'Tathea and Ishrafeli have just arrived here by sea. They knew nothing of our troubles,' Phraxus explained.

Allomir glanced at Tathea, then his eyes rested on Ishrafeli and he looked at him with growing intensity, as if he were certain he must know him but the memory eluded his mind. 'Who is to defend?' he demanded, his voice harsh, and yet there was a timbre to it which commanded attention. 'No one is prepared to step forward and commit themselves – at least no one of legal stature.' He spread his hands jerkily. 'Plenty of soldiers will, and young men who espouse Cassiodorus's cause, but without a proper advocate the trial cannot succeed.'

'Succeed?' Ishrafeli said quickly. 'What would success be?'

26

'Ah!' Allomir let out a sharp bark of laughter. 'There is no success.' He chopped his hand sideways in the air. 'If he is found innocent then we have granted him the first step towards despotism. We have ratified his corruption of power and we cannot then refuse him the next stride, and the next, and so on until he has the reins of government in his hands, and his admirers with him, which include the rashest and most brutish elements of our army.' He looked at Ishrafeli earnestly. 'At the last call, there is nothing between the best of man and the worst but the will to master his instincts in the face of law, in the interests of his fellows. Override the common consent, rule by strength alone, and we have thrown away all that has given us dignity and raised our souls above the beasts.'

'And if he loses?' Ishrafeli asked quietly. Darkness seemed to touch his face, a very slight tightening of the lips.

Allomir stared at him as if there were no one else in the room. The fierceness of the emotion in his angular body was almost mesmeric. It seemed to Tathea as if for Allomir Ishrafeli were the most important person in the room.

'If he loses, he will fight.' He spat out the words. 'He has strong support from his own soldiers, and anyway the young men of the city, those with no wives or children, second sons without property to be ruined if there is war—'

'There won't be war!' Phraxus protested. 'He wouldn't do that! He may be arrogant, impatient of the old ways and what they can cost, but he is still Parfyrian.'

Allomir swung round to him. 'And we cannot breed tyrants?' he demanded with stinging anger. 'We are not born good, Phraxus, we become good because we learn the law, we perceive its strengths, and I dare say its weaknesses, but we choose to obey it.' He shrugged his bony shoulders sharply. 'And if we can choose to obey it, then we can also choose to disobey it. That is what we are: creatures within whom lies the measure of all things, for good and for evil. It is the law which determines.'

Tathea stared at him. Was this strange, ugly man with his narrow face saying what she had come to learn? But who determined the law?

'Do laws change?' she asked him. 'Who interprets them? Is it written in pure words you can refer to? Or is it accumulated from all the wisdom and experience of the past? Where I come from it is the latter. There are judges throughout the Empire, but in capital cases there is an appeal of last resort, to the Isarch himself.'

He turned to her, a sudden interest flaring in his eyes. 'You know much of this law, Madame?'

'Yes,' she answered without hesitation. She had sat beside Mon-Allat often enough when he had heard the cases that came to him.

Allomir saw the certainty in her face. 'Our law, too, is built on the

27

wisdom of the past. How is it you know your own law? Do women judge in your land?'

'No . . .' She had not considered the possibility before, but why not? An educated woman would know as much as a man and her power to discern would be as great. 'Not legally,' she amended. 'But in effect, sometimes. I counselled my husband, and the verdict he rendered often sprung from my words to him.'

Phraxus glanced at her, then back to Allomir.

Allomir was deep in thought. Behind him the window was filled with the night sky, wind-driven cloud covering the stars.

'Do you really believe that if Cassiodorus loses he will seek war?' Ishrafeli asked softly, his voice troubled. 'And risk destroying all this?' He moved his hand to include everything about them.

'No, of course not!' Phraxus replied.

'Yes,' Allomir contradicted with equal certainty. 'He is a man who sees only his own needs. He will not believe it would be destroyed. He will think his influence and following is sufficient to bring victory without so high a cost.' His lips twisted, misery in every line of him. 'He knows there are enough among us who would rather see Parfyrion in his hands than watch the beauty and the dreams of a thousand years shattered by the sword.'

'It won't come to that!' Phraxus shook his head, his voice sharp. 'He is ambitious but he is not a fool.'

'If he loses, what will his punishment be?' Tathea asked.

'Exile,' Allomir answered.

She said nothing. She knew too well what it was to leave all you loved, everything sweet and familiar, and begin the long journey to nowhere.

He misunderstood her silence. 'Exile from Parfyrion is everything,' he said abruptly. 'It is his birthright, his identity. What more can a man lose and yet be condemned to live, or accept death by his own hand?'

It was Ishrafeli who spoke next, gently. He had a broad mouth, strong, but now his lips were touched with sadness. 'To be an exile from what you know is sometimes the beginning of finding the true measure of yourself, that part which has lain asleep because you did not require it. We seldom grow unless we are forced to.'

This was beyond Allomir. 'You do not understand!' he said urgently. 'Exile from Parfyrion is to leave behind you all that is beautiful of mind and spirit, all that enlarges the intellect and refines the soul. It is a kind of death, without the peace of oblivion.'

Ishrafeli did not argue. Whatever it was that he knew lay silent inside him.

'If we do not have an acceptable advocate for Cassiodorus's defence,' Allomir continued, facing all of them again, his voice rasping

28

with anxiety, 'the trial will not satisfy the letter of the law. But far more important than that, the people will not accept its verdict, and therefore its sentence. I can find no one.' He swivelled back to Phraxus. 'I come to you as a last resort. I know you are a soldier, not a lawyer, but at least you could offer an argument for him, and he would accept you. You have served under him and seen the reality and the ruin of war. You can speak of it from knowledge.'

'I can't!' Phraxus looked beyond them out of the window. There were torches in the streets below as groups of men moved about, though here, high above, they could not hear if there was shouting or a clash of arms. 'I am a witness,' he continued. 'Any defence must call me. I shall be seen as self-serving. You must find someone else.'

Allomir clenched his fists, his shoulders rigid. The shadows cast by the lamps made his nose huge and his eyes so deep-sunken there was no light in them. 'I have tried all the arguments! I have spoken to every advocate.' There was an edge of despair in his voice. 'And no one will accept.' He waved his thin arms. 'I have told them that they do not serve Cassiodorus, but the ends of the law. The only one who would have agreed to defend him is Styanax, but he is too old and too ill. He can barely hobble about. His voice is a whisper, and even that costs all his strength. But he understands that the law is greater than the individual cause, and we must argue both sides for the balance to weigh truly. If we do not, we ourselves have corrupted the law and tainted the truth.'

'I know that,' Phraxus agreed, leaning forward, 'but I cannot serve.'

The silence weighed heavy in the room. Tathea looked at Ishrafeli. His broad brow was smooth, as if the emotion in him was biding its time.

'I hate him!' Allomir said with sudden, deep pain, his voice shaking. 'And I hate him doubly for awakening that feeling in me! It is against the spirit of everything we have built and taught.' He turned to Phraxus, jabbing his finger in the air. 'Have you seen what is happening to the people? We are becoming divided, father against son. Where there used to be respect, now there is anger and contempt.'

'I know—'

'Even natural affection is eaten away,' Allomir cut in, the tide of his anger sweeping aside even agreement. 'All the tolerance we thought was at the heart of what we loved.' His voice choked. 'But how real is it, Phraxus?' he demanded. 'If one man's ambition can tear it apart, is there a greater power of good: honour, pity, self-mastery, enough humility to obey the common will and not permit one man to destroy the old decencies? Or is it all only a sublime delusion?' He moved his hands in agitation and the lamps made his shadow dance on the walls.

'I hate myself for my doubt. That is what I have let Cassiodorus do to me! Were we already so corrupt that it needed only one evil man for

29

us to fall like rotten fruit?' Now he was speaking to Ishrafeli, as if he felt impelled to convince him. 'I know he's guilty! But without a defence, we cannot convict him, and above all we cannot punish him! It will be an invitation to every brash, articulate youth who thinks to try his hand. The truth is that we should have stopped him sooner, but we were too complacent to see the danger. He was handsome and brave, a golden man.' He spat the words, filled with self-contempt. 'And we were loth to curb him and risk his temper when we needed him most. We accepted what he offered, without asking the cost.'

Phraxus looked at Tathea, frowning, reaching for a thought in his mind. As if already understanding it, Ishrafeli looked at her also.

Allomir swung round. 'Yes?' he said suddenly, hope pitching his voice high. 'You have counselled the supreme judge of your own land, wherever that is. Will you speak for Cassiodorus, that justice may be satisfied? For Parfyrion, for the law?'

Tathea turned to Ishrafeli. She had known him only a short while – it seemed incredible that it was only hours – but he was her guide and she remembered the emotions she had seen in his face, the courage and the vulnerability. She would do as he said.

But when he looked at her, smiling, there was no answer in his eyes.

'Please,' Allomir urged. 'I will counsel you in the Parfyrian law. Phraxus will acquaint you with the facts and the arguments, and a list of witnesses who can be called to substantiate what Cassiodorus may say.'

She looked at Phraxus. He nodded in affirmation.

There was no time to weigh the issue. She must decide now. They would need all night to prepare. There was so much to learn.

'Yes. I will do what I can.'

'Thank you!' Allomir's ugly face shone with gratitude. He reached forward as if to touch her, then changed his mind. 'Then we must begin to prepare. Listen to me . . .'

There was time for only an hour's sleep before they began the day with bread, fruit and a cheese flavoured with wild rosemary. Sunlight poured through the great window, making the lines of the room hard and clean, full of polished wood and smooth marble. Through the window Tathea could see knots of people moving about without purpose. The city was restless. Nobody was trading in the streets, and again there were no women or children.

Allomir left first, and Phraxus, Ishrafeli and Tathea followed a short while after. It was already warm and the road smelled of dust and stone and every so often as they passed a gateway the sweetness of damp earth.

Tathea was nervous. She saw everything with a new clarity, as if she would remember each exquisite carving and weathered stone. Their preservation might rest on her ability to speak for Cassiodorus with exactly the words which would serve justice and yet show Parfyrion that he was indeed guilty of a blasphemy against all they believed.

She had been given a Parfyrian robe so she would not appear too obviously foreign, and they entered the corridors of the large hall of justice without attracting more than casual interest.

'I must speak with Cassiodorus,' she insisted. 'I must hear his argument from his own lips.'

'Of course,' Phraxus agreed quickly. 'I would have taken you even had you not asked.' He guided her past the public galleries, where they left Ishrafeli, and through an archway along a smooth-sided passage to a door, guarded by men dressed in grey tunics. There were no marks of rank upon them, and the armour bore no scars, as if it had never been used in battle. It was a peculiar reminder that the charge was blasphemy, not treason.

Phraxus explained who they were and they permitted Tathea to enter but, expressionlessly, they barred Phraxus from following her.

The room was bare except for a cot bed and a single chair. The man seated on the bed looked at least as tall as Phraxus, and as broad, but there any similarity ended. His hair shone like gold, springing up from a wide brow. His nose and lips were fleshy, his eyes the boldest Tathea had ever seen, as if they would strip all pretence from her, even all privacy. She was chilled with an inexplicable fear, even though the room was warm. She stopped as far from him as she could. He remained seated where he was on the bed.

Oddly, he did not ask who she was. Perhaps he did not care.

'I am going to speak for you,' she told him. 'We have an hour in which you may tell me the most important things you feel I should know, and say. Is there any witness I should call that you have not already mentioned?'

There was laughter in his eyes. 'Have you got Phraxus on your list, lady?'

'My name is Tathea. Yes, I have.'

'Ah, good. The noble Phraxus.' He said it with a curl of his lip, full of contempt, as if he knew something that Phraxus did not. 'He will speak the truth, because he cannot climb outside his nature. And it will hurt him, because he would prefer the lies.'

'Anyone else?' she pressed. 'I have several soldiers here, and men who have lost their homes and their possessions in the wars with your enemies, tradesmen who can now profit from the peace, and benefit the city because of it. There is a matriarch who has lost five sons in battle. She will speak for many others.'

His heavy-lidded eyes were too wide apart, the bridge of his nose too thick. It gave his face power, and robbed it of sensitivity.

'You have done well!' he said, still half jeering at her. 'It seems you

31

really mean to defend me. Why? Are you afraid of what will happen if the old men try to gag me and drive me out?'

It cost her an effort of will to meet his eyes. 'Should I be?'

'Oh yes,' he said very quietly. 'I shall destroy what I cannot have.'

She had heard bravado before, and certainly she had heard threats. But his words ran through her like ice, as if the hand of death had touched her. She stared into his eyes and saw the laughter and the power in them. She wanted to look away, but she felt her strength of will seep out of her.

His smile grew wider.

She wanted to lash out at him, strike him, and force that smile away. But she was here to defend him. She had promised Phraxus, given her word. The law was greater than the anger or vanity of one person. It was certainly greater than Cassiodorus. He might destroy Parfyrion, but it would not be because of her failure to uphold its law.

'That is your weakness,' she said calmly, surprised to hear her voice sound unafraid. 'It is not mine.'

Without warning rage boiled up inside him. He rose to his feet, towering over her, his face dark and his lips ugly with hate. Then just as suddenly it was gone again. His smile returned, but now his eyes were veiled.

'We'll see,' he said, going back to his seat on the cot. 'It is only the beginning, the very beginning. You cannot conceive how far the journey stretches ahead of you.'

She did not answer, but turned and took her leave. When she was outside in the passage and the guards had closed the door, the papers she had brought slipped from her stiff fingers and scattered on the floor. She found her clothes were soaked with sweat, and she was shaking.

The trial was held in a room with a domed ceiling open at the top for the sunlight to stream in. The walls were decorated with carved and painted friezes in soft earth colours. The public benches were packed, she could not see a single vacant space.

Five green-robed judges sat in the centre, facing Cassiodorus who stood, manacled by each wrist, in a railed box with guards on either side. Tathea searched for Ishrafeli, and with a sudden surge of pleasure, almost relief, she saw him sitting close to the front.

The proceedings began with Allomir putting the argument for the prosecution. Everything was smaller, more intimate than in Shinabar. There was no searing desert heat, no bitter tang of herbs on the wind, but rather the faint smell of salt. But the mind of it was the same: the conflict, the weight of judgement, the issues of right and wrong, and the law.

Memory crowded in on her. The past seemed all around, yet

32

beyond her reach, gone for ever with all it held that was dear past measure.

'We have observed honour without arrogance,' he said in his harsh voice that could not be ignored. 'Each man has known his own freedom, and been a servant to the common weal. I will show you that Cassiodorus, in his negotiations with the enemy, has cast aside our ways and sought to make himself the arbiter of what is good.'

There was a rumble of anger from young men in the room. Tathea saw Cassiodorus lean forward in his box and whisper something to a golden youth beside him and he in turn spoke to his neighbour. An ugliness passed from face to face.

'Whether that is treason need not be argued,' Allomir went on, with a glance at Tathea as if he had noticed her attention wander. 'We have not accused him of treason, but with a defiance of that modesty, that bridle to the power of the individual, which the gods have placed upon us from the beginning, and which has made us what we are.' His voice lowered. 'It cannot be broken without a terrible cost, one which we and our children's children will pay in blood and in tribute all our lives.'

Through the blue heat of the day they argued and paraded witnesses. Allomir showed that Cassiodorus had negotiated the treaty without reference to the people of Parfyrion, their judgement or their wishes. The facts were simple. No permission had been sought. No debate had taken place.

Tathea called witnesses to the long deprivation of the war, its detrimental effect on the welfare of the city and its people, how its art had grown stale, its political life strident and repetitive, its creativity directed only to weapons of war.

The following day she called the women who had lost their husbands, their brothers and their sons in the conflict. They spoke with dignity, but it was their grief-stricken faces that had most power to move.

In questioning the women and drawing from them their pain, Tathea laid naked her own. The desolation she had felt riding across the desert, the loneliness that still haunted her and her restless questioning of the past as if somehow she could have changed it, all poured through her own words, brief as they were compared to the witnesses'. The judges listened to her and watched.

When she glanced at Cassiodorus in his railed-in dock, she saw the brilliance in his eyes, the probing, exultant knowledge of her wounds, and she felt as if something dirty had crept inside her. There was an evil in him that terrified her. She tore her gaze away and looked for Ishrafeli but could not find him in the crowd. Her vision swam, the individual faces blurred and she had to close her eyes to steady herself.

'Are you well?' It was Allomir's voice, concerned, oddly gentle. Had he seen in Cassiodorus the same terrible evil that she saw? No, of course not. Cassiodorus was simply a man whose overbearing pride and ambition needed curbing, for the sake of everyone in Parfyrion.

And she was defending him! He was laughing at her, because he knew she hated it, just as he knew she could not escape. He was using the people's honour against them, such was his contempt for it, and for them. Perhaps there lay his weakness. She decided to call one more witness, one that Allomir had mentioned, a historian and lover of the old ways.

'I call Styanax.'

Cassiodorus stiffened. He moved his hands and she heard the clank of the manacles. She found herself shivering, in spite of the sun pouring through the heart of the dome.

Styanax was an old man, white-haired, gaunt-faced. He looked at her guardedly and with dislike, holding on to the rail to steady himself, his thin hands blue-veined and spotted with age.

'You accuse Cassiodorus of blasphemy,' she began solemnly. 'How are you sure that it is the gods' will that the majority should decide all issues, even those which they do not understand because they have neither the information nor the experience? No one has denied that Cassiodorus is the best soldier Parfyrion has had in four hundred years. You have not even questioned that this treaty is both timely and fair.'

Styanax smiled very slightly, only a curve of the lips. 'It is a good treaty,' he replied with great gravity. 'If Cassiodorus were to rule Parfyrion, his decisions would be far better than the Council's, at first, and certainly swifter.'

'At first?' she prompted.

'Like all men, he will in time make mistakes, misjudgements. But by then there will be no one left strong enough to make him reconsider. And those who question him he will see not as counsellors but as enemies, traitors to his peace and order, his prosperity for the people. It is the age-old pattern of all tyranny.'

It was a risk to ask, but she had to. The purpose was lost if she stopped now. Her hands were still trembling. 'Then why did Allomir not say all this? Surely it is part of his argument, if it is true?'

'Because it has not happened yet,' Styanax answered, his eyes holding hers steadily. 'Cassiodorus can deny it, and there are many who will believe him. The young are impatient.' He smiled thinly, and she wondered if he had sons of his own. 'They would rather have his efficiency,' he went on. 'They are tired of the sobriety of the old way, the eternal argument and the discipline. Allomir has not accused him of treason against the state; and it would not advance his prosecution to prove it, even if he could.'

34

Should she stop now, while she had at least half made her point, or continue and risk losing it all? She could feel Cassiodorus's eyes on her, and the brilliant jubilation in him. She made her decision.

'Have you not had other heroes in the past who were admired by the people and were not always modest in the heat of their praise?'

'Of course—'

'And were they a threat to Parfyrion?'

There was a cheer from the crowd. A young man waved his arm. Tathea cringed inwardly.

Styanax inclined his head. 'Some were, and we countered the threat by use of balance and the law.'

'Did they always take advice well, even on the occasions when they were right, and others less brave, less skilled, were wrong?' she pursued.

'It is not a question of being right or wrong,' he explained with weary patience. 'It is a question of power. If you grant any man power over you that you cannot remove from him should he abuse it, that you cannot curb, and in the end cannot even question, it becomes tyranny, and then finally enslavement. You have ultimately lost your freedom of conscience, and that means you have lost your soul.'

She turned to Allomir.

He understood. His beaked face was transfigured with the beauty of it. He rose to his feet, smiling at her, then turned to Styanax.

'Is that not the greatest blasphemy of all?' he asked softly, but his voice filled the room.

Styanax sighed and the anger and despair left his body. 'It is,' he replied.

Cassiodorus's features were contorted with fury. His rage filled the vast room and washed round it, spilling over everyone, feeding on the pride and outrage of the young men who were already preparing for violence. The noise in the room was a low rumble like a gathering tide.

Tathea turned to the judges. Their decision was plain in their faces, but they pronounced it with due weight and in the traditional words.

'Cassiodorus, son of Critos of Parfyrion, we have found you guilty of blasphemy, and we sentence you to depart these shores and never to return as long as you shall live. You have betrayed your trust, and your name shall be removed from among us.'

Cassiodorus raised his manacled hands, his body leaning forward, bull-like, menacing, and stared around the room at the hushed crowd.

'My name will never be removed! Parfyrion will know me centuries after you are dust in the streets, and your children's children after you.' He looked at Allomir. 'You speak for an age that is locked in the past, without ideas and without life. You will perish with it before tomorrow comes. And you!' He swivelled to stare at Tathea. 'Woman,

35

you have betrayed me.' Suddenly his voice was soft, intimate, for her alone. 'I know who you are. I have written your name on my hands, and I shall remember you in all the days that are to come. You will pray on your knees that I should forget, but I will not. Your God cannot protect you from me.' He jerked his head sideways derisively. 'Ask Ishrafeli! He will tell you!'

She wanted to answer him, but her mouth was dry and her throat almost too tight to breathe. The words pounded in her head but would not reach her tongue. She meant to defy him but she was seized with silence.

Cassiodorus threw his head back and wrenched his arms up, away from the guards, and smashed them down, splintering the railing. It was not an attempt to escape, simply a demonstration of his strength and a rallying cry to the young men in the court who had already risen to their feet and were pushing aside the older and weaker or more hesitant as they forced their way out. Other youths stood silent and afraid.

Cassiodorus was escorted away. People moved to huddle together in anxiety. A shadow had settled over the room.

Allomir walked across the floor to Tathea. 'You have done well,' he said gravely. His black eyes searched her face, trying to gauge how far she had intended her victory. 'Parfyrion is in your debt.' His lips tightened. 'But walk carefully, lady. Cassiodorus will not forgive you.'

'I know,' she said hoarsely. She wanted to sound confident, but it was beyond her power.

The judges thanked her also. She turned to leave, uncertain what she had done, or what she had learned. If this was part of the truth she sought, she was far from understanding it.

She saw Phraxus coming towards her, his brow furrowed. He did not speak until he had reached her.

'You meant to do that!' His voice lifted with admiration as if he could scarcely believe it.

She did not know what to say. She was assailed by doubt. Where was Ishrafeli? She wanted to speak to him, to be near him. His opinion mattered intensely.

'It is not the truth?' she asked, finding her voice at last, but it sounded like defiance, not a question.

Phraxus's face was suddenly bleak. 'Yes,' he answered quickly. 'Perhaps I should have known sooner. I have fought beside him often enough, but I read the signs for what I hoped was true.' He offered his arm. 'Come. We should leave. You must be hungry, and tired. And I think it would be safer for you not to remain.' He guided her through the milling, jostling crowd outside into the sun and the bright air. Allomir was on the steps a few yards away, his robes gleaming white.

She saw Ishrafeli coming towards them. He had been waiting here for her. His eyes searched her face.

There was a cry. They all swung round. A young soldier had darted forward, sword drawn, and lunged at Allomir. Allomir looked down, eyes wide as scarlet blood gushed from his chest. The moment seemed frozen as he stood perfectly straight, dazzled by the sun, then gradually he buckled at the knees and slid forward on to the stones.

A woman screamed. A slow rumble of horror went up from the crowd, increasing until it was shrill with rage and a deep, underlying terror.

Phraxus was white-faced, his eyes hollow. He stood rooted, too stricken to speak.

Tathea felt a touch at her elbow. She knew without looking that it was Ishrafeli.

The crowd was beginning to break up. Men were running forward. Several had drawn weapons. Blind anger surged like a trapped wave of the sea, creating a vortex which sooner or later must consume everything. Fear was so sharp Tathea could taste it, acrid like the smell of sweat. There was shouting, women were screaming. Someone was calling out orders. Several people ran around, blindly. Others huddled together. Then the fighting began.

Tathea turned as if compelled, and above their heads she saw the towering figure of Cassiodorus, the same brilliance in his eyes, the curl of triumph on his thick lips.

She swung round to Phraxus. He, too, was staring at Cassiodorus, his old commander. The sun was on his face, the wind in his eyes. Around them was the heat and dust of the city square, the tumult of milling people unaware of the challenge being cast down.

Cassiodorus was free of his guards and he was armed. Carefully, very deliberately, he drew his sword, the light glistening on its blade.

Ishrafeli pulled Tathea a step backwards, away from Phraxus. Somewhere a woman was sobbing in terror.

Phraxus lowered his hand until it rested on the hilt of his own sword, the sun on his bare arms, catching the fine gold hairs. He hesitated a moment, knowing that if he drew it there would be no turning back. Then he completed the movement, brought the bright blade out and held it up. It was civil war.

There was a roar from the crowd. A man shouted his allegiance, then another, then a score.

Ishrafeli gripped Tathea's arm, she felt the pain of his fingers on her flesh, and she had no choice but to follow him as he pushed his way out of the square and along the broad street down to the harbour. Behind them the noise was growing uglier. Along the pavement doors were closing. A child started to cry, standing in the middle of the road, its face twisted with fear.

Tathea hesitated, longing at least to see it was safe.

A group of youths came out of a side street ahead of her. Two had broadswords. They spread out to bar the way, their faces surly, eyes bright.

Ishrafeli stopped, half pushing Tathea behind him.

The first youth swaggered forward and stood splay-legged a yard in front of them, sneering. But it was Tathea he was looking at, recognition in his face.

'It's her!' he said loudly, jerking his head to his companions. 'She's the one who betrayed Cassiodorus!' He fingered his sword. Then he swung it and lunged forward.

Ishrafeli dodged without apparent effort, lifted his arm, feinted, and caught the youth a blow at the back of the neck, sending him sprawling to the ground where he lay still.

One of the others let out a yell of rage and started forward with his sword slashing. He showed more skill and far more preparedness.

Tathea was horrified. She hurled herself forward to the fallen man, seized his sword and threw it to Ishrafeli.

The fight was swift and violent, and left the youth mortally wounded and Ishrafeli ashen-faced, his arms and clothes stained with blood. He snatched Tathea by the arm and started to run, dragging her stumbling down the steep slope past the fading beauty of the buildings to the harbour where the tide was high and their skiff riding easily. He almost threw her in, loosed the rope, pushed the weight of his body against the hull for a moment, then leaped over the widening spread of green water to land in the stern.

'The sail!' he ordered her. 'Unbind that end!' He pointed and with fumbling fingers she obeyed. Behind them Parfyrion was ochre, fire and gold in the setting sun. Already the sky was stained with smoke. Together they worked, muscles straining, hands bruised and grazed, to lift the sails and catch the faint breeze.

They gathered speed over bright water like a sheet of bronze, purple sails wide. She looked at Ishrafeli where he stood holding the ropes. His face was copper in the burning light. He seemed older than she had thought before. In the set of his lips there was grief as ancient as heaven.

Only when Parfyrion was a smoking blur smudged across the horizon and the fire of the sunset burned heavy in the west did he lash the ropes and come to her, kneeling in front of her, touching her cheek with his fingers.

'You wanted the truth,' he whispered. 'Did you imagine it would come to you without labour or pain?'

'I don't believe that was the truth.' Her voice choked in tears.

He smiled at her, and softly put his hand over hers, warm now, but he said no more.

Chapter Three

Tathea woke with a gasp, giddy with relief to see the black cavern of the sail above her, swallowing the stars as the skiff pressed forward on the wind. She had been dreaming of Cassiodorus, his bold eyes tearing the privacy from her mind, intruding, stripping her thoughts and promising he would know her and hate her for ever.

Now she was cold, even under the silk cloak, and she shivered and pulled it closer to her.

Her movement caused Ishrafeli to turn; all she could see of him was a dark silhouette against the sky. She wanted to talk to him about Parfyrion, but she did not know what to say. They had been there barely two days, but the loss of it was sharp, like unshed tears. So much nobility of thought, high dreams broken by arrogance, and one man's will leading others too young to see its destruction.

'Is truth all about power?' she asked.

He came to her and sat on the boards. She could feel the warmth of him faintly.

'In part.' His voice came out of the darkness. 'You can never reach the measure of your creation until you know how to use power, and how and when to lay it down.'

The rush of the water was soft about them, an incessant whispering vastness.

'Who is Cassiodorus?' she asked.

'Don't you know?' His voice was soft.

She strained to see his face, but the starlight was too dim.

'No.'

'What do you think?'

She shivered, memory chilling her more than the night and the wind. 'I feel as if he is . . .' She struggled for something sensible, and found nothing. 'I feel as if he is some great everlasting enemy!'

He slid his hand over hers. 'He is only a shadow of the Great Enemy, a breath from the ice.'

She sat silent for several minutes, memories filling her, of sunlight on the stones, a statue with perfect grace, Phraxus's face in the upper room, and again the moment of decision as he drew his sword against Cassiodorus. She heard Allomir's voice, vibrant with the passion of belief in him, and felt the terrible loss of his death.

'Truth is about courage too, isn't it?' she said. 'And cost.'

'Yes,' he agreed and there was no hesitation in his voice.

She shuddered and pulled the cloak tight round her neck.

'Are you cold?' he asked.

'Yes. The air has changed. It smells different, stinging, as it did when I was coming towards the Maelstrom. Are we coming to another maelstrom? We are not going back, are we?' Why did that thought hurt so much?

'No.' There was tenderness and pain and laughter in his voice. 'We have a long way to go yet, but not through another maelstrom, at least not in the manner you mean. But I think there may be terrible seas and perhaps some will drown. There are many kinds of waves, and many ways of drowning beneath them.'

There was no sound but the whine of wind in the rigging and the rush of water around them, but the pitch had changed and she knew they were travelling at far greater speed.

For a long time they sat together without speaking. She was comfortable in the knowledge of his presence. There was a peace within him that outer turmoil could not touch, and something of it spread through her when she was close to him. She was not sure if she slept or merely let the darkness and the safety of being with him ease her into half dream.

When she opened her eyes the sky was paling in the east, water-green under the hood of the night. She turned to Ishrafeli. His eyes were closed. In this glimmering half light his features were smoothed of emotion, only the strength of the bones showed, and the curve of his mouth. His cloak had fallen down a little, and she pulled it up to keep the cold air from his neck.

He smiled.

'I didn't mean to wake you . . .' She was momentarily abashed to be caught in such an intimacy.

He sat up, glancing at her, then turned to the horizon ahead of them where the dark line of land was just visible.

'Where are we going?' she asked.

'Bal-Eeya,' he replied. 'We must shorten sail.' He looked up at the sky and the fast spreading light. 'If this wind goes on rising we'll capsize. Here, hold this.' He passed her a rope. 'Pull hard. It's strong.'

She was glad to help, and they worked side by side reefing the sail and tacking and veering to avoid the troughs. The waves increased steadily until full daylight came, bleached winter-pale across a wind-washed sky, cloud racks massing darkly on the horizon. The air stung her skin with flecks of ice and the brilliance of the light on the choppy water hurt her eyes. The tide was running hard, driving them before it whether they would or not.

40

They were swept round a headland and it took all their combined strength, and Ishrafeli's skill, to come about and ride the current into Bal-Eeya's harbour. What she saw was nothing like Parfyrion. There was no warmth, no mellow stone and wide streets. They were closed around on three sides. Skirting the harbour itself was a rock-built wall leading to a jagged island so that it formed an almost complete shelter. Only the south where the clouds now covered half the sky lay unprotected.

On the shore the buildings were of painted wood, clean as snow, full of straight lines and scrubbed colours. Wooden boats lay at anchor, their masts jostling as the sharp seas swung their hulls. Seabirds wheeled and mewed overhead, and men working on the wharves were muffled in coats with fur collars and hoods. Occasionally one would raise his head and look out to sea towards the darkening horizon.

They drew the skiff in close enough for Ishrafeli to call out to a group of men, 'Where may we moor?'

One of the men dropped what he was doing and came to the edge of the wharf. His straight hair was swept back from a broad brow. It was the face of a man used to command, yet he spoke gently.

'You will need the inner harbour, friend. Your vessel is light, and there is a storm coming. The tone of the wind and the smell of it make me fear it will be one of the worst we have yet seen.' He pointed with outstretched arm. 'Go to the end of the staging and hard right. In the inner harbour there you will find a row of berths. The fourth one along is mine, and is presently unused. You are welcome to it.'

'Thank you . . .' Ishrafeli hesitated.

'Itureus,' the man answered, then looked beyond them at the sky to the east, shading his eyes not from the sun but from the wind. 'You had better make haste. The weather is worsening fast. Have you friends in Bal-Eeya?'

'No.'

'Then may I offer you the hospitality of my house? You will need shelter and food, and you are welcome. I will take you, when I have spoken to Patro. There is still much to be done.'

'Thank you.' Ishrafeli stepped back to the ropes and guided the skiff carefully along the wharf, standing well out as the water grew choppier and the current threatened to carry them against the pier stakes and crush them.

It was a difficult task negotiating a course to the inner harbour, but once there the right berth was easy to find and Ishrafeli made the skiff fast. Soon Itureus joined them, followed closely by another, far younger man, whom he introduced as Patro, the leader of Bal-Eeya. Patro bade them welcome, exchanged a few more words with Itureus, then took his leave.

Tathea and Ishrafeli hurried with Itureus along the quay and up the

41

grey stone streets, shivering with cold. The buildings on either side were shingle-roofed, boards scoured by salt and wind, painted in the pale, cold colours of the sky, blues and greens and the greys of twilight. There were no groups of people talking as there had been in Parfyrion. Here and there a lone man hurried about some business, head forward. Long, woollen, fur-trimmed cloaks gave gravity and a sense of height, even to the most ordinary.

Tathea saw no statues, no carving or embellishment of any sort, and there were no theatres. But as they strode up the hill, she did begin to see that the buildings had a kind of spare beauty. White bell-towers marked out churches, airy and shimmering in the thin sunlight and rising wind, the steep-pitched roofs at a multitude of angles.

Itureus led them to a fine house with a walled garden a little distance from the centre of the town. In its lea grew laurel bushes with thick, shining leaves and under them a profusion of smaller plants with grey-white feathery leaves and white flowers.

They were welcomed as soon as the door opened. The woman who greeted them was beautiful with a fair, smooth face and golden-brown hair. Her dark blue eyes swept over them in only momentary surprise, then as Itureus explained their situation and introduced them, she smiled and stepped back to open the door wide for them. Her name was Dulcina, and she was Itureus's wife, although seemingly at least twenty years younger than he was.

'You must be cold and tired.' She looked at Tathea's silk cloak. 'May I lend you a wool dress? And warmer shoes? I am afraid the coming storm is going to be very bad.'

'Thank you,' Tathea said gratefully. She was shaking with cold and her feet were numb.

'Patro is afraid it is going to be far worse than last year.' Itureus fastened the door, leaning against it to secure it from the wind.

Dulcina smiled, but there was a kind of impatience in her eyes. 'Patro is only trying to persuade you to help him,' she said, then turned to Tathea. 'Itureus was the leader of Bal-Eeya for twenty years and everyone trusts him,' she explained. 'He has managed to save the city from the sea every year. Every year for twenty years he has laboured to help build up the sea walls and ensure that all the beasts are gathered from the shores and penned inland, that every ship is lashed and battened down, that everyone has food, and that the watch is kept. If you have not been in Bal-Eeya during a storm, you have no idea what work that is.' She was speaking to Tathea as one woman to another, excluding the men. 'I have sat alone here so many nights when the weather was closing in. I worked with the other women, of course, in the hall preparing emergency rations, blankets, bandages and splints. But at night I have come home and slept alone, hearing the wind rise, holding my child, knowing my husband would always be

42

the last to leave his post, and then only when the danger was over. He has earned the right to step back now and allow someone else to lead. It is Patro's turn. He is perfectly able to do it.'

Itureus put his arm round her. 'My dear, he is only concerned for his responsibility.'

She glanced at him with a smile, then back at Tathea. 'Come, let me show you the room where you may change, and where you may sleep, if the wind allows it.' She turned to Ishrafeli. 'Would you like a woollen tunic and cloak also?'

They were in what was apparently the main room of the house. It was wide and light with a stone hearth in it surrounded by grey and white marble, bare and clean, but possessing a beauty of texture on which ornament would have been superfluous. The walls were a shade of blue as indefinite as the evening sea, but the colour was warmed by the deep bronze of the hangings and the reflection of the firelight.

'Thank you,' Ishrafeli accepted. Then he looked at her curiously. 'Is this really a worse storm than usual?'

'I doubt it.' She shook her head and lifted one shoulder in a dismissive little gesture. 'It is merely that in the heart of the summer we forget what they are like. Patro is new and he is nervous. He will learn –' she glanced at her husband – 'if he is allowed to! Come, please. Itureus will show you your room, and I will take Tathea. Then you must have something to eat. It has been prepared for nearly an hour.'

She led Tathea up shallow wooden stairs to a room at the top of the house. It seemed to be a kind of turret with windows in three sides, full of white wood and blue light, as if the sky enveloped it. The floor was carpeted in woven sea grasses, bleached by salt and wind to almost the colour of bone. The only ornaments were great shells with hollow hearts of primrose and gold. Dulcina brought her a soft cream woollen robe and tunic and leather shoes, and left her to put them on.

When Tathea went downstairs again, she found Ishrafeli already there, and Itureus standing by the window looking up at the sky, his brow furrowed, his mouth pulled tight.

'It always whines like that,' Dulcina said. Her hand rested on the shoulder of a small boy of perhaps four or five years. His hair was fair like hers but he had the steady eyes of his father. The slender nape of his neck and his narrow shoulders caught Tathea with a thrust of searing pain for Habi. For a moment she was paralysed with grief. She could not draw her breath, her heart was tight inside her and the hurt was beyond bearing. The room dissolved around her and she was in the palace again in the desert night, Habi lying in her arms.

'Does it?' the child asked, his voice cutting through her mind. He looked from one to the other of them. 'Elnid said it was worse than ever before.'

'Nonsense, Kori,' his mother said reassuringly. 'Patro will make sure that all is well. There is no need to be frightened. And this time your father will be with us to look after us here at home.'

Tathea tried to regain her composure and return to the present.

Kori looked up at Itureus.

'Of course,' Itureus answered, his face softening. 'But before the storm strikes, we must go and bring all the animals in. The sheep are still out along the shore. I must help with that.'

'Can we help too?' Ishrafeli offered quickly. 'It is small return for your hospitality.'

Itureus did not hesitate. 'Thank you. All hands are welcome.'

Ishrafeli looked at Tathea. He could know nothing of what was inside her. None of these people could. She must hide it, go forward and find what she had come to seek, the meaning, and the value to it all. She could not go backward. Was there somewhere ahead, which would fulfil the sage's promise? She had to believe it . . . for Habi's sake! She must know . . . for him.

'Yes . . . of course.' Her voice was hoarse. Ishrafeli looked at her curiously, but he did not ask, and she could not tell him.

First they ate. Tathea was surprised that she could. Then she put on a heavy cloak Dulcina offered her and went obediently with Itureus and Ishrafeli out of the house and back towards the city where they found Patro. His young face was anxious until he saw Itureus, then his face ironed out and he straightened up, as if a leaden weight had slipped from his shoulders.

'The wind has dropped!' he said with a catch in his voice. 'That means it will break soon – doesn't it?'

'Perhaps tonight,' Itureus agreed, putting a hand lightly on Patro's arm. 'Don't worry, you will know what to do. You've seen many storms before and helped me often enough. Now we must get the animals in. I will take the south shore. Ishrafeli and Tathea will help me. You see to the harbour wall. There are many sandbags to be placed yet.'

'I know, I know.' Patro ran his fingers through his hair distractedly, and turned away.

Itureus smiled, but there was no unkindness in it. 'Come.' He took Tathea by the arm. 'We must find all the beasts or we shall lose them.'

The air was sharp. The wind scattered wisps of slate-coloured cloud like mares' tails across the cold blue of the sky. As they walked the narrow paths up over the headland, the dry grass rippled and bent as the fingers of the breeze tugged at it. Tathea heard the sound of the surf even before they came over the breast of the rise and saw the long spumes of white roaring up the pale sand, hissing and folding under, sucked back into the dark body of the ocean.

She drew in her breath in surprise. It was terrible – and beautiful.

There was a kind of music in it like the beating of the blood. And it was as clean as the beginning of time, before anything had been soiled.

She lifted her face to the sky. White birds soared across the emptiness of it, sliding and skating through the tunnels of the wind. Suddenly there was a hunger and a hope inside her. She hardly dared acknowledge it, in case it was no more than an illusion.

Itureus was talking, but his words were drowned by the thundering surf. He waved his arm to the left, and then touched Ishrafeli and pointed to the right where sheep were scattered across the low grass, unprotected from the sea. Ishrafeli nodded and Itureus went down on to the strand to the left.

'Come, we are going along there,' Ishrafeli shouted to Tathea, pointing to the pale sand stretching away in front of them to the right where the wind whipped the surf and blew the spray in white manes. He took her arm and they ran and slid down to the shore, all but knocked over by the wind as they came out of the shelter of the hill. It was bitterly cold, but the pounding water and the endless roar of the surf filled her with exhilaration, a freedom, almost a unity with the wheeling birds and the torn and streaming clouds driving in from the east.

Suddenly Ishrafeli began to run, swinging his arms wide, not caring if the wind banged and buffeted him. Tathea hesitated. She wanted to join him, but she could not let go of the grief inside her.

He was leafing her behind. She ran to join him, skipping over the stones and dark patches of weed, the blood surging and singing in her veins. A nameless laughter beat in her ears, filling her as the wind filled the sky.

Finally, far along the shore, Ishrafeli stopped and held his arms wide and she ran to him. He held her and she clung to him for a wild, wonderful moment, feeling the strength of him flooding through her. Suddenly she was seized by a soaring joy. Anything was possible. Heaven itself was within reach!

He stepped back and took her hand. His grasp was hard and strong. 'Come, we have work to do,' he ordered. 'Not a sheep, not a lamb must be lost. If we do not find every one, they will drown.'

She was happy to obey. It seemed a good and precious thing to do. She was more than willing to walk until her legs ached and her hands and feet were cold and bruised. They worked all day, driving the nimble, long-fleeced sheep inland to the high pastures. They stopped only long enough to sit in the lee of a stone wall and eat the bread and drink the water Dulcina had given them.

As the light faded they went back to the shore a last time to check that they had left no animal behind. They stood together on the headland as the sun set in a crimson orb behind a furnace of clouds, staining them with a glory of flame and gold crossed by dark, ragged shadows like smoke.

'It looks like the fires at the end of the world,' she said softly. 'Is the storm behind that?'

'Yes. It will come before morning,' he answered. The sky reflected red on his smooth cheek and brow. 'Patro is right,' he added, putting his arm round her shoulder. 'It is going to be worse than ever before.'

The splendour filled the west until even the air glowed amber and red, and the darkened sea reflected like a pewter shield the funeral pyre of the sun.

She thought of Parfyrion, and Cassiodorus, and the power of ice and rage within him. The shadow of the Enemy, Ishrafeli had said.

'Is it anything to do with me?' she asked, and the wind whipped the words from her lips.

'I don't know,' he replied, his hand tightening on her shoulder. 'But yes, I think so.'

They reached Itureus's house as the wind rose to screaming pitch. Garden trees were bent double, branches thrashing. Even wearing thick woollen cloaks, they were numb with cold.

Dulcina welcomed them, looking quickly from Tathea and Ishrafeli to Itureus, searching his face.

'All is well,' he assured her quickly. 'The beasts are gathered and the people are prepared. The sea defences are complete.'

She relaxed and smiled. 'I told you Patro would do all that was necessary! There was no need for you to go. Now, you must be hungry.' She included them all in this last remark and led them through to the large room with the bronze hangings. The fire blazed in the hearth, vivid, consuming the wood and dark peat as the wind drew it. On the table was a large earthen pot with delicious-smelling steam coming up through holes in its lid.

They ate companionably but without speaking. The pitch of the wind rose a little higher, and even in this stone-built house and with the leaves dashing against the windows, they could hear the dull boom of the surf on the shore.

After they had eaten, Tathea helped Dulcina carry away the dishes. She had never done such a thing before, but here it seemed quite natural. These people were the leaders in Bal-Eeya. They had offered hospitality, but not service, and she could not comfortably have accepted it.

'Thank you,' Dulcina said with a smile, washing plates swiftly and putting them away. 'You have no idea how different it is for me to have my husband beside me during a storm instead of overseeing everything, worrying about everyone.' She worked with quick, practised hands, scouring the pot clean. 'When it was all over, he would be so exhausted he looked like an old man. No one can bear that responsibility for more than a short number of years. They asked too much of him, but he would never refuse them.'

'You must be very relieved now his term of office is over,' Tathea sympathised, taking the pot from her and drying it.

Dulcina washed the last bowl and set it on the bench, then turned to face Tathea. 'It wasn't only the time,' she explained. 'It was the danger too. In Bal-Eeya we are all used to the power of the sea. We know it can kill at any time, and probably will, but the leader always takes the greatest risks. He is the first man to dare the dangers, the last man to leave the barricades, like the captain of a ship. He never commands a man to do something he would not and has not done himself.'

'But you must be proud of him,' Tathea said earnestly. 'Even in the hardest and worst moments . . .'

Dulcina turned away. 'I'm glad they're over. I want him to be here with Kori and me. It is someone else's turn now.'

Tathea did not answer. She had no right to judge in a land of which she knew so little. If it could have saved her child's life, she would have given up the throne of Shinabar without a thought. She wished with all her strength that someone had offered her that choice!

Dulcina stood very still. Her face was very beautiful, ageless.

Tathea smiled at her, all thoughts of judgement vanished.

The tension left Dulcina's body and, at ease with each other, they returned to the main room.

Ishrafeli was sitting close to the fire. Itureus lay back in his chair, his eyes closed, as if he was asleep. The lines of worry were smoothed out of his face and Tathea could see him, as he must have been years earlier, before his leadership in the long struggle against the sea. In a way it was like a military campaign, and he the general leading his army against an implacable enemy who never tired, who never sustained losses, and who could not be killed. They might win this or that skirmish, but the war itself would never end. The ashes settled and Ishrafeli stoked the fire. Outside, the wind shrieked with a thin, piercing sound growing steadily a note higher, a note sharper.

It was a few minutes before they realised the banging on the door was someone trying to gain their attention rather than simply a branch or flying debris. Itureus opened his eyes and rose to his feet.

Dulcina stiffened, her expression suddenly wary.

They heard Itureus unbar the door and a moment later he returned with Patro, his face whipped and bruised by the wind, his body shivering under his mahogany-brown cloak. He turned to Itureus immediately.

'It's already worse than anything last year!' There was fear in his voice, brittle-edged and urgent. 'The sea has gouged out great hollows in the shore to the north. It's almost up to the grass. It will take part of the land, even the low pastures this time!'

'No, it won't,' Itureus assured him, leading him further into the room, closer to the fire. 'It always looks worse than we remember. The storm carries the sand along to the East Point, but when the wind veers, it brings it back. In the spring the neap tides carry it up and smooth it out. We just forget.'

Patro shook his head. 'I've never seen one like this before.' His voice was sharp, a note of panic close beneath the surface. 'The water is higher. It's over the outer wall already, and we don't know if the wall's only submerged or has been washed right away.'

'It's only submerged,' Dulcina said a little impatiently. She gestured towards the darkness beyond the window. 'You couldn't see anything in this anyway. It always seems worse when you can only half see, and there's such a noise. You've watched Itureus scores of times. You know what to do.'

'The whole of Bal-Eeya stands or falls in this.' Patro's fear was barely under control, his body was shaking. 'I need Itureus's experience to guide me. He can look at a wall and see its weaknesses where I have to measure and test, and I still might be wrong.'

'You won't be wrong!' she answered firmly, her voice steady, her body standing square to his. 'You must learn to trust your judgement. If people see you are afraid, they will be afraid too, and that is when accidents happen because fear eats away confidence and decision. This storm is no different from all the storms you have known all your life in Bal-Eeya. It only seems different to you because for the first time you are leading the people, not Itureus.' She moved to stand closer beside her husband, and linked her arm through his. It was a familiar gesture, gentle and possessive. 'He has earned his right to rest, and I have earned the right to have him with me.' She smiled up at him, then turned back to Patro. 'Go and fulfil your destiny, Patro.'

He drew in a deep breath, shaky, unconvinced.

Itureus looked quickly at Dulcina, then put out his hand and took Patro's.

'She is right, my friend. Your judgement is excellent. The people trust you, but you must also trust yourself. Of course you are afraid. Do you not think I was afraid, every time? Afraid of the storm, afraid of the sea, and above all afraid I would let everybody down and others would suffer for my mistakes.'

Surprise filled Patro's eyes. 'Thank you,' he said warmly. He hesitated a moment. 'I still believe this is more than the usual storm, but I will go and do all I can.' He looked quickly at Ishrafeli, then at Tathea. 'Goodbye. I hope all is well with you this night.' And he turned and left. Itureus went with him to the door and then barred it behind him against the wind.

They blew out the lamps downstairs, damped the fire and crept up to their beds, but sleep was no more than fitful. Tathea lay in her turret room and listened to the high, thin shriek of the wind and the trees thrashing below her. She pulled the soft blankets over herself and drifted in and out of dreams, but always the violence was around her, enormous, threatening, destructive. Sometimes in her confused, half-sleeping mind it was not the elements that tore at the skies and sea, it was multitudinous armies of barbarians, shrieking and howling blind hatred. They threw themselves against the borders of the sane and beautiful world with a madness that would destroy everything made by man. Sometimes it was the great shadow behind Cassiodorus, a darkness that would swallow the light and devour the soul, because it hated with a misery that could never end.

She woke with the sweat cold on her body, and found with relief that it was only earthly wind howling in the sky and pounding breakers thundering on the shore.

As she lay grasping the covers, afraid to close her eyes again in case the nightmares of sleep returned, lightning tore across the sky and for long, terrible seconds the whole room was lit with a blue, shadowless brilliance. The darkness that followed was more intense, like a cave beneath the earth, and the noise even greater.

The lightning came again and again. Then there was a crash of splintering glass, and a scream . . . within the house . . . human.

Tathea threw herself out of bed and without bothering with a blanket or robe, ran from her room and all but fell down the stairs. A single lamp was burning down in the main room but its shadows flickered wildly, though it was covered with protective glass.

Cold air touched Tathea's flesh even before she reached the bottom stair. She swung round and saw Dulcina crouched over Kori in front of the shattered window, her face white, her eyes staring desperately through her wild hair.

'Help me!' she cried as soon as she saw Tathea. 'Help me! He's hurt! He's bleeding badly!'

For a moment Tathea could not move. The crumpled child, legs and body stained with blood, hurled her back into the tearing loss of the past. She was looking at Habi again, her eyes knowing he must be dead, her heart refusing to believe it, and already the grief piercing her with hurt beyond bearing.

Kori moved, no more than a twitch of semi-consciousness.

It broke the spell. Tathea flung herself across the floor which was littered with branches and leaves and other debris of the storm. She knew much of medicine. It was a Shinabari art. She pushed Dulcina away and swiftly ran her hands over the child's body, seeking the site

49

of the bleeding, and searching for broken bones.

'Get me cloth!' she ordered. 'Something light and smooth that won't get caught in the open flesh. Quickly.'

'What are you doing?' Dulcina demanded.

'I'm going to stop the bleeding first,' Tathea answered without looking up. The wavering light made it difficult to be certain, but it seemed as if his body was unhurt. The bleeding appeared to be from the legs, one of which was definitely broken. The gash was deep, and around him lay several long shards of broken glass, all splashed with scarlet. He was very small, his body lying curled over so she could have cradled him like a baby, and his limbs were so slender her fingers would close around his arms.

'Cloth!' Tathea demanded sharply.

At last Dulcina responded. She tore her own skirt and held out the pieces.

Tathea rolled one into a pad and with the other tied it over the deepest wound. The rain was lashing in through the shattered window. The floor was wet. 'What happened?'

'Is he going to be all right?' Dulcina stared at her.

'I think so.' She kept her voice steady. 'What happened?'

'I don't know. He must have woken up and come down here. I didn't know until I heard the glass break. I couldn't sleep. I came instantly, and found him. He must have been dreaming.' Dulcina shook her head, pushing her hair out of her eyes. The wind was driving in and it was bitterly cold. She was shuddering as she spoke, her teeth chattering. 'He never comes down alone! It's the storm.'

Itureus was on the stairs. 'What is it?' he asked, coming into the room. Then he saw Kori and ran forward. He stared at Dulcina, then at Tathea, wordless with fear.

'The window blew in,' Tathea said quietly. 'I think he's going to be all right, but we must keep him warm and set the broken bone in his leg, and keep the wound from bleeding.'

Dulcina went to pick him up. Tathea held her arm hard, hurting her. 'No, you'll make it worse. Get me something to splint the leg. Anything straight and firm will do.'

Obediently Dulcina stood up and began to look around for something.

Itureus reached for a slender-legged chair and in one movement snapped off one of the legs and handed it to Tathea.

'Have you any herbs for cleaning wounds, or for restoring strength?' she asked, taking the wood from him. 'And I need more clean linen, cut in strips for binding.'

Dulcina was shaking with fear. Her face was twisted with anguish and almost without colour, as if it were her own life seeping away. Tathea felt for her with a pain Dulcina was unaware of; it was too raw a wound to share with anyone. Tathea worked quickly and alone in the face of Dulcina and Itureus's ignorance of subtler medicine. Ishrafeli was apparently asleep, and there was no purpose in disturbing him. She did not need his counsel in this. It was one of the few practical arts of which she was mistress. No Shinabari was considered too noble to learn it, certainly not the daughter of a desert prince.

It took her an hour to bathe the wound with cloths soaked in an infusion of herbs she found in the kitchen. She splinted the leg, packing the raw edges of flesh with a cleansing paste made from crushed leaves and berries she hoped were of the same genus as the ones she knew. Then she prepared a lightly restorative drink and gave it to Dulcina to feed to Kori. All this time she kept him as warm as possible, wrapped in blankets.

When she finally went back to bed, she was wet and shuddering with cold, and drained with the horror of seeing an injured child, holding him in her arms, and knowing she could never heal her own son. She crept under the covers and pulled them tight about her. Outside, the wind seemed less, but she no longer cared. She felt the slow, hot tears run down her cheeks in grief that could not be eased.

When she awoke it was already day. The room was filled with a green, sickly light. All around her through the windows she could see a sky shredded with clouds. She rose and wrapping a blanket over her shoulders, went to the window and stared out. The bells had been removed from all the church towers. They looked bare, bereft. The only sound was the thin wail of the wind and the boom of water crashing against the sea walls and the white surf exploding.

Her first thought was of Kori. She washed and dressed hastily, and went down to see how he was.

In the main room she found Itureus and Ishrafeli. They were beginning to clean up the shattered glass and the debris.

'Is the storm over?' she asked, looking around to see how best to help them.

'No,' Itureus answered with a slight, wry smile. He pushed a weary hand through his hair. 'This is the lull before the heart of it strikes. I fear Patro is right after all and it will be one of the worst we have known. There is something in the colour of the sky, the smell of the wind, which is different.'

Ishrafeli glanced at Tathea, then away again. He was busy picking up branches and leaves, but his attention was not on it.

Tathea stood still. 'Worse than last night?'

'Yes. That was only the preliminary,' Itureus answered grimly. 'The real storm is still out there. I should say two or three hours away.'

'Then we must board that window.' Ishrafeli straightened up and walked over to it, staring at the garden where several trees were down, even within the shelter of the walls. He frowned, as if something in the garden troubled him.

Tathea went to where the branch lay which must have broken the glass that had been the cause of Kori's injury. A heavy stoneware jar also lay among the glass fragments. The lid was broken, but the jar itself, exquisitely simple in shape and coloured pale blue and green like the sea grasses, was only chipped. She felt a sudden regret for its loveliness. Perhaps with skill it could be mended. She would have to find the missing chips before they were swept up and thrown away with the other wreckage.

She righted the jar, placing it where it could not be knocked over again, and began to search. At first she examined the floor where it had fallen, then in slow circles she searched wider and wider, without finding them. She had actually given up and was helping Ishrafeli nail up the boards when she saw them. She was standing outside the window on the stone paving, because the boards needed to be fixed externally, or they would merely blow in again. She looked down and the pale, triangular pieces caught her eye. Puzzled to see them there, she bent down to examine them: four small chips of stoneware, bone pale on two sides, pale blue and green on the third. There was no mistaking them.

Ishrafeli was waiting. She slipped the pieces into her pocket and then returned to her task of handing him the long iron nails one by one.

They had finished only a few minutes when Patro returned, his long robe torn and stained. There was no mistaking his fear or his urgent, painful anxiety. He made no attempt to hide it, speaking immediately to Itureus.

'It is worse than before. I know the wind has dropped now, but the sea is higher than we've ever seen it. If I stood on the old high water mark, it would be over my head. When the wind comes again, we may not survive it. Please come and judge the defences before it is too late. The people need you. I've done all I can, but I don't know the sea as you do.'

Dulcina appeared in the doorway, her hair loose on her shoulders, her face pale, and dark shadows under her eyes.

'You can't go!' Her voice was strident with fear and anger. She swung round to Patro. 'He's led you all these years without ever once thinking of himself. He's laboured out there on the defences hour after hour, day and night, to keep you from destruction. Now it's your turn for the danger and the cold, and for your family to wait, alone, never knowing if you're coming back or not!' She jerked her hands. 'It's your turn for your wife and children to face the storm without you to help or comfort them. Go away and leave us! Your place is out there!' She flung her arms wide. 'Not here, bothering us!'

'My dear,' Itureus began, but she faced him with blazing eyes, and he stopped and looked at Patro. 'I'm sorry,' he said softly. 'What my wife says is true. You should have more faith in yourself.'

'It is not like other storms,' Patro argued, desperation naked in his blue eyes. 'We need you!'

'We need him too!' Dulcina took a step towards Patro. 'Kori is hurt, badly. His leg is broken and he has bled for hours. Itureus cannot leave.'

Patro's face was very white, but he did not retreat. 'I am sorry,' he said with deep sincerity. 'But the sea does not have morality or compassion—'

'Does that mean you don't either?' she cut across him wildly, her eyes glittering.

'It means I will do all I can to save Bal-Eeya,' he answered, but he looked as if she had struck him, so white was his young face. 'All of us, not just a family here or a house there. Itureus has wisdom I lack.'

Itureus looked at his wife, then at Patro, then back at his wife. 'My son is injured,' he said huskily, emotion tearing at him. 'I cannot leave now.'

Dulcina sighed and her body seemed to release a little of its terrible tension.

Suddenly Ishrafeli spoke. 'I'll come with you,' he offered Patro. 'I don't know Bal-Eeya, but I know the sea. I can be of some help.'

'Thank you,' Patro accepted, but it was courtesy, not relief. Ishrafeli was a stranger. Patro barely looked at him. It was Itureus he needed.

Tathea felt cold, even though the window was boarded up. The wind was sharper again. The calm was coming to an end. She hunched her shoulders and pushed her hands into the pockets of her borrowed tunic. Her fingers met the chips from the vase.

'Kori was hurt,' she said, looking at Patro. 'Very badly. He could have been killed. A branch came through the window, shattering the glass and knocking over a great jar which stood inside. He broke his leg and it bled a great deal.' Her voice choked. 'He is only small.'

Patro accepted defeat. The rising wind told him he had no time to argue. 'I'm sorry. That is terrible. There are a few trees down but not any others in walled gardens.'

Ishrafeli looked at Tathea quickly, then at the window, his eyes questioning.

She pulled the chips out of her pocket. They had been outside, not inside where the vase was. The branch was too long to have come through the frame of the window except end first, but it had not lain that way on the floor. If it had knocked the vase over, then the chips would have been inside. Someone had gone out and used the vase to break the window. Without the chips no one would ever have known. Itureus or Dulcina? She knew the answer before the question formed, even though her mind rejected it. She could never have hurt her child to keep her husband with her! But then she had not loved Mon-Allat. She could not have injured Habi even to save her own life!

She looked at Dulcina and saw the truth in the hollow of her eyes.

Should she speak? How bad was the storm? Would it really drown Bal-Eeya, or was Patro simply a man afraid of a task he had not yet tried?

'Is it really worse than before?' she said aloud.

Dulcina stared at her. 'No, of course it isn't!' she snapped. 'Patro is afraid, that's all. He doesn't want the burden of responsibility. Now that it's on him, he realises how heavy it is. He wanted the glory and the pride, but he doesn't want the cost if he fails, or the danger. Can't you see that?'

As if to answer her, the wind dropped its tone.

'Yes, it is worse,' Itureus said quietly, his mouth tight and pinched. 'It is there in the colour of the sky. When it breaks, it will be terrible.'

'How do you know that when others don't?' Tathea argued. 'It sounds as if it's blowing out.'

He gave a little shrug, rueful, sad. 'You don't know the sea as I do,' he said wearily. 'I can smell the heaviness and feel the shift in the pattern of it.'

'Then you should go.'

He looked past her to Dulcina. 'I can't,' he said. 'Not this time. I owe . . .'

Tathea held out the chips in the palm of her hand. 'I found these outside on the stone paving.'

'What are they?'

'Pieces of the vase which was broken – when it was used to smash the window which injured Kori . . .'

There was no sound in the room but the moan of the wind. Dulcina stared at Tathea with a searing hatred.

Itureus looked from Tathea to his wife. His eyes betrayed his knowledge, and his pain. For long seconds he struggled with his decision.

'I must go,' he said at last, his voice soft and filled with hurt. Without another word he walked out ahead of Patro. Ishrafeli followed.

Dulcina turned to Tathea, her eyes dark holes in her head, filled with knowledge and hatred, in them an infinite understanding of weakness and fear and need, and how to manipulate them, and a blind incomprehension of honour. She had used every power she had, and it had failed. She had wanted Itureus to love her before all else, even his soul.

She raised her arm. In her hand she held another jar. She smashed it against the table and held up the jagged end.

'You have taken from me what I want more than anything else,' she said through gritted teeth. 'I shall destroy you for that.' But she did not move.

Outside the wind rose again and the pitch changed.

Tathea stepped backwards. She must get out of the house. She would rather be crushed by the wind or drowned by the sea than face that monstrous hatred. It was like being with Cassiodorus again. It dizzied her senses and made her limbs heavy.

She backed into a stool, bruising her legs.

Dulcina started to laugh. 'You won't escape me! I'll find you wherever you go. I'll find you again, and again, for ever.' She came forward slowly.

Tathea fumbled for the door and threw it open.

Dulcina fell against the stool herself and the shard of glass cut her arm. The flesh was spongy, bloodless, like old rubber.

Tathea flung herself out of the house. She started to run. The wind tore at her, whipping her hair into her face, blinding her. She was blown to her knees, grazed and bleeding. The sound of the wind was like nothing she had ever heard before, not a shriek any more, but a deep-toned roar like the sound of a great organ, and it filled the air.

She climbed to her feet and plunged on, weaving as if she was drunk, falling again. She crawled up the breast of the hill on her hands and knees, clinging to the grass, dragging her body to the crown. Ahead of her was a sight which transfixed her with its obliterating power. The eye of the storm lay dark over the moiling face of the ocean. The sky was cocooned in clouds drawn out like shadows strung round to circle Bal-Eeya in a violence that sucked up everything that dared lift itself from the hard surface of the ground. The water rose in huge, grey walls of fury, towering like moving mountains till they overbalanced, crashing in torrents of boiling spume. It was like the wrath of creation itself, as if it would destroy and remould the earth.

Tathea dared not move. She huddled like an animal, crouching flat to the ground, grasping it with her hands, her face hidden. Even if Dulcina had found her, she could not have moved. All day the storm roared around her, the sky ripped across with lightning, the earth battered by the wind and devoured by the raging sea.

With the fading of the light, the violence finally exhausted itself. The last clouds shredded purple and indigo across the west and the arc of the sky became limpid aquamarine. Tathea was so cold she could barely move. Her limbs ached and her muscles were locked. To move shot her whole body through with pain.

It was Ishrafeli who found her. She did not see him until he was kneeling beside her. He lifted her, easing her racked body over, holding her in his arms. In the wan light of the sinking sun he looked exhausted. His black hair was wet and his face was marked with strain, the lines around his eyes and lips deeply etched.

'Is it over?' she asked, her voice rough, her body juddering with cold.

He held her carefully, rocking her a little, moving her limbs gently from their agonised crouch. 'Yes, until next time. But I think there will not be another one like this again, not here.'

'Somewhere else?' she said, searching his face, fearing she knew what he meant.

'Oh yes,' he answered. 'There will be many such storms, in different ways.'

She said nothing for several minutes. He took her stiff, aching legs and rubbed the life back into them, kneading her muscles with his fingers, then her arms, until at last she felt able to move. He stood up, helping her to her feet, taking her weight, and she turned to look at the shore. The sea was a strange, pellucid green, heaving as if still troubled far beneath its surface, but there were no white breakers, and the golden splash of sunset stained a path across it right up to the wreckage of the strand.

'But Bal-Eeya will be all right?' she asked him. She had been here such a short time, and yet it mattered fiercely.

'Yes.' His voice was grave. 'There are many injured, and some dead, but without Itureus's wisdom they would all have been lost.'

'Dulcina is . . . she tried to . . .' She found it curiously difficult to tell him, to bring it from fear into the reality of words. 'Like Cassiodorus.'

'I know.' He looked at her very directly. His eyes were so dark they looked black in this surreal light. 'You were warned it would have cost.' He was very close to her. The strength of his hand on her arm rippled through her. He urged her forward through the sea grasses back towards Bal-Eeya and the harbour where the skiff was waiting. This was not what she had sought; part of it perhaps, but not all. They must go on, out on to the waiting sea again. Her body ached, every step hurt, but she lengthened her stride to walk beside him and he let go of her arm and took her hand instead.

Chapter Four

They said farewell to Patro, who was exhausted but standing straight-shouldered and calm, and to Itureus, weary to his soul and unable to say more than to wish them well. They left Bal-Eeya in the dark, crossing water that was black and heavy as molten lead, and with the breath of ice still in the dying wind.

It was hard work steering the skiff out of the harbour through the wreckage of the storm. The swell carried them more swiftly than Ishrafeli would have liked. In the starlight Tathea could not see his face, only the outline of his body, straining against the surge of the tide and the power of the wind in the canvas. Neither of them dared sleep until the land was far behind. She wanted to say something about Itureus and Dulcina, to ask what lay ahead for him. The tragedy in his eyes haunted her, but she knew Ishrafeli could not answer.

She woke at dawn with the sea and sky like the heart of a great shell, the flaring roof of heaven fine drawn with mackerel clouds, opal and gold in the rising sun. Ishrafeli was asleep, the helm lashed. She stared across the sweep of the water, white-patched with drifting foam, even this far from Bal-Eeya. There was nothing else to see on the smooth face of the ocean. She shivered and pulled her cloak tighter. It was still cold.

Ishrafeli stirred and sat up, smiling at her, but he did not speak. He leaned over the side and splashed sea water on his face, then looked up at the sails and the sky. He tested the ropes and found them satisfactory, then he unwrapped the bread and apples he had brought with him from Bal-Eeya, and offered them to her.

They ate in silence.

Then after a long time they spoke of other things, some that mattered because they were beautiful or precious, or because they involved people she had loved. She told him of things that were unimportant also, moments of laughter, fleeting thoughts that seemed foolish so long after. It was sharing them that mattered, not what they were.

He spoke to her of places he had seen, great forests with ancient trees, wild valleys in the sun, upland wastes beautiful in lean starkness, shining pools, reed-speared, reflecting the sky. He did not tell her where they were, but he described them with a fierce tenderness in his eyes, as if he had loved them long.

Later, in silence again, she watched him as he sat with his head high, face lifted to the sun. He held the sail ropes in his hands, feeling the wind as if it were a living thing. His hair was swept back from his brow and in the harsh, clean light reflected off the water, she could see fine lines of his face, the marks of a lifetime of passion, and hope and pain. There was strength in it, not the raw drive of youth, but a thing tempered by fires whose heat is in the soul. She had doubted it before, but now, in this immense, wind-washed cavern of sea and sky, she was certain he understood the truth she sought, as if he knew its author face to face. Tathea was glad to sleep.

When she awoke it was bright morning and Ishrafeli was singing softly as he watched the sails. It was a lilting song, full of joy. The sun was high and warm, shining on blue water, and on either side hills soared straight up into the bright air, their slopes patched with vivid green between the great scars of rock and scree.

'Where are we?' she asked. After the experiences of Parfyrion and Bal-Eeya, she was wary of new places.

'Malgard,' he answered.

She searched his eyes to read the humour or sadness in them and know what was ahead, but she saw only that it was immediate and real, and that it could not be changed.

She turned to face the long inlet as the skiff veered and tacked on the wind and the hills opened into soft valleys, here and there clothed with woodland. It was spring. There was sweetness in the air.

They had to veer and tack three more times before the skiff came to rest next to a wooden pier. Behind it was a small town of colour-washed stone, pinks and peaches and primrose yellows, roofs slanting steeply upwards. Patches of flowers spread lavishly across the grass and trees hung heavy with blossom.

People were crowding down the pier to see them. At their head was a young man with wind-burned skin and wide, liquid-dark eyes. His face was beautiful, fine-featured with a high-bridged nose and broad brow.

'Welcome to Malgard!' he said with a quick smile. 'You must have come for the festival! We have never had visitors before. This is wonderful! We are so happy to see you. My name is Salymbrion. What are yours?'

'Tathea,' she answered. 'And Ishrafeli.'

'Welcome to Malgard,' Salymbrion repeated, holding out his hand to help her ashore as Ishrafeli made the skiff fast. The people crowded round, all eager to see the newcomers and to offer whatever assistance or hospitality they could. It was quickly established that they would stay with Salymbrion, but everyone was eager to show them Malgard and to explain the festival.

'We hold it every year,' Salymbrion said to Tathea, walking up the wooden quay beside her, matching his step to hers. 'We celebrate every art, but music and poetry are the greatest. You will love it. The laurel is the highest prize in the world.' He laughed and shrugged his shoulders. 'I have competed seven times. Last year I was second, but I think I might win this time. I shall put my whole heart into it.'

'What is the laurel?' she asked as they stepped off the quay into the quiet streets. There seemed no places of trade, only of work, a blacksmith's, a carpenter's, a blower of glass and a potter. Gardens spilled over with flowers of all colours. Leaves and vines climbed walls and hung across arches, heavy with perfume. The sound of falling water was broken by birdsong. A small brown dog pattered along the street, tail wagging. The only thing missing was the laughter of children, but she saw none. Perhaps they were at study.

'The laurel?' Salymbrion's brows furrowed. 'It is the prize for the greatest singer and poet of all.'

'But what is it made of?' she persisted.

'Why, leaves!' He did not understand her question. 'Laurel leaves. Of course they dry out in time, but they do not wither.'

'I see.' She did not, but it did not matter.

He accepted her answer with a smile. It did not occur to him to doubt her. She had the sudden conviction that she could have told him anything, and he might have thought her mistaken but never that she deliberately lied. His innocent trust was like a child's, unspoiled by the wounds and disappointments of life. A wild hope filled her that this was what happened to the souls of those who died in their infancy, like Habi, before they had had the chance for good or evil.

Without thinking, she turned to Ishrafeli, expecting to see in his expression whether or not this was so. But he was listening to a young man and woman who were telling him about the mulberry orchards where the silkworms fed, and he was for the moment unaware of Tathea.

A deep calm lay over everything, so sweet and unbroken it seemed to be within the very nature of the land itself, as if in time it could resolve all ugliness and sorrow and melt grief as the spring melts snow to feed the birth of flowers.

Salymbrion's home was set in its own wide garden where apple trees hung low over drifts of crocuses spearing through the grass. Bees droned lazily in the sun and Tathea glimpsed hives through the branches.

'This evening there is a party at Ikthari's house,' Salymbrion told them as he showed first Tathea then Ishrafeli where they might rest, and later sleep, after the celebration was over. Sunlight bathed the walls in soft colour, blending the peaches and pinks with yellow.

'Who is Ikthari?' Tathea asked.

59

Salymbrion looked up quickly. Obviously the question surprised him. She must be the first person he had encountered who did not know.

'He is our leader, only he is far more than that. He is our guide, our protector, our adviser and friend. You will meet him this evening, then you will understand.'

She was offered fresh clothes to wear for the celebration and she accepted them gratefully. There was no glass to see her reflection, but the robe's simplicity needed no ornament and its golden apricot tones flattered her dark skin and dense, black hair. There was happiness in Salymbrion's eyes when he saw her, as if he knew he had chosen well, but he made no comment. Ishrafeli smiled, and he too said nothing.

Tathea was eager to meet the man who was the leader of such a people. As they walked through the twilit streets she was aware of the blossom in the trees above her, the sweet scent in the evening air, the call of night birds and the distant laughter of people as they all converged on Ikthari's house. She wanted to know all about him.

'How did he come to be your leader?' she asked. 'Did he inherit the calling, or did you choose him, elect him?'

Salymbrion was puzzled. 'Inherit?' He repeated the word as if he did not know its meaning.

'From his father before him,' she explained. 'Or his mother.'

'He has always been our leader,' he replied. 'There has never been anyone else.'

She was about to argue but checked herself. She was in a strange land, and not everything had to be explicable in her terms. Perhaps these people lived longer lives than in Shinabar, and kept no recorded history – although Salymbrion himself looked to be no more than thirty years old at the most. In fact nobody she had seen looked older, or younger. Maybe they did not age here.

'Do you have cold winters?' she asked instead.

'A little,' he replied easily. 'Sometimes there is a frost, but it does no harm. In fact it is good for the earth. It breaks it, ready for seed time.'

'And droughts in the summer?'

He looked surprised. 'No. It rains every few days, mostly after dark, but not always. Does it not rain where you come from?'

'No, it never rains.'

'Then how do you live?' He was fascinated.

'There are underground rivers,' she replied, 'running from the mountains hundreds of miles away. They feed cisterns under the city and we channel water to where we need it.' She remembered Shinabar with a distant kind of ache, as if it were no longer entirely real, although she could recall the scorch of heat and the fine, scratching irritation of sand in everything quite clearly, and the moon over the desert and the smell of bitter herbs on the wind. She did not want

Salymbrion to ask her about it. She changed the subject. 'Is Ikthari your ruler, your judge?'

'You mean for the festival? No.' He seemed to find the idea amusing. 'We judge by common consent.'

'I mean in civil matters,' she corrected. 'In disputes, or if there is a crime.'

'A crime?' It seemed another word he did not know.

'If someone does something wrong,' she explained.

'We make mistakes sometimes, of course. Yes, Ikthari would correct us. He has been our guide always.'

They were at the entrance to a house slightly larger than the others around it, and people were streaming in, each one welcomed at the arched doorway and yet passing through quickly.

Tathea looked around for Ishrafeli, but she could not see him in the crowd. Then she and Salymbrion had passed through the archway into a great room strung with bright lanterns. To one side a table was laden with dishes of fruit, nuts, flowers and bread baked in a dozen shapes. Jars of clear honey looked like jewels of amber and gold. Beeswax candles burned with aromatic perfume, flames steady in the windless air, light falling on the fire-coloured skins of fruit, purple-black grapes, velvet peaches, wine-dark plums and berries like drops of blood.

Ikthari sat in a huge, carved ebony chair wrought with figures of fishes and birds. At first his face was in shadow, and all Tathea could discern in the candlelight was that he was a broad man with thick, heavy hair.

Salymbrion introduced her.

'Welcome to Malgard,' Ikthari said softly. His voice flowed over her with a languorous warmth which made her at once feel at ease. 'What brings you here?' he asked.

She was uncertain how to answer. The truth was far more than he had requested, and too intricate to share. And yet she found herself afraid to lie to him, as if he would know it and be angry.

'I am seeking knowledge,' she replied tentatively. 'And experience.'

He smiled. She could see little more of him than thick, wide lips and a flash of teeth. 'You seek wisdom.' It was a statement, and his tone seemed to hold both amusement and anger.

'Yes.'

'Yet you are frightened to look,' he said softly.

His smile grew wider. He rose from his carved seat, moving his head into the light. He was huge, and magnificently ugly. His features were broad and sensuous, his black eyes brilliant with intelligence. 'You must allow me to show you all that we have in Malgard, and share it with you.' He was looking at her intently. 'All that we possess is for sharing.'

61

'Thank you.'

'Where shall we begin?' The question was rhetorical. He was staring across the room, not looking at her. His face was still wreathed in the same wide smile. What he saw pleased him intensely. He gleamed with satisfaction.

She followed his eyes and saw fifty or sixty people talking and laughing together. Even in the flickering and shadowed light, the contentment in their faces was unmistakable. Nowhere did she see the angular tensions that would have been evident in such a gathering in Shinabar. In her mind's eye she could see the great hall of the palace in Thoth-Moara filled with the generals, ambassadors and merchant princes, their postures of arrogance and domination, the lowered eyes of the nervous and dependent, the exchange of favour, flattery and half-truths.

She saw no cynicism here in Malgard, and she smelled no breath of fear.

'Have you always had the festival?' she asked Ikthari.

'Yes. It is good that people should strive to excel. It is even better to praise what is lovely, and give song to our gratitude for it, and to the god from whom it came.' His heavy robe stirred a little as he moved, swinging wide. 'To take for granted one's blessings is a damage to the soul, and in time one will lose them, simply from lack of care. One should never tire of nourishing and treasuring all that is lovely.'

She turned quickly to look up at him, catching the sweetness of truth in his words.

'Come, let me show you more of Malgard.' He took her by the arm, his eyes shining. His touch was light, but immensely strong and for an instant it frightened her. She had to exert an effort of will not to pull away. To do so would have been unforgivably rude, and quite ridiculous. Why should she be afraid? Everything she had seen here was filled with beauty. Were those she loved destined for a heaven like this? Perhaps that was the darkness at the edge of her mind, that she did not belong, that Habi was not here, or her mother, or her father with his fierce desert beliefs.

'Come,' Ikthari repeated, his hand still on her arm. 'We love to share what we have. Malgard is for all who choose it.' He said it very deliberately, giving weight to each word.

She walked with him in silence, questions hammering in her brain. How did they choose? When? Had Habi been given the choice?

Ikthari led her out of the main room through a passageway that opened into an arcade whose slender arches looked out on to a garden bathed in moonlight. It washed the air with silver. White magnolia petals gleamed in the soft radiance and were reflected like fallen stars in a motionless pool. There was barely a breeze, only a faint stirring, as if the earth breathed night-scented jasmine and something sharper and cooler, like narcissus. Suddenly a bird sang with the piercing sweetness of the nightingale. It came again, like falling crystal, and then the silence closed in, soft as balm.

'Will it last for ever?' she asked impulsively, turning to Ikthari.

He stood still, looking at her for several minutes before he answered, and she was overwhelmingly aware of the power in him.

'Oh yes,' he said at last. 'No one has ever wanted to leave.' His voice was rich with unfathomable satisfaction. 'Everyone here knows how precious this is. They may appear young to you, even naive, but they are possessed of great wisdom. They know God's plan for mankind, and they have chosen to be here, to have this and never to trouble or spoil it.'

She could believe it easily. The thought of leaving this place was unbearable. There was a peace here deep and calm as the summer day, and an innocence that made lies or betrayal impossible.

'Do you cast people out if they commit an act of ugliness?' she asked him earnestly. 'What if someone is dishonest, or cruel, or covetous?'

He took her by the arm again and led her down the step into the moonlight.

'No one is dishonest,' he answered her, his voice a soft rumble in his throat. 'Why should they be? People only tell lies when the truth is disagreeable to them, or frightens them, or to cover sin. There is nothing here to be afraid of.' He gave a tiny shrug. 'So there can be no need to lie, no desire to.'

They were entering an arbour at the end of which was a lawn bordered by great trees. The scent of cedar and new grass mingled with the perfume of flowers. He waved a large, broad-fingered hand to encompass all they saw. 'What is there to envy? Everything is here for all.'

'But what about the old, or the sick?' she persisted, thinking of beggars she knew of in Shinabar, how the aged were revered by good sons and daughters, but all too often ignored if they were ill or troublesome, or stood in the way of ambition. And there were always those who had no one.

He smiled, his teeth glinting in the moonlight. 'You ask from your own fears. Do you see any illness, any infirmity among the people of Malgard?'

'No.' A fierce hope seized her that she hardly dared acknowledge, that this was indeed some heaven that she had been permitted to see, a perfect place where the righteous might live for ever without pain in body or soul.

'Exactly . . .' He breathed the word like a sigh on the breeze. 'I think, child, that you are beginning to understand. Come up to the crown of this little hill. I will show you the city of peace.'

She kept pace with him up the shallow incline and the flower-strewn steps, unable to avoid treading on the leaves, so the air was filled with the pungent aroma of wild thyme. At the top he stopped and turned. She turned also and saw below them the houses of Malgard spread across the valley, the pale blur of blossom trees, the glass-like reflections of still pools and the whisper of fountains. In the distance the sea gleamed in the radiant air like a pale silver shield, barely rippled by the breath of night. Only the stirring of leaves and the distant call of a bird, clear and sweet, broke the silence.

'It is perfect,' she said gravely. 'Now I have seen it, I do not know how one could desire anything else.'

'It is a true glory, is it not?' he agreed, and again she heard the profound and abiding satisfaction in his voice.

'Your guests will miss you,' she said. 'I think you are as much the guest of honour as the host.'

His eyes were wide in the folds of his extraordinary face. 'You are quite right.' He nodded very slightly. 'I should return. We both should. Come with me.' And he held out his arm to escort her, but loosely now, inviting her simply to lay her hand on his. She went down the steps with her head high. For the first time since she had woken in the palace with the sound of screams filling her ears, she felt the knots of pain inside her ease and let go.

That night Tathea's sleep was deep and dreamless, a last releasing of all the fears left by every old wound and scar in her memory, stretching back long before the assassination.

She awoke in a room filled with the sun's brightness. She rose and dressed. Downstairs Salymbrion was nervous and excited about the festival. He tried to keep his mind on offering his guests food and drink and assuring himself of their welfare, but he kept forgetting what he was doing halfway through a task, and laughingly Ishrafeli would complete it for him.

'I'm sorry,' Salymbrion said with a blush of embarrassment. 'I want to win to much that I can think of nothing else. No, that's not entirely true,' he corrected. 'I want to do my very best, to stretch myself as never before and create something of such beauty it will be a joy to everyone who hears it.' A shadow crossed his face. 'Am I grasping for too much, do you think?'

'No,' Ishrafeli said instantly. 'You should always reach for your highest dreams.'

Salymbrion laughed; the answer clearly pleased him.

At mid-morning they joined the crowds entering the great amphitheatre and took their seats. As guests they were given the best.

Ikthari rose to open the proceedings, and there was instant silence in the amphitheatre. He stood in the centre of the stage in a black and golden robe with the moon and stars embroidered on it. He announced the first contestant and then stepped back to allow a young man in a green robe with a flute in his hand to take centre stage.

He began to play gently, plaintively, with an aching sweetness. Then he took the instrument from his lips and sang of the rebirth of nature after the winter's sleep, the first melting of the ice from the grip of frost, the swelling of buds beneath the bark of birch and oak, and the awakening of the squirrels and hedgehogs. His voice was clear and his words full of tenderness and wonder.

When he had finished, the applause was tremendous. He bowed, flushed with pleasure, and withdrew.

Tathea glanced at Ikthari, and saw him watching her. His smile widened minutely before he looked away as the second contestant, a woman, appeared. Her instrument was the lyre, beautifully carved. She sang of her love for the animals. There was laughter in it, gentleness, exasperation, and a wealth of joy. She, too, received warm applause.

A man with a bass voice, deep and soft as the growl of far thunder, sang of his days on the mountainside as a shepherd, of his care for his sheep and the grace and perfection of the wild creatures and the abundance of the earth which supported and nurtured them all.

A thin man with a radiant smile played a lute and sang softly of his love for woodlands and gardens, how he watched the changing seasons. He sang of the delicate first leaves of spring, the pale, cold scent of hyacinths. The languorous profusion of roses and the whisper of ancient trees rising into a cloudless sky. He moved to the splendour of autumn, ending with the sweet pungency of wood smoke, the dancing sharpness of winter and the perfect circle of life.

All day singer followed singer, some more excellent in their words, some in the loveliness of their voices, some in their skill with their instruments. They sang every kind of song; with passion, gaiety or sadness but always with love.

At last as the sun sank in the sky and the light in the amphitheatre turned amber, Salymbrion stood up to sing. There was a breathless expectation. He was the last. Would he also be the best?

He stood motionless, smiling a little, his smooth face like bronze in the glowing light, his hair black as ink. There was a calm and exquisite joy about him. Slowly he lifted his harp and began to play, a few falling notes like the first light of dawn, so soft one wondered if they were no more than imagination. Then he began to sing of sunrise over the sea. His voice was clear and pure, seemingly effortless in its soaring notes, his words were so delicate and full of joy that as he sang Tathea could smell the sweetness of the wind, the dew on her skin and the kiss of the cool air.

His voice grew stronger as he sang of the leap of the sun above the horizon and the blue brilliance of the day, of setting his boat out on to the glass-smooth water. He held the harp gently as if it were a living thing that he loved, and sang of the silence of the sky and sea and wind. There was no shadow in him, as if the light filled his soul.

Not a person in the audience moved. Every eye was on him.

At last he sang of the homecoming as the light burned gold and waned, and the soft haze of dusk purpled the sky, as it was now in the amphitheatre. The final notes fell away and there was silence, utter and complete, before the thunder of applause.

There was no need for a debate or a casting of votes. By common consent Salymbrion had won. The thin man with the flute was the first to come forward, his face full of awe for the beauty of the song he had heard. There was no shadow of envy in him, only the love of music. He held out his hand. Salymbrion hesitated a moment, then with a flush of happiness clasped it. The man in the green robe was next, then a woman, then another. Not one withheld their praise or their pleasure for Salymbrion.

At last Ikthari himself came forward, the wreath of laurels in his hand. He lifted it high. For an instant his eyes turned to Tathea, seeming to bore into her as if he would split open her mind and read it. Then he turned back to Salymbrion and amid rising excitement in the huge crowd he set the laurel on his head. A roar of approval filled the amphitheatre.

When at last it died away, Salymbrion picked up his harp again and joined Ishrafeli and Tathea.

'You are the first strangers come to visit Malgard,' he said shyly. 'Won't you sing for us, Ishrafeli, and tell us of your land? Tathea says your voice has great beauty. Please? We should be honoured to hear. It would complete our joy.' It was a gracious invitation, made with a whole heart.

Ishrafeli did not reply.

Others added their voices. 'Please! Sing for us!' They were all turned towards him, faces eager.

Something in his face flickered for a moment, as if the decision were impossibly hard.

'No . . . no, thank you.' He seemed hurt; it was subtle, no more than a change in his eyes, and the way he held his body. Tathea saw it and did not understand.

'Please,' Salymbrion urged, offering his harp. 'But if you prefer a flute, or a violin . . .'

Ikthari stepped forward between them, some strong emotion clouding his dark face. 'Do not press him!' he commanded. 'Not everyone rejoices in song. It is cruel to pursue where a refusal has been given.'

'He does sing!' Salymbrion answered him innocently, still holding out the harp. 'He is merely modest . . .'

'You have asked, and he has declined!' Ikthari snapped, his tone rising with an echo of darkness Tathea had felt long ago, somewhere else. It sent a breath of fear through her. 'He is not of Malgard,' Ikthari went on quickly. 'You do not know what it is you ask. Be still, he has said no.' His gaze burned on Salymbrion's face and there was a new kind of stillness in the air, as if the decision were momentous, immeasurably more than the mere matter of a song.

Salymbrion seemed oblivious of it. He had won the laurel. His joy overflowed and he longed to share it.

Ikthari turned to Ishrafeli. They were so close to Tathea she could have touched the embroidered hem of Ikthari's robe.

'You do not need to sing,' Ikthari said slowly and very distinctly. 'The choice is yours, not ours.' He was speaking to Ishrafeli, but it was as if the huge audience was what mattered to him. He lifted his heavy hand, the dark sleeve falling away. 'You are our guest. That relationship is sacred.' He lowered his head a little, fixing his eyes on Ishrafeli's. 'We would not trespass on that for the sake of a song.'

Ishrafeli rose to his feet. He stood face to face with Ikthari. Ikthari seemed almost to grow bigger. He raised his huge shoulders an inch or two and his cloak spread wide around him, massive, as if it were solid. He said nothing.

Tathea sat frozen. The two men were locked in a battle of wills so immense and so savage they were oblivious of their surroundings. Then Ishrafeli looked from Ikthari to Salymbrion's eager, generous face. At last, very slowly, as if there were an enormous weight upon him, he took the harp. He walked to the centre of the stage and softly touched its strings with his fingers.

There was silence right to the very furthest reaches of the amphitheatre. The evening sky was purple, pricked with the first stars. Torch flames lit the stage.

Ishrafeli's voice was quite different from Salymbrion's. It was dark, full of passion and a low, aching sorrow that thrilled and stirred hungers for things unknown. His fingers on the harp strings plucked a melody that returned again and again, each time subtler and more familiar, as if drawn from the memory of the soul. It was the song of a man cast out and alone, a man fighting all evil and despair with no word of hope, no light in the sky, only a blind love of what he knew was good. He sang of the grief of friends lost, of betrayal that stuns and amazes with pain, until the notes were wrung from him like a cry, anguish that could be tasted in the air, heard with the skin and the flesh and the bones.

He sang of the dark night of the soul when a man turns at last to face his inmost self and fights his own devils with no weapon in his hands and no friends beside him.

Then gradually the notes began to rise. There were new cadences, they became stronger and surer until at last they soared upward in sublime, full-throated ease. Tathea was filled with a glory that was

67

more than sound. Her whole body ached with the passion and the ecstasy of it, as if she trod the tumult of the stars and heard the angels speak her name.

When the final notes died, the silence was like a bereavement. She did not move. For minutes they sat, each one alone with their thoughts.

The first one to break the terrible stillness was Salymbrion. With a face as white as that of a man who had looked into the abyss, he took the laurel from his brow and placed it on the ground in front of Ishrafeli.

'I thought I could sing,' he said very quietly, his voice catching in his throat. 'I can't.' He swallowed. 'Life has carved me shallowly, a cup that holds too little of joy, or of pain.' He took a shivering breath. 'The power that protected me from hell has also denied me heaven.' There was despair in his eyes as he looked at Ishrafeli, but no hesitation. 'I have heard the holiness of man in your song, and I cannot be complete until I have found it for myself. My voice is worthless beside yours, empty of meaning, and it will remain so as long as I live in Malgard . . .'

Ikthari lunged forward, his black robes flying, his face twisted with rage. 'You cannot leave Malgard! If you do, you will die!' He swung his arms wide to encompass the crowd stretching beyond sight into the indigo night, and all the sleeping land beyond. 'Everything good is here! Love, plenty, innocence. A whole people of pure hearts – your people, Salymbrion!'

Salymbrion stood silent, his eyes wide.

In Ishrafeli's face was reflected all he had sung, the glory and the grief.

Tathea waited with her heart pounding, the muscles of her body knotted so tightly the ache filled her, and yet she was barely aware of it.

Ikthari took a step forward towards the edge of the stage and the crowded people. The torchlight glittered gold on his embroidered sleeves. 'Out there is only ugliness and pain!' His voice thickened with hatred. 'Violence, deceit and disillusion, and in the end the certainty of corruption. You will find nothing but the long, lone journey towards death, and your own dissolution, thoughts that have never entered your soul before, loss you cannot imagine. And there will be no one to save you!' There was almost triumph in his face.

Salymbrion turned to look at Ishrafeli, but he did not speak. He had heard his song. He needed no more. The knives of suffering were already carving his soul into a larger vessel, even as they watched.

Tathea was numb. Why had Ishrafeli sung? His voice held all the unimaginable beauty of heaven. She was ravished by the glory of it and the hunger to hear it again would never leave her. But the happiness of Malgard was shattered for ever, shown to be superficial, a delusion.

Salymbrion looked at the black fury of Ikthari. For the first time in his life he tasted fear, and yet he found the courage to meet it.

'I must go,' he said levelly. 'It is time for me to move on. To stay here would be to die.'

'You will die if you leave!' Ikthari grated between clenched teeth. 'I promise you, you will know day by day, hour by hour, the slow disease of the flesh and the despair of the spirit, and at last the ashes of death will choke your mouth!'

'Then I will die seeking the greater light of a God whose name I have heard tonight,' Salymbrion replied, his head high. 'I will not die the soul's death here.' He swung round to Ishrafeli and met his eyes in a long, unwavering stare. The silence pounded like a heartbeat. Slowly Ishrafeli extended his hand, and Salymbrion grasped it and held it hard and close. Then he let go and walked away, off the stage and out of sight towards the darkening sea and the boats.

Ikthari turned to Ishrafeli, his eyes hideous in their hatred, his wide lips drawn back from his teeth.

'See what you have done!' he said with a scalding rage. 'You have touched innocence with the hand of death! A myriad souls will despise you throughout eternity for this. You will taste the fruits of hell and remain unforgiven because you know what it is you do!'

'Of course I know what I do,' Ishrafeli said very quietly, his lips soft with pain. 'I have broken a dream with the hand of awakening.'

Ikthari swivelled to face Tathea. 'You seek the burden of truth, woman,' he said to her, and there was something in him which was terrible. 'Once you find it, and take it, it may lift you up to the glory of heaven or it may take you to a damnation far deeper even than that which awaits you if you do not. Promises must be kept.' Now he whispered, and yet his words filled the night. 'If you break your covenant with God, you will belong to me, and my vengeance will be hideous. The first beginnings of the knowledge of it would shrivel the life from your body, but your spirit cannot die! There is no escape in the furthest reaches of time or space. Think well on that before you go with Ishrafeli!'

'But I have heard the voice of heaven,' she said through her tears. 'For one moment God spoke my name to me. What greater darkness could there be than to lose that?' She breathed in deeply. 'I will pay what it costs.'

She did not hear Ishrafeli sigh, nor see his body relax and his lips smile in the dark, but she felt his hand in hers, and she turned and went with him out of the amphitheatre and into the streets of the town. As they walked, the air grew colder. The first milk-white blossoms withered and fell petal by petal from the bough. No birds sang. By the time they reached the waterside, a thin rime of ice coated the stones.

Salymbrion was waiting by the skiff, shivering, his eyes wide and frightened. Tathea was racked with sorrow for him.

'You were warned the price was high,' Ishrafeli said softly in the darkness. 'Did you think the pain would not be real?'

'I thought it would be my pain!' The words were torn out of her, choking. At this moment she hated his glorious voice that harrowed up the soul and left it forever changed. 'You didn't tell me it would hurt so many others!'

He touched his warm lips to her brow. 'Of course it wounds others. Our pain is incomplete if we suffer only for ourselves. Salymbrion chose the truth, as you have. You cannot protect him from life, and neither can I. Not even God can do that.' He stepped away over the gleaming ice to unfasten the ropes of the skiff. 'Come, we have a long way to go yet.'

Chapter Five

They sailed from the shores of Malgard in darkness. There was no fierce wind, no premonition of storm, only a steadily increasing coldness. They each slept a little, huddled in the stern together, wrapped closely in the woollen robes they wore and the silken cloak Tathea still had from the Lost Lands.

Tathea and Salymbrion woke stiff and shivering, moving reluctantly to sit up. The air held the breath of ice in it, and the blue of the bottomless water was chill to the eye, shadowed by steep cliffs and soaring peaks, white-crowned, climbing to the fragile sunlight above. Pale windflowers and burning lichen on the stones seemed an illusion of the summer they had so recently left behind.

She looked at Salymbrion, frightened, feeling his innocence and aching to protect him but helpless to do it. He stood up beside her, his face towards the light, eyes wide with amazement. He had no conception of what was to come and nothing from which to imagine it, or prepare himself. He was as vulnerable as Habi would have been.

She looked at Ishrafeli, but he was busy working the skiff towards the shore, his hands clenched on the ropes, knuckles white. He, too, was shuddering with cold.

What kind of city or people could they be seeking in this bitter place? What more experience awaited them? After Malgard, what more was there to learn? Were they now entering that terrible darkness of the soul, of which Ishrafeli had sung, so that they might find the indescribable glory of joy at the end? If so, then she would go forward with fear filling her heart and mind but without hesitation. No price could be too great because, once seen, the light of God could not be forgotten, and no other sweetness could assuage its loss.

Salymbrion knew that just as she did. He, too, had heard Ishrafeli's song and it had driven him from Malgard.

The settlement was tiny, a village of no more than a few houses. They did not stay. Ishrafeli purchased fur-lined clothes, hoods, boots and sharp, curved knives for them, and oil with which to cook and to give light in small, portable lamps. Then they set out across the icy scree towards the mountains. This was the Land of the Great White Bear, and they were to travel northward.

71

They journeyed without speaking. All their strength was needed in the labour of movement, and they kept their faces covered against the steadily increasing cold. They ate fish caught in streams and cooked over fires built of dried bog peat and wind-blasted wood from long-dead trees. They slept at night close together in a tent made of furs and skins they carried.

On the third day they climbed a high ridge and looked out on to a vast landscape of snow, every escarpment, peak and valley as far as the eye reached was dazzling, mantled in unbroken perfection. The silence was absolute.

Tathea looked at Ishrafeli, then at Salymbrion. She saw in both their faces the same awe she felt.

Ishrafeli turned towards them. His eyes were soft and troubled, but he did not speak.

Salymbrion drew a deep breath and nodded.

'Onward,' Tathea agreed.

They continued through snow and over freezing rock and then under pines dark in the shade and dazzling white in fantastic, motionless towers above, until twilight cast long shadows across the snow and they met a group of men, apparently a hunting or war party. Their leader stepped forward. He was of less than average height, strong and lean. His skin was dark, his mouth subtle and humorous. It was a face of both intelligence and power, but there was reserve in it, and the knowledge of grief. He did not speak, his demand for explanation was in his silence and his unwavering gaze.

Ishrafeli saw the warning in it and stood still with his hands away from his sides and the knife in his belt.

For long, icy seconds they stared at each other, then the other man relaxed.

'Who are you? Where are your other followers?' he asked.

'I am Ishrafeli, and I have no others but Tathea and Salymbrion whom you see. We travel for the love of knowledge.'

The other man's face quickened. 'Knowledge? What knowledge is it you seek?'

'The knowledge of all things good and evil, the bitter and the sweet, that is called wisdom,' Ishrafeli replied.

The man's face broke into a slow smile. 'My name is Kolliko. We go north. This land is easy. It will be terrible where we go, but we must follow Tascarebus to the eternal night if we do not catch up with him before then. He raided our houses and took the woman Sophia, and we are pledged to free her from him. If you come with us, you must serve the same cause and give your obedience without question. We know this land and how to survive in it. Otherwise go your way alone.'

'We will go with you,' Ishrafeli answered. 'Your quest will be ours also.'

72

'Good.' Kolliko nodded. 'Then eat with us, and sleep, and tomorrow we shall begin again.'

The food was sparse but well cooked, and afterwards they sat huddled together, sharing the warmth of each other's bodies. A lean, wind-burned man with eyes as green as sea ice played a small instrument of hollow horn. Tathea had never heard music like it before. It was a deep, rounded note of mournful sound, pure and haunting, and the tune he played was unbearably melancholy. He lowered the instrument and began to sing. It was an ancient tale of love and betrayal before the beginning of the age of ice which had overtaken the world and would end all things.

Tathea looked around at the faces in the flickering lamplight. The song was not a new one to any of these men. She knew that from their calm eyes, the impassive, almost comfortable ease with which they listened to the words of despair. For them there was a familiarity in the returning rhythms of the refrain and the falling half notes.

She turned to Salymbrion. His face was shadowed, but in the line of his brow and the curve of his lips she could see confusion and the beginning of a new kind of hurt. He had never encountered quiet, courageous despair before. He could hear the pain in it, but all the rest was mystery. She had seen it far from here, among the old, the ill, and the dispossessed in the heart of Shinabar. Then it had seemed merely an inevitable part of life. Now it was sharper, and the individual reality of it hurt. Perhaps it would always be so now because of the joy that she had seen for those few moments in the amphitheatre in Malgard.

In the morning they continued northwards with Kolliko and his companions. Travel was hard, there was no strength to spare for anything but the effort of setting one foot before the other. If Salymbrion was exhausted, he did not complain. If the endless waste of ice and rock frightened him or crushed his spirit, he hid it, although Tathea saw the lines of weariness and fear in his face. His innocence was gone.

The terrain grew more mountainous, great gleaming blades of rock like sword-edged backbones of the earth shone white in the sun, dazzling the eyes. Storms blew up suddenly, darkening everything within moments. Vast-bellied clouds tore themselves open and sleet and snow whirled around them, buffeting and shrieking with high-pitched whine and roar. They staggered on, close together, footsteps muffled in a virgin landscape.

On the fourth day at noon they climbed to the top of an escarpment and ahead of them opened a valley, at its centre a motionless lake as green as jade. Beyond it a glacier curved upward in a lazy arc towards massive peaks in the distance. Between it and where they stood, the vast expanse of ice was scored with crevasses spattered with perilous mounds of snow and stained with dark moraine at the edges.

Tathea's heart sank. 'How do you know Tascarebus passed this way?' she demanded of Kolliko. 'Who is he?'

'I do not know if he passed this way,' he answered. 'There is an easier way, but this is shorter.'

'Who is he?' she repeated, staring at his weathered skin and figure leaning forward into the wind.

'He takes that which he has not earned,' he replied without turning look at her, his eyes narrowed against the light as he searched the way ahead.

'He destroys what he has not built,' Vartreth with the green eyes added.

'He kills without need.' These words were from Shaki, a man who had chosen to walk beside Ishrafeli and stood now sharing water with him, as Kolliko did with Tathea, and Vartreth with Salymbrion.

'What will you do when you catch up with him?' she pressed.

'Whatever is necessary to free Sophia,' Kolliko replied, taking the water bottle and fastening it to his belt. It was heavy to carry. 'Then we will return home. You would do well to do the same. There is nothing beyond here but ice, and the gates of hell.'

They trudged onward through the heavy snow that clung and weighed down their feet. The sky above was a dark, cold blue, as though it swallowed the light, yet some far glow radiated into it. Perhaps it was the reflection of endless snow beyond the horizon. The green lake, when they came to it, was milky with ground ice. Ahead of them the glacier roared and groaned as it shifted in its infinitesimal journey downwards.

They were climbing up a steep slope towards a pass, beyond which lay a plateau, when a slow rumble broke the silence.

Kolliko stopped, his body rigid, his head towards the sound as it gathered in intensity.

'Avalanche!' he shouted, flinging his arm out towards a buttress a hundred yards ahead of them.

Ishrafeli grasped Tathea by the arm and dragged her forward through the heavy snow. She looked around for Salymbrion and saw that Vartreth was with him.

'Run!' Ishrafeli shouted, hauling her upright as she stumbled. They were all lurching and falling in their haste. Above them millions of tons of snow loosed and gathered speed as it roared down the mountain, consuming everything in its path.

They reached the lea of the buttress just as the first white torrent swept over them in a howling, thundering darkness. They huddled together, Tathea in Ishrafeli's arms, feeling the strength of his body holding her, shielding her from white, smothering, primeval death. On and on the torrent crashed, deafening and blinding as if the whole world were collapsing in on them, entombing them for ever in snow.

At last the tumult ceased and there was silence, utter and total. Not a crystal of ice moved. Wordlessly Kolliko stirred, uncurling his body inch by inch until he was on his feet. The others followed his example, and then very gently, handful by handful, they began to dig their way out, moving only a little at a time, in case they began another slide.

Tathea did not count the time it took them to tunnel their way to freedom. She was bitterly cold. Even in the heavy fur gloves her hands were numb. She was aware of Ishrafeli beside her, and she kept turning to Salymbrion to see that he was all right and not too frightened or exhausted to continue. His back was bent, his dark face pinched with cold and concentration. Only once did he look up and meet her eyes, and in that moment she could see his thoughts, the immensity of his surprise at this vast and terrifying world outside Malgard with its physical violence and crushing weight of despair. He had never known danger before, or loss. It was still like the brilliant blade of a knife whose wound he could only imagine.

She smiled at him.

He smiled back, and went on working.

They emerged into an unrecognisable landscape. Everything had changed. A great gouge had been ripped out of the mountain and the valley floor was filled with walls of impenetrable, blinding whiteness.

A sudden panic overwhelmed Tathea. She was dizzy. They would be locked in here for ever! This shifting mountain would fall again and cover them, buried and frozen into eternity. It was as if in the silence of this lifeless cold she could hear Cassiodorus's laughter and see Dulcina's blazing eyes. This was the paralysing ice of endless hate. She stared at the band of men, Ishrafeli beside her, Salymbrion blinking in the light. She saw in his face a momentary reflection of all she felt, the same horror, the same weakness. Then he straightened up. Kolliko was already moving forward with Vartreth, Shaki and the others.

In her heart Tathea heard the echo of Ishrafeli's song, and as Kolliko moved off, she leaned her weight across the snow and followed.

For four more days they travelled, always northward into the ice, building shelters at night and sharing the warmth. There was nothing to hunt and food was rationed: frozen meat, thawed over small oil lamp fires and scrupulously divided. The land was too harsh for anything but elemental survival. Each man protected his neighbour. Nothing must be done alone. Salymbrion watched with fascination and a kind of awe. He had always shared with generosity; selfishness and envy were not in his nature. But he had no knowledge of interdependence, where life itself rested on sharing born of necessity. The land was beautiful, but it punished every mistake, without exception and without mercy.

75

As Tathea travelled beside Kolliko, her admiration for him grew. He was not without error, but he knew how to recognise and retrieve his mistakes. Whatever terror, pain or doubt he felt within himself, he never permitted it to show in his face, for the momentary weakness of the individual could become the weakness of the group.

It was a stark and pitiless land. Between the ridges, shallow lakes reflected the colour of the sky. At sunrise they were apricot and such a shade of green it seemed there must be sunken forests within them. At sunset they became purple and bronze and a pink so fierce the water seemed to burn.

At dawn on the fourth day after the avalanche, cold and aquatic blue with the wind from the north, heavy with the smell of snow, Tascarebus struck. Tathea's first awareness was the thud of spearheads landing in the ice and the scream as a man fell, the shaft sticking out of his back. She watched in sick horror as scarlet blood stained the white fur of his coat.

She looked up. A score of men breasted the ridge ahead of them and charged down its slope, weapons in hand. She stood paralysed. Ishrafeli seized her and forced her inside the rough square Kolliko's men were already forming. Salymbrion stood still, dazed. He had no idea what was happening. He had never seen violence.

'Salymbrion!' Tathea screamed at him.

He swung round. Vartreth caught him by the hand and hurled him into the square, still uncomprehending.

They stood back to back, swords outward, ready to fight. For a long moment there was silence. The sky arched milky blue overhead. All around them gleamed the white sheet of ice, and over it moved the attacking men, as if caught in some radiant dream. Then the illusion snapped. As they came closer it was possible to see their hate-twisted faces and the glint of raised steel. The clash of metal soon followed, and the cry of pain as steel bit flesh.

The fight was fierce and long, but the square held. As one man fell another took his place. The wounded were hauled to the centre to join Tathea and Salymbrion. Tathea knelt to do what she could for them, binding their wounds with strips torn from their own clothing. Salymbrion stared at her without understanding. She realised with a new sense of shock and sharp pity that he had never seen physical injury in Malgard. He knew the word for 'death' because Ikthari had spoken it, but he did not know the reality. He was only now truly beginning to taste the first terrible comprehension of the choice he had made.

'Help me!' she commanded him.

Obediently he knelt beside her, his face twisted with knowledge of his own uselessness.

Another injured man stumbled into the square, bleeding profusely, and Tathea eased him down on to the snow.

'Stick your fist into that wound!' she ordered Salymbrion. 'Tear the corner of his coat and pack it in to stop the blood.' She worked with her knife to cut strips from her own jacket.

Salymbrion stared wide-eyed, as one man's life slipped away and there was nothing they could do to save him.

'What happened?' he asked, bewildered as a child. 'He's gone! Why?' He swung his arms wide to embrace the battle only a few yards from them. 'Who are they? Why are they doing this?'

'He's dead,' she said quietly. 'We must help the next one.' She crawled over to a man with a broken and bleeding arm.

Salymbrion stayed where he was on the ice. 'But what about him?' he demanded. 'We can't leave him!'

'Yes, we can,' she answered. 'He's dead. Come and help me here.'

'But where is his spirit?'

'I don't know!' she shouted, suddenly sick and horrified and racked with nausea at the sight of so much blood. In the freezing air she could not smell, not as she could have in Shinabar, but her mind supplied what her senses could not, filling her nose and throat with the stench till it stifled her. 'Help me!'

He heard the panic in her voice, and the despair. Frightened, he came over and did as she commanded.

Eventually Tascarebus withdrew, wounded but not beaten. The men stood in twos and threes, bloodied and weary, except for four who lay unmoving in the snow, never to rise again. Shaki bent over one of them, his face bleak, eyes narrowed to stare at the lowering sun, silent as one who sees the light fade and does not look for dawn.

For a moment Tathea did not comprehend, then realisation came like a wound to her own flesh, shocking her, robbing her of breath. Kolliko was dead.

Each man looked at his neighbour, then at the bodies of the fallen. The shadows across the snow were long and there was a thin, warm streak of light across the western sky.

Shaki straightened. 'Vartreth,' he said, and a moment later the name was repeated by a score of throats.

Salymbrion was close beside Tathea. 'What is it?' he asked with a frown.

'Kolliko is dead,' she whispered back. 'A new leader is needed.' She looked at his face and the dawning grief in it as he thought of the wounded men they had watched die, and knew that this too had happened to Kolliko. The wonder of loss was in his eyes, amazement at the pain.

There was no time to hesitate or think. The night and the cold would wait for no one. Vartreth accepted leadership. He detailed two men to bury the enemy's dead. Tathea continued to do what little she could for their own injured, working with stiff fingers and a desperate

77

urgency. Shaki began the ritual for the dead. With a knife he cut a small piece from each man's clothing, shaved the fur from it and stitched it into a pouch. Then they all stood facing the westering sun, to attention, as if for inspection by a prince.

Vartreth called each dead man's name and asked if there were a kinsman among those left. That man then stepped forward and drew his sword. From its horn hilt he cut a small wedge and gave it to Shaki with the words, 'He was my brother.' Shaki put it in the pouch, tied it tightly and knotted it round the dead man's neck. If there were no kinsman, then the man who had fought at his right hand took his place with the words, 'He was my friend, he stood beside me.'

When this was done the jackets of the dead were filled with stones from the lake edge and they were cast into the water, to disappear almost immediately into its murky depths.

For Kolliko it was different. The sun was turning to flame on the horizon and the sky above arched green when they came to him. Tathea stood between Ishrafeli and Salymbrion as one by one the nineteen men remaining came forward and each cut a notch from his sword handle and gave it to Vartreth with his own words: brief, raw, final as death itself.

'He led me in battle with perfect honour.'

'He marked my way through an unknown land.'

'His sword was my shield.'

'He never failed me.'

When it was Salymbrion's turn, he walked forward and looked down at the motionless face, the spirit already gone, the flesh calm, empty of that which had made it unique and marvellous.

'I was not prepared for this,' he said quietly. 'But I am wiser and richer because I knew him, and for that I thank the God who made us both.'

The man looked at him anxiously, puzzled by such strange words.

Ishrafeli was last. Tathea was a woman and she did not count.

He bent forward and touched Kolliko's brow. 'My friend has gone his way well, and kept his first estate. I shall miss him.' And he stepped back again.

Vartreth signalled and they lifted Kolliko and carried him to the water. They laid him on its bitter surface and let him go. Vartreth faced the last of the light and spoke.

'The days of the sun are short, the summer flowers abide only a little time. We make life what we can. These men lived with courage and honour. They never took what was not theirs, nor turned aside from the path of duty. They did not quail before the enemy. They shared the good and the bad with us. We shall be together in the sleep of eternity when the world ends.'

'So be it,' the men answered in unison.

'So be it,' Vartreth finished.

They stood in silence. The sun streaked across the shadowed snow. The sky above was far and blue, a hollow cavern whose gate was the fast closing furnace of the west. The lake's face, unrippled by breath of air, was flat as a copper shield. Vartreth, with his back to the sun, was a black outline.

'We have a short time to sleep, only until the new light,' he said. 'Then we must move. Tascarebus will strike again.'

They continued northwards, crossing the trail of Tascarebus more often. Now they were fearful not only of attack, but of the hazards of the land, ice bridges that gave way and plunged into crevasses, loose snow that moved in small avalanches. There were blizzards which would bury a man standing outside a shelter, flying snow and ice which tore the skin and blinded the eyes. And always there was cold, hunger and exhaustion. Each man's life was in his neighbour's hands. They shared food and labour with utter honesty, even the warmth of one another's bodies in the bitterness of the lengthening nights. Weariness, pain and hunger were constant companions. No one complained. No one spoke of turning back. Tascarebus must be fought and beaten. Sophia must be freed.

At night they watched in pairs, safeguarding the company and each other. Sometimes Tathea watched with Salymbrion. They spoke little. In the bitterness of the polar night they crouched back to back, to see both ways, and kept all but their eyes covered against the wind and the ice.

She wondered if he thought often of Malgard and what he had left behind, the life in which the word 'pain' had no meaning. If he did, or if he regretted his decision, he did not speak of it. She looked at his eyes but could read nothing in the glimmering, snow-reflected half light. They discussed the men around them, and what manner of woman Sophia must be that these men of the Land of the Great White Bear were willing to travel through hardships such as these in order to find and rescue her. There was no certainty of success, and yet they journeyed without question or complaint.

Salymbrion did not remark that this was a nobility beyond all others, because they had not heard Ishrafeli sing. They knew of no unimaginable glory at the end of their seeking. But one day when they stood a little apart he spoke to her quietly.

'Even if they endure all things with a spirit made bright and wise, gentle and clean of all malice and selfishness, what sublime courage is asked of them, when they do it without hope!' There was wonder in his voice, and awe. 'They believe there is nothing at the end of all this . . . except an eternal sleep in the all-conquering ice . . . a world returned to the ultimate death.'

79

She asked Ishrafeli why he did not sing for these men. 'They know there is hell,' she said. 'Why do you not let them see for a moment that there is heaven also?'

'This is not hell,' he said. 'This is a land without life and without mercy. It is like the spirit of the Great Enemy, but it is not hell.'

'That is not an answer!' she protested angrily.

His eyes smiled. 'Heaven and hell are of the soul,' he answered. 'Regions far beyond this. They will find their own path upward. You cannot find it for them, nor do you need to.'

'I don't want to find it for them, just to let them know it is there!' she argued. 'As Salymbrion does. As I do!'

Ishrafeli turned away towards the horizon and did not reply, and she was left alone, not understanding.

When Tascarebus struck again, it was as sudden and violent as before, but instead of swords, this time he used the land. Vartreth had misjudged how close they were, and the weight of the snow on the slopes above them. First there was a sudden shout which echoed across the valley.

Vartreth froze. Then he whirled round and cried out for everybody to go back. For a second, a hanging, trembling instant, no one understood. Then obedience took over and they turned and ploughed back the way they had come, Vartreth at the rear.

But the last few were too late. The snow came like a wave breaking from the sea, higher than ten men and roaring like a great ocean in torment. It caught them and buried them as if they had never existed.

The rest stood huddled together, stunned for loss. Far above on the crest, Tascarebus waved his arms, then disappeared beyond the ridge.

'The ice has them in the last sleep,' Shaki said so quietly his voice was barely audible. 'We will each cut a notch from our swords for the fallen, and one for Vartreth. He was a good man.'

The others looked at Shaki, but he turned his face towards Ishrafeli. 'It is yours to lead. Tascarebus is ahead of us. Which way do we go?'

Ishrafeli looked surprised. His eyes widened. It was the first time Tathea had seen him faced with something he had not foreseen.

'Which way?' Shaki repeated.

Tathea stared at Ishrafeli. For a moment there was indecision in his eyes. Then he lifted his chin. 'Forward,' he said quietly.

It was noon of the third day after Vartreth's death that they caught up with Tascarebus again. The sun was midway up the southern sky and before them lay a wild and dreadful valley, hemmed in by mountains which cast strange, depthless grey shadows that distorted distance.

The attack came totally without warning. This time Salymbrion fought too, wielding a borrowed sword with a fury he had never experienced before, slashing, piercing, stabbing, heedless of his own safety. He seemed suddenly to understand that all he loved was threatened and he must kill to protect it or it would perish here in this terrible wilderness.

Ishrafeli fought solemnly and with loathing for what he did, but he did not flinch. He was filled with anger at the men who came at them again and again out of the snow, as if the great white world around them was of no importance and all that mattered was to slay. He did not hesitate to drive the fatal wound, and perhaps in this unforgiving land this was a mercy. Only the slightest of scratches failed to kill in the end.

Shaki sustained a deep wound to the shoulder, and it took all Tathea's skill to bind it till it stopped bleeding. Two others were injured, five lay dead.

Fourteen of Tascarebus's men were killed, leaving his band a tattered and miserable few, happy to escape towards the high pass ahead, and the fast approaching storm.

No one had even glimpsed Sophia.

They stood close together. The wind was keening with a high-pitched whine and already snow flurries were being whipped up off the ground. The snow would bury the dead, but they looked to Ishrafeli to speak for them.

He looked down, his face solemn, full of grief. He said nothing to the survivors, offered no explanation or comfort, but his bowed head acknowledged responsibility for the deaths.

'You fought well, for a just cause which will not die,' he said in the half light. Ahead to the north the sky was so dark it threw eerie shadows, making the ground seem almost luminescent in contrast. 'When the glory comes, it will be yours as well as ours, and we shall meet again at the last. Until then, abide well.'

Tathea wondered what he meant, but there was no time to ask. Leadership had set him a little apart and she could no longer walk with him as before. Now the men were all waiting for him to make his decision.

'Forward,' he said, turning to the north where Tascarebus had disappeared, and obediently each man leaned into the wind and began the hard journey. Within moments the sun vanished and the world was opaque, directionless. Everywhere, before and behind, above and below, was a screaming whirl of grey-white ice, buffeting, bruising the skin.

Like animals fleeing before the wrath of God, they tore at the snow and hollowed out a shelter for themselves. Others carved the boulders of ice to form walls and a domed roof, then at last, exhausted, almost paralysed with cold, they crawled in, spreading their extra furs on the floor and keeping their bodies as close as possible. There was little food left, and little oil, but not to use it would be to die.

Tathea lay next to Salymbrion, acutely aware of him although even turning sideways she could see only the outline of his head and the profile of his nose and brow. He did not often meet her eyes. Perhaps he was afraid she would read in them regret for his decision, the enormity of what he had done. The reality was so much more than he could have imagined. Ikthari had warned him, but his words were shallow compared with this. Salymbrion had never complained. He had not once spoken sharply to Ishrafeli, or murmured against him or questioned his leadership, as well he might have done when he considered the laughter and peace of Malgard compared with this icy despair.

Tathea moved her aching body a fraction and looked across at Shaki, his lips pinched with the pain of his wound, his blue eyes tired but calm. This was what he expected of life.

Ishrafeli was beside him, the light of the oil lamp yellow on the planes of his face. He had lowered his mask of furs and his mouth and chin were visible. He was deep in thought, and Tathea could see that the sorrow in him was different from that which he had felt for Parfyrion or Bal-Eeya. He looked up at her once, and she saw his pain. It was raw with doubt and grief. The shadow of a smile crossed his face and then vanished. It was self-mockery, a knowledge that he, too, was learning something he had not imagined before.

She wanted to move closer to him, to touch him, but she could not. Apart from the physical difficulty of climbing out of the spot in which she was wedged and disturbing everyone else, it would have been inappropriate. There was no dignity in it, and dignity was perhaps all they had left. So she lay and thought about him, wondering what journey of the soul he was making, how like her he might be, or how different. It mattered. In all this painful learning he was the one constant hope. He was far more than the one whose belief had made him a voyager who would climb the stars and make the joy and the glory real. There was a secret core to him that she had never touched. Was he ever truly and wholly afraid, sick with the misery of despair? Or did that bright vision heal all his darkness? She did not know and there was nothing in his eyes or his lips to tell. But she remembered the passion of his song, and believed his hell was as wide and as deep as everybody else's.

The storm raged through the night. There was no morning, only a lessening of the gloom while the blizzard continued to howl. They remained in the shelter, each alone with their thoughts. If any man tasted terror or despair he hid it, and presented only the face of blind courage. Tathea looked at them one by one, and loved each of them. Every one had taken blows meant for her, or shared his food or his oil with her. Each one had at some time cried out a warning, lent her an arm when she slipped or was weary.

She caught Ishrafeli's eyes for a moment and saw reflected in them the same tenderness. He smiled at her briefly, uncertainly. She ached to say something, find a word that would tell him how she felt, but there was none, and they were not alone.

Another night passed before the storm eased, then Ishrafeli dug his way out of the shelter and motioned the others to follow. Crawling out, muscles shot with the pain of cramp and cold, they beheld a world utterly changed. The sky was heavy grey, clouds obscuring the mountains so they could have lain in any direction. All the landmarks were unfamiliar. Ridges and promontories of ice had disappeared. Drifts had covered old monoliths, and valleys were scoured out where there had been plains before.

Which way should they go? How could anyone follow Tascarebus in this new land? They waited for Ishrafeli to speak.

Without thinking, Tathea moved forward to stand beside him. If there were any fault, any blame, she would share it with him. The wind still blew, flicking snow and ice into her face, and the sky was so dark she could only guess which way was south or north.

She looked at Ishrafeli's face, and saw for the first time fear in him. He knew no more than she did. Suddenly, overwhelmingly, they were equal. Tascarebus was leading them on until either he or the land killed them all, then he would return south, leaving their bodies to the ice. The Great Enemy would have won. Heaven was only a dream, a song sung in another world which they had forfeited for ever.

She put up her hand and tucked her arm in his, and felt an answering pressure as he squeezed it. He took a few steps forward. He must be seeking the cromlech which had been there before the storm. Surely it had been too huge for any blast of the elements to have moved it. It should be there . . . or perhaps a few yards further on . . . to the left a little? The mountain pass was beyond that, on its right shoulder mark.

Ishrafeli loosed his arm from hers and went forward alone. As she stood and watched, he disappeared through the scurrying snow.

'He should not have gone alone!' Shaki said urgently, eyes straining to follow Ishrafeli. The whine of the wind rose a note. The storm was not over.

Panic rose inside Tathea. Sweat broke out on her skin and instantly froze. Ishrafeli had made a mistake. He had gone alone to look for the cromlech which marked direction, and he was lost. She swung round to Shaki, despair choking her.

There was no direction. In the grey, ice-leaden air, light diffused until everything gleamed and reflected back from glistening surfaces. The wind was rising again, but it seemed to come from everywhere, one minute one way, and the next another.

He moved forward, head down, a little lopsided from his wounded shoulder, and in an instant the gloom swallowed him too.

She stood unmoving, eyes straining to see Shaki, oblivious of the cold, aware only of the terror inside her. Was this the end? Was she to die alone in the ice, separated from Ishrafeli by an error of judgement? Ishrafeli, who had promised heaven, had in the end failed. His joy was an illusion. Salymbrion had forfeited his innocence for nothing. Not all her passion or prayers could protect either of them from this last, dreadful truth.

She saw something move in the restless gloom ahead, a figure bent over, supporting another, coming towards her. Hope rose inside her like a winged bird. She lurched forward, calling "Ishrafeli!" uselessly as the wind tore the words from her mouth and the tears of relief froze on her cheeks.

Shaki staggered out of the whirling snow, half supporting Ishrafeli's weight.

Instantly others surged forward also. A dozen hands stretched to help, lifting each man, carrying them into the shelter and rubbing limbs, breathing on lips, on eyes. Tathea held Ishrafeli in her arms, surprised how slender he was, how easily she could clasp him. She let the breath of her mouth unfreeze his eyes and his lips. His eyelids flickered open and recognition lit them, and knowledge of his fault.

She found herself smiling, relief like light after a great darkness.

He struggled to sit up. 'Shaki!' he whispered, trying to turn to look for him.

Tathea could see him, and even before she took in the wax-like skin and the scarlet seeping through the bandages on his shoulder, the peace in Shaki's face told her he was beyond the reach of life.

Ishrafeli stared at him and his grief and despair clouded his eyes. He tasted the bitterness not only of sorrow and failure, but of guilt as well. Shaki had rescued him from his error and it had cost him his life.

Outside, the wind roared. Inside, the oil lamps flickered, the precious liquid burning lower and lower. They were lost, there was no food left and little fuel. Over half the men had been killed. Tascarebus was still somewhere ahead of them, but no one knew where. And no one knew if Sophia was even any longer alive.

Tathea ached to help Ishrafeli, but lies were useless, and there was no word of truth that was any comfort at all. There was no light ahead, nothing that redeemed the total loss. All she could do was sit beside him in silence, her shoulder next to his, touching him lightly, and love him in silence, while he walked alone through the dark, inner night of his soul.

Perhaps it was a change in the wind which at last broke his trance. There was no hope, nowhere to go, but he rose to his knees and faced them, his eyes soft with grief.

'It is time we moved forward,' he said clearly. 'Maybe there is nothing left to gain, but at least death will find us still seeking, not sitting here.' It was a ridiculous speech, full of courage without hope, and purpose without reason. He took out his sword and prised the jewel out of its hilt. He laid it on Shaki's body, inside the breast of his coat, where the blood had stained the fur. Then he turned and left the shelter. One by one they crept out of the shelter after him, sealed it over with ice, and began on the journey after him, towards they knew not where, nor why, except that it was better to be beaten than to surrender. To travel without hope, but still without fail, was the last and ultimate courage.

They walked until the sun reached its height and began to sink again. Tathea knew Ishrafeli had no idea where they were, nor what lay ahead. She could see it in the blind grief in his eyes, and in the line of his shoulders, the way he faced the light. Again, there was nothing she could say, only meet his gaze without blame or question, smile when he looked at her, hide from him her own fear and despair. And curiously, her own loss of heaven hurt far less than her pain for him. It was his wound that gouged out the soul-deep scars in her.

The light was fading when Tathea became aware that they were not alone. At first she thought it was an illusion of the snow, a denser wall of white. It was moments before she realised it was a living creature, huge, thick-furred, with the power to defy even this terrible land. Its head was sleek, its muzzle a single blade as it wove through the murk . . . a great white bear, bigger than ten men.

A shudder passed through her at the sight of it, its strength and its breath-stopping beauty – and because it was another living thing in this mouth of hell.

It turned and stared at them for a moment, then swung its sleek head north, into the wind, and began to move forward.

Ishrafeli plunged after it, calling to them to follow.

Salymbrion and Tathea were the first to move, more from instinct than thought. Tathea had no idea where Ishrafeli was going, or why he followed the bear, but she would follow him. Salymbrion went to protect her, and because he, too, would go where Ishrafeli led.

The great beast moved up the incline like a ghost, no more than a deeper whiteness in the gloom, and they moved after it as rapidly as they could, exerting all their strength to keep it in sight. Now and again Ishrafeli stopped to make sure they were not falling behind. Once he came back to help Tathea, then ploughed on again, half pulling, half carrying her, until at last they breasted the pass and began the descent. Suddenly the wind ceased, the snow settled, and before them was a wide valley. And in the valley, black against the snow, lay Tascarebus's camp.

They stood together, arms about each other, and stared in the moonlight. They had no idea where they were, but the air was calm and the goal of their quest was ahead of them. They each stood a little straighter, heads high, smiling in spite of bodies that cried with pain.

The great beast ambled away across the ice, its huge, dark muzzle turning one way then the other, its feet silent on the ground as if it had no weight. With a shock of disbelief Tathea saw that it left no footprints behind it.

Then as she stared across the ice towards Tascarebus's camp, the round moon dazzling the snow, filling the air with radiance so intense she could have read from a page, she saw a figure set out towards them. It was slender, not very tall, pale furs reflecting the lumines-cence of the night.

Tascarebus? Surely not! One of his soldiers? Why? Not for mercy, not for alliance. Treason? Gain? Murder even? Ishrafeli put his hand to his sword and she saw his fingers almost unconsciously touch the empty socket where the jewel had been.

She watched while the figure came closer, but it was not until it was only a few yards away that she realised it was not a man but a woman. She put up her hands and pushed back the great hood of her cloak. The night was so still that not a breath of wind stirred the thick fur.

Ishrafeli drew in his breath sharply, his face filled with recognition, wide-eyed, amazed. He stepped back.

Tathea felt her heart lurch.

But it was Salymbrion who went forward to her, as if compelled, his feet crunching over the snow.

The woman's hair was streaked with white, knotted behind her neck. Her features were perfectly balanced, her eyes purple-dark as the night, and she was old. Her face held passion and pain, strength, and immeasurable gentleness. In the line of her mouth was the knowledge of all human endurance. She spoke to Salymbrion, as if he alone had sought her. .

'My name is Sophia. You have come very far to find me.'

'You are . . .' His voice died away, confused and bewildered.

'Old,' she finished for him, smiling as if there were secret laughter inside her. 'You thought I was innocence . . . purity . . . that you had come to rescue me? I know. She is at home, tending a good hearth and serving her neighbours.'

'But Tascarebus . . . took you . . .' Salymbrion floundered, still staring incredulously at her, searching her eyes, her lips.

'No,' she answered softly. 'I came here of my own will so that you would seek me.'

He stared at her in the moonlight, his face transfigured with wonder.

But she put her hand out to his and clasped it. 'You came to seek the upward path, to learn of life and death and the journey of the soul,' she said very gently. 'You have begun well. The rest still lies far ahead of you, but what you have learned here you will never entirely forget, and it will serve you when you need it most, and perhaps expect to find it least, in your second estate, when you will have forgotten this.'

'I shall never forget you.' He said it with absolute conviction. 'I will stay here, and serve you in whatever way I can.'

'Here? In this land?' There was laughter in her voice again, and surprise.

'If this is where you are, then in this land – or any other,' he replied.

She looked at him steadily and he returned her gaze.

'Good,' she said at last. 'Then abide with me.' She withdrew her hand and walked over to Ishrafeli where he stood a yard in front of Tathea. Tathea saw the depth of beauty in Sophia's face and caught a glimpse of the reason why Salymbrion knew so swiftly and without question that he would stay with her, even in this terrible place.

'You came to teach them the way to the stars,' she said softly to Ishrafeli, her voice little more than a whisper. 'To understand the heart of God, and His inheritance for His children. But it is harder than even you could know, and there are few who climb all the way.' She touched his face with awe. 'You will be one of them. Never again will you taste the full bitterness of soul that you have known here. I will take the men back to their valley in the south, every one of them, except Salymbrion, who has loved me above all else. I will guide you and the woman back to the shore, from where you will voyage to Sardonaris. There joy and sorrow await you, and victory and death. Come.'

Salymbrion swung round. 'But what of Tascarebus?'

'He will always steal what does not belong to him,' she answered. 'And he will always lose it, sooner or later.'

'Always?'

'Always. The Land of the Great White Bear will never be free of him – until the end.'

Tathea stared at her. The moon was very bright, every detail of her face was clear, and beauty flowed from her and settled in the soul like a great light.

'My name is "Wisdom,"' she said gently. 'To follow the word of God even when you cannot imagine an end and there is no light to your path, that is courage, and the beginning of understanding.'

Chapter Six

Tathea and Ishrafeli left the Land of the Great White Bear in the skiff in which they had arrived. She had learned enough about handling it now to be of considerable help, and they worked together to manoeuvre the boat down the narrow channel between the ice floes. The water was shallow and green with reflected light. There was little wind and they made way only slowly at first, until the current caught them and took them out into the dark blue water of the ocean beyond.

The sail filled and the bow cut through the water, spilling foam on either side. Ishrafeli lashed the helm and came to sit beside her near the stern. They had not spoken of Shaki, or the bear, or Salymbrion's decision to remain. These were experiences too big to be encompassed by words, nor was it necessary. The defeats shared were a deeper bond than the victories, the failure and the grief told more of love than the beauty understood, or the parting.

They journeyed sometimes in silence, sometimes speaking lightly of things that did not matter. He would tease her and spin tall tales which she nearly believed, and they would laugh.

They approached Sardonaris as the sun was descending in the western heaven, and the air was filled with a radiance of gold. The city was built round a vast lagoon, the wind barely rippling its blue-green water. Tathea held her breath in wonder. The city seemed to float on the sea's face, its pale marble and amber stone glowing in the evening light. It was an old city, weathered by sun and salt, mellowing as its summer decayed into autumn. The heat was gone but the softness still hung in the air, the warm colours, the balm in the wind.

Fishing boats plied their trade across the lagoon. Others carried passengers. Some, like long-legged beetles, dipped their oars swiftly in and out of the water, weaving between the great galleons moored to the west.

As they came closer, Tathea realised that the city really was set upon the water. Most of its thoroughfares were actually canals, and it was possible to penetrate into the heart without stepping from the skiff. Quickly she helped Ishrafeli reef the great purple sail and unlash the top half of the mast so that they might pass beneath the numerous bridges crossing the canals. Ishrafeli produced a long single oar, which he turned expertly, balancing in the stern as he worked. From the look on his face and the ease with which he handled the oar, Tathea realised with a rush of surprise that he knew this place. It was the first time she had had such a feeling, and it pierced her with a sense of excitement, but also of loss. Was this to be the end of her journey? Would she find here the revelation she sought? And would he then leave her?

She remembered the sage's words that there would be a terrible price. How blindly she had agreed to it! She knew now that leaving Ishrafeli was a payment she was not willing to make. She would rather be with him, even in the Land of the Great White Bear with its horror and grief, than in the aching beauty of this city.

She looked up at him where he stood with his face towards the sun. It was low now. The buildings around them cast dark shadows across the water. His eyes and mouth bore the marks of his suffering, the pain of the ice was there, and the knowledge of his failure and what it had cost.

With a vividness that jolted her as though the silence still echoed it, she heard again his voice as he had sung in Malgard. If only she could have understood it all, the truth had been there then, eternal, terrible, sweet – and familiar as a voice whispering her name, beautiful as the light.

They were moving slowly, almost drifting. She stared at the white palaces where the limpid water lapped into their steps. In the shadows it was full of browns and golds, dark stains of weed on the sunken stones beneath. Sometimes bridges arched over from one building to another, a few were covered with secret fretted windows through which the light fell in patterns like lace.

They passed many flights of stairs with their lowest steps disappearing into the water, visible in wavering, dappled outlines beneath. Sudden vistas opened up of half-hidden gardens, arboured in rose and crimson blossom, and burning yellows.

And always the shifting, whispering water reflected light in ever moving patterns, giving the illusion that the whole city was floating.

Here and there in niches in the walls Tathea saw statues, many of them quite small and intimate. They did not idealise the nobility of man, like those in Parfyrion. They were not dreams in stone, but portraits of individuals. Each had its human imperfections, but of such passion and grace that time and again she all but cried out to stop and look more closely at the courage or hope in a marble face, the tenderness of a hand or the anguish in a bent head.

When at last she did speak it was because she could bear the burden of silence no longer.

'Ishrafeli . . .'

Just as he turned to look at her, the sound of a voice on the near bank distracted him. A man in an embroidered doublet spoke to another whose sleeves flashed scarlet in the sun. Then they embraced and parted. The man in the doublet ran along the path at the water's edge and up a shallow flight of steps, worn low in the middle by centuries of use. He glanced around, his face closed and malicious, then slipped a folded piece of paper into the cross-shaped slit in the top of a gleaming, jewelled reliquary. He ran back down the steps, pulling his velvet hat forward over his brow, and darted into an alleyway towards another canal, narrower and darker, beyond the sun's reach.

Tathea turned to Ishrafeli, questioning.

'The Stair of Sorrows,' he answered, his face shadowed. 'He has just put the name of his friend into the Traitors' Box.'

'What will happen to him?' she asked, although with a breath of coldness she knew. She had lived through twenty years of Shinabari civil politics. She had seen betrayal too often – and yet not clearly enough! It had still taken her by surprise when it was her turn.

'He will be arrested,' Ishrafeli answered. 'Tonight or tomorrow.'

'And tried?' There was a flicker of hope.

He looked at her with sorrow and his voice was strained. 'Not that anyone else will see. The verdict is always the same. The sentence depends upon what bargain the accused makes with the Oligarchs who rule Sardonaris. If he agrees to become an agent for them, he will live. If not . . .' He did not bother to finish.

'That is vile,' she said bitterly. 'He could be innocent, his accuser could be envious, or in debt to him, or any of a score of things!'

'It will make no difference.' He leaned on the pole and pushed hard. 'The Oligarchs rule in secret and by fear.'

'Why do the people bear it? Why do they not rebel?'

'They do.' He looked down at her with a gentleness in his face which frightened her. 'Some with courage and sacrifice, others only with violence.'

'Then there is great evil here!' Disappointment burned inside her, dissolving into the same bitter disillusion she had felt when the loveliness and hope of Parfyrion had disintegrated into war. Perhaps after all there was no truth to find except courage and human wisdom and endurance. Maybe the only glory was to live. There was nothing more necessary to it all than to stumble through with as much honour as possible. The thought was desolate. There was no plan, no purpose, human or divine. They were alone in the universe . . .

'Yes,' Ishrafeli agreed quietly. 'There is great evil here.' He worked at the oar again, and moved the boat smoothly over the water.

Tathea shivered and sat further down in the boat.

On a bridge two lovers stood, their hands barely touching, their faces radiant in the last light. He wore a green cloak, and the marks of time and suffering were deeply printed on his face. She wore blue, caught under the bosom with silk and beads. Her throat was still slender, her cheekbones high and pure, but she had waited long for this moment and there was grey in her hair.

Tathea was overtaken by the longing to share that same closeness with Ishrafeli. Who else could understand the hope and the destruction they had known, the passion and the dreams lost? Who else could grasp the knowledge of their journey of the soul, with its hunger and its pain, and the glory they had glimpsed in Malgard? It was impossible to think of loving anyone else, except in the bonds of friendship and the love for all living things.

Suddenly looking at him, the curve of his shoulder, the way he was balanced in the stern, his hands on the bar, she understood something that filled her with fear. He was as vulnerable as a candle in the winds of the night.

She swallowed, unable to speak.

Ishrafeli brought the skiff to rest beside a flight of steps and tied it to a stone bollard. The tops of the walls were still warm in the sunset, but the water was dark and in the east the sky was indigo.

Quickly she climbed ashore and together they set out through the narrow, torchlit streets towards the main square where they could hear singing and loud laughter. It struck her ears jarringly. It was vulgar, bawdy, the words blurred with drunkenness and the harsh, high sound of unreason.

Ahead of them a blind man with a begging bowl felt his way along the wall. An old man in a worn cloak and thin shoes drew level with him. He opened his purse and emptied the last gold coin out of it into the bowl. Then he hurried away, without seeking thanks. Just as Tathea and Ishrafeli reached the end of the street and turned to cross into the square, a youth with a narrow, secret face knocked the blind man down and took the bowl and everything in it.

'Thief!' Tathea cried out in anger.

Swift as a cat, Ishrafeli turned and ran back after the youth who scrambled up a vine-covered wall and over the top, Ishrafeli behind him.

Tathea bent to help the blind man to his feet.

'Are you hurt?' she asked gently, supporting him as he struggled to find his balance. He was thin and lame, as well as sightless.

'No, thank you,' he answered patiently. 'Do not concern yourself.'

'But he took your money!' she said with a catch in her throat, hating having to tell him. 'I have none, or I would share it with you.' She held him more tightly, feeling his wasted arms. 'Ishrafeli will catch him, if anyone can.'

The blind man smiled. 'Perhaps . . .'

She eased her hold, in case she bruised him. 'The last coin was gold.

91

Did you know that?' She thought of the thin shoes and the worn cloak of the man who had given it, and suddenly she could have killed the thief with her own hands.

'There is much goodness here,' the blind man said quietly. 'And much evil. Thank you for your help.'

'I'll stay with you until Ishrafeli returns,' she promised.

But fate did not permit her to. A group of revellers came staggering and laughing round the corner, men with loose-lipped mouths and flasks of wine in their hands, women with skirts awry and naked bosoms. They saw Tathea and the blind man and hooted with derision.

'Hey, what's this?' one of the men called out. 'An old fool and his daughter. Hey, old man, is she a virgin? What's she worth, eh? I'll give you a groat – that'll get you a bottle of wine to warm you belly!'

'I'll give you two!' another yelled, and then howled with laughter.

'Why give him anything?' a third jeered, his raddled face hideous in the torchlight. 'The old fool's blind. He'll not report me. Get her!' He made a lunge towards Tathea.

She must defend the old man. He was helpless against them. She struck back, hard, with a clenched fist. The man staggered, his breath let out in a belch.

'Run!' Tathea shouted. 'Anywhere!' She swung to hit out again, but caught a blow in her side which sent her reeling. She glimpsed the person who had hit her – a large fat woman with a painted face and bulbous breasts. Tathea could smell the sweat on her body. She kicked her as hard as she could and heard her scream. Another man, his skin white, cheeks rouged, was weaving drunkenly towards her, a blood-stained knife in his hand.

The blind man was gone.

Tathea turned and fled too, not caring where she ran, anywhere to be away from their obscene, grasping hands and their devouring eyes. She heard their bellows of outrage only dimly above the pounding of her heart. They began to chase her, but they were too drunk and their legs buckled, sinking them into the gutter amid a shower of vicious oaths.

'Stop, thief!' one of them called with a stroke of brilliant malice. 'Stop that woman!'

Other people took up the chase and Tathea ran in terror, turning first one way and then the other, until her breath rasped in her lungs and her legs ached. At last she was cornered. Behind her were her pursuers and ahead only the black water of a canal. But she would rather drown than have those filthy hands touch her.

She was about to plunge in, bracing herself against the shock of the cold, when out of the darkness a boat appeared, a slender skiff like Ishrafeli's, except in it was a young woman in pale clothes.

'Come!' she said quickly. 'Jump! Don't you know what will happen if they catch you?'

Tathea did not hesitate. She leapt and landed awkwardly, gashing her shin on the wooden crossbeam that formed the seat. She was aware of pain, but little more. The skiff rocked violently with her weight and she crumpled on to the floor of it, her strength gone. The girl twisted the oar with a swift movement and they glided out into the engulfing night.

Tathea slowly raised herself up until she was sitting, conscious of an ache in her chest and blood running down her leg.

'Thank you,' she whispered.

There was no sound but the gentle hiss as the bows cut through the water. Ahead of them was a patch of light from torches on long poles at a landing stage. Instinctively she shrank back from it.

'It's all right,' the girl said softly. 'They won't follow you here.'

The skiff slid across the black silk of the tide and into the shadows again. The journey seemed endless. Tathea was shaking with cold and pain by the time they at last pulled in at a landing stage. The girl alighted and tied the skiff's mooring rope to a carved stone post.

'Come,' she invited. 'You will be safe in our house, and you are welcome.'

Tathea had little choice. She had no idea where Ishrafeli was, nor how to find him. She was injured and exhausted and so cold she could not keep her body still.

'Thank you,' she accepted and climbed with difficulty on to the narrow, damp stones. She was very weak and it hurt to breathe.

'Can you manage?' the girl said with concern.

'Yes . . .' It took an immense effort of will to follow the girl up the flight of stairs. Tathea clung to the wall as she mounted the steps which curved round a tower. At the top they crossed a bridge, high above the water, and went in through a beautiful studded door.

Inside, candles were burning and the room glowed with the soft light. The furniture was simple, polished wood, although one large chest was intricately carved. But it was the girl herself who commanded Tathea's attention. She had the loveliest face Tathea had ever seen. Now it was filled with concern.

'You are hurt! I did not realise you were injured.' She came forward quickly, as if Tathea might fall, and indeed she was swaying as waves of pain shot through her chest and up her leg. She felt strong arms round her and was glad to be eased down into one of the chairs.

'My name is Ellida,' the girl said. 'I'll wash and dress your wound. I have some skill in the art of healing. Please trust me.' She knelt in front of Tathea and regarded her gravely. 'You will be safe here, I promise you. This house is very well guarded, and it is secret. The Oligarchs do not know of it.'

Tathea was too tired and bewildered with pain and an overwhelming loneliness to care. Ishrafeli's absence ached inside her more fiercely than any physical injury.

'Thank you,' she said numbly, looking down with surprise at the amount of blood seeping from her leg.

'What is your name?' Ellida asked, rising to her feet and going to the far side of the room where she poured water from a jug into a bowl and dropped a tiny spoonful of liquid into it. Tathea could smell the pungency of it from where she was sitting.

'Tathea,' she answered. Where was Ishrafeli? How would he ever find her here? How could she have allowed so stupid a thing as a street robbery to separate them?

Ellida returned with the bowl and several cloths and a jar of ointment. She searched Tathea's face carefully then felt her brow. She glanced down at where the woman had struck and pulled aside Tathea's clothes with soft hands. Her mouth tightened and she did not touch the abrasion. She made Tathea lie down and began very gently to clean the wound in Tathea's leg, then placed on it a bandage with some unguent, which stung.

Tathea sank into a daze of pain. She winced.

'Sorry,' Ellida said with a wry smile. 'But it will stop the bleeding.'

Tathea was doubtful. Nothing she knew of in Shinabari medicine, and she knew a considerable amount, could stop bleeding like this, except a pad held firmly for some time over the blood vessel. But there was no purpose in saying so, it would be rude, and the girl was doing her best. Obediently she drank the potion she was offered, trying not to wince at the bitterness of it.

Ellida removed the empty cup, then helped Tathea over to a couch and eased her down.

She must have drifted off into sleep because she awoke with a start to find two more people in the room. One was a young man, slender and dark, who moved with an unusual grace. The other was shorter and fair-haired, and judging by his crouched posture and the extreme pallor of his face, he was in great pain. As she watched, Ellida went to him swiftly and she and the dark young man helped him over to a pile of cushions.

'What happened?' Ellida demanded urgently. 'Pandolf?'

The fair man gasped, clutching a bloodied hand to his chest and shoulder and Tathea could see that the wound must be deep, so thick and dark was the stain seeping through his fingers.

'The secret police caught us at the end of the passageway going down to the Stair of Sorrows,' he answered between stiff lips. 'They were waiting for us. We got two away, but they killed Arrigo. Radamistus rescued me.'

Ellida turned to the dark man. 'Are you sure Arrigo is dead?'

94

'Yes,' he said without hesitation. 'I would not have left him in their hands alive.'

'God protect his soul,' Ellida whispered.

'That is another one of us gone!' Radamistus looked at her, his eyes narrow and anxious. He glanced beyond her to Tathea on the couch. 'Who's she?' There was alarm in his voice now, and suspicion.

'A fugitive,' Ellida answered him, and her tone allowed no argument. She turned to Pandolf. 'I must clean your wound and dress it. Talking can wait.' She worked in silence and Tathea watched.

Radamistus went over to the window and stood with his back to them, staring out over the domes and rooftops into the night. Either he had no skill in medicine, or he was not needed.

Ellida looked around for more linen. There was a roll of it on the small table. Without thinking, Tathea stood up and fetched it for her. It was only after she had done so that she realised that she felt only a dull throb in her side and her leg, and she was perfectly clear-headed. She had no difficulty in breathing either. The fear was still there, and the desperate knowledge that she had no idea where Ishrafeli was, nor how they could find each other. But she was quite well. Amazement slipped through her like physical warmth, tingling her skin, loosening her knotted muscles. She must help, not stand here as if paralysed. She bent and picked up the soiled cloths Ellida had been using, cleared away the bowl and fetched fresh water.

It was several more minutes before the task was finished and Pandolf lay back on the cushions, the sweat glistening on his skin, a faint smile touching his lips. Would he recover, or had he already bled too badly before he got here?

Ellida stood up. 'Thank you,' she said graciously to Tathea, moving towards the far end of the room.

Radamistus turned. 'Can you do it this time?' he said very softly so Pandolf could not hear.

'Yes,' she replied gravely and without hesitating.

He looked at her. 'Can you be so sure?' He did not disbelieve, it was surprise that lifted his voice.

'Yes,' she answered without turning to him or stopping what she was doing. Her face was very grave, very certain.

He bit his lip. 'Do you always know?' His expression held such an intensity of emotion he seemed to be asking far more than the words held. There were layers of meaning beneath this exchange of which Tathea knew nothing.

Radamistus swung round without warning, his dark eyes probing her thoughts.

'My sister has the gift of healing. But perhaps you know that.'

Tathea was caught by surprise. 'No. I know nothing about her. I was attacked by some . . . ruffians . . . in the street. She rescued me.'

'But you were injured,' he pointed out, glancing down at her bandaged leg.

'Yes. I did that when I jumped into her boat. And I was hurt below my ribs. But it is not as bad as I thought. It feels far better than it did even an hour ago.'

A flash of humour lit his eyes. 'Of course it is better. I told you, Ellida has the gift of healing. Pandolf will be better very soon too, since she says she is quite sure we got here in time. She knows when she has healed.'

Tathea realised he meant literally that she had a gift, not simply that she was wise in herbs and knowledgeable in anatomy. She looked at Ellida with a new, sharp respect, and curiosity.

As if reading her thoughts, Radamistus answered the question that had flashed through her mind. 'Yes, it is a burden. And not without danger. We are terrified the Oligarchs who rule Sardonaris will find out about it. We are at war, but I presume you know that. If you didn't before, you have seen it now in Pandolf. And it seems you tasted a little of it yourself.' His eyes flickered down to her leg.

'I thought they were just . . .' She stopped.

'Street robbers?' he finished for her. 'They probably were. But if the Oligarchs ruled by law, not by fear, then such events would not be rife.'

Ellida looked up from tidying away the herbs and bandages. 'Our city is corrupt,' she elaborated. 'Those who should administer the law and protect the weak take money to turn their eyes the other way when the depraved indulge their appetites – for anything. That is why your cries for help would not have been heard. But that is enough talk of grief tonight.' She made herself smile. 'Come, it is time to rest. Pandolf will thank us little if we keep him awake all night. And you must be ready to sleep. We have a room you are welcome to. There is a bed, and blankets.'

Tathea accepted gratefully. She was so weary the oblivion of sleep was the only haven from her pain and loneliness. Ellida showed her into a small room opening on to the water, and the smell of the night air was cool and welcome. The bed was made, and there was a ewer of clear water on the table and a small bowl of bread and fruit. There was even a clean cotton gown to wear.

As soon as Ellida had gone, Tathea washed and undressed and lay down, thinking she would sleep immediately, but her anxiety for Ishrafeli would not let her rest. Then gradually above the murmur of water she became aware of voices beyond the door. Ellida and Radamistus.

'You don't know who she is!' he was saying angrily. 'You have no right to bring her here. You endanger us all!'

'Where else could I take her?' Ellida demanded. 'She was being chased by the bawds from the brothels on the Green canal. You know what they would have done to her.'

'Yes, of course I do!' There was resentment in his voice. 'But you should not have brought her here. You could have put her ashore somewhere else – anywhere.'

'She was hurt . . .'

'And you are the great healer!' Now there was mockery in his voice. 'You never miss a chance to remind me, do you? You've paid for your gift by forgiving me, and you'll never let me forget it.'

'You never let yourself forget, Radamistus.' Her answer was suddenly cool and steady. 'I helped her because I wished to. I healed her because I have that gift. And I chose to forgive your betrayal of me willingly, for you as well as for myself. You are my brother, I want to be able to love you freely, with a whole heart and will.' Her voice dropped a tone and Tathea could only just hear her. 'I want you to prove yourself as brave and as true as anyone in the resistance. You can't do that if we don't give you the chance.'

'I don't want any chance given me as a sop!' he said with profound bitterness, his voice sharp and low.

'Then earn it!' she answered instantly. Lying in the dark, Tathea could hear the pain in her voice, and the regret, even if Radamistus could not.

There was silence.

'I'm sorry. I . . . I hate having to prove myself. I feel as if everyone is waiting for me to—'

'No one is!' she responded swiftly. 'No one else knows of the first time, except me.'

'Don't you ever get tired of being the leader?' There was surprise in him now, and something that might have been pity. 'Doesn't the weight of decision crush you, and the knowledge of pain and death, like Arrigo's? If you had given different instructions he might still be alive.'

Her answer was almost a whisper. 'You do not need to tell me that. I do the best I know, and live with my mistakes. I would also die for them, if that is what is called for. I brought the woman back because I thought it was right. I still do. Now go and sleep. We have much to do in the morning. You saved Pandolf. Be glad of it. Goodnight.'

Tathea did not hear his reply. Perhaps he made none. Perhaps he touched her, gently, in understanding and gratitude. She wanted to think so.

When she awoke the sun was streaming into her room. The sky, framed by the golden stone of the window, was azure. Drifting up from the water below came the voice of a man singing to himself, a limpid, lyrical song of tenderness.

Ishrafeli! She leaped out of bed and ran over, leaning out across the sill, memory and joy so sharp she could all but feel the touch of his hand and see the light on his face.

But it was a stranger who poled his boat away across the still surface of the canal, and beyond the echoing walls his voice was not so like Ishrafeli's after all, it had not the subtlety or the power, and it was far too light.

She went back to the bed and dressed in the gown that Ellida had left for her. She moved slowly, not because her body hurt any more – it was completely healed – but for the consuming ache of loss inside her.

Downstairs breakfast was waiting: bread, cheese and huge purple plums with glistening skins. Ellida and Radamistus were there, and Pandolf, looking rested and almost well again. The colour had returned to his face and he sat upright at the table, if a little stiffly. They exchanged greetings, and asked after each other's recovery, then the conversation returned to the business of the resistance, but so coded as to be almost meaningless to Tathea. Only the fierce emotion in their faces betrayed their concern.

She had her own preoccupations. She must find Ishrafeli. Even in this beautiful room she felt imprisoned and she was chafing to leave and begin her search. When Ellida rose at last and left them, Tathea followed her to the landing stage. The day was already brilliant, the stones warm in the sun. A faint breeze whispered in from the lagoon, clean with the morning tide, as if the sins of the night had been washed away. The water lapped against the buildings, an incessant, whispering presence. A barge laden with fresh fish passed by, followed by another carrying bales of silk in splendid colours, indigo and saffron and hot reds. Tathea's gaze swept over the fine houses with their courtyards, pillared arcades and flowering vines, the squares whose statues had less than perfect grace, less dignity than those of Parfyrion, but more of the agony and the bliss of human life. At the furthest edge of the lagoon where the blue of the water met the haze of the sky, the sun flashed momentarily on the white dome of what looked like a palace.

'Where is that?' she asked Ellida as she followed her into the boat. 'Is that Sardonaris too?'

Ellida did not answer. Without a word she untied the ropes and took the oar, guiding them out along the narrow canal and into the main thoroughfare now teeming with boats. Many were carved with heraldic beasts and painted with coats of arms. In some, ladies sat on cushions, proud and idle. Many were obviously courtesans.

A boat passed them carrying a woman whose thin features had the calm of perfect faith, and suddenly the courtesans' beauty seemed like blistered paint.

The corpse of a man drifted by, face downward, the death wound between his shoulders, knife gleaming in the sun. No one else took more than cursory notice of it. Tathea was gripped by a sickening fear that Ishrafeli too had been killed and was floating in some dark canal, jostled by passing boats indifferent to his death. It was so blinding that the sunlight seemed harsh, the sounds of voices and splash of oars beating in her ears as if she were shut away from them in an unreachable world of loneliness.

And then she saw him, walking easily down the street towards them, smiling as if he had never worried, never been touched with that sick terror for her that she had felt for him. He stopped on the stairs above them and looked down. His eyes searched to see she was whole, unharmed, but if he saw the torrent of relief in her, or the anger that he should be so casual, he gave no sign. Instead, he turned to Ellida, and like the light coming from behind a cloud, something quickened in him.

'Thank you,' he said softly to her. 'Thank you for looking after Tathea. I chased a thief to get a blind man's money back, and we became separated.'

Ellida, too, seemed to have been seized by some new emotion. Her face was flushed, her eyes brilliant. Her gaze on him did not waver. It was as though they were the only two living creatures on a painted stage.

'It was the natural thing to do,' she answered him simply. 'My name is Ellida. Are you also a stranger in Sardonaris?'

'My name is Ishrafeli,' he replied, as though that satisfied the question.

'Have you somewhere to stay?' The upward lift of her voice made it an invitation. 'My brother and I have a house, in the Tower of the Vines.'

'Thank you.' With an easy movement, he jumped down lightly into the boat. He did not take the oar from her but sat and watched as she turned the boat back the way they had come. Whatever the original purpose of her trip had been, it was clearly no longer important. Neither spoke to Tathea. Several times she opened her mouth to say something, but Ellida was busy guiding the boat, and Ishrafeli did not take his eyes from her. By the time they stepped ashore and began climbing the long flight of steps upward and round the tower, Tathea felt as if any notice they took of her was a courtesy, empty of meaning.

She was numb with desolation. She was alone here in this beautiful and violent city, bereft of everything familiar, everything precious and sweet from the past, certain of only one thing in all the shifting patterns of doubt – Ishrafeli was at the core and heart of everything she loved. And even as she reached the studded door, he had already gone inside with Ellida and she was left outside, forgotten.

It would pass. It must. They had barely met! They had not shared the death of Allomir, the desolation of Parfyrion's loveliness and hope, the terrible, destructive power of the sea in Bal-Eeya, Malgard's sterile innocence and Salymbrion's towering decision, the Land of the Great White Bear with its fellowship of courage beyond hope, all the passion and the tenderness and terror of this whole journey of the heart . . .

And yet when she pushed the door and went inside, they were standing together, shoulders almost touching, and she felt an intruder. It was the most terrible pain she had felt in her life, consuming everything else.

Pandolf and Radamistus were there also, sitting at a table, talking. They were discussing some miscarriage of justice by the eleven Oligarchs, a rivalry, a doomed love, and a murder.

Ellida joined the debate. 'She can't have known!' she said with fierce denial, her voice raw with pity.

'Of course not,' Pandolf agreed. 'It was Tallagisto again. He used her and betrayed her, as he does everyone, sooner or later. It would amuse him to do it that way. The irony would suit his humour.'

'And they are both dead?' Radamistus asked.

'They are all three dead now,' Pandolf answered. 'And Orlando is injured and will die. The only thing to be savoured from it all is that Tallagisto's man Skibus is wounded too, badly enough to die also.'

Ellida turned away, her face pinched with regret. 'I wish I could have reached Orlando. I might have saved him.'

Ishrafeli looked at her quickly, his eyes wide.

She answered him as if he had spoken. 'I have the gift of healing.' She did not explain any further, expecting him to understand.

He smiled slowly, his eyes full of gentleness. 'That is a great gift . . .' He hesitated, tenderness about his lips. 'It comes with a heavy price.'

'I know,' she answered steadily, and Tathea remembered the over-heard conversation with Radamistus the night before, his anger and her words of forgiveness. She was beautiful, wise, brave, and generous. She fought for justice, and yet she would forgive even betrayal. Tathea knew it, she could see it in her as plainly as the clean light on the water, and it pressed on her heart like a stone lid.

'No, you don't,' Ishrafeli said so softly his voice was no more than a whisper. 'All you have paid so far is little compared with what you will give in time.'

She stared back at him in silence, not daring to speak.

He slid his hand over hers for a moment, then withdrew it.

The conversation resumed. They spoke softly. Their trust was absolute. It had to be. One whisper to the secret police and they would disappear into the prisons of the Oligarchs and only reappear in the shifting tide, face down.

The day was the most wretched Tathea had ever endured. It was worse even than being lost in the ice, because her heart and soul were cold. They went out in the boat again, Tathea in the centre, Ishrafeli and Ellida in the stern, their hands touching as they drifted on the water. He met her eyes and understood what was not spoken. He laughed easily, and at the same things she did. At sunset they stood on the tower steps and stared at the dying fire over the western sky. They seldom seemed to speak, as if their thoughts were so perfectly attuned they were beyond commonplace words.

Watching them, with the soft light in their faces, Tathea would have given up every journey of the soul, every truth or glory at the end, to be back on the shores of the Lost Lands and not to have found the sage or asked him for knowledge. If the end of all the passion and the cost, the courage and the hope did not include Ishrafeli, then it could be no more than a sham, a second best, shot through with loss.

On the third day, a little after noon, Tathea was alone in the tower when she heard a sharp rap on the door. She opened it without interest. There could be nothing that mattered.

Outside stood two men in sumptuous clothes, with slashed and embroidered sleeves, soft velvet hats and doublets laced with ribbon. They both carried daggers and their hands rested idly on the jewelled hilts. There was a narrowness in their eyes, and a certain tension in their bodies as if they were ready to move quickly. She could sense power in them, smell it as though it was an odour in the air, like sweat.

'Yes?' she said quietly.

The taller of the two adjusted his weight and smiled at her though misshapen teeth. 'Is this your home?'

She was about to deny it and explain that she was merely a guest when the whole answer was there in her mind as plainly as if she had understood it from the moment she entered the lagoon of Sardonaris, even before she met Ellida or heard of the Oligarchs.

'Yes.' In a word she committed herself irrevocably.

One of them pushed past her, flinging the door wide, but the other remained behind, cutting off all possible escape. Not that that was what she thought of. There was now only one acceptable path and every move must be made correctly, or it would all be in vain.

With trembling legs and dry throat she followed him into the room and went to stand by the table on which stood a bowl of fruit and jugs of wine.

Both men stared at her, eyes bright, lips curled in the faintest of sneers.

'Where is your brother?'

'I don't know,' she said defiantly. There was no need to pretend the fear; it was real enough in her clammy hands and lurching heart.

'Never mind,' the taller replied. 'It is you we want.' His face showed weariness rather than pleasure. He was bored with tortures. He had

101

seen too much, and time was short. He stepped towards her.

She must move now or it would be too late and there would be no warning for the others. She swivelled round and swept her arm across the table, knocking the bowl of fruit over and smashing the dish. She grasped the largest wine jug and flung it at the man, soaking him, splattering wine on the floor. One of the velvet curtains was stained.

The man swore at her and grasped her viciously, wrenching her arm. Pain shot through her but what did it matter now? Nothing they could do would hide the signs of a struggle or make the room as it had been.

Sullenly, trying not to show her eagerness to be gone, she submitted to them. They must not be here when the others returned or the whole purpose would be lost.

Held tightly by both arms, a dagger pricking her side, she was led down the winding steps to the landing stage. A long, black vessel was waiting, with a third man at the oar. It was not an open boat, like Ellida's, but covered by a heavy, dark awning. No passer-by would see her, or hear her cry out.

She sat silently as they moved out on to the water. When the others came home they would see the wreckage and realise what had happened. The secret police would not know they had the wrong person. Perhaps the plan to overthrow the Oligarchs would succeed. Far more than that, Ishrafeli would have what he longed for: Ellida, safe. If the secret police had taken her there would be no happiness for any of them. This way was better. She had wanted to give him her own love, her life, her laughter, her hope and her pain, but he had not wanted it. The one thing she could give him was Ellida. At least he would love her for that.

The boat stopped and she was led out. They were in a narrow canal with walls on either side rising sheer from the water. A staircase led up to a crested iron door which opened from the inside as they approached it, and clanged shut with a dead finality after them.

She was taken along bare passages past windows of fretted stone, which overlooked the water, bright patterns from its movement rippling across the ceiling. They went down shallow, broad steps, this time carpeted, until at last they came into a great room hung with red and gold tapestries. At the far end, behind a table, sat a withered man in a tall, crimson hat, his heavy-lidded eyes deep sunken. He was Tallagisto, the eleventh, the hungriest, and the cleverest of the Oligarchs.

'The woman Ellida,' her escort announced. 'She was alone there.'

'Pity,' Tallagisto said drily. 'But she will do.' He looked at her with interest. 'She is not as beautiful as I had heard – or as young.' His lip twisted slightly. 'But fiercer! Your pride will earn you nothing here, mistress.' He looked beyond her at the men. 'Enough. You can go.'

She heard them step back but if the door closed, it did so silently. She met Tallagisto's clouded, stone-like eyes without flinching. He could hurt her, perhaps terribly, but in the end all he could take was her life. He could not take her purpose.

'As I said, proud,' Tallagisto murmured. 'Your brother said you had courage, but he did not speak of the fire in you, or the strength.' His voice sank in tired contempt. 'He is a fool.'

She looked at him with a sick realisation. It was Radamistus who had betrayed them – again. She saw the age-old hate in Tallagisto's eyes, the same bottomless hunger she had seen in Cassiodorus, and Dulcina, and Ikthari. The recognition was like a terrible nausea. Perhaps this was the last confrontation.

'You are right,' she agreed. 'He is as great as fool as a man can be. He has betrayed not only me, but infinitely more than that, himself – what he might have been, and what he has become.'

The old Oligarch gave a crooked, wizened grimace. He had a high, domed forehead and a nose like a great bird's beak.

'A philosopher as well as a fighter and a healer! Well, I have a task for you. It is the price of your life. One of my friends, Skibus, is mortally injured. Heal him, and you may live too. Fail, and I shall kill you.' His lips curved back. 'Not necessarily quickly.'

It would be brave to refuse him. The name of Skibus had been mentioned. He was a bully and a torturer. Should anyone, even in the name of mercy, heal such a man so that he might kill and maim again? She had no choice. Her Shinabari arts were good, but no more than human. She had not Ellida's gift, which was of God.

She lifted her face and forced herself to meet the old man's eyes. 'No.' Her lips were dry and the word scarcely audible.

Tallagisto leaned forward in his scarlet chair and struck his hand across the side of her face, his ring gashing her cheek. The power in him was startling. She was sent reeling backwards, falling heavily, wrenching her ankle. Pain throbbed through her. He leaned forward and she could feel his breath on her face.

He struck her again. This time she remained on the floor, the taste of blood in her mouth.

'Heal Skibus for me and I shall reward you richly, Ellida.' His voice was whisper-soft and cold as the grave. 'You will be safe. I shall give you your brother's life to do with as you will. You shall have wealth and honour if you want them. Refuse me, and you shall have nothing, not even a martyr's death.'

She did not doubt that he meant it.

'No . . .' The word was a sigh, her mouth too sore to speak clearly. Tallagisto rang a tiny gold bell beside him. The door opened.

'Take her,' he ordered. 'Kill her. Slowly.'

She was half carried, half dragged out of the great red room, along a different passageway and down into a bare cell.

Another figure was waiting for her there, lean and sparse, dressed entirely in black from the hooded mask over his head to the ridiculous, curl-toed shoes with tiny silver bells on them.

'She's mine now,' he said softly to the guards. 'Go your ways.'

She heard a sniggering laugh, and then the door closing.

She faced the man in black, terror tightening her throat until she could barely breathe. She prayed that in spite of Tallagisto's orders he would do it quickly, while her courage lasted. There was nothing left now but to die.

He bent forward, crouching on the floor. There was a faint noise. He pulled up a trap door. Panic filled her as if this were the mouth of hell. An eternity of horror engulfed her. Very slowly she looked. A flight of stone steps led down to the faint glitter of water.

'Hurry!' he whispered in her ear. 'They will return, and they must not see you alive!'

She was dazed with incomprehension.

'Hurry!' he repeated, taking her arm. 'Down the stairs to the boat. The tide will take you. Go!'

'Thank you!' The words were swallowed in the darkness as she fumbled her way down, dizzy with bruising, the taste of blood still in her mouth.

Chapter Seven

The boat carried her slowly at first, through glimmering darkness broken only occasionally by the light from latticed windows as she passed other passages, other dungeons. She lost all count of time. She ignored the blood running down her cheek. It was of no importance. She was under the city, and if she was on the current of the tide, she must be going out towards the sea, at least until it turned.

Why had she been released? Who was the man in black? One of the resistance? Had he also assumed she was Ellida? Could she now find a ship and escape Sardonaris altogether?

What was the truth she had come for? Sacrifice? That everything had a terrible price, and in the end she was alone?

She fell asleep still being carried outward between grey walls through tunnels echoing with the lap of water and the endless drip of water on to stone. She woke to see the blue of the sky arching far above her, touched with the breath of evening. A seabird wheeled and caught an eddy of air, soaring upward, wings gleaming, then careened down the long expanse of the wind.

Very slowly she moved. There was no pain, no bruising where she had been struck. She put her hand up to her face, expecting to feel blood and raw skin, but her fingers met a smooth cheek that was not even slightly tender.

She was in the centre of the lagoon. She sat up and looked around. Behind her Sardonaris lay gold above the turquoise of the harbour, its warm stones crumbling gently, the sun apricot on the west-facing walls. She stared ahead where the current was taking her. The bright sheet of the water was pellucid, charged with shadows, and above it rose the pale marble pillars of the island palace.

She was moving more swiftly now. The evening air was cool on her skin, and sweeter than anything she had known. There was no sound but the faint whisper of movement.

At last the skiff bumped against the stone and she climbed out, tying the bow rope to a bollard. She went up the shallow steps until she was at the threshold of a long, pillared gallery stretching westward towards the fading light. A small black and white cat with a pointed nose and jewel eyes curved itself gracefully round the base of a column, then stopped and stared at her.

Ahead was a door at least twice the height of a man, with scenes of passion, hope, courage and pity wrought on its panels. She walked over to it. It was ajar and she pushed it wide enough to slip through.

The room inside was hung with tapestries. Ahead was another double door, this time of cedar, polished and hinged with brass. It, too, was ajar. She stood against it, listening. There was utter silence. She looked round it, into a hall so vast, its far end was beyond sight. It was thronged with people, legion in number, wordless, motionless. They were all facing towards an open space to the front, and there was an urgency in them, a straining of such intense eagerness it was like a charge in the air, a tingle creeping over the skin and making the hair prickle.

Tathea held her breath, her heart pounding. She followed their gaze to the high, recessed seat on which sat a man whose face shone with such beauty its radiance dazzled her and she looked away, but the glory of it remained within her like a peace never to be forgotten.

There was a movement in the throng, a heightening of emotion, an eternity of expectancy at last come to fulfilment. A man stepped forward from among the crowd, the light gleaming on his smooth, brown hair and catching the fine lines of his face, marked with the essence of all reason and excellence of mind.

'Man of Holiness,' he addressed the figure seated in the great chair. He spoke clearly, calmly, but to Tathea it was as if he stood beside her, even though he was at least fifty spans away.

'Speak, Savixor.' The answer was only two words, yet the sound of it was like a whisper of heaven in the soul.

'We have asked what the plan for mankind shall be,' he began confidently. 'What manner of mortal life shall he have that he may take flesh upon him, that his spirit and body may be united for a space that shall be as a probation for him, before he is resurrected for eternity? We have asked what the nature of his world shall be, what his destiny. I have thought well . . .'

There was a faint sigh, the outgoing of a myriad breaths.

Savixor raised his hands a little, as if to display some invisible thing that rested in them. 'His world should be as the worlds we already know, made of the same elements. There will be heat and cold, ocean and dry land, rocks, trees, herbs of the field, and beasts and fishes and birds . . .'

There was a rustle of impatience from the assembly and another figure stepped forward, pale-haired, with ice-blue eyes and a fierce countenance.

'This much we already assumed!' he said angrily.

'Silence!' Savixor's reproof was terrible. He did not raise his voice, but it boomed around the hall like the backwash of the sea after a

106

great wave has broken. 'I have been given leave to speak! Who are you, that you dare to interrupt?'

The man stepped back, his face haggard but for two spots of burning colour high on his lean cheeks.

Savixor turned to the people again. 'Man is the most marvellous of all creatures; the fire of his mind, the boundlessness of his imagination, the excellence of his reason. Love of beauty, of order, and of wisdom, are his birthright.' There was a murmur of assent as if the words had struck some chord of universal meaning. 'Set man in his world and he will strive until he learns the workings of nature and the marvels of the land, the water and the air, and the forms of life that have their being in each. He will discover the place and the purpose of all. He will chart the stars and learn the seasons, build cities and till the earth. But far more than that, he will create loveliness of his own. He will paint pictures, carve statues, sing songs and write the dreams of his soul in words.' He flattened his hand across his chest in a deprecatory gesture. 'He does not need gods!'

There was a momentary stillness in the chamber, and then consternation in the air, a shivering like the silent breaking of icicles.

'He is sufficient to himself,' Savixor pronounced. 'Leave him to pursue his own destiny. He will realise his full measure, and come into his own.'

There was a stirring, a questioning in the faces of the throng. Some shone with approval, certainty bright in their eyes, but still no one spoke. The air hung thick and silence beat on the ears. A slow smile spread over Savixor's countenance.

Then another stepped forward and for a moment Tathea's heart lurched and the pulse in her throat almost suffocated her. It was Ishrafeli! She recognised the smooth sweep of black hair, the angle of his shoulder, the grace. He looked towards her as if he must surely see her at the door, listening uninvited to this great council. But his blazing eyes were blue, and in the shadows she might have been invisible to him. She was nothing, merely one figure among countless.

She forced herself to remain where she was, her fingers clenched on the door, unseen. He was so like Ishrafeli, and yet unlike him. His bones were the same, as though in some unimaginable beginning they were cast from one mould, but time and passion had altered him. His winged brows were tighter, his vision not wide like Ishrafeli's, but narrow, closed in by bounds of the spirit within. His mouth had no tenderness, no laughter, the hunger was all inward, not a longing to receive but a drive to devour. A nameless terror gripped Tathea.

'I am Asmodeus,' he said quietly, and the echoes of his voice trembled to the very furthest walls of the chamber and every figure stiffened, listening intently. 'I am Asmodeus, and I have a plan that is better than Savixor's. I will save every soul that is given me. Not one of all the millions shall be lost. Not one shall perish or fall into sin!'

The silence was so intense Tathea could hear her own breath like the rasping of a saw.

'I will create a world for man where he can live in peace and safety, not only of body but of spirit,' Asmodeus continued, his voice like dark honey. 'I will not afflict him with harshness of climate, with fierce winters or summer droughts. Every season will come in its fullness and bring its fruit and its harvest.' There was a smile on his lips. 'The sun shall not smite him nor the frost wither him. The rain shall not fail, nor shall flood consume his house or his goods.'

Now many people smiled and nodded in approval. There was a murmuring, a beginning as of movement, yet no one departed.

'The creatures shall be his servants and his friends, the beasts of the field shall obey him, and the fish of the sea shall fill his nets. The bees shall give him honey and the cattle shall yield him milk, and the trees shall bear fruit, each in its turn. He will never taste the bitterness of failure; he will never be despised or rejected. He will never see darkness or know sin and the horror of its bondage – nor will he need repentance, because he has no knowledge of the law, so he cannot break it.

There was a sigh of breath through the hall like a summer breeze passing, faint and sweet, so light the cheek caught it rather than the ear.

Asmodeus knew it and his smile widened.

'Man shall be born and grow to strength without pain or disease. His limbs shall be straight and strong, and his mind innocent. He will commit no ill.' He lifted his shoulders. 'There will be none for him to commit! He will live from day to day into his maturity, and then pass peacefully from mortality back into immortality again, as sinless as he came.' His head high, his face shining, Asmodeus turned to the sublime figure in the carved seat.

'I will bring back every soul as perfect as I received it, therefore follow my plan and let me have dominion over them – and the glory!'

Silence hung in the air as though the world trembled. Tathea was cold to the bones of her body, and yet the sweat stood on her skin.

Then the light around Asmodeus dimmed and the last figure came forward. This was Ishrafeli. The recognition was instant, sweet and sure, without shadow, yet as she had never seen him before. His face was as calm as the dawn in a perfect sky. There was passion and faith and honour in it that made all else disappear from the heart. All memory of pain was washed away. All price became nothing.

'I am Ishrafeli,' his voice filled the silence and touched every soul, 'and I speak not my own words, but those of our brother who has already redeemed the flesh of all worlds from the corruption of physical death.' He leaned forward, urgency in the lines of his body, his outstretched arms.

'But what of the death of the soul? Asmodeus would save man from the first death but only by denying him true life! Man without knowledge of good and evil is a child, and in bondage to his ignorance. He will never choose wrongly, because he will have no choice at all.' He spread his hands, beautiful, sensitive. 'He will have neither sin nor virtue. There will be nothing for him to fear, so he will never be a coward. He will never flee from duty or pain, never betray rather than suffer, never lie to escape, never twist and deceive – never attack rather than wait to defend.'

There was pain in his face so raw it cut the heart. His voice was soft. 'Neither will he ever master his own quaking flesh and sinking soul and face the night of his terror.'

The myriad faces watched him, white with anguish, and the beginning of an understanding so beautiful it transfixed them.

Ishrafeli's voice was unrelenting, filling every heart. 'He will never mount the steps of sacrifice with trembling and sweat of fear, and yet not flinch to pour out his own life, that others may be preserved. He will not labour and toil and bleed to protect the vulnerable, secure justice and see that truth is spoken aloud.

'He will not sin – he will have no need of repentance. Neither will he know how to humble himself before God his Father, and plead to be forgiven.'

He turned further towards the great seat, and the Man who sat motionlessly upon it. 'He will not be happy to eat the bread of humility, to wipe out all his own dreams and imaginings, and allow God to create in him a new heart, wiser and gentler than before. And because he has not understood the utmost bitterness of sin, he will neither fear it nor flee from it. Nor will he understand how to forgive others. His heart will not ache with pity, nor his love flow outward over the distressed and those who mourn and come on bended knee in contrition.

'He will not know the humility of failure, nor the grace of gratitude, nor from whom his gifts have come. He will have no need to seek God, or to learn who it is that loves him without condition and without end.

'His soul will become a crippled, shrivelled thing, a promise unfulfilled.' His body expressed his pain, his devastating knowledge of loss. 'He will know neither sorrow nor joy, neither darkness nor light; he will remain for ever a child, imprisoned in eternal infancy.' Ishrafeli turned to the figure in the great chair, his voice a passionate plea.

'Give him choice! Let him see the pleasure and pain, good and evil. Teach him the law! If he understands it and turns his back to the light he will live in his own shadow. But if he learns to keep the law, however slow and faltering his steps, however often he needs to repent – and repentance is sure, though his sins be scarlet and cry out to heaven – yet in bitterness and in pain his tears may wash them out, through God's grace.'

He lifted his head, his eyes shining.

'Then at the last he will reach the fullness of his purpose and his creation, and become whole, as he was born to be. The price has been paid! Let this be the plan: a world where every good and every evil is possible. Let man choose for himself, and the glory be thine.'

The great hall grew brighter and brighter till it shone with a perfect light, and the Man of Holiness rose from His seat and stepped forward.

'Let man choose.' His words filled the air in an eternal benediction. 'Prove him, that he may work his own salvation, and inherit glory and dominion and everlasting joy, for this is indeed why he was born.'

Tathea was transfixed. This was the truth. This was what she had been searching for and paid such an agonising price to know.

It was infinitely precious, beyond anything and everything else. All other good was encompassed within it.

Behind her the room seemed different. She was no longer sure which way she had come in. Huge torches burned in brackets high on the walls, shedding their light over tapestried hangings and carved tables. On one of them lay a book covered in beaten gold and set with chrysolite and pearls. She went to it, as if drawn by an unseen hand. Its beauty was marvellous, its workmanship unlike any she had seen. Its great hasp was set with a single star ruby. As her hands touched it, an ineffable sweetness ran through her. She hesitated only a moment, certain that the words in it, once known, could never be denied. Then she opened it and read:

'Child of God, if your hands have unloosed the hasp of this Book, then the intent of your heart is at last unmarred by cloud of vanity or deceit.

'Know this, that in the beginning, throughout the dark reaches of infinity, was the law by which every intelligence has its being and fulfils the measure of its creation.

'When God was yet a man like yourself, with all your frailties, your needs and your ignorance, walking a perilous land as you do, even then was the law irrevocable.

'By obedience you may overcome all things, even the darkness within, which is the Great Enemy. The heart may be softened by pain and by yearning until love turns towards all creatures and nothing is cast away, nothing defiled by cruelty or indifference. The mind may be enlightened by understanding gained little by little through trial and labour, and much hunger, to perform great works. Courage will lift the fallen, make bearable the ache of many wounds, and guide your feet on the path when your eyes no longer see the light.

'When your spirit is harrowed by despair and all else fails you, compassion will magnify your soul until no glory is impossible.

'By such a path did God ascend unto holiness.

'But the law is unalterable, and unto all, though the tears of heaven wash away the fixed and the moving stars for you, though God has shed His blood to lave you clean; each act without love, each indifference, each betrayal robs you of that which you might have been. Eternity looks on while you climb the ladder towards the light, but neither God nor devil takes you a step up or down, only your own act.

'If it were not so, where would be your greatness at the last? Would God rob you of your soul's joy? Of that day when you stand before Him in eternal life and say not as a stranger but as a citizen, "I have walked the long path, I have conquered all things, thou hast opened the door for me and I have come home".'

Tathea stared at the page until the words swam before her eyes. She had no need to read further. This was everything, all there was to seek or to find. She did not know how long or how steep the path would be, but to climb it was the only goal.

Gently, reluctantly, she closed the Book and lifted it. It was heavy but not beyond her ability to carry, and the metal was warm to the touch. She would take it back to the world, share with everyone this treasure, this key to all happiness.

She walked out of the chamber, the Book in her arms. Outside, beyond the door, the sky was pricked with the first stars as the purple of night overtook the heavens. Holding the Book tightly, she went out through the colonnades and down the shallow marble steps, pale in the limpid light. Below her the skiff rested against the lowest stair.

Ishrafeli was already there, standing silently, waiting for her.

The words she had planned died on her lips, all the questions, the explanations slipped from her. Even the bruising fact that she loved him found no voice.

'So you have the truth,' he said gently.

'Yes.'

'And you have taken the Book.'

Suddenly her breath hurt and a chill spread through her. 'Yes . . .'

He came to her, putting his hands over hers. 'You have made your choice, now you must abide by it.'

'It is the truth, I know that.' She did not elaborate. 'I must take it back to the world. I must share it.'

The barest smile touched his lips. 'I know. But it is heavier than you can dream, heavier than you can bear alone.'

'But you will come with me!'

His hands tightened over hers, warm and strong. 'I cannot. You

111

have chosen truth. You have taken the Word from Heaven to give it to men. I brought you here because above all else you wanted to come, enough to pay whatever price was asked. Now you must go back to the world, with all its risks, its pain and its glory. But my time is not yet.'

She asked the question because it was beating in her mind, crying to be answered. 'Who are you?' Her voice was no more than a whisper in the enormous cavern of the sky.

'I am an angel. Did you not know that?'

'Then can I not stay here with you?' It was a cry torn from the heart.

He smiled, a great tenderness in his face, and perhaps for an instant a reflection of the same searing loneliness that swept over her. 'You know you cannot. You have taken the Light of Heaven.' Slowly he let go of her hands and stepped back.

Some faint and fearful glimpse of what she had done lit her soul. He saw it in her eyes. He held out his hand again. 'Come,' he whispered.

Silently she followed him back up the steps, then walked beside him through a different hall, still clutching the Book to her breast. At the far end a door opened into a room whose radiance was pure beyond all power to imagine and the air held a sweetness which was the breath of all life.

In the centre stood one Man alone, and in His face was the love that has created worlds, and before whose beauty the stars tremble.

Tathea bowed her head and sank to her knees, her spirit filled with light. She felt the touch of hands upon her head and the peace of God rested within her, and with it came the certainty that never again, through all time, need she be alone, or afraid.

His words filled her ears and were written on her soul: 'I bless you to go forth in the world and teach My Word to all the people of the earth, that they may know they are My children, and may become even as I am, and inherit everlasting dominion and glory and joy. But they are agents unto themselves, and in all things they must choose.

'I have loved you from the beginning, and shall love you without end. I shall walk beside you, my arms shall encircle you and my hands bear you up. I cannot protect you from pain, because only through hurt and labour will you grow, but your name is before My eyes, and I shall not forget you, nor shall I leave you alone.

'Rise now, my beloved, and continue your journey.'

The touch vanished from her head and she knew He had gone from the room. She waited a long time, then at last she stood up, still holding the Book, and made her way through the door and down some steps to a grassy sward.

A man stood before her and this time she knew instantly he was not Ishrafeli, for all that he resembled him. He was cloaked in the colours of the night, blues and violets shot with sudden sparks like the light of forgotten stars. It was Asmodeus, the Great Enemy. He looked at the Book in her arms, and his eyes glittered with a hatred older than time.

'So you know truth from falsehood,' he said slowly. 'But you will not win. You have not the strength, nor the courage. You will not endure. I will rob you of that which is dearer than you know. I will wound you where you will not heal. You think love will protect you?' He laughed, a terrible sound, like the end of all light and life.

Ishrafeli came down the steps slowly and stood on the grass a little distance from Tathea.

'Love is enough,' he answered. 'You do not believe because you do not understand it.'

Asmodeus swung round to face him. 'So you would fight with me? Over this Book, this woman?' His lips curled. 'She is nothing! As frail as grass, here a moment and gone again, withered by the first blast of reality. But so be it! We will fight with real weapons, the eternal weapons of light and darkness!' He flung his arms wide, fingers stretched skywards, and opened his throat in a wordless, terrible scream.

The light was wan across the sky, the air filled with a glow like wine, and into it came a winged creature scaled in shining gold, its head like a man's, its body that of a lion, its tail barbed with quills, the tip the sting of a scorpion. It was huge, bigger than a score of men, and it glittered as if forged in the fires of the dying sun. Tathea felt the heat of it burn her skin.

It pranced upon the ground, its eyes bold, staring at them one by one. Then its gaze rested on Ishrafeli as if it knew its master's prey. It shot its golden quills like arrows, spearing the ground, leaving the darts embedded where they struck.

Tathea was helpless. She knew what it was, the Golden Manticore, the spiritual creature of pride. The sin was as old as time, and as real as the heart of man.

Ishrafeli stood staring at the monstrous thing. Tathea could do nothing. Such battles can only be fought alone; the time for help or comfort was over.

But Ishrafeli knew the long winter of the ice, and had learned the depths of his own soul. He had overcome terror and despair, and found beyond them wisdom and the love of God. He understood the combat, and sought his own weapons. He concentrated his mind on gratitude for every good thing of his life, for every opportunity to learn, to perform some act of grace or love, every sin for which he had been forgiven – and the longing to walk with the Man of Holiness, and to know and be known by Him. And out of the twilight came another creature, white as milk, like a mighty horse with a single horn on its brow.

The Manticore screamed and shot its shining barbs, and they fell

113

blunted to the ground. It clawed with talons and gnashed its bloody teeth – but the Unicorn's hooves broke its bones. Back and forth they swayed, dust flying, the ground scored up. Then as they closed in the final struggle, the Manticore's scales were gashed, its scorpion tail writhed and darted futilely on the Unicorn's impenetrable hide.

Its horn pierced the golden scales and the Manticore's lifestream gushed out. It gurgled and choked thick in its throat. Its body fell and lay twitching and helpless.

The Unicorn withdrew its horn, unstained, and stood a moment in the lambent afterglow. Then it swung its exquisite head and leaped into the air as another might scale a flight of stairs.

The Manticore shimmered and seemed to dissolve until there was nothing left of it but a scar of burning on the earth and a sickly smell in the air.

Ishrafeli was on his knees, his skin pale and his hair streaked with white. Asmodeus was contorted with fury, his body twisted, his face a mask of cunning and rage. Not once did his eyes turn to Tathea. He flung his head back and cried out, this time a roar like terror and agony beyond enduring.

The sky grew darker, and out of the south, hideous as nightmare and the cold-sweating dreams of madness, came another creature on black wings, ragged, its skin stretched taut over its skeletal frame. Its head was birdlike with cruel beak and glaring eyes. On its bald crown a cock's comb glowed red, the only colour on a body as dark as rotted wood, with clawed feet and leather-like tail.

It was Basilisk, the beast of fear. To look upon it crippled motion, froze warmth from the heart, and brought panic and the violence of chaos to the brain. Its fearful wings beat over Ishrafeli's head, darkening the air; it screeched with an eldritch voice that numbed the mind and drowned the soul in terror.

But Ishrafeli remained firm. His heart remembered the battles in the ice, remembered shame and defeat and loneliness, and how he had found the courage then to rise and follow the star he had seen once; and know the truth of all things that are good.

And out of the north like a moving mountain of snow, like a storm on the wind, came a white bear so huge it dwarfed both men. When it reared up on its hind legs, only the Basilisk's blood-red comb rose taller than the Bear's lean head. With a giant paw the Bear struck the Basilisk and tore one black wing from its socket and left it dangling, crumpled and repulsive.

The Basilisk roared and let out a belch of breath like the air of rotting graves. All human death was in its eyes, and the slow torture of injury and disease.

But the Bear reared up again and struck a second time, sending the creature reeling backwards, falling, flank torn open, joints awry.

Round and round they fought, the Bear wounded, blood staining its white fur, and the Basilisk vainly flapping one wing. Courage and cowardice reeled as the last clouds faded on the horizon and the first star showed a glimmering light in a flawless sky. The human figures stood motionless.

Then the Bear struck a tremendous blow, and the Basilisk lay motionless on the ground for a long, breathless moment, then its body dissolved and left only a stain upon the earth.

The Bear reared up and lifted its white face to the sky, paws spread wide. Then it turned and moved swiftly, disappearing as it had come, like a pale storm racing northwards.

Tathea gazed helplessly, drained with emotion.

Ishrafeli's hair had turned white across the crown and his face was haggard from the mighty effort.

She turned to Asmodeus and saw in his eyes the first dawn of knowledge that he could fail. His hands clenched and unclenched. He let out a thin, piercing wail like all despair, and at his command came the last beast of sin from the darkness of the inner mind, the Dragon of Sloth. It represented everything that desires to win without struggle, to take the lesser, easier path, that seeks to reap without having sown, that deceives and begets lies because the truth is labour and pain.

It came out of the north where its cold sleep had made it sluggish. Its awakening was primeval, torpid, it clung to death and the slow disintegration of the world back to darkness and the void before there was light.

It stared at Ishrafeli with an evil so intense it seemed he must be consumed by it. Its form was indistinct, lost in the vast shadows of the night, reptilian, lizard-eyed, its size too great to measure. It had no weapon but its immeasurable weight, as if it would crush out life merely by touching it.

Ishrafeli made as if to move, but his limbs were paralysed. Sloth had crept into them and he knelt immobile as the beast lowered its snout and fixed implacable eyes upon him. Ishrafeli bowed his head. Tathea watched with unbearable grief as his body crumpled and grew weaker and smaller. She could do nothing. The Dragon folded its huge forelegs as if to roll over and crush him to pulp.

Then out of the calm west on wings lit by the last rays of the vanished sun flew a white swan, radiant as moonlight. Its shadow fell on the Dragon, and its grace and ineffable loveliness seared the beast's flesh. The Dragon's cold, sluggish blood boiled and burst its skin in agony, hissing and bubbling down its flanks like lava. Its cries were like the voices of the damned come forth from hell.

It turned and lumbered away, crashing into rocks and pulverising them to a fine, choking dust. And all the while its thin, primal scream

115

filled the air until even its shadow vanished into the jaws of night.

The bird circled once, twice, and a single feather fluttered down. It flew low once more, then was gone.

Tathea stooped and picked up the feather. She knew what it was: compassion, that unconditional love through which man comes closest to God.

Ishrafeli was broken. His hair was a shock of white, his body withered with the mighty effort of battle. But he had won, he had called forth out of his soul the Beasts of God. Asmodeus lay upon the ground without sense or breath, his robe stained by dust and sweat, his hands grimed, his face blank. His spirit had fled for a season – the likeness of death descended on him.

Tathea's prison was broken. She went to Ishrafeli and knelt beside him. She placed the Book in his arms and cradled him against her. He felt slight, wasted away like an old man, and there was no strength in him. She touched his brow, stroked back his hair. She held him closer in her arms and let her tears bathe his cheek. She kissed him softly on eyes and lips.

His eyelids fluttered open.

'You must go,' he whispered, his voice no more than a breath. 'Go while you can. This is a battle of the soul we shall fight many times before the end. Remember, you are not alone . . . never alone . . .' And with a smile he drifted into sleep as soft as the white swan's feather.

She kissed him once more and then let him go.

The skiff was waiting and she had the golden Book. The tide was already beginning to turn.

Her body was aching and her eyes were blind with tears as she walked through the starlight down to the boat and climbed in. She collapsed in the stern, hugging the Book to her, and let the sea take her where it would.

She awoke in a magnificent dawn. The roof of heaven was bathed with light and the sea floor gleamed translucent blue and grey shot with bars of silver. She was lying curled up in the stern of the small boat with the single sail barely touched by wind.

She sat up, staring around her. Ahead was an island shore, so close she could see the pale bar of sand, and behind it a rising mound of green with a town folded in its crevices. A few ships with brilliant sails, spots of saffron and flame and rust, showed bright on the water. There must be a harbour beyond the point. But the wind and the tide were carrying her to the beach, and the ropes were tied too fast for her to undo and change course.

The bow crunched on to the sand with a bump. She clambered to her feet. There were seabirds crying overhead and the faint fragrance of wild asphodel and sea pinks drifted to her from the land. A small house stood in the dunes.

But before she left the boat she knew there was something she must take with her, something so precious that life was of no value or purpose without it. She stood motionless, unable to remember. Then slowly she picked up a flask of water, a small box which had contained food, a pillow, and lastly a large silk cloak. Under it was a golden book. For a moment its beauty dazzled her, but its true worth, she knew, lay in what was written inside.

She picked it up, put on her cloak, and stepped ashore. She knew where she was now. The house belonged to the sage who had told her to go and wait on the sand, and beyond the hill was Orimiasse. She could remember going, waiting all night until dawn, as he had told her to, but what had happened then?

Ghosts of memory trailed across the edge of her mind, but no vision came, only an ache of passion and a knowledge of grief. It was something to do with great loveliness and its dissolution, the break up of old and treasured things. And dimly there were flights of the imagination, and loneliness, desolation and violence of nature.

Then sharply, very clearly came a stillness that was evil, a denial of life and growth, great courage, something of a city of desperate, irretrievable beauty and corruption, of honour, sacrifice, and unendurable pain. But she could not call back the meaning of it, only the scars it had left, the understanding of doubt, and a knowledge of what it is to fail. Most clearly of all she had a sense of having left behind something which was dearer than anything else, a part of herself.

But she had the Book, and she must go back to Orimiasse, and find the ship she had arrived in.

First she should thank the sage. She followed the path between the dunes and tussocks of wild grass and the sweet scent of sea pinks to the lone house.

He was waiting for her at the door, smiling. He looked at her, and at the golden Book in her arms, and then at her eyes. There was wonderment in him, and a deep fire of pain because an age had ended and a new one had begun. He was a man whose inner vision had seen the future as well as the past.

'So you have taken the Word from Heaven,' he said very softly. 'I knew one day someone would. When I saw your face, when you came yesterday, I thought perhaps it would be you.'

'Yesterday!' she exclaimed. 'No . . . no, I came long ago . . . a season . . . or more. I have been . . .'

His smile was very gentle. 'On a journey of the spirit.' He shook his head. 'It takes no time at all. Guard well what you have found, child. It is the light by which the stars burn, before which all darkness flees, both across the wastes of the universe to the farthest echoes of the mind of God, and in the secret depths of the soul within, where is the hope and the despair of man.

'Be true to the light. Never deny it or turn your face from it, and though the darkness encompass you and the Great Enemy tread upon your heels, your foot shall not stray from the path, nor your heart perish.' He raised his withered hand in a blessing and closed his eyes. A great smile of peace touched his lips as gently he sank against the door post and slid to the ground where he lay huddled in a small heap, no bigger than a child, and relaxed gradually into the sleep of death, his long task done.

For a moment she was frightened. She knew the Book was precious above all, but the knowledge had been close within her, unconfirmed by anyone else. Now his words made it an overwhelming fact, and his silent body at her feet, released from an age-old vigil, was a testament of its power.

The sea wind stirred the grasses and blew against her, like a warm hand pushing her. There was nothing she could do here. The old man was at peace, he had no need of her.

She turned and climbed up the headland. She did not look back at the bay and did not see the skiff float gently out into the blue water, slowly gathering speed as if by sunset it would be no more than a dark speck on the horizon.

Chapter Eight

Tathea walked slowly down from the crest of the hill towards Orimi-asse. To them she would not have been gone long, a day and a night. For her it was a time without measurement. The world around her was the same, the sharp feel of the sandy ground under her feet, the aromatic smell of the herbs and the grasses, the wind off the sea. But inside her everything was different. She was filled with emotions whose origins hovered at the edge of her mind. The harder she grasped at them, the more intangible they became.

There was only one certainty, absolute and unchangeable: the Book clasped in her arms was the source of all that was beautiful and precious, the beginning and the end of everlasting joy. The power of the universe was in its pages. She must share it. Everyone must know.

She had reached the outskirts of the town. Her feet were no longer on earth but on smooth paving stones. Men and women passed her, going about their business, planning tomorrow, as if the world had not changed.

How did she tell them? She had looked at the Book only momen-tarily on the shore before she left the sage and his eternal peace, but it was enough. In it was a staggering new truth. It was not God who made the laws, nor could He break them. The law was immutable. The very stars would fall apart, worlds disintegrate, chaos destroy the universe if it were broken. Meaning itself would disappear. God would cease to be God.

And vast in its immediacy, wonderful, and yet almost too hard to bear, was the understanding that He was the Father of all mankind. They were begotten in His likeness, however unrecognisable now; just as an infant, full of weakness and fears, helpless even to stand, was still in embryo the titan it could become. It was of the same kind and carried in its frail and foolish soul the seeds of Godhood. The journey from the beginning was immeasurable to man, but known to the last step by God. And He expected that the full course be run, year by year, victory by victory until the stature of the giant be reached.

How should she begin?

She passed a woman who glanced at her curiously.

She must protect the Book. It was beautiful. People would see it as precious, perhaps for all the wrong reasons. She took off the indigo silk cloak and wrapped it round the Book, hiding its gold.

And to succeed she must survive. With that knowledge came the return of the twisting pain of loss inside her. For an instant it was so sharp she stumbled. She remembered Habi's limp, blood-soaked body, felt his slight weight in her arms as if it had been only moments ago. She could hardly breathe.

She was utterly alone. Whoever had murdered Mon-Allat and all the others would be aware that she had escaped. They would not rest knowing she might form the core of a rebellion against them. The wrongs inflicted on Shinabar must be righted, justice must be done for the dead and, even more, for the living. But to achieve this she must have power herself, more power than the knowledge of truth, however bright and all-encompassing, however beautiful. She could not return to Shinabar, not yet.

She did not want to go back to her mother's family. She had a responsibility to survive, and to protect the Book. She would be wiser to remain alone. There were many in Shinabar who knew her mother had come from the Lost Lands. It would not require a great leap of intelligence for them to assume she might have sought refuge here, and follow her.

She must leave again, as soon as possible. But where should she go?

She was standing in the street close to the quayside. She could smell the salt and the sharp odour of tar and weed. She had kept with her the leather pouch of jewels Kol-Shamisha had given her. She could leave now, without telling anyone. Where would her enemies in Shinabar be least able to look for her? Where was Shinabar's power and influence weakest?

Camassia. Perhaps others would come to the same conclusion, but it was still the best answer. It was the only power in the world that might one day rival Shinabar's. A faint smile touched her lips as she thought how soon that day might be. That had been the fear of Mon-Allat's enemies, perhaps the reason he had been overthrown. On the borders of Shinabar, to the east and the south, barbarian tribes had amassed in the last decade, gaining strength. The number and violence of their incursions into Shinabar had increased steadily. In Thoth-Moara many chose not to believe it. Shinabar had not been successfully invaded in a thousand years. They could not imagine the possibility.

But Tathea knew it was real. She had seen the emissaries from the outlands and heard in their own words the tales of slaughter, of more and more men armed with better weapons. And there were attacks further north too, in the plains beyond Irria-Kand. One day soon the barbarians might threaten the expansion of Camassia as well. That was why Mon-Allat had sought to mend centuries of enmity and sign a treaty with the Emperor of Camassia. It was an alliance of civilisation against the waves of darkness beyond the edge of what was governed by laws, even if those laws were sometimes flawed and unjust.

She could remember the months of diplomatic argument, then the elation when at last the treaty was agreed. The Emperor Isadorus had sent over some of his most senior representatives to sign it. The Lady Eleni, the Emperor's sister, had come with the delegation.

Would Eleni remember her? Yes, of course she would! One does not forget queens, whatever their change in circumstances. That is where she would begin. She would travel to the City in the Centre of the World, to Camassia, and find a way to speak to Eleni.

Tathea grasped the Book more tightly and walked across the wooden boards of the quay towards the nearest ship.

The voyage to Camassia was long and she spent the time studying the Book. It was written in the ancient tongue which was the root of all the languages in the world, and it required intense concentration for her even to begin to understand it. She also knew that if she hoped to share what was written in the Book with the world, she would have to translate it into a more modern form, and to do that she must learn its meaning thoroughly. But with each day she felt more deeply its strength and the power of its beauty. And with each day, too, she became more keenly aware of a presence, almost a tenderness, that enveloped her, and she felt at moments as if she could have reached out and touched the person who was the source of it.

They docked in the City, which was not as ancient as Tarra-Ghum but had the magnificence of the Empire clearly stamped on it. Buildings of rich-coloured stone, warm as sunlight, stretched beyond sight over the hills. Cypress and lemon trees showed in patches of dark green, olives silver grey. Here in the harbour she was surrounded by fat-bellied ships laden with cargo from all over the world, sleek warships, triremes and quinquiremes, busy fishing skiffs, and elegant barges. Everywhere was movement. Shouts echoed across the water.

Tathea went ashore and walked up the worn stones of the quay into the streets, past storehouses and shops, and then on past people's homes. She had been educated to understand Camassian speech, but it sounded alien, the cadences different from her own. And the smells were different, sharper, touched with the salt and the damp of the sea air, nothing like the hot desert wind of Thoth-Moara.

She must find lodgings. She must not be alone in the streets at nightfall. The Book was once again wrapped in her blue cloak, but she had no other clothes, and no possessions other than what was left of the jewels. And she had no way to defend herself. She must sell one of the gems to raise some money.

It was difficult. This was not a task she was used to. Never before in her life had she had to consider the daily necessities of food and shelter. They had always been provided, and like the air she breathed, she had taken them for granted. The Camassians regarded her oddly, not for her dark Shinabari looks – they were used to every race on earth – but because she was a foreign woman travelling alone, and only too obviously unused to it.

The first few weeks passed slowly. She was a stranger in a land she did not know and among a people to whom she was of no importance. She was merely one more face among the tens of thousands that thronged the streets. On the ship it had seemed like an excellent idea to approach the Lady Eleni. She was the one person in Camassia who knew her. But in the past they had been equals, or almost. Tathea had been Empress, Eleni merely an Emperor's sister. Now Tathea was a fugitive, possessed of nothing but a handful of jewels and a gold-covered Book written by the hand of God. But surely that should be enough.

Sometimes it seemed so, when she was rested, when the sun was high, when a man or a woman smiled at her in the street. But when she was tired, when darkness came and she climbed the steps of her lodgings and heard the voices of people laughing together and speaking a language that was foreign to her, then it was not. The worst was always when she saw children, young children with wide eyes and slender shoulders, the way the soft hair grew at the back of their heads and their delicate necks. Then nothing was enough, nothing comforted. She crept into her room, bolted the door, and wept.

She sold more of the jewels Kol-Shamisha had given her and purchased a house on the Hill of Cypresses, near the Imperial Hill. She hired servants. She bought good Camassian clothes, long-sleeved dresses caught high under the bosom with rich, embroidered borders in bold patterns of blues and greens and golds, fit for a lady to be seen in. A small black and white cat with a pointed face sauntered in one day and took up residence with her, a companionable creature that sparked a flare of joy and memory in her that she could not place. She quickly learned to love it. She became used to the daily life of the City, and grew familiar with the customs and values of its people. They seemed less sophisticated than the more ancient Shinabari. They were harsher, hastier to judge, less tolerant of eccentricity. But they were also less cynical, and they were angered by corruption in a way Tathea wished her own people had been. They still believed they could eradicate it. Their ideas were raw, unpolished by experience, sometimes short in the understanding of life's trials and failures; but they were also untarnished by disillusion. There was no weariness of heart or soul.

At times she felt very apart from them, and much older. There was an aching loneliness in being separated from the subtlety and wisdom of her own culture, refined as it was over millennia. The Camassians did not understand Shinabari wit, the multitudinous variations of

122

meaning in an old and exquisite language, full of nuances lent by legend and literature. She had no one with whom to share sudden moments of laughter, self-mockery or joy at tiny things made beautiful by time and knowledge.

She concentrated on the golden Book and prepared to teach its light to others. She did not alter her plan to begin with the Lady Eleni.

She had been in Camassia nearly sixty days when she first saw the Emperor Isadorus. She was part of a crowd lining the streets as he processed past. It was a celebration of some victory in the provinces, an excuse to please the people and proclaim a holiday. The day was warm with the haze of the fading year. There was a smell in the air of cypress, dust and fallen leaves. A certain depth in the quality of the light mellowed the colour of the stone buildings. There was no glitter, no distraction to the eye.

She waited with the rest of the crowd, pushing forward, a baker with flour on his hands to one side of her, a woman with a child on the other. She wanted to see the Emperor's face, not from admiration or the sense of unity which possessed those around her, the pride of belonging to the heart of the world, but because she hoped to read in his features something upon which to base her judgement as to how she should approach him. If she failed there would be no second chance.

There was a stir of movement around her. Someone made a joke and everyone laughed. There was the sound of feet slithering as people jostled each other, and the clinging smell of dust and sweat. Far along the massed heads, up the broad road between the palaces and halls of government, the cavalcade of the Emperor was coming. Shouts went up, trumpets and bugles blew and the air was filled with noise.

Tathea pushed forward, determined not to be elbowed away from the front. Soldiers appeared, dressed in leather tunics reinforced with metal plates. It was not ceremonial armour such as Shinabari soldiers wore on state occasions but heavy and practical, designed for war. Scarlet plumes decorated their bronze helmets and scarlet cloaks swung from their shoulders. Instead of the halberds and curved swords of Shinabar, they had spears and short, broad blades in scabbards at their sides. They marched in perfect unison, like a walking wall, legion after legion of them, tens of thousands of men from every province: broad-shouldered and sunburned from the south; narrow-eyed, high-cheeked men from the east; taller men with fair skins and heavier bones from the north; blue-eyed men from the west, Islanders from the Edge of the World. They carried their battle standard aloft and held its Imperial insignia with pride, as if their unity in this vast, conglomerate whole was more to them than their individual part.

The noise of cheering thundered on every side, drowning the tramp of feet and the clank of armour. Tathea was bumped and poked, her feet trodden on, her sides bruised. The sun was high and getting hotter. Somewhere a child was crying, tired and frightened, perhaps lost. Tathea felt suffocated as people surged forward.

After the legionaries came soldiers on horseback. They rode beautiful beasts with arched necks and high-stepping feet, their hooves clattering on the stones. The sight of them brought Tathea a violent ache of homesickness. They were desert horses, bred in Shinabar, brought here under the treaty signed by Mon-Allat.

But there was no time for the indulgence of pain. The Emperor's guard was passing, proud men with bronze breastplates gleaming in the sun and scarlet-crested helmets. Alone behind them rode Isadorus himself, on a white horse, saddled as if for war, and armoured like the guard. Did he actually lead his troops in battle, as once the Isarchs had, a thousand years ago? He rode comfortably, with the grace of a man long used to the saddle. But it was his face Tathea stared at, trying to pierce the outer mask and read the nature of his mind behind the broad brow, the long straight nose. She was not close enough to see the expression of his eyes, but to her the mouth was the key – wide, mobile, intelligent, with enough fullness for passion but too little for indulgence. It was the face of a man whose power lies within him. If birth or chance had not given him dominion, then he would have built it for himself. There was no cruelty in it, no rashness, no weakness for a courtier to manipulate.

The cheering rose in a wave of sound, battering her ears. Tathea had never been in a throng like this before. In the processions in Thoth-Moara the people were held back to allow her to pass. Here she was shoved from side to side, a person of no importance. It made her feel alien and overwhelmingly alone.

She turned and tried to force her way out, suddenly desperate to escape, to return to her home and solitude to hold the Book in her hands, read its now familiar words and allow its spirit to sink into her soul as if its Author's hand had touched her.

She stumbled and would have fallen but for strong fingers grasping her and taking her weight. Her first instinct was sheer panic at being held. She tore herself free and stared at the dark face of the man in front of her. He was lean, smooth-cheeked, with a long, straight nose and delicate lips, Shinabari dark, and no more than twenty years old.

'Ta-Thea,' he said gently. 'Majesty . . .'

She froze, her body rigid, a wave of sick terror surging through her.

He smiled, touched his finger to his brow between his eyes, then lowered his head, still looking at her. 'My name is Ra-Nufis, and you will always be Majesty to me, no matter what usurper sits on the throne of Shinabar – for now.'

She did not know him. The name meant nothing. Her first instinct was to deny who she was, but she dismissed it. He looked so certain, and if he were Shinabari he might well have seen her dozens of times.

124

She did not recall the face of every courtier or supplicant. And had she really lost so much that she had sunk to the indignity of denying her identity?

She straightened up, meeting his eyes. 'Who is he? Do you know that, Ra-Nufis?'

He kept his hands by his sides but began slowly to follow the crowds who were moving up the hill. She kept pace with him.

'If you mean his name, yes I do,' he answered gravely. 'Mon-Allat's nephew Hem-Shash sits on the throne now. But who prompted the assassins I do not know, or who speaks through Hem-Shash.' He turned to look at her. 'Perhaps I can find out. They are usurpers, all of them, and their rule is oppressive.' His voice was urgent and he kept close to her, shielding her from being brushed by the people streaming along beside them. 'But they are nervous, they constantly look over their shoulders, as the guilty always must. They see plots and counterplots even where there are none. Guards are tripled, people arrested without warrant or cause.'

The sound of his speech with its familiar cadences brought the old memories flooding back and Tathea longed above all to go home, to feel the dry heat and the prickle of sand, to be among the people she knew.

'Knowledge of a few names won't change that!' she said harshly, more to herself than to him. She must not indulge in dreams. Thinking of Shinabar was painful. Hearing of the changes there, predictable though they were, hurt her more than she would have expected.

Ra-Nufis caught up with her, but keeping a respectful mien, hands at his sides so he did not accidentally touch her, just as if she had still been his Empress.

'I agree,' said Ra-Nufis quietly. 'The names of assassins are of no importance. History will deal with them. Of infinitely more value would be the names of those who are still loyal, those who have enough courage and love for their country to work and fight to restore justice, even to die for it if necessary.'

She stopped abruptly and turned to stare at him. He met her eyes without flinching, a long, steady gaze. He was so young, his face showed no lines of anxiety or temper yet. Her heart lurched for his innocence.

'What are you saying?' she asked huskily.

'That you are the last rightful heir to the throne of Shinabar, Majesty,' he answered. 'And that I will do anything to protect you and return you to your country, where your people need you. Many of them remain loyal to your house, and as the abuses increase, so will their number.' His face was alive with urgency. 'I will find them. I will build knowledge, fact upon fact, name upon name, until you have enough to act.'

Dared she believe him? Had the same power that had given her the Book also sent Ra-Nufis to help her return to Shinabar with it? How could she be certain?

She looked at him steadily, ignoring the last of the crowds drifting past them, chattering about the procession, their families, the next day's business.

'I no longer believe in all the old ways,' she said, watching his eyes. How much of the truth should she tell him? She must tread carefully.

He was confused. 'What do you not believe?'

Not yet. It was too soon. Learn to know him a little.

'Many things,' she said lightly, letting him know by her smile that she was setting her answer aside only temporarily.

In the days and weeks that followed, she did indeed learn to know him. He offered her help in all manner of small ways, found her a perfect chair for her home, chose a blanket for her in warm colours like the desert, discovered which market sold the best bread and dates, and they laughed together over Camassian notions of Shinabari cuisine.

One day in the small garden of her home she told him something of what she believed they should be seeking.

'We should be climbing always a step upwards,' she said, 'towards the kind of courage which can face the knowledge of agony and despair and failure without turning away, the kind of wholeness of heart and mind in which there is no division of purpose, no lies, no self-deceit.' She watched his face, motionless in the sunlight. 'Towards the kind of love which can cherish and nurture – forgive even the most wicked, the ugliest and most callous,' she finished. 'Which is the love of God for the World, and yet keeps the law of creation and is the power which begets all the souls of men and wills that they shall have joy.'

Ra-Nufis looked across at her, his eyes shining. 'Where did you learn that?' he asked.

She smiled. 'I have a Book in which it is written—'

'May I see?' he interrupted, then blushed, looking down and blinking. 'I'm sorry. That was . . . brash of me. I should not be so—'

'Of course you may,' she answered quickly. 'It is for sharing. You are the first, but it is for everyone.'

'The first? Me?'

'Yes.'

'When?'

'Now, if you wish.'

'I wish . . . more than anything else on earth.'

Tathea stood up and he followed her inside to the cupboard where she kept the Book. She unwrapped it from the blue silk cloak and held it out to him.

126

He took it from her with trembling hands, moving his fingers slowly over the gems on its surface, as if he were afraid to open it. He looked up at her, then down at it again.

They sat down and she waited.

He opened the cover to the first page. He began reading. He read for an hour without even glancing at her. When at last he did raise his eyes to hers, they were bright with tears, and a brilliance of wonder shone through.

'It is everything!' he said simply. 'I can hardly begin to understand all it means, but I know its beauty is the heart of the universe, the power and the meaning of all that exists. We must take this back to Shinabar . . .' He did not even realise he had included himself in the task. 'Let me go first and begin to gather information.' His fingers moved gently over the surface of the Book. 'This must not be taken there until we have overthrown the usurpers and restored justice. Few people know me. I can move about unseen.' His voice was rising with urgency. 'I can find out where your support is, learn military, political and economic information which you will need to gather forces here. It will take time.' He stood up slowly, holding the Book out to her. 'I had best begin to plan now.' He did not even consider the possibility of her refusing. He knew what was in the Book, and he knew she knew it even more profoundly. There could be no turning back.

By the beginning of winter Ra-Nufis had left Camassia. Tathea decided she must hesitate no longer in seeking the Lady Eleni. The best course would be to approach her in the open. The forthcoming chariot races should provide an opportunity.

Accordingly Tathea selected her best Camassian gown, dark wine-purple with gold cord under the bosom and a deep embroidered border at the hem. She regarded herself critically in the long, polished glass. She was too dark to look Camassian, but she did appear a woman of dignity and some importance. She could not be dismissed lightly by the Imperial Guard.

She stood with the Book open in her arms and read the first page again, as if she was communicating with the One who had written it, then she closed it, placed it in the chest under her clothes, and locked the chest, pocketing the key.

She had made her decision. There was no purpose in pondering it any more. She left the house.

It was a cool, bright day. The circle of the race arena was crowded, tier above tier fifteen storeys high at the outer rim, and five hundred yards across.

Tathea stared around her. There must be a hundred thousand people here, of every trade and occupation, a dozen races, a score of creeds, all packed elbow to elbow, shouting and cheering. Wagers were being laid, arguments waxed hot and furious. The air was heavy with the odours of meat, the pungency of lemons and quince spices and the sweetness of honey. People called out greetings, challenges, encouragement to favourites. The sound of a dozen languages swirled around her.

In spite of its size, the circuit the horses would run was tight enough to be dangerous at speed. There was always the risk of mutilation or death. It required skill and courage to compete, and wealth.

There was a rustle of excitement and a sea of faces turned towards the Imperial stand. Tathea looked too as the Emperor Isadorus came into view, raising his arms in salute. Beside him was a woman of stern, patrician handsomeness, her gestures gracious but cool, as if she took little pleasure in the crowd's adulation or the prospect of the races. That must be Barsymet, the Empress. It was certainly not Eleni.

Tathea felt a moment of alarm. Where was she? If she had not come, the plan was foiled. It might take months to approach her through intermediaries, and it could be dangerous.

The beginning of the parade of chariots in the arena interrupted her thoughts. There was a roar of excitement. People craned forward, yelling encouragement. The horses were beautiful, prancing in their eagerness, heads tossing, bodies shining in the sun. The charioteers wore military uniform, scarlet tunics with polished leather armour to their knees, but their arms and shoulders were bare to allow freedom of movement to handle the reins and wield the whip.

As they passed the Imperial box, each chariot turned and the driver saluted the Emperor. One drawn by black horses with eagle crests was level with Tathea and the charioteer looked up. His head was high, his arms extended. He swayed very slightly with the chariot's movement. In his pride and skill he was as perfectly beautiful as his beasts. His face was aquiline, arrogant and intelligent. For a moment she forgot the present. In his ancient unity of man and animal he could almost have been Shinabari.

He moved on, and she recalled her purpose with a new urgency. She swivelled round to look back up to the Imperial box. She must speak to someone, whatever the risk.

Then she saw Eleni, smiling, leaning forward, watching the same charioteer she had noticed. Eleni was just as Tathea remembered, soft features, honey-warm complexion, the sweep of auburn hair. Tathea smiled to herself. For all the differences between them in race and culture, and now in circumstance, the woman in Eleni was responding to the charioteer in exactly the same way she herself had done. Eleni was just as vulnerable, just as human.

The chariots were lining up for the signal to begin. There was a roar from the crowd, then the thunder of hooves and a cloud of dust as three score horses charged, throwing their weight against the harnesses, and three score wheels dug into the ground and hurtled forward.

It was a wild sport, thrilling, dangerous, conducted at breakneck speed amid yelling and stamping and cheering. Women were squealing with excitement.

Early on there were casualties: wheels jammed, drivers toppled, chariots overturned or careered off the track. At great peril to themselves men ran on to the track to rescue fallen competitors, sometimes carrying them bodily if they were badly injured or senseless. Others waved arms or coloured sticks and shooed the loose horses aside before catching them and leading them away. All the time the roar of the crowd rose as the climax neared.

In the final circuit only six chariots remained. The black horses with the eagle crests were among them. Tathea leaned over the rail, holding her breath. She wanted him to win, but far more than that she was terrified he might be injured.

The chariots thundered past for the last time, sweat-streaked, spattered with sand. A giant man in white and green finished first, the man with the black horses only a yard behind. Disappointment washed over Tathea, and vanished, overtaken by relief. She was weak with the sudden relaxing of strain. It was over and he was safe. The throng roared its approval as the last chariots crossed the line. A woman beside Tathea was waving her arms above her head in jubilation. Already people were beginning to leave their places to collect wagers or take refreshment, calling out to friends.

In the arena the winner bowed before the Emperor, and Isadorus saluted his victory, throwing down a laurel which for an instant as it arced in the air woke a memory in Tathea, which vanished before she could place it. Then he tossed a purse of gold.

After him came the other charioteer, meeting the Emperor's eyes boldly, and caught the purse of silver thrown to him. He bowed. If he was disappointed, there was nothing of it in his expression or his bearing, but Tathea knew from the set of his shoulders and the swagger of his walk that he would try again and again, until he won. In spite of her fear for him, she was eager that he should. She would have been disillusioned if he had been content with second place.

The next race was beginning. Should she try to see Eleni now? If she waited until it was all over Eleni might leave and it would be too late. Or would she resent being interrupted? Might it sour the possibility of friendship?

Tathea looked up at the Imperial box. Isadorus was watching the race, but his face was impassive, as if only part of his attention were on it. He knew what was expected of him and would never give less, but his thoughts appeared to be elsewhere. Beside him the Empress Barsymet was talking to a youth of perhaps twenty-two who resembled her so much he must surely be her son, the Emperor's heir, Merkator. The darker youth behind him would be his younger brother Tiberian. They both stood close to their mother, shoulders half turned towards her, away from Isadorus.

Could she interrupt now? Behind the Imperial family stood soldiers in the purple-bordered tunics of the Household Guard. A few months ago, not half a year, she herself had sat in an Imperial box to watch the drama of the theatre. A different Household Guard had stood behind her, dressed in bleached linen with blue and turquoise sashes and beaten copper helmets. Outside, the desert night had dried the moisture from the skin, and sand had crept whispering over the stones.

The race ended and another began. She had missed the moment.

Two horses passing in front of her collided at violent speed, both falling, hurling their riders clear. Neither man was seriously hurt and both scrambled up, shaken but whole. One horse rose to its feet and trotted off, but the other, a beautiful beast, pure Shinabari from the fine, intelligent head, struggled to rise and fell back again. It was hideously apparent that one of its legs was broken.

The rider staggered over to it, his face streaming tears, his agony unashamed. He called out to it as if he could ease its fear, pleading with his gods to save his beloved animal at any cost.

Tathea was sick with horror. In the desert a horse was life. She understood the bond between man and beast and she felt for the rider as if she had been in his place.

A figure came down from the Imperial box, vaulting over the divisions of the rows, and finally jumped from the lowest, past where Tathea stood, and landed on the sand, his knife already drawn to end the horse's pain. He knew the rider could not bring himself to do it. It was the charioteer with the black horses and the eagle emblems. Of course, he was a member of the Imperial family; she should have known.

Tathea gathered up her skirts and scrambled over the rail too, landing hard on the sand. There was nothing she could do to help, except stand with the rider whose face was filled with agony as if he would sooner it were his own bones that were broken. Over and over again he spoke his horse's name, his voice choking.

'I'll be quick,' the charioteer promised, his face full of pity.

The horse lay on its side, its body shuddering, head up, eyes rolling with terror and pain.

Tathea moved towards the rider but he did not even notice her.

The charioteer turned back to the horse, steeling himself to do the deed, his shoulders rigid, his hand shaking in spite of his purpose.

From the steps Eleni appeared, running across the sand, her skirts flying. She pushed past the charioteer and fell to her knees on the

130

ground beside the horse's head. She took the reins in her hand, speaking to it softly, as if it was a child. Then with her eyes closed she reached out and touched the splintered leg, running her hands down it softly, barely caressing the skin.

All around them the vast crowd was silent.

The charioteer tried to reason with her, standing close, his hand on her shoulder. 'Eleni, waiting is only making it worse, for the animal as well as the man. Let me end it.'

'No!' She did not turn towards him.

The rider stood motionless, ashen-faced, paralysed with grief.

Eleni straightened up and turned to the charioteer. Her face was calm, her eyes wide and amazed. She seemed to radiate a kind of joy she herself could hardly grasp.

'You won't need it,' she said quietly, looking at the knife in his hand. 'The bone is not broken. The skin and the bruising will heal.'

'Eleni, it is in pain.' His voice was gentle, full of hurt. 'Don't prolong it . . .'

'It is all right!' she insisted, not loudly but with an authority that stopped him even as he went to step past her. She turned to the rider, smiling at him. 'Take him home. Clean the wound, and in a few days it will heal.'

They all stared at her, then as one they swung around to the animal as it lurched to its feet. Slowly, unsteadily at first, it walked over to the rider and nuzzled his shoulder. He threw his arms round it and buried his head in its neck, his body shaking with sobs of relief.

'I could have sworn it was broken,' the charioteer said with a look of bewilderment.

It had been. Tathea knew it with absolute certainty. And just for an instant, as if in a time utterly apart, she stood in another room and watched a woman extend her hands in miraculous healing, but that woman understood her gift and used it knowingly, and accepted that it came with a price.

Then the moment vanished and the present filled the air again, the sand and sweat of the arena, the roar of the spectators as they realised what had happened and rose to their feet, cheering. Eleni and the charioteer were both looking at Tathea, waiting for her to say who she was and why she, too, had come down from the tiers of onlookers.

It was time.

She moved forward to Eleni, her head high. She must be believed.

'We met in Thoth-Moara . . . before my husband was overthrown.' Her voice sounded strange and dry out here. 'My name is Ta-Thea.' She gave it the Shinabari pronunciation.

Eleni stared at her with disbelief, her eyes puzzled. Then recognition came, and pleasure, and pity. 'You survived!' She came forward quickly, both her hands extended. She searched Tathea's face. 'How can we help? Have you shelter, a home, people to care for you?' She swung round to the charioteer. 'This is my husband, Alexius. He did not come to Shinabar with us. He was with the army in Caeva.' She did not explain to him who Tathea was. He would already know.

'I escaped with sufficient to provide for my immediate needs,' Tathea replied. What a ridiculously formal phrase for what had happened! She should have guessed the charioteer would be married . . . but to Eleni! It hardly mattered. In fact it was nothing at all. She dismissed the pang of regret she felt with anger. The Book was all that was of importance. 'But I have something of uncountable value, beyond measure, which I would share with you.' She hesitated only a moment then went on, 'It will explain something of what happened here today. You have a right to know, and I think perhaps a need.'

Alexius glanced across at the horse, still held in an embrace by its rider, but Eleni's eyes did not leave Tathea's.

'Yes . . .' she said slowly. 'Yes, I do need to know.'

Tathea went to the Imperial Palace. It was far smaller than the palace at Thoth-Moara, but it had a magnificence of proportion which gave it great beauty. It sprawled over the crown of the hill amid olive and lemon trees, and dark cypresses. The first time she went she did not take the Book. She told Eleni the story of her escape from Thoth-Moara, her flight across the desert and the beginning of her quest, the passion, the need which had impelled her to the Lost Lands, and the shore to await whatever might be, and how she woke in the skiff as it scraped the sand, with the Book in her arms.

Eleni listened intently. They had met only once before and they were divided by different cultures, yet they shared the privileges and burdens of high birth, its loneliness without privacy, and now its violence and also its loss. There was no one else Tathea could have told who would have understood so deeply.

'And the Book?' Eleni said at last. 'May I see it?'

It was what Tathea had been waiting for, yet now the moment had come she was afraid. So much rested upon it. But there could be no retreat.

'Of course. When shall I bring it?'

'Tomorrow.'

Tathea spent weeks in the palace. Every day she read with Eleni. The beginning was easy to understand, though its meaning became subtler and more profound with each repetition. The work was an exchange of views between two great persons, the light and the darkness of pre-mortal creation whose origin lay before the foundations of heaven. As Tathea read it again, seeking to explain it to Eleni whose quick mind hungered to grasp every shade of meaning, she began to appreciate that her own understanding was yet infant.

She liked Eleni more each time she saw her, but coming to the Imperial Palace was a strange and often troubling experience. In Shinabar it would have been she who received or refused. The servants, who here looked her in the face and directed her where to go, would not have raised their eyes to her in Thoth-Moara. They would have worn her livery with pride. The Household Guard would have lowered their weapons as a sign of submission. There would always have been a steward close at hand, whose sole duty it was to anticipate her wishes. Here in Camassia she waited for admission. The guards and servants had no idea who she was, except that the Lady Eleni chose to receive her, and the two of them sat for hours at a time and refused interruption.

Tathea first met the Empress Barsymet quite by chance. She came in casually, leaving her waiting women at the door. She was exquisitely dressed in shades of green with jewelled borders to her gown. The draping of the folds emphasised her height and grace. Her gestures were easy and she spoke without great formality, but there was little warmth in her eyes.

Eleni introduced Tathea, but made only the most passing mention of the Book.

'Indeed,' Barsymet said with a single smile. 'We commiserate with you in your misfortune. I am glad you have found asylum here in Camassia.' Then she turned to Eleni and spoke of some state affair they were to attend.

Tathea watched both women as they faced each other in Eleni's gracious room overlooking the herb garden and cypress walk. Barsymet stood very upright and a little stiffly, her shoulders high. In her youth she must have been a beautiful woman, but there was discontent in her face now, and the fine lines around her eyes and mouth were not those of laughter.

Eleni was less patrician, and the curve of her lips was softer. When she smiled it touched her eyes. She stood comfortably, as though she feared nothing. The two women might have been bound by family and circumstance, and yet looking at them Tathea was increasingly certain they were divided by a gulf that had never been bridged.

Another woman who called during those days was Alexius's sister, Xanthica. She swept in, beginning to speak almost before she was through the door. The affection between her and Eleni was obvious, and Tathea was introduced immediately and her presence explained.

Xanthica regarded the Book, lying open on a small table in a pool of sunlight.

'Really?' she said curiously. 'May I?' She did not wait but walked over and glanced down at the page. She read with gradually furrowing brow. She turned the page and read on, then swivelled around. 'What

133

is it?' Her eyes were wide, clear hazel.

'I believe it is the Word of God to mankind,' Eleni answered before Tathea. 'He is explaining to the Great Adversary who we are, and what we may become; that we can attain an everlasting joy, one that will have no ending in all eternity.' She spoke without hesitation or doubt. Perhaps it was in that moment that she committed herself to it.

Xanthica stared at her. Puzzlement flickered across her eyes. 'What is the price of it, this joy?'

Eleni regarded her gravely. 'It is not something you are given so much as something you become.'

'I don't understand.' Xanthica looked for a moment at Tathea, then back again to Eleni. 'You can't merely will yourself to become happy,' she protested. 'If you could, it would have little to do with God.' She laughed, but there was a hint of nervousness in it. 'You say it as if there were only one god. Do you mean to do away with all the others?'

Eleni's eyes widened. 'If you put it like that, yes, I do. The others are more like reflections of us . . .'

'Oh, that's nonsense!' Xanthica moved quickly, dismissing the idea with a wave of her hand. She walked over to the window. Soft spring rain was falling outside.

'We do not have the powers we attribute to them,' Eleni persisted, 'but we invest them with our ideas, our desires. We believe they behave as we would, had we their power. We suppose they are stronger than we are but not wiser or nobler. We use the word "holy" to describe them when what we mean is "clever".'

Xanthica turned back to the room, shrugging. 'You are delving too deeply. All I need to know is what to obey. That's all most people need. I have no wish to be a philosopher.' She smiled at Tathea to rob the remark of offence, and after a little while took her leave.

Tathea did not see Alexius again. Several times she was on the point of asking Eleni if she had spoken to him of the Book, but the opportunity to do so without it seeming forced never arose. Always she kept her sights fixed on meeting the Emperor himself. He held the power to help her return to Shinabar and take the Book with her, to teach her own people its message. Every time she came into the Imperial Palace with its beauty and grace, its newly gained Imperium, she remembered Thoth-Moara and the ancient glories she had left behind, the familiarity, the happiness and the pain she had known there and the violence which cried out for redress.

She eventually met Isadorus not in the palace but in the great courtyard on the slope of the hill just below it. One of the military legions had just returned from a period of service on the eastern frontier. Isadorus was receiving a public offering of tribute from his latest subjects, presented by the general in command, and also giving praise and reward to soldiers who had marked their duty with exceptional courage or sacrifice.

It was a sharp, windy day with patches of sunlight sweeping across, followed by spattering rain. The scarlet plumes on the helmets fluttered and the occasional cloak flapped loose.

Isadorus stood on a stone step, Alexius beside him, light catching his fair hair. It was the first time Tathea had seen him since the chariot races. He made the same profound impression on her as before, but now she knew him as Eleni's husband. Eleni was her friend, the one person in Camassia who had shown her warmth and a fellowship of understanding. And, above all, she believed in the Book.

Eleni was here now, standing well behind her brother and her husband, but lending a grace to what could otherwise have been a stiff affair.

Tathea shivered in spite of her voluminous cloak. She was not used to the cold, and the damp made it bite so much more deeply. No desert night had ever been as cold as this.

The congratulations of the leaders were finished and the fourth soldier was coming forward to receive his commendation for courage when a gust of wind tore at one of the battle standards, catching it and carrying it out of the bearer's grasp. The flapping cloth startled several of the horses and one reared up, squealing. The rider regained control within moments, but not before another man had been badly trodden; his foot was crushed and bleeding.

A murmur of horror and sympathy went up from the watchers. The injured man made no complaint, but he could not hide his agony.

Alexius went across to him, shouting over his shoulder to send for a physician.

Isadorus turned to Eleni. She moved to join Alexius. He hesitated, looking at her, searching her face. He saw in her something that made him straighten up and step back.

Eleni bent and touched the injured man's foot, running her hands over it. Again the miracle happened. The pallor disappeared from the man's face and slowly his clenched body relaxed. A look of wonder filled his countenance. He stared at Eleni as if the rest of the gathered lines of soldiers had disappeared; not even the Emperor seemed to register on his consciousness. The ranks of the men behind him were silent, their eyes on Eleni, their faces filled with awe and a swift-dawning reverence.

Tathea walked towards them, compelled by something too indistinct to be called memory, but a need to be there, to warn.

Alexius noticed her first. His eyes met hers, searching for explanation, a long, steady gaze.

Isadorus swivelled round and followed Alexius's stare. 'Who are you?' he demanded.

135

'Ta-Thea,' she answered. 'Of Shinabar.'

Understanding was instant in his face. 'And this?' he demanded, gesturing to Eleni and the soldier. 'Do you understand it?'

'Yes,' she said without hesitation, certainty absolute inside her. 'It is one of the great gifts of the spirit which has been given to the Lady Eleni. It is rare, and precious . . .' She stopped, frightened to say the rest of the truth that was becoming clear in her mind even as she spoke.

'And?' Isadorus said levelly.

Everyone waited, the soldier, Eleni, biting her lips, Alexius beside her, a protective hand on her shoulder, his eyes still on Tathea.

A horse shifted its weight. Leather creaked. Not a man in the courtyard moved.

Tathea struggled with indecision. She risked anger, disbelief, Isadorus's rejection of her and everything she might say afterwards. And yet the compulsion inside her to warn Eleni overrode everything else.

'And there will be a price to pay for it,' she answered. Her mouth was dry, the breath caught in her throat, but she knew what she said was true. 'A great price.' She swallowed. Her body was shaking. 'The only price greater would be to refuse it. That would be to deny yourself, to refuse to accept who you are, who you have become.'

There was a minute's silence. The wind gusted a spatter of rain across the yard.

'A gift from whom?' Isadorus asked. The question demanded an answer.

Tathea looked into his grey eyes. 'From the God who is the beginning and the end of all things,' she replied. 'There is no other God, only visions and beliefs.' She turned to Eleni. 'The gift is yours. It is for you to choose whether you take it or not.'

Alexius's grasp tightened on Eleni's shoulder. His hands were strong, beautiful.

Isadorus opened his mouth to speak, and then changed his mind. His face was gentle when he looked down at Eleni. There was no command in him, no overt desire.

It was the soldier who moved. He lifted his hand and touched his damaged foot, then smiled at Eleni, a slow, sweet smile, unwavering.

'I could not refuse it,' Eleni answered. 'It would be a kind of death. I am as sure of that as I have ever been of anything.' Then she looked at Tathea. 'Thank you,' she said softly.

Chapter Nine

At first Tathea was afraid, the task of presenting the Book to the Emperor and persuading him of the truth of it was so great, the price of failure too high. Now she doubted her ability. She had been too arrogant in her plan.

She looked at the Book where it lay on the table and was overwhelmed by her charge. Then in the silence of her heart she heard the words that were written: 'I give no commandment except I make a way possible for you to fulfil it, if you will walk in obedience and trust in me.' A shining peace blossomed inside her. She could almost touch a memory of joy unimaginable, but she had no idea where or when it had been, simply that it had.

She met the Emperor on the balcony of one of his many private apartments in the palace. He leaned against the balustrade and regarded her levelly as if they were two strangers who could have nothing to fear from each other, only from their own failure within.

Slowly he smiled. His body relaxed a little. 'Now you look more like the Empress I have heard of,' he said with a flash of amusement. 'No more hovering on the edge of events, averting your eyes and hoping not to be challenged.'

It was just. Until now she had behaved like the fugitive she was.

He saw the acceptance of it in her eyes, and for a moment his expression softened, but he made no apology. He straightened up and walked across the chequered marble floor towards the table and chairs, the sun catching the purple and gold edging of his robe.

'Tell me about this Book you have been sharing with my sister. Where does it come from and what is it? Why do you not share it with your own people?' He was regarding her closely, with the perception of a man who could afford few mistakes. He had inherited the throne from his father Baradeus, who had won it by force of arms, and Isadorus held it by skill and the power of his own character and judgement.

She smiled at him. 'I did not have it when I was in Shinabar. But I will share it with my people, as soon as I am able to return home.'

His brows rose very slightly. 'You expect to?' He gave nothing away of how much he knew of the overthrow or current Shinabari politics.

She did not look away from his eyes. 'Yes, I hope to. Wouldn't you?'

He smiled. Strange how much the strength of a man could show in a mere smile. She could see strength in the ease with which he moved his supple soldier's body beneath the embroidered tunic and robes, but it was the calm in his face that told of his true inner power. He was a man who had tested and mastered himself.

'I think if the throne of Camassia fell, I would not be alive to attempt a return,' he said drily, watching her eyes to see how she should react. 'I would be dead, as Mon-Allat is dead. But if my wife survived me, I doubt she could plan such a thing. But my sons would, that I would swear to on my life.'

'My son is dead,' she said harshly, her voice rough-edged. It was still difficult to say, as if the words reinforced the reality of it. 'He was only four.' Without warning the tears choked her throat. She refused to look away from him. It was not an emotion to be ashamed of.

He was caught unaware. It was something he had not known, and there was a swift, naked pity in his face.

'Then you will have to act for him,' he said gently. 'If you can.' The emotion vanished. 'But tell me of this Book.' He indicated with his hand that she might sit down. 'You brought it here to my Empire and you told my sister that it speaks of the God who gave her the power to heal wounds.' He remained standing, looking down at her. 'And at the same time you warned her that there will be a price for her gift, a high price. I require an explanation of that.'

She swallowed away the tears in her throat. She forced pride into her mind. She had been Empress of an older throne than his! 'I went seeking the knowledge of who I am.' She waved her arm, encompassing the palace and the City beyond. 'Stripped of the power of office and possessions, of lands, family and identity in the eyes of others, who are you?' She allowed it to be a challenge. 'If you were to stand naked before heaven, what answer would you give that question?'

A flash of laughter lit his eyes, self-mockery, and amazement. 'And are you going to tell me?'

'You are a child of God,' she said unwaveringly. 'And that means you must learn to behave like Him. It will take time unimaginable, but you must begin now.'

He looked at her steadily and slowly understood the certainty in her. 'Indeed? And is this Book of yours going to tell me how?'

She answered with certainty. 'It will tell you something. Much of it you must learn for yourself, by experience and error. These things cannot be told by one person to another.'

He raised his eyebrows, the tug of amusement again showing at the corners of his lips. 'Then what is in this Book that I should bother to read it? That life cannot be taught? Only a fool, or a philosopher, imagines it can!'

'Truth can be taught.' She smiled back as she said it, but she did not allow her voice to be light. 'And wisdom, the reason for things, and the hope. Then you will understand what experience offers, and instead of confusion and despair, you will learn faith and obedience.'

'From a book of rules!' He shifted his weight, shrugging a little, but he did not look away from her. 'Do this, don't do that!'

'By the knowledge of who you are,' she returned. 'Where you began and where your choices will lead you.'

He moved to sit on a wide, cushioned stool with carved wooden sides. 'Who wrote this Book that I should believe it?' His expression was bright, sceptical but not unkind.

There could be no answer but the truth. 'I asked the sage in the Lost Lands. He told me truth was a heavy burden, but if I was ready to hear it, I should wait by the sea. I remember being there all night. A skiff came in with a man in it.' Even recounting it brought a sense of peace, a calm radiance inside her, and her voice rang with certainty as she continued, 'He asked me again if I was certain. I told him I was. After that I don't remember anything until I awoke on the same shore, with the Book in my arms. I don't know where it came from, but it is the truth. Touch it and you will know that too, whether you want what it tells you or not.'

'Rules?' he repeated, but the disbelief had gone from his face. His voice was surprisingly soft.

'No,' she answered. 'A conversation between God, who would have us grow to fill the measure of every possibility for power and laughter and joy, and our Adversary, who would keep us eternally dwarfed, dependent, and spiritually unborn.'

'Bring it to me,' he whispered. 'Let me read this myself!'

Tathea spent many days with Isadorus as he studied the text of the Book. He asked questions about the nature of the Adversary, and she struggled to answer, occasionally chilled by a sense of darkness as if just beyond her knowledge some immense evil waited, but she did not try to delineate it for him. It was an awareness of the soul, not of the mind.

The torches were flickering in their brackets on the walls, sending shadows across the floor as he closed the Book and turned to her.

'There is hope in this which is different from anything Camassia believes.' His hand lingered on the gold surface of the cover, as if he were loth to leave its warmth. 'There is a pity and a love. But it is also very terrible to have the possibility of hell, and the knowledge that damnation is of your own creation. What the Great Adversary says of fear is true.' Unconsciously he had lowered his voice. This tranquil room was too far from the rest of the palace for domestic noises to intrude. There was only wind in the lemon trees and the evening sky.

'It will cripple many of us. We will make promises we cannot keep. I want it to be true, but I am afraid of it.'

'So am I,' she admitted, smiling at him and biting her lip, acknowledging the irony of it, and her own vulnerability. 'He knows we will do much that is wrong, and make mistakes. He says so. Our life in the flesh is a journey, not an arriving. If there were not repentance, it would be unbearable.'

'I know! I know!' He nodded quickly. 'There is the Beloved One who made that possible in a way I don't understand. It is a better belief than ours. It is a better social law because it does not depend upon the ability of man to judge or his power to execute sentence.' His wide mouth lifted in a wry smile. 'An arrogant man may think to defy humanity. And I could name a score of those without going beyond my own court. I dare say you could too.'

She thought of them and their simple, heavy robes decorated with purple and gold borders, their solemn faces. They were the courtiers, the Archons. Their asceticism was a kind of pride in itself.

'I could,' she agreed wryly.

He grunted, leaning back in his seat. 'And the devious ones may deceive. Perhaps you know more of that than I do. Or is it only my unsophisticated Camassian idea that the Shinabari are subtler than we are?'

'Oh no!' she said softly, meeting his eyes. 'We are far subtler. Just sometimes we don't show it, so you are left uncertain. Then at other times we do, so you imagine we are far cleverer than we are.'

It was an instant before he understood. Then he laughed openly, with unaffected amusement. It was the first time he had let slip his guard and permitted the man beneath to show.

The light faded from the sky. Torches glowed yellow, casting thick shadows. Servants brought food and wine.

They talked long into the evening, sharing random moments of past loneliness, doubts and joys, unexpected betrayals and weaknesses long seen or suspected. He told her of his early years in the army when his father had been on the throne, of the isolation that always set him apart as the heir to a power that was envied but not understood. Fleetingly, by omission as much as anything, he touched on his dark moments when he questioned the old values of self-discipline, of duty and honour where courage was the greatest virtue and loyalty the ideal. There was little warmth in it, and no mercy for the weak of spirit, no second chances. Even the glory at the end of it was a poor thing compared with that promised in the Book. But there was also no Adversary. Not only was hell smaller, but heaven also.

After that evening, their relationship altered. He was less guarded with her. He had accepted the philosophy of the Book, even though his

140

understanding was yet limited. In front of his household as witness of his intent, he covenanted with God and with man to walk in the teachings of the Book and keep its word. He asked Tathea to move her household into apartments in the Imperial Palace, where both she and the Book would be safe, just in case her growing reputation should attract Shinabari attention. She accepted, taking her own few pieces of furniture, and of course the black and white cat.

Late one evening towards midsummer, when the torches were newly lit and smoking a little in the wind, and the heat of the day was heavy in the air, Tathea was walking across the courtyard and she saw Isadorus. He was leaning back on a long cushioned bench, his face raised towards a woman who held out a bunch of bright berries in her hand. His body was totally relaxed. The pleasure of his face betrayed his loneliness, his need to escape the weight of duty. With this woman he was merely a man.

She said something, and he laughed, reaching out towards her. She did not play the coquette. The way she responded to him laid bare their long familiarity.

Tathea stopped. Coldness welled up inside her, and confusion, followed by a stinging loneliness. The moment's intimacy excluded everyone else; certainly it excluded Barsymet. You could not love two women in such a way – not at once. Mon-Allat had never loved her like that. Tearing her memory apart, she could bring back no such simple tenderness, nothing so spontaneous or unguarded. Even in moments of passion, and the calm afterwards, he had never permitted her to creep inside his shell of self-awareness. Always he kept the core of his identity apart. Had he touched his mistress Arimaspis with the quick warmth that Isadorus now showed this woman, unafraid of rejection, trusting her gentleness in return? Tathea had been a good Empress, but he had not loved her, not with fire or tears or laughter or an ache of incompleteness if she were absent, even for a day.

Mon-Allat had shared the burdens of state with her only because it was his duty, and her purpose. She understood them. No doubt Barsymet understood also. But he had not shared his hopes or his pain, his weaknesses or his needs, his dreams. Had he shared them with Arimaspis? Had she known him as Tathea never had? Did she mourn him even now, and lie awake alone in her bed, missing his warmth beside her, and weeping for him? It was a new thought, and a bitter one. Until that moment it had not even occurred to Tathea.

But the Book spoke of integrity, of wholeness of heart. She did not need words to detail that Isadorus's was divided. However well understood, however sanctioned by emotion or mitigated by love, it was not a heart single to the purpose of God.

How could she tell Isadorus? In doing so, might she lose the one

141

man whose belief she must have if she were to gather the power to return home?

But he had sent for her so she must present herself. Suddenly afraid, she continued her way across the courtyard and into the light of the torches.

Isadorus saw her shadow before she reached him and he turned with a smile. The woman stepped back, but only a pace. She was almost as dark as Tathea, but beautiful in a subtle and gentle way, startlingly feminine.

'This is Tissarel,' Isadorus introduced her. He said no more, assuming that Tathea would guess her position. 'There is no harm in her hearing what is written in the Book,' he added, seeing Tathea's face. 'Soon all Camassia will hear it.' He indicated where she should sit, and Tathea obediently did so.

Tissarel stood a little apart, listening. She did not interrupt, but more than once Tathea glanced up at her and saw her eyes, the tension and the shadow in them, and knew that she understood the weight of what they were saying, and that it would demand from all of them decisions from which there would be no escape.

Eleni was interested in the culture of Shinabar, the arts and sciences which were more sophisticated than those of Camassia.

'Tell me about them,' she said, 'if you don't mind speaking of them. Does it help, or hurt – or both?'

'Both,' Tathea replied unhesitatingly. Remembrance of the past sharpened the sense of being alien here in the City. But it was also a reaffirmation of the forces and the love which had shaped her, and of days which had been lit by happiness. Later tragedy of deeper knowledge should not spoil that pleasure. It had been sweet in its time.

Eleni, in turn, enjoyed telling her about Camassia and showing her its art, such as the coloured mosaic pavements, quaint in their beauty and so full of life the artist's dream spoke from them. Sometimes they were to be found in public squares, but the most individual, and to Eleni the best, were in small courtyards and on private pavements.

They also went occasionally to the theatre and Tathea had to swallow her reactions to Camassian drama, which she found unbearably stiff and self-conscious. It rigidly conformed to rules of art without apparently understanding that those rules were there to discipline and give power to inner passions, they were not an end in themselves. Camassian ideas had no subtlety and no wings. Its culture was young. Its virtues were bound up in honour, courage, duty and loyalty. It seemed no artist had yet dared to challenge the boundaries of thought, or tread the unmarked paths of the soul. There was good humour, but none of the incisive wit of an author who dared mock or challenge.

142

Visits to the theatre were agreeable, and certainly they were fine social occasions, but Tathea found the plays essentially boring. It was only the presence of Eleni's sister-in-law, Xanthica, who gave the evenings interest. She was full of vitality and usually paid more attention to her fellow theatre-goers than she did to the play. She always knew many people in the audience and would nod greetings to other aristocratic women.

'Calvia,' she would whisper. 'That's her fourth husband walking behind her. She smiles at everyone, and has a tongue like acid.'

The woman swept past them without a glance.

'And that one hasn't a penny with which to bless herself,' Xanthica said of the next woman. 'She takes young lovers, and keeps them because she can make them laugh. Everyone likes her.'

The woman caught sight of them and smiled. She was dressed outrageously, with blazing colours and considerable panache. Xanthica smiled back, raising her hand in an elegant little salute. Eleni did the same.

'That is Marella,' Xanthica continued, indicating with a tiny gesture a large woman dressed in red and gold. 'She has five sons, for whom she has immense ambitions. Everything about her is overstated.'

'Including that dress,' Eleni added. 'Her jeweller should be shot!'

'Don't say that aloud or he probably will be!' Xanthica hissed back with a grin.

Tonight's play was a standard work which they watched only in snatches. After a particularly stilted scene of pious judgement, Xanthica turned to Tathea. 'What would your Book make of that?' There was laughter in her eyes, but behind it a hunger to know.

'It is only through pain and knowledge of what it is to sin that we can learn how to forgive,' Tathea replied, smiling also to lighten the gravity of her words.

The interest sharpened in Xanthica's eyes, and later she asked other questions about purpose and failure, and Tathea answered them.

After the performance they returned to Xanthica's home, and a most excellent late dinner of fruit, wine and light pastries. Xanthica's husband, Maximian, joined them in the wide room where they sat facing windows that looked over the City. It was a balmy evening with a touch of autumn in the air, and the windows were wide open. He was a handsome man with strong features and a streak of grey in his heavy hair. He was dressed in the purple-bordered robes of an Archon, and he carried his weight of office with conscious dignity but with the ease of one who is long accustomed to it. He regarded Tathea with interest and some sympathy.

'I feel for your loss, my lady,' he said with an inclination of his head, as if he were speaking for the government of Camassia as a whole, yet there was warmth in his voice, which was gentle and personal. 'It is the world's misfortune that the steps towards peace between our nations have been reversed, but your own bereavement is separate and apart. I hope the City in the Centre of the World has made you welcome.'

'It has,' she answered with equal gravity. She had known too many ambassadors not to be familiar with the formality of his speech, or to mistake it for the artificial. 'I have found both safety and generosity, and I am deeply grateful for it.' She could say so without resentment. Eleni's friendship was too wholehearted to allow pettiness. They had been candid with one another, laughed at absurdity. They had climbed the Hill of Cypresses together, and both realised they were tired at the top, and the view barely made up for aching legs and blistered feet. In front of anyone else Tathea might have refused to admit it, but a glance at Eleni's face and they had both laughed, and with a groan sat down in the sun.

Xanthica offered her husband food and inquired after his day, though she did not need to hear his answer. She read what she needed to from his face. They were comfortable with each other as people are after long intimacy, although for her there was still a quality of eagerness that lifted it above habit.

They discussed the play they had seen, and Tathea very quickly realised that Maximian perceived no lack of art in such works. For him the values they taught were paramount. He felt exactly as the playwright had; that love of duty was sublime. The hero who denied his errant family in order to die for the common good had scaled the heights of nobility. That he lacked subtlety or laughter, that he did it without the flaws of human weakness or need, that he never doubted or was tempted did not reduce his stature in Maximian's eyes as it did in hers.

Tathea thought of all the arguments that would have portrayed him with wounds of the heart, with weaknesses and failings as well as victories, and would have given him the flesh of reality. More importantly they would have placed him within the empathy of ordinary men, even have made his sacrifice the greater. Then she caught Eleni's eyes and saw her shake her head minutely.

Xanthica shrugged. 'Florius is a fine actor,' she said wryly. 'But he always seems to me a little as if he is addressing a public meeting.'

'He is,' Maximian smiled. 'What could be more public than the audience in a theatre?'

'The Hall of Archons,' Eleni replied without thinking.

'Very few people attend the Hall of Archons compared with those who go to the theatre,' Maximian pointed out. He looked at her with amusement. 'I suppose you will say that is because we are very dry speakers . . .'

'I wouldn't dare to!' she responded, her eyes bright with laughter.

'My dear, it is clear in your face. And I fear you are right, at least most of the time.'

'You can be marvellous,' Xanthica defended staunchly, then grimaced. 'The trouble is we never know when these times are going to be!'

Maximian accepted the chaffing without offence.

Half an hour later, Alexius joined them. He came in swinging off his heavy red cloak which he flung casually over the back of one of the long seats. He touched Eleni with easy affection and greeted Xanthica with a kiss on the cheek. There was gentleness in his gesture towards Xanthica that reflected an elder brother's tolerant, protective care. He spoke briefly to Maximian, then turned to Tathea, his eyes widening with surprise. The last time he had seen her was when Eleni had healed the soldier, but he must have known that she had spent much time with Eleni studying the Book. His curiosity was sharp in his eyes, but it was of the intellect, far quicker and more probing than Maximian's.

'How are you, my lady? Did you enjoy our Camassian theatre?' he asked politely. Was it a glimmer of amusement she saw in him, or did she only imagine humour because she wished it?

How should she answer? Courteously, because she was a guest in his country, and in Maximian's house, or honestly, as one would respond to a friend and an equal? It mattered to her more than she wished it to. 'It was different,' she chose the words carefully, aware of them all watching her. 'I have not learned the conventions well enough yet to see the subtlety beneath.'

'It is stuffed with conventions,' Alexius agreed drily, glancing at Maximian. 'I am not sure if the playwrights themselves know them all yet. I have a suspicion they make up more as they go along.' He walked over to one of the long couches and sat down, relaxing into it, and Tathea noticed the easy power of his body beneath the robes.

'They spring from the need for discipline.' Maximian was compelled into the argument in spite of himself. There was heat in his voice as he spoke of something which apparently touched his beliefs deeply.

'There should be room for a little more inspiration,' Eleni said with a smile, but the quick turn of her head and the timbre in her voice warned that she, too, was serious.

'You mean sudden impulse?' Maximian raised his brows.

'No, I don't,' she said instantly. 'You make it sound frivolous, and that's not what I mean at all. I want imagination, stretching beyond the known to explore the possibilities beyond. You should read some of the Book Tathea has brought. There is so much we don't know.' Her face was alight now with the vision within her. 'Things of unimaginable power –' she waved her smooth arm to indicate a universe beyond the window – 'worlds of the mind and the spirit, a morality wider and deeper than our dreams . . .'

Alexius was watching Tathea, his grey-blue eyes studying her face. She avoided looking back, self-conscious, aware of her hands as if suddenly she did not know what to do with them.

'That sounds like mysticism,' Maximian said patiently. 'It is hardly news. All the old religions of the south have practised some version of magic for generations.' He did not say he despised it, but his eyes and his voice conveyed it more profoundly than words. 'We have a cleaner morality than that, built on accountability, and the old virtues of courage and honour and the human duty of man to his fellows.' He turned to Tathea. 'I do not intend to insult you, my lady, but I cannot pretend I admire the philosophies of Shinabar. They seem to me an excuse for self-indulgence and the evasion of that kind of integrity I believe is at the core of all that is of most worth in man. I look for no magic and no excuses.'

Xanthica turned to Eleni then back to her husband, indecision in her face. Tathea knew that the hope and the vision of the Book had caught her mind and awakened in her something she found piercingly sweet. Yet it was manifest Maximian thought it effete, debilitating to the purity and strength he loved.

'I suppose it is.' Xanthica turned away, hiding the quick disappointment in her face. 'I only know a little bit, but it just seemed . . .' She did not finish.

Maximian put his arm round her. 'Easy answers that depend upon some greater power,' he agreed, his fingers tightening gently on her shoulder.

Alexius looked at Tathea, waiting to see if she would fight for her belief. She was acutely conscious of him. It should have been Eleni's judgement that mattered to her, and she understood that even while she thought of Alexius, whom she barely knew.

'The answers do not depend upon anyone else.' Tathea looked directly at Maximian, but she knew the others were listening to her and their belief might hang directly upon what she said. She felt terrifyingly alone. How could she do justice to the burden of the truth she bore? Maximian's face was full of polite disbelief, but he did not interrupt. His courtesy and innate kindness forbade it.

'Every human soul has the agency to do as it will,' Tathea went on. 'Every act of courage or honour, of secret compassion or forgiveness enlarges the soul.' She wanted to look at Alexius, to see what he thought, but she studiously kept her eyes on Maximian. 'Every deceit or evasion, every cruelty, great or small, diminishes you. Every lie or turning aside erodes what you are. Not even God can alter that.' She heard the certainty ringing in her voice. 'What you make of yourself is all you have. What seems mysticism to you is only the love you do not yet understand. Neither do I!' she added hastily. 'But above everything

146

else in life, I want to learn. I am horribly aware of the enormity of what I do not know.'

Without meaning to, she had turned to Alexius sitting opposite her. The flicker of a smile crossed his mouth. He looked at Maximian, his eyes questioning. 'Do you know the answers then?'

'No, of course not,' Maximian acknowledged. 'But I don't believe they lie in this Book.' He faced Tathea. 'But I will defend your right to believe it. Camassia has never denied any man the right to pursue truth anywhere he finds it, as long as it does not mar his duty as a citizen. That would be treason.' He said it lightly, and there was no harshness of judgement in his face, but it was Tathea he was speaking to, before he turned again to Alexius.

Xanthica moved forward and quite deliberately broke the tension of the moment by changing the subject.

An hour later, long after midnight, Tathea stood alone before the open window, gazing across the City where a few random torches showed; only the great public thoroughfare was lit. Moonlight shone grey on the olive trees and black on the dark columns of the cypresses.

She was aware of someone behind her and knew without turning that it was Alexius. The faint clink of metal on leather told her, and the clean masculine aroma.

'Is it very different from Thoth-Moara?' he asked quietly.

'Yes,' she answered, looking ahead into the night. 'Thoth-Moara is flat, and of course far from the sea. The desert stretches around it, beyond the horizon. The wind is always warm, and prickles with sand. It smells different, aromatic, sharp. The skyline is simpler, even in the dark.'

'And the plays are more complex,' he countered.

'Yes.'

'You were very civil to Maximian.' There was an echo of humour in his voice. 'You didn't say Camassian drama is a deadly bore.'

She smiled, although he could not see it. 'Of course not. I am a guest in his house.'

'But you preach the Book even when you know he thinks it effete and dangerous,' he pointed out. He was standing close behind her. She could feel his warmth.

'It is prudent not to disagree with him in more than one thing,' she replied. 'I picked the one that matters.'

His voice changed, the banter was gone. 'Do you really believe it is the power spoken of in this Book which gives Eleni her gift of healing?'

Unreasonably, she was hurt. He was not seeking truth for himself, he was questioning Eleni's belief.

'Yes. I know it. Doesn't she say the same?' Her voice was more brittle than she had meant it to be. She hated being a stranger here, trying to convince people who belonged, when she belonged nowhere. They were kind to her – heaven knew, Eleni was generous beyond all need. But if she left for Shinabar tomorrow, Eleni's life would still be perfectly whole without her. Isadorus would miss her, but only because she had brought him the Book. It was the law in the Book he loved, its justice beyond the flawed judgement and the limited passions of men. It provided a better faith for his people, and he had the wisdom to see that. It offered hope to the afflicted, and retribution for the evil which escaped temporal law.

'Yes, she does,' Alexius answered. If he caught the change in her voice, he did not react to it. 'But she knows immeasurably less of it than you do. One day you must teach me something of this Book, if you will.' It was barely a question. He knew she would teach anyone, and most assuredly him.

Isadorus was finding the burden the Book heavy upon him. The passages that caused his grief were those concerning loyalty, honour, and above all the mystery of appetite and the hungers that drive men to both good and evil. For days he had tried to avoid the realisation which now stood before him. Barsymet, in all her cold dignity, was his wife. The generous, laughing Tissarel was his mistress, a servant in his house.

He had argued with himself that all men were equal. This naturally included all women. Love was superior to status. It was the great power, the great commandment. The God of the Book had created man to be joyful. Barsymet did not love him, and he was not deceiving her. There was no lie involved. The pleasure of Tissarel's company, her gentleness, the warmth of her body, all enabled him to be a better man, kinder and more patient with others. He needed such moments of humanity.

But all such arguments were excuses. By repeating them he was separating himself from the Book and from what he now knew without question to be the truth, the pure fire of everything he wanted to be.

He stood by the window, staring down at the City, waiting for Tissarel to come. He must tell her himself. A few months ago he could not have imagined that he would feel ashamed before her, or in her debt. And yet now he did.

He turned as she entered. She looked as she always did, laughing and eager. There was no premonition in her eyes.

He felt the knot of guilt twist inside him. She did not deserve to be discarded in this way. Nothing she had said or done, or failed to do, had brought this about. It was his doing, his internal struggle and decision, but she was going to pay part of the price. She would no longer be the Emperor's mistress.

He looked at her familiar beauty with his usual pleasure, and a new keenness for its loss.

Then suddenly, with an ice-cold amazement, he realised that perhaps the rewards for her were her physical safety and recompense, the relative luxury in which she lived, the clothes and jewels few other men could have afforded to give her. It was quite possible she would feel no emotional wrench, no loneliness whatever. And it startled him how much that thought hurt.

She came towards him slowly, sensing something was amiss.

He stepped backwards. 'Tissarel . . .'

She stopped. She had never presumed, never been the first to move. She had never, even in their most intimate moments, forgotten that she was at his beck and call, not he at hers. Had he ever considered she might have needs he had not met? Not really, nothing more than a passing moment of jealousy that she might have desired a younger man, and even that had not lasted long. He was at the peak of his physical power, and he knew it.

'Tissarel . . .' This was even harder than he had feared. Excuses would offend both him and her. 'I believe the words in the Book that the Lady Tathea has brought.'

'I know that,' she answered. 'I have seen it in your face for a long time, since the second or third day she brought it here.'

'You've listened?' He should not have been surprised.

She took it as criticism. A flush rose up her cheeks, but she did not deny it. 'Yes,' she said simply.

Without thinking, he stepped forward and took her hands. For once there was no response in her. Her eyes searched his.

'Then perhaps you will understand why I must forego the things which give me pleasure,' he said very quietly. 'And do instead those things which are right.' Should he tell her that he did not love Barsymet? It might be of comfort to her, and it was certainly true. It was also an unnecessary disloyalty, a poor beginning to any reconciliation he could try. 'For years I have followed my own hungers,' he went on. 'I have been moderately discreet. I have not dishonoured my wife before the people—'

'I understand,' she interrupted. She looked at him steadily, and for a moment they were equals, not Emperor and servant, but man and woman. He had no idea how deep her wound might be, but it was deeper than he could see, and more than he had earned any right to know. He wanted to add something, but she turned away. 'It is right,' she said softly, hiding her face from him.

He moved after her, swiftly, barring her way.

'You must leave the Imperial Hill, but don't leave the City. Everyone you know is here. You have . . .' How could he tell her without condescension that she had given him laughter and gentleness, been worthy of trust. 'I wish this . . . were . . . not necessary . . .' For the first time he could recall, he was floundering for words. He

149

wished he knew what she felt. Was her pain anything for him, or simply loss of a position many women might envy? Was the rigidity of her back insulted pride, or the need to master loneliness? Was it a parting that mattered to her as deeply as it did to him?

He could not ask her. And even if he did, how would he know if her answer were the truth? It would be easy enough to say yes, of course she loved him. What else did one say to Emperors?

'I understand the Book,' she said, her voice thick with tears, then she brushed past him. He could have put out his hand and kept her with him, but it would only prolong the inevitable and be unfair to her as well as to himself. He let her go.

The room became colder, darker. He knew what he did was right, but he was far less certain he could bear it. He found he was shivering, which was absurd, because the fire was burning and there was barely a chill in the air.

It was two days before he found the right opportunity to speak to Barsymet alone. It was early evening and he had spent most of the day with ministers and ambassadors. He was still at his desk when Barsymet entered the room.

He gestured to the other chair where until a few minutes ago an ambassador had sat, talking of an incident of Shinabari arrogance at sea. The days of the treaty were most definitely past.

She sat down slowly, as if it had been an order not an invitation. She kept her gaze lowered. He could not undo years of coldness in a single evening. It might take months.

'What would you like to eat?' he asked.

She made a slight dismissive movement. 'Whatever you are having.'

He told her of the incident with the Shinabari.

She was not surprised. 'They would like war with us. The only thing that holds them back is fear they might not win.' There was contempt in her expression. 'They have grown soft. Their great days of conquest are long behind them. And there are serious barbarian incursions on their southern borders.'

'How did you hear that?' He had not realised she had any interest in political matters. But it was years since he had bothered to talk to her about anything but trivialities.

She flashed him a quick, cold glance. 'What do you imagine I do with my days?' she said bitterly.

He was too abashed to answer, and she knew it. The shadow of a smile touched her lips. 'Are you still studying the religion that Shinabari woman brought with her from . . . wherever?'

He resented her reference to Tathea in such terms. In the past he would have crushed her for such language, but he was trying to build some reconciliation between them. A quarrel would make it even harder.

'I have reached my conclusion on it.' His voice sounded harsher

150

than he wished, his anger showed very clearly. 'It is the truth. I will try to live it . . . and teach my people.'

She stared at him. Her eyes were large and grey, very steady. They should have been beautiful, but there was bitterness in them which frightened him.

'Will you?' she said with interest. 'You mean to live it yourself?'

'Of course!' he snapped. 'I told you, I believe it is the truth. And I can hardly preach it to Camassia and not embrace it myself.'

'Of course you can,' she retorted. 'People do it all the time. Most religions are a means of government, not a matter of example.' There was laughter in her eyes, sharp like moving shards of glass. 'But if you wish to impress the Hall of Archons and the nobles, then you will have to be seen to live it, whatever you think privately.'

'I believe it!' Certainty burned like fire in his mind. 'It may take a long time, but I intend to understand the teachings and to live them.'

'Purity, honest of heart, loyalty?' she asked with a lift of sarcasm, her fine lips faintly sneering. 'Freedom of conscience for others?'

He leaned across the desk towards her, ignoring the papers and the ink and sand. 'Yes. I will not compel you, or anyone, to come with me.'

Her eyebrows rose. 'Not even Tissarel?' The question cut across the air swift and sharp as a knife.

'Tissarel has gone,' he answered softly. 'I told her of my decision, and she understood.' Why did it hurt so much to say that, and to Barsymet of all people? He felt as alone as he had at twelve, when he had first left home to join the army. He had sat huddled into himself then, cold and frightened at seeing the watch fires in the darkness, and hearing the laughter of strangers. This woman was his wife, and he was Emperor of the greatest power on earth. He was in his own palace, warm, secure, admired. He had but to give the word and a man lived or died.

He leaned back again and sighed. 'You must do as you please, Barsymet. I will follow the Book.'

'Oh, I shall support you,' she said immediately. 'It will be good for everyone. I wish she had come with it twenty years ago. Then perhaps you would have shared it with me.'

He did not answer. What was there to say?

Chapter Ten

Ra-Nufis entrusted messages to no one, so Tathea did not hear from him while he was in Shinabar. It was now well over a year since she had come from the Lost Lands and the City was familiar to her, but she was still alien here and she missed Shinabar as keenly as ever. And in spite of Eleni's friendship and the many hours spent with Isadorus, there was a certain loneliness of heart.

The season was turning. The coolness of autumn was delicious, but the constant chill and the shorter, darker days of winter were oppressive. The first time she had felt rain it was strange, even exciting. Two or three times a week it was no pleasure at all. Wet clothes, wet feet were a misery she could not get used to.

In the palace she was treated with courtesy and the fact that she was a guest, not its mistress, no longer unsettled her. Only now and again, on first waking in the morning if it was a bright day, and she saw the sunlight slanting across the marble floor, did the shock of memory return. It was not Mon-Allat she missed, but Habi. His limp, bloodstained body still tore at her with a grief she did not know how to bear. Yet she could not let it go. To try was like attempting to deny his life, as if he had not been, and she had not loved him. There were nights when she woke in the dark, thinking she had heard him calling, then remembered, and turned over in her bed and wept.

But there were also times of laughter, especially with Eleni. Alexius was away with one of the frontier legions, and Eleni seemed glad of her company and always eager to learn more of the Book. They shared many other things also, ideas, appreciation of beauty or drama, sympathy for others, pleasure in gowns and jewels, ornaments, new furniture, linen, trivial gossip and jokes.

Still she was eager to see Ra-Nufis and hear news of Shinabar, and to speak her own language with its rhythms and imagery of the life she was born to.

He came in the evening to her apartment in the palace. She had removed some of the heavy, ornate Camassian furniture and it was now more like the surroundings she had been familiar with, simpler lines, a greater sense of space, and warmer colours, a gold, a rose, against the greyer light.

Ra-Nufis looked at it only briefly, then his eyes searched her face.

'How are you?' she asked, indicating the wide chair for him to sit. His skin had been darkened by the desert sun, his features honed to leaner, harsher lines by wind and the fatigue of travel. She guessed that he also felt the strain of constant vigilance. 'I'm glad to see you safe.'

He smiled, his eyes bright. 'And I to see you,' he said fervently. 'Never forget, my lady, that you have enemies for two reasons: you are the true Isarch's widow, and so the only one who could lead the people against the usurper, but far more than that, you are the Keeper of the Book. If there are forces of light, then there must be forces of darkness also, or there would be no struggle.' His eyes narrowed. His face was touched with pain. 'Shinabar has changed, even in one short year . . .'

She walked over to the table under one of the torches and poured wine into two dark glass goblets. She returned and offered him one.

'Will you eat?'

He shook his head fractionally, he was too eager to speak to her to think of such things.

'There is a secrecy there,' he continued, leaning forward and holding the goblet in one slender hand. 'A kind of creeping malaise I have never seen in the past. The energy is dying.' He sipped the wine and his face puckered although it was sweet. 'Or perhaps it has been dying for a long time, and I just didn't see it before.'

She watched him with dread for what he would say next. This was not a Camassian view, slanted by the perceptions of people who did not know or love Shinabar, but an intimate understanding, the instinct of a native. He would catch the small, unseen straws in the wind even the subtlest ambassador could not.

She picked up a bowl of almonds from the table where the wine jug was, and placed it in front of him.

'I have learned all I can about the assassinations,' he said softly, his eyes on her face, knowing it must hurt her. 'It was committed by elements in the Household Guard, but you knew that. The men immediately behind them were caught within weeks. The usurper was arrested and executed.' He sipped the wine and took a handful of almonds. 'Tiyo-Mah saw to that. She was tireless in her vengeance. No one escaped.'

Tathea laughed abruptly. She had known the Isarch's mother most of her life, and feared her. She could picture her copper-coloured face with its curved nose and hooded eyes, her skin like old leather, soft and creased, her full lips. She had a curious quality of stillness, allowing others to come to her as if she had the power of will to command them, whether they would or not. Even Mon-Allat had never defied her. But there had not been a woman on the throne of

Shinabar in all the millennia of the past. Tathea's nephew, Hem-Shash, would be Isarch. He was the only male of the royal house left.

'There is dissatisfaction,' Ra-Nufis went on. 'It is small now, but it will grow. Economic times are good, but greed will erode that. The pattern of it is there already. The belief in instant reward. There are more and more officials to deny responsibility for everything but who seem to have the power to obstruct.'

He put the goblet down. Outside, the rain was falling gently on the lemon trees and the smell of damp earth came in through the open window.

'The knowledge and the love of beauty is dying,' he said quietly, his mouth pinched, a tiredness about his eyes. 'We are forgetting our past and who we are. We no longer know what we believe. No people ever needed the clean sanity of the Book more than ours. We need its hope, its truth. How can we strive for heaven when we have forgotten what it is?'

Ra-Nufis's words burned like fire in Tathea's mind. She had allowed herself to become comfortable in Camassia. She had forgotten the urgency of her calling. She should have been anxiously engaged in planning her return to Shinabar, taking the healing of the Book to her own people. She had studied its words every day. How could she have been so blind?

The next day she sought audience with Isadorus and found him in the company of a soldier named Ulciber, a man whose golden fair face was smooth and comfortable even in the presence of his Emperor. A fire burned in a huge, marble hearth, and the dogs lay sprawled before it.

She would rather have spoken to him alone, but Isadorus offered her no choice. If he sensed her desire for privacy, there was no sign of it in his face. Ulciber was a trusted favourite, and Isadorus now wished to share all matters of the Book with anyone who showed the slightest hunger to know.

'What is your concern?' he asked, inviting her to sit.

'I have heard much news from Shinabar lately,' she answered, not wishing to tell him from whom. If he knew or guessed, that was another matter. 'All of it is ill.' She detailed what Ra-Nufis had said to her, and he listened in silence. His ambassadors must have told him similar things; his spies certainly would have, even if they had not Ra-Nufis's skill, nor his interest in seeing the old order restored.

Ulciber remained silent, looking first to Tathea, then to Isadorus, watching their faces.

'I grieve over it,' Isadorus answered her at length, and indeed there was a darkness in his face, a gentleness when he looked at her. 'I wish I could comfort you for your people, but all I hear confirms what you say.'

'But there are many who would support an overthrow of the old regime, and peace with Camassia,' she argued.

'Hem-Shash is of the old blood,' he pointed out, meeting her eyes steadily.

She had expected that. 'I know. But he is young, and will always be weak. Those who were behind the coup rule through him. There is corruption and apathy in the country. The army is disorganised and losing morale. Government is increasingly oppressive.'

'And that should trouble Camassia?' he questioned. There was no anger in his face, only a probing sadness she did not understand.

It was Ulciber who answered. 'My lord, the Lady Ta-Thea –' he gave it the Shinabari pronunciation – 'has no doubt also heard the rumours of increasing barbarian incursions on the borders of Shinabar. As we have from our own legions.' He leaned forward a little, closer to Isadorus. 'We need allies who are not only strong in armies and navies, but whose governments will not fall to internal chaos and civil strife. If Shinabar crumbles, then we are threatened on all sides.'

It was the last quarter from which Tathea had expected support, and a sense of unease troubled her, but she ignored it. Isadorus was, above all, Emperor of Camassia. Its prosperity, its glory, its safety lay at the heart of all he did. She had watched him over her year and a half in the City. He was a better statesman than Mon-Allat. He had had to fight to hold his power, and he understood its strength and its limitations far more profoundly than any man who was born to sovereignty could. He took nothing for granted. She had seen how no friend or political favourite stood in the way of his judgement. These were lessons she should learn if ever she were to return to the throne of Shinabar.

'Better we should be threatened from all sides beyond our borders,' Isadorus said quietly, 'than be eaten away by corrosion within.'

A flash of disappointment crossed Ulciber's smooth face. His blue eyes widened in momentary surprise. He leaned back again and looked at Tathea.

'I will teach my people the law of the Book.' She pressed the one argument she knew Isadorus would not refuse. Already he was spreading the word himself, opening up ways for all manner of men to hear and to learn. They were rudimentary, merely groups who met to study and to discuss the principles with each other. There needed to be much organisation yet, and he had spoken to her of it. 'It is for all people,' she added urgently. 'All nations, all tongues.'

One of the dogs stirred and whimpered in its dreams.

'I know.' His voice was even softer, scarcely above the flicker of the flames. 'But we have much work yet before it is ready to take to the world. It must be translated into a common language, codified for the ordinary man to understand. And when that time comes, it will be taught not by force, but by example.'

She was stunned. 'I have no intention of forcing it upon anyone!' she protested. How could he even think such a thing of her?

'You would take it to them on the heels of your conquest,' he pointed out. 'You would overthrow the usurpers of your throne. Tell me you do not want justice for your dead.'

She started to answer, but Ulciber spoke before she found the words. 'Justice, not revenge, my lord. She would seek your aid to restore a rightful order and establish peace where men are not afraid to espouse a new faith, if they choose to. It will not only be to Shinabar's good, but to Camassia's also.' Again he leaned forward, the firelight gold on his smooth cheek, the curve of his lips. 'We have enemies enough. If Shinabar believes the law of the Book, then they will be our allies against whatever darkness or violence threatens us, from any quarter.'

Isadorus rose to his feet and walked towards the window, speaking with his back to them. 'I know Tathea is our ally, Ulciber. I know your advice has my good at heart; but the law of the Book is the sanctity of choice. You cannot teach truth in the wake of force. If I send Camassian armies into Shinabar to restore Tathea to the throne, she will be listened to for the wrong reasons. What may begin as justice will end as revenge, because passions will run too hard and too high to stop. Where is the end of retribution?'

Ulciber's face tightened and something in his eyes flashed for a moment, as if it were he who had sustained a defeat, and not Tathea. But he said no more. He was a counsellor, even a friend, but he knew his boundaries and was wise enough not to overstep them.

Tathea also recognised defeat, and although all her passion cried out against it, her anger was too hot for her to trust her tongue. She had asked for help, and been denied it. She withdrew before she betrayed her emotions. If sense did not move her, at least pride did.

She dreaded telling Ra-Nufis of her failure. But after initial surprise, he contained his frustration with dignity, and entirely without blame towards her.

'There will be a way,' he said with absolute confidence, standing in the sharp winter sunlight in her room. 'If not now, then later. The Word will prevail. The Power that gave it to you will open up another path. Events may occur which will cause Isadorus to change his mind.' He bit his lip and shrugged his shoulders very slightly. 'One thing you may be sure of, conditions will grow worse in Shinabar. That alone may be sufficient.' He looked down, then up again quickly. 'This I do know, the Word will not fail.'

It was enough to return her to her study of the Book, and gradually a peace grew within her, a deeper knowledge of her own fallibility, and a resolve not to fail Ra-Nufis again, or all those people who did not know the burden with which she was entrusted but who depended upon her.

It was well into spring when Alexius returned to the City from the border wars in Irria-Kand. It had been a hard season of campaigning and the barbarians beyond the eastern plains seemed greater in number than previously, and better armed. Camassian legions were holding, but their losses had been considerable, and it was mixed news he brought back to Isadorus.

Alexius was used to life on the march and on the battlefield. He did not enjoy physical hardship, but it did not trouble him as it did many. He had long ago learned to master not only the exhaustion, the cold and the hunger, but also the fear of the enemy in daylight, and that worse fear born in the imagination when at night he lay under the stars, hearing the cries of injured men, and knowing what the morrow could bring. He knew how to discipline his dreams. He had seen enough of death and of mystery to imagine the divine.

Nevertheless he was startled on his first audience with Isadorus to find him so changed by what he had read in the Book. He had seen Eleni's gift of healing for himself, and it had disturbed him deeply because of its overturning of the natural order he had come to expect; it spoke of deeper powers than he had believed in before. It also disturbed him because it was his own wife who possessed the gift, a woman he had known all his adult life. He had shared all manner of experiences with her. He thought he knew her as well as he knew himself. Now, without warning, she was the channel for something greater and beyond them both.

He left Isadorus and went home. Eleni greeted him with the old, familiar warmth; quick to laughter, gentle to touch, as easy in response to him as she had always been. It was as if nothing had changed. And yet within hours he knew it had. There was a secret joy in her from which he was excluded. All night he lay beside her in the darkness, feeling his separateness.

It drove him to seek the Shinabari woman and find out for himself what the Book said, and why it mattered so profoundly to those he loved.

She was alone in a room overlooking a walled courtyard of the palace with cypress trees and a pool for lilies. He had thought he remembered her face, but when he saw her again it was with surprise. She was darker than he had recalled. Her features were stronger. Only her mouth was soft, and the long curve of her throat. He noticed with surprise that she had beautiful ears.

She stood in the middle of the floor. She was dressed in hot earth colours bordered with bronze. All the joy and pain of her belief were naked in her extraordinary face.

157

'I came because I wish to see the Book,' he began. 'I want to learn of it from you, not from one of those who know little, except that they believe its power.'

She did not point out to him that Eleni had been studying the Book for close to a year, or that Isadorus was more than familiar with it now. That was not what he meant, and perhaps she knew that what he needed was to come to the source.

'If you wish,' she agreed, watching him steadily. She made the slightest gesture with her shoulders. 'I will fetch it.'

'Thank you,' he accepted, coming further into the room. For the first time he glanced around. It was filled with her presence, her different, subtler nature. There was no Camassian ornament, only the architecture was native. On a small table stood an alabaster horse. It had not the complex lines of a live animal, but was simple, fluid, with the imaginative grace of the artist's dream. In its power it was truer to the spirit than to reality. He knew without question that it was Shinabari.

Tathea was coming back with the Book in her arms and its beauty caught him by surprise. The gold of it was warm, the pearls gleamed soft as milk but with a radiance as if they held the light rather than merely reflected it. The great star ruby in the hasp burned like fire.

He had come intending to inquire, not to argue. He knew enough of mystery to be prepared to believe, but he had not expected to feel awe, and yet now at the moment of reaching to touch the Book, suddenly he was hesitant.

'Take it,' she urged him with the barest flicker of amusement in her eyes.

The gold was smooth beneath his fingers. He sat down on the chair she indicated, then opened the Book and read the first page, then read it again. It was what he had already heard from Eleni, but seeing it written awoke in him a new feeling. He lost all awareness of the room around him, even of Tathea standing a yard away. He was alone in a pool of light with the words and he was unable to draw his eyes from them.

He turned the page and read on.

When he looked up she was still standing. She had not the warmth of Eleni, and the gentleness that he loved, but there was a grace in her unlike any other. It came of hunger and pride and loneliness and, he realised with surprise, an intense ability to be hurt. He looked at her with sharper curiosity.

'He says He gives no commandment without making a way possible to obey,' he said. 'And yet He seems deliberately to have written confusion. When you face the extremity of life and death, hunger, pain, terror, bereavement, you are truly alone with yourself. Dreams fall away. Mysteries crumble and leave nothing. All that stands then is truth, and the law.'

Her eyes did not waver. 'I know that,' she answered him. 'You speak as if you are the only one who has faced death or despair. Do you imagine the Book fell out of the sky and landed in my hands?'

It was a just rebuke.

'I apologise,' he said sincerely. 'But that is not an argument. The Book is still complex and unclear.'

'And if it were clear, would you value it?' she demanded.

He was about to answer that he would, then he recognised the challenge in her voice and thought again. 'Do you see some virtue in obfuscation?' he asked.

She took it up as if it had been a gauntlet thrown down. There was certainty in her as if she were inspired by something beyond herself. He had never seen anyone with such a passion of the mind. It sparked a ripple of excitement inside him.

'Do you value what is given you, or what you have laboured for?' she challenged.

'I should labour to understand this?' He touched his finger to the Book, but he did not take his eyes from her face.

'You are a child of God, but not a baby to be fed with a spoon!' she returned.

He laughed abruptly. 'You don't honey your words, do you!' He leaned back, looking up at her.

'Wasn't the bare truth what you wanted . . . General?' He saw in her eyes a world of memory lying behind her use of his title. She was reminding him of the battlefield, of his implied condescension to her as a woman, because he knew hardship and courage, and he thought she did not. With a ripple of surprise, and something curiously like pleasure, he recognised in her a spirit of remarkable strength.

Forgetting time, he sat opposite her, turning page after page of the Book, picking out passages and questioning her, arguing, wresting one meaning from the words, testing it and finding another, seeking to understand.

Always she kept up with him. Her mind was logical, incisive and agile. She gave no quarter in pursuit of truth, and seemed to feel no resentment on the rare occasions when he found flaws in her reasoning. It amazed him that she grasped new thoughts with such eagerness. The clarity of her ideas and the sheer power of her mind excited him. It was like the physical exhilaration of a wild gallop along the shoreline with a perfect horse beneath you.

He was astonished when he caught sight of the hourglass and saw it was after midnight. He opened his mouth to apologise, then knew he would be a hypocrite to express sorrow, even superficially, for what had been superb, a time filled with tumultuous, burning ideas he would never discard or forget. Words of any sort were unnecessary. She did not care that it was nearing the first hour of morning. They had explored eternity. He found himself resenting the duties which must keep him away for several days.

'May I return after the festival?' he asked as he stood at the door. She was in the centre of the room, distanced from him, from the simple furniture. The light was gold on her lips and the hollow of her neck.

'Of course.' She looked at him with an expression he could not read, as if she both wished him to return and at the same time felt pain at the prospect. He thought how little he knew her. Her mind was as clear as sunlight to him and her heart a territory unmapped and unknown.

He had intended to tell Eleni in detail about his time with Tathea, but somehow the right opportunity did not come. He referred to it only obliquely, and then only in terms of his interest in the Book, not his discussions with Tathea.

He found thoughts of the Book and his visit to Tathea occupying his mind more and more. The ideas in the Book consumed him. He returned to see her after the festival, and again after that. There was a beauty of justice in the teaching, from which he could not turn away. He struggled through the complexities of the language towards a kind of sublime reason in all things. It was always there, just beyond his grasp, beckoning to him, revealing new fragments of the whole each time.

And she was the perfect companion. The breadth of her imagination astonished him. The courage of her spirit never failed. Nothing was too difficult, too powerful or too subtle for her to attempt. Her hunger to read the mind of God matched his own.

It was late summer and a sudden squall of rain was lashing the cypresses in the palace gardens when they came to the end of a long discussion on the nature and purpose of power. They had argued furiously, but with the pure pleasure of duellists, rejoicing in each other's skills and never doubting for an instant that they sought the same truth.

'I still think there could be a better way,' he said, leaning back in his chair with a smile. 'The power to heal –' he thought briefly of Eleni – 'to turn stone into bread and feed the hungry, anything that relieves pain or loss, would do only good.'

'No, it wouldn't,' she responded instantly. She was sitting opposite him in a matching chair, the dark blue of her gown spilling gold at the hem. She no longer bothered to pretend patience with him. He regarded it as a measure of their honesty with each other. It was at the core of his ease with her, and the refreshment of heart and mind he knew in her company.

'A miracle is a product not a cause,' she went on, looking at him

160

earnestly. 'None of those gifts to heal, to feed or clothe, to command the elements, even to raise the dead bring any souls nearer to the knowledge of God.' She leaned forward a little, bringing her face further into the light, deepening the soft shadow of her hair over the nape of her neck. 'If it could teach you love, or courage, or integrity of heart, do you not think God would do it himself? Then there would be no need for life or learning!'

He regarded her closely. There was an intensity in her which made her face the most beautiful he had ever seen. Without thinking, he reached out and touched her, only an instant, and withdrew again. The warmth of her ran through him. No one else had the same fire in the soul, the same blazing courage of heart.

He did not bother to say he understood her. She had seen it already in his eyes.

It was some time after that that the subject arose of Isadorus's rejection of her plea for troops to return to Shinabar. Summer had turned to autumn. The leaves were turning, the cypresses were dusty. They stood together on the bare earth of the lemon grove, the fruit hanging golden ripe.

'Do you know anything about war?' he asked mockingly. 'Do you even know which end of a sword to hold?'

'I can ride well!' she answered.

'Riding well is for running away,' he retorted with a smile. 'If you plan a military campaign you should learn something about warfare, even how to hold a sword.'

'Teach me,' she asked immediately, her gaze unflinching.

He was uncertain for a moment if she was serious. He should not have been. He knew it the instant after. The doubt in her eyes was whether he would do it, not if she needed the knowledge.

It was rash. He looked at her. She was no warrior queen. In her plain, dark green robes he could see how slender she was. There was nothing of the athlete about her. One good blow would have broken her in half.

She sensed his refusal and disappointment filled her eyes.

'Of course,' he said quickly. 'It is a small thing in return for all you have taught me. We'll start tomorrow.' He laughed suddenly. 'Sabres at sunrise!'

They met in the gymnasium where the Household Guard practised, but shortly after dawn, before the Guard arrived. Tathea was dressed in a borrowed tunic and a padded cotton tabard to protect her body.

Martial skill did not come to her naturally. She tired easily, and Alexius had to work hard not to hurt her merely by his far greater strength. To begin with she was hesitant to strike out. Over and over again he told her to lunge, and she failed to. In the end he had to make her sufficiently angry. He caught her with the flat of his blade

161

until she lost her temper and finally struck back, awkwardly, losing her balance.

He guffawed with laughter as she scrambled up, cheeks burning. This time she slashed at him with more skill, remembering what he had told her.

'Bravo!' he said, still laughing and sidestepping with ease. He caught her again, a clean score, but gently.

Her lips tightened and she began to concentrate, moving her feet with more agility, her body with more grace. He saw the determination in her. He needed to defend himself with a trifle more care.

When they were finished, she was breathless and exhausted, leaning over her sword, her hair failing out of its ties, but she could not keep the smile from her face and her eyes shone with victory, not over him, but over herself.

Military strategy was a far different thing. They studied in the palace map room where all the Camassian Empire, its provinces, dependencies and neighbours, were built in clay, down to the last valley, river and hill. She grasped the elements in an instant, indeed sometimes she was ahead of him in perceiving his purpose. He never had to explain any tactic more than once. She understood, before he elaborated, the need to know the terrain of a battle, to be familiar with an enemy commander's history, the experience of his men, their morale, and also the weather. It was barely necessary to touch on the importance of supply lines for food and weapons, of care for the wounded and evacuation if possible, of the maintenance of discipline and at all times of respect for the command, and the belief in victory.

It was extraordinary to be speaking of such things to a woman, and yet in a way her gender was irrelevant. She was at times the most comfortable of people to be with.

When they spoke of the Book, she still startled him with the daring of her imagination. It soared to heights he could barely think of. She stood with her face to the light, her passion so intense she seemed almost unaware of him. Then as suddenly she would turn and look at him, forcing him to climb the untrodden paths with her, to reach for thoughts no man had grasped before, ideas in the mind of God Himself.

Eleni's study of the teachings in the Book was quite different. For her its reality was in the acts of mercy in daily life. She, like Isadorus, had been born while their father was a soldier and she knew the reality of ordinary men who risk their lives. She had seen wounds, hunger and exhaustion as closely as she now saw the splendour of court. She also knew the frailty of power.

For her the truth of the Book lay in the relief of individual pain. The gift within her was of God. She had never doubted it, from the moment she had first felt it flood through her into the injured horse in the arena. The act of healing was the purest joy she had ever known, like the flight of a bird soaring upwards on effortless wings, the grace of doing what she was born to do.

But afterwards she was drained. Frequently she had to sleep. She awoke refreshed, and with a sense of peace she thought nothing would disturb.

She learned her mistake in a place she had never imagined. She went to visit Tathea. It was now almost winter, and she had not seen her since early autumn. The servant told her that Tathea was not in her apartments but in the Guards' gymnasium. Eleni was surprised, but intent upon speaking with her she made her way back down the steps, across one of the dozens of courtyards, to the gymnasium. She opened the door and saw Alexius, stripped to breeches and chest armour, shoulders and arms bare, holding a sword in his hand and laughing. Opposite him was Tathea wearing tunic and light armour, her legs also clothed in breeches, leather boots on her feet. Her black hair was tied hard back from her face and she, too, held a sword.

'Better!' Alexius said, choking back his amusement, but his voice was soft with approval. 'Now try again.'

Tathea lifted her weapon. She was not easy with it, it was obviously heavy for her, but she showed some skill.

Alexius feinted and moved quickly.

Tathea ducked and tried again.

There was a clash of metal, and another. He was very obviously measuring his attack precisely to her ability, laughing at her, encouraging, sometimes praising, at others offering specific criticism.

She was determined, intent upon learning, correcting every mistake, trying to be quicker, stronger, anticipate his move. Neither was aware of Eleni in the doorway watching, or even of the Guards beginning to arrive. They were alone in a world in which no one else had a part.

Tathea dropped her sword, exhausted. She sank to her knees, running her hands over her face and through her hair, smiling up at him.

Alexius let his sword fall also and went over to her, crouching in front of her, leaning towards her till his knees almost touched her.

'Better,' he said softly, his eyes searching her face. It was a single word he might have used to anyone, but there was an intimacy in it, a tenderness that left Eleni stunned.

Without making any deliberate decision, she backed out of the room silently. Outside, the air felt cold on her face as she turned and walked away. She could not bear to speak to them now, not yet. She must gather her thoughts. She needed to be alone.

She walked quickly across the open yard. Her first feeling for Tathea had been pity. She was a woman robbed of all the things anyone would hold dear, family, home, country, position. She had become a stranger and a fugitive with no one to trust, no one left alive who loved her. It was that last bereavement which had cut Eleni most deeply for her. No gift or burden of knowledge could make up for that.

Now she realised that the many griefs which had awakened her pity, and the qualities of courage, imagination and humour which had made her like Tathea, were also the same ones which made her dangerous. Even if she did not mean to be, if she was unaware of it, a voyager compelled to follow her dream, she was still a passionate and lonely woman. The fire of her spirit would burn many. Eleni should have seen it from the beginning.

She almost stumbled over the step and regained her balance only with difficulty.

Was that the price of her gift of healing, that she should lose Alexius, in heart even if not in body?

She started up the shallow flight of stairs, brushing past people she knew, hardly aware of them. The sunlight was harsh, the angles of the walls and roofs sharp. It was a price she had never imagined, and she was not prepared for it.

Was it God's bargain, or was it Tathea's? Who was Tathea, that she had this power? Why would she exact such a payment?

No, that was ridiculous. The gift was of God. What Tathea did was her own choice and she was accountable for it. If she took Alexius, if she could, then that was human weakness.

Eleni had studied the Book and understood its spirit well enough to know that God knew the hearts of men and might well foretell what they would do, but He did not cause them to do it. The great, sacred truth at the foundation of all things, the soul of the law, was that every spirit ever born had a right of choice, which God would never remove.

She bumped into someone, and apologised without looking at them. She was not going anywhere. She was escaping.

Was she still free to make her choice, to give back the gift and let everything be as it was before Tathea had come? Or was it already too late?

She stopped on the steps at the end of the cypress walk, facing the City. It was cold. The wind wrapped her robe round her body and unravelled a little of her hair. From here she could see across the rooftops as far as the bay and the haze of the horizon beyond.

She knew the answer already, and refused to accept it. Perhaps she could face Alexius, ask him for the truth, rather than argue with herself. Argue about what? She had been married to him for over twenty-five years. She had not misread the way he had looked at Tathea or the softness in his voice when he touched her. She could see it again, with her eyes closed against the light, and the wound hurt more than before. There was no numbness now to dull it.

And her choice was already made. If she were to give back the gift, assuming she could, she would be denying herself and all she believed. She would be denying who she was. She did not want to live with that. But even if she did, it would not win Alexius's admiration or his love. Laughter and tenderness, the sharing of dreams could not be bargained for.

She remained staring at the sea, the wind tugging at her hair. She was shivering, but it did not matter. She must keep the gift, whatever its cost proved to be. It was part of her. It was a hard, bruising knowledge, but there was no escape from it, however fiercely she wished for one.

Tathea was unaware of Eleni's pain, but she was not blind to Isadorus's.

Barsymet was civil to him, on public occasions even warm. She enjoyed the new experience of being the only woman to whom he had any bond of loyalty or affection. All the court knew Tissarel had gone and not been replaced. But at a banquet in honour of the new ambassador for Tirilis, a politically delicate situation, Tathea saw something that confirmed Isadorus's loneliness in her mind.

He was speaking to the new ambassador and he turned to draw Barsymet into the conversation. Tathea could not hear what they were saying, but she saw Barsymet smile and answer, and rest her hand very lightly on his arm, just for a moment, the light catching on her rings, then withdraw it. It was a proprietorial gesture, but there was no tenderness in it. It was for public consumption.

The evening was long, full of ritual and formality. Not until the early hours of the morning were the guests free to retire.

Isadorus saw Tathea as she was leaving. He moved towards her, a moment of pleasure in his face. His eyes met hers with a quickening of warmth. 'I hear you are becoming quite a warrior,' he said softly. 'To what purpose? I don't know how you will take the Book to your people, but it will not be in the wake of armies.'

She drew in her breath to find some argument.

He smiled. 'If you do it by force, what value is it? God could force us all, and rob His teachings of purpose by robbing us of the chance to choose.'

'But . . .'

He touched her arm. His hand was light but she was startled by the strength of his grip.

'Tathea, listen to the voice of the Great Enemy as well as to the voice of God!' he said earnestly, his eyes wide and steady. 'We have it for a purpose. It would be easy enough simply to have the word of God and all the commands about what we should do, what we must avoid. The voice of destruction is sometimes a stronger warning

165

against evil than anything spoken by one who loves us.'

Like the smell of a charnel house, her mind filled with the memory of hatred, of eyes that saw inside her with such intimacy that it was a violation of the soul. The hall around her became a small room, a prison cell closing her in, tight, claustrophobic. She could not breathe. Only Isadorus's hand on her arm kept her from falling.

'Tathea!'

She remembered bright sunlight, and death.

'Tathea!'

The stench faded. She thought she saw Alexius for an instant, holding a sword high. Then she realised it was Isadorus in front of her, in the hallway.

'Yes . . .' she gulped. 'Yes . . . I'm sorry.'

'Are you all right?' There was sharp concern in his face.

'Yes . . . I just felt . . .' She was about to lie, to make some trivial excuse of politeness, but the words faded. He deserved better than evasion. 'You are right about the Enemy . . .'

'Never forget him.' His voice fell to a whisper, urgent and very close. 'He will never forget you, Tathea.'

This was a truth more real than the marble floor on which she stood or the stone pillars on either side, the crowd beyond or the soaring dome of the ceiling.

The moment was broken. Barsymet came up the steps and saw Isadorus. Her face was smooth and polite, but cold. Then she recognised Tathea and the coldness deepened, mixed with a consciousness of irony. It was Tathea who had brought the Book that had restored her to her place at Isadorus's side – in the world's eyes, if not in his heart.

'Good evening, lady,' she said courteously. 'I am pleased you were able to honour the occasion with your presence.'

Behind her the soldier Ulciber stood to attention, his eyes not on Barsymet but on Tathea. He smiled very slightly. It had no warmth, no beauty.

Tathea's throat was dry. She sought for words and her lips would not move.

Alexius appeared. He saw Tathea's face and strode forward.

'Take her to her rooms.' Isadorus was pale, as if he had understood something beyond the outer shell of meaning.

'What happened?' Alexius demanded, his eyes dark with apprehension, his voice urgent. He turned from Isadorus to Tathea, questioning.

'A moment of . . . of remembering,' she answered. That was the truth, although of what or when she did not know.

Alexius assumed it was the assassination. His expression was bleak with anger and pity and a fierce tenderness. He put his arm round her

166

and had she not moved, he might even have picked her up. She would have been glad if he had, except for the absurdity of being carried in front of Barsymet and Ulciber. She leaned against him, close to the warmth of his body, his strength and the familiar touch and smell of him.

She barely saw Eleni as she watched them leave, and she was only dimly aware of Ulciber's smile widening till his face seemed to shine.

Chapter Eleven

Eleni saw Tathea leave with Alexius and her heart chilled inside her. She knew Tathea had suffered some kind of shock or illness, and that any man capable of care or respect would have helped her. It was not that Alexius did so but the tenderness in his gestures that caught her with renewed pain.

She barely heard the conversations around her, Barsymet's questions, and Isadorus's affectionate goodnight. He seemed to have seen nothing. She turned and walked alone, making some polite and meaningless farewell.

She did not sleep. She lay alone in the darkness. When Alexius returned she remained motionless, breathing regularly, eyes closed. He spoke to her softly, and she gave no response at all. Inside she was numb, her mind racing in futile circles, hurting herself over and over again by deliberately remembering. If she did it often enough, perhaps it would develop a different meaning.

She woke before he did, and rose immediately. She still did not want to speak to him. She would have to in time, of course, but she needed to heal first, find some way in her mind to come to terms with the anger and the fear that filled her. Until then she must hide it from him. If he knew, he would find it ugly and unwarranted. They would be strangers, because he would, for the first time in their lives, be repelled by something in her nature. Or, worse than that, he would understand only too well. He would be torn by guilt. She could not bear the thought of that. Standing on the terrace in the morning light, she began to shake and a sickness welled up inside her.

She decided to go to the hospice where she had frequently worked with other women to help care for the sick and injured. If she must pay such a fearful price for her gift, at least she would use it. That one fierce, sweet power of giving was untouched by the passion of loss. It depended on no one else.

She walked quickly through the cold, early-morning streets, passing bakers and deliverers of fresh milk and fruit hurrying on their way. The air was clean after the night, and the pavements still wet.

The hospice was not far, no more than ten minutes away at a brisk pace. They were delighted to see her. There was always too much to do, and too few to do it. The night had brought its usual tragedies and Eleni knew well that daylight only made the suffering harsher and more real. There were many who found waking the hardest time, the hours too long until they could hope for the oblivion of sleep again.

She worked steadily, hard, forcing from her mind her own sense of betrayal. Tathea, of all people! Tathea whom she had befriended, who had taught her the secrets of the Book!

Or was that it? Was that what Alexius loved? The beauty and breadth and perfection of the Book, not Tathea herself.

What was the difference?

Eleni was tending a woman who had a fever. It was nearing crisis. She was bathing her in cool water, trying to keep her temperature down, and gradually she became aware through the turmoil in her thoughts that she was failing. The woman was slipping into delirium.

The physician came to her shoulder, his lips pursed. 'No one can help her now but you, my lady,' he said gravely. His voice was full of trust.

It was the moment. She had almost let it pass. She placed her hands gently on the woman's face and concentrated her thoughts upon her, waiting for the familiar power to run through her, the bright knowledge of joy.

Nothing happened.

The physician was holding his breath, expecting the miracle, awed by it, although he had seen it many times before.

She must channel all her strength towards the sick woman. She must will her better.

Still there was nothing.

The physician cleared his throat.

With darkness inside her, Eleni knew it was not going to happen. She had wanted the gift to be gone; the burden of it was too heavy, the price more than she was willing to pay – and God had heard her! It was gone.

The sick woman's breath rattled in her throat, and then stopped.

Eleni felt as if it was her own death she had seen. She withdrew her hands slowly. They were stiff and cold. This was not what she had meant. She had lost something of herself which had nothing to do with Alexius or Tathea or anyone else. It was between herself and God, and she had broken a trust.

The physician closed the dead woman's eyes then put his hands on Eleni's arms, very gently, trying to turn her away.

She did not move. This was worse than anything she had imagined. There was a darkness inside her where there had been light before, an emptiness she knew nothing else would fill. Alexius could not, because it was within her. She had denied herself.

'Come, my lady. You cannot help her now,' the physician said more firmly, his words at last penetrating her mind.

She looked up at him, making herself see the disappointment and the confusion in his eyes. It was not only the dead woman she had failed, and herself, it was all those who had believed in her power, and perhaps those who had trusted in the Book because of her. She should have known this would happen from the first time they had looked at her with such awe. They had expected the impossible even then. It had frightened her, but not enough, or she would not have allowed this to happen.

She permitted the physician to lead her away. She wanted to be alone, to return to the Book, do anything that was necessary to be given another chance with her gift. She had, for a moment, denied the light. Had she given away her own nature, even her soul, in doing so? She had to know, and only within the Book could she learn.

Tathea did not hear of the incident in the hospice. The physician's passion in life was the healing of the sick, both in body and in soul. He knew that the loss of hope killed as many as the nature of injury or disease itself. He spoke of it to no one.

As winter passed into spring and early summer, the teachings of the Book spread rapidly in the City, and here and there beyond it into neighbouring cities, carried by traders and soldiers, tax gatherers and government officials as they journeyed. It was accepted and rejected with many degrees of faith, and sometimes of scepticism, and for many reasons.

Alexius struggled with the details of the teachings in the Book, but he had no doubt whatever that it was true. Understanding might take all life long, or more, but it was beginning already. Eleni knew it. She had no need of instruction from him. Perhaps she knew some of its heart better than he did.

His sister Xanthica was different. She was five years younger than Alexius and he had loved her, bullied her, taught and protected her to a greater or lesser degree all her life. He could not now fail to share with her this treasure of the mind and soul.

He began slowly. He knew her resistance to instruction. She had always loved him, but her loyalty was to her husband Maximian, as it should be, as Eleni's was to him.

She listened to him, agreeing easily. It was a lifetime's habit, but he knew it was only words.

They were in the lily garden one early evening when he destroyed her evasions at last. The sun was low as the year waned. The almonds and olives were ripe. Nestlings had long since flown.

'You keep saying you agree,' he charged. 'But you won't commit yourself. You talk about mysticism, but that is not what you mean. I've answered every argument on that.'

She kept her face averted. They were moving slowly between the beds of regal, wax-like flowers, their perfume heavy in the heat.

'I suppose it frightens me,' she said quietly. 'You keep on pressing, and I don't know how else to answer.'

He caught up with her and put his arm round her shoulders, but after a moment she pulled away, turning to face him, her eyes angry.

'Have you noticed Eleni lately?' she accused. 'Sometimes I think you are blind! She's wretched! That gift of healing she has may be marvellous but it's drawing every last bit of happiness out of her!'

It was true. Eleni had tried to hide it, gloss over the misery inside her, but he knew her face too well to be deceived, even though he had tried to disbelieve it. But that was because he did not want it to be true. He loved Eleni, and he loved the Book. Without realising it, he had looked for only happiness in it, and her pain caught him unaware. It confused him. He did not understand her gift. He possessed nothing like it, nor did Tathea, the only other person with whom he could share the depths of the Book's meaning.

Xanthica was regarding him critically. 'It is too hard.' She pursed her lips. 'If it can hurt someone as good as Eleni, what will it do to the rest of us?' Then as he did not reply, she went on, 'I don't want it! I don't want to challenge an enemy who says he can cover the face of the earth with ruin and war, who can reap the last grain of destruction – and that is what the Book says!'

'I know,' he agreed quickly. 'But for those who endure, there will be the joy of God, and peace which has no end. Is that not worth any price?'

'No!' She did not have to think about it. 'I like what I have, Alex.' She moved her hand expressively to indicate the garden and the City beyond. 'I don't want the sun and the moon and the stars. I am perfectly happy with the ordinary mortal earth I have, with Maximian, with honour and wit and a decent life from day to day, with kindness and diligence and honesty between one man and another. That is what the best in Camassia have believed and lived by for generations, and it is good! I don't know why you want something else.' She looked at him earnestly, struggling to understand.

Why did he? She deserved an unequivocal reply.

The sun was warm on lilies and the perfume heady, the drone of bees lazy and far away.

'I've seen something brighter,' he replied with the simplest truth. 'And I can't forget it.'

She shivered, annoyed with him. His stubbornness was causing unnecessary pain. 'What's brighter about it?' she demanded. 'It is full of threats as well as promises. What about the world crashing around our ears and death and despair in every land? I don't want that for myself or for those I love – or anyone at all! I don't want sacrifice, or all the years of labouring and learning and trying to understand.'

There was anger in her voice and defiance in the way she stood. She was frightened. He had no doubt of it. He moved towards her, taking her hand gently.

'It is possible to achieve,' he promised. 'He is not some demon mocking us by commanding things we cannot do.'

'Some of us!' She snatched her hand away, her rings catching roughly against his skin.

'No, all of us,' he corrected. 'He expects from each of us only what we can do. He is a God of morality, not just of power.'

'He wants everything!' She was not in the least mollified. 'You say in one breath that there is a sacred freedom of choice, then in the next you say we must obey, or be punished. And if we don't obey everything, sacrifice, tribulation, suffering and labour, then the alternative is to lose it all!'

He kept his patience with increasing difficulty. Had it been anyone else, he would not even have tried. But there was a bond between them he could not break. He could not leave her behind, and still be whole.

'No, that's not true,' he persisted. 'Everyone will be rewarded according to their acts and their desires, what they would have done, had they the power, for good or evil. But if you turn away from the best, the utmost you can do, then your reward will be only part of what you could have had.'

She stepped back on the paving, away from him and almost into the flowers. 'I'm perfectly happy with an ordinary reward. I don't want to be a god, now or ever! I think it is arrogant and, frankly, ridiculous.' Her voice was sharp. 'I'm a human being. I have faults and weaknesses and I probably always will have. I don't mind it. And I'm happy with other people who are the same.'

He knew why she was angry. The last sentence held it all. Some part of her feared that the Book held the truth, but she did not want to be alone. Maximian did not believe. He did not see in the Book anything beautiful or sublime. He saw only mysticism and confusion, the clouding of reason, the loss of self-discipline and that code of duty which had made Camassia great. Xanthica had caught a glimpse, however small, of the light in the words, but she would not risk losing any part of Maximian's love, or his approval. Had she already tested his reaction were she to accept the Book? Or dare she not even do that?

Alexius had argued with Maximian himself, and met polite but total resistance. He was too courteous to insult another person's belief, or even to refuse to listen, but he listened with the ears, not the mind. Talking to him had made Alexius realise just how great was the gulf between them. He had never appreciated before how unlike they were.

Maximian was of an ancient family, and in his own sober, drily humorous way he was intensely proud of it. His praise of the old ideals was no mere lip service. He lived by them, and would have died for them as willingly as any lover of the Book would live or die for it. He made no passionate speeches, nor did he attempt to persuade anyone else, but it was no less deep in his blood and bone for that.

'Why don't you say something?' Xanthica demanded. 'Don't just stand there accusing me!'

'I'm not accusing you,' he answered quietly. 'You must choose as you wish, I only want to be sure I have explained it to you well, so that—'

'You have,' she cut across him. 'Several times. I don't want to talk about it any more.' And she started to walk down the path towards the steps and the carved animals on the ascending wall, her bright, terracotta skirts sweeping behind her, embroidered borders catching the light.

Isadorus had asked Tathea to simplify the teachings in the Book and set them forth, in Camassian, in a manner all people could read so that they might find in them a way of life and a structure in which they could teach and support each other. There were now many hundreds of believers, and they required more than solitary reflection upon its philosophy, which was at the moment random and in no order of increasing complexity.

Tathea had argued with Alexius that one values only what one has struggled to grasp, but she understood very well that those whose nature did not drive them to study and to seek were still worthy of all the knowledge the Book could offer. The ancient language in which it was written was unfamiliar to the vast majority of the people. There was an element of it which was universal, but it was too easy for even scholars to misinterpret.

'Make of it something I can give to anyone,' Isadorus urged. It was not a command but a plea, and she could not refuse, nor did she want to. He gave her scribes and promised assistance from anyone whose help might further the work.

It was not merely a matter of translating the Book into daily Camassian understandable to all. That might have been relatively easy. It must also have the power and the beauty to move men and reach into their hearts, and she must be certain that she did not unintentionally corrupt its meaning. For that she wanted more than scribes, however skilled. She must read it over and over again, ponder it in her mind, walk alone and search her memory for those fragments of joy that lay just beyond recall, the peace that filled her and gave her soul wings when she saw the light arch across the sky in a particular way, or reflect back from water. She must allow the peace to settle within her until she could feel the certainty blossom warm inside her that she was right.

She needed to work, to converse, to argue and test every sentence against the judgement of someone else who grasped its truth, and who would measure her work without fear or favour.

Alexius was that person, and Isadorus spoke his name before she did. She would work with the Book and at regular intervals Alexius would read what she had written and weigh it against every argument he could bring to test its strength and probe for weakness, ambiguity, clumsiness, omission.

They were given a long room on the top floor of the palace, overlooking the wing where once Baradeus had counselled with his generals. There were windows all along the southern side and the light was excellent, even though it was now approaching winter – the fourth since Tathea had come to Camassia.

They worked with pleasure. There were always scribes present at the other end, but in spirit it was as if they were alone. Usually they worked in the evening after Tathea had spent the day wrestling with the text and Alexius had completed his military and diplomatic duties. He usually wore not a uniform but a long tunic and robe like an Archon, but without the purple border.

'This passage about miracles,' he said one night, looking up from the page in his hands. 'You have made love plain, but not the law.'

'Yes, I have.' She leaned forward and indicated where she had written it.

He shook his head. 'It is not strong enough. It would be too easy to believe from this that love and belief are sufficient. If you go back to the original . . . where is it?'

She turned back a page in the great Book on the table and found it, reading it aloud.

'You see?' He met her eyes. 'The power of the law is given greater weight. People can convince themselves to believe all kinds of things if they want them badly enough. You are leaving too much room for mistaking desire for faith. And then when the reward does not come, abandoning the truth will have its ready excuse. It will appear that the promises of God were broken.'

'People will do that anyway,' she said with wry memory, 'if that is what they wish. We can justify anything to ourselves.' Then she saw something deeper in his face, an emotion behind the thought, a softness about his lips. He was thinking of someone he loved. She did not want to hurt him.

There was no sound in the room but the faint scratching of the scribes' pens across paper.

'There is a difficulty,' she said slowly, trying to choose her words so they were both gentle and honest. He was the last person who would appreciate a moderation of the truth, even in compassion's name.

He laughed quietly, looking at her, the lamplight catching gold on the fine hairs on his cheek. 'Only one?'

Was he aware of her understanding? Searching his eyes, then lowering her gaze again to the page, she was certain he was.

'One at a time,' she responded with a smile, her voice catching a little. 'How to balance law and hope, justice and love. We must be honest in warning, and yet not so rigid as to frighten people away.'

'It is deeper than that.' His voice held anxiety, and hurt. He was watching her.

She knew it, but did not look up. 'How deep?'

'Those who do not know the law cannot be accountable to it.' He was seeking the words as he spoke them. 'If you love someone . . . and we should love all people . . . and you tell them the law, show them the precise path, then you have laid on them the burden to choose. If they refuse it, even though they have seen, then you have helped them to a condemnation they would not have deserved had you kept silent.' He hesitated, his emotion naked in his voice. 'Have you helped them or hurt them?'

She knew exactly who he meant – Xanthica and, beyond her, millions of others through all the ages past, and to come, who would see something of the truth and turn away from it because of its cost.

She had no answer.

'You say nothing,' he prompted, leaning a little closer. He needed to know. He was afraid of the answer but he was long schooled in courage and he would not allow himself to turn aside. She knew so much of him. She had learned to anticipate his thoughts, to know his instinct. And yet there were other ways in which they were strangers. There were vast areas of his life of which she knew nothing at all, multitudes of facts, experiences she could only guess at from the results carved into his nature. Just as he knew her as she was now but had no conception of the Empress she had been in Shinabar and could barely comprehend the power she had held then. Yet he seemed to grasp something about her love of the Book that even Isadorus and Eleni had not. She had never told him, because she was only reaching after the knowledge herself, but she had fought for it, and paid dearly. She had waged and won some war of the spirit which held real and terrible dangers. And perhaps it was not over.

' "It requires all that a man has," ' she quoted softly, looking up into his clear eyes. " 'To the height and depth of his soul, but it does not require more. I give no commandments except I make a way possible that they may be accomplished." '

She tried to read how far he wished to go. She would insult him if she did not pursue it to the end, and hurt him if she did. She hesitated, clenched inside.

'Say it!' He half smiled. He was so close she could smell the warmth of his skin. 'The law is from eternity to eternity, and even God must obey it, or cease to be God.'

She could not argue, it was a direct quote from the Book, in the plain words everyone understood.

'And where there is law there has to be the possibility of obedience to it,' he went on. 'And of disobedience.'

'Yes.' She knew what he was going to say next, and she did not say it for him.

'And where there is obedience and disobedience, there must be reward and punishment or, if you prefer, cost,' he stated. 'Otherwise there is chaos, and the Adversary has won. There is no meaning to anything.'

'Yes,' she said again. There was no disagreement possible. 'But you must remember there are great variations in agency and power to understand, let alone to obey. Millions will live and die without ever having heard any of the law. We are judged according to the light we have. To whom much is given, much will be required.' She knew that with a passionate and absolute truth as she heard her own words as if from the lips of a stranger. 'Judgement is just. The desires of the heart are measured. We are weighed for what we would have been, had we the chance, as much as for what we are. There are many who would do good, or evil, but circumstances prevent them.'

Outside, the wind was rising a little and the room was growing colder. One of the scribes left his table to place another piece of wood on the fire.

Alexius looked at Tathea very steadily. The sand trickled through the hourglass and she did not speak. He kept his eyes on hers. Only his lips moved, to form a slight, sad, self-mocking smile, full of gentleness.

'I'll say it for you,' he said. 'There is no escape.'

'No . . .'

He sat silently for several minutes, then stood up and walked towards the windows and the panorama of the dark City beyond Baradeus's council rooms. 'What should we tell people, Thea? How much? If they hear the truth, and turn away from it, their condemnation is far worse than that of anyone who didn't know. So I ask again, have we helped them, or hurt them? Without us they could have claimed innocence. We are responsible, either way.'

'We are responsible for their knowledge, not their choice,' she answered.

'Don't be a sophist.' He did not turn from the window. 'That's not an honest argument, and you know that. If we didn't force them to hear the truth, they wouldn't have had to make the choice, right or wrong.'

176

She leaned a little against the polished table top, watching him. 'I don't think it is sophistry. The choice will have to be made. Sooner or later, in this life or after it, everyone will have the truth.' She shook her head. 'And if they don't, isn't that what the Great Enemy wants – ignorance, to remain for ever in the womb?'

He half twisted from the window, the light on his face again, showing the pain and the confusion in it. 'Yes . . . yes, I suppose it is. But . . .' He stopped again.

'I know,' she whispered. 'It hurts and will go on hurting when those we love choose the other way. I don't know another answer. Can we have two rules, one for those we love, and another for those we don't? God loves us all.'

He closed his eyes. 'I know! And if we know and don't speak, then we are taking from others their right to choose, we are making the judgement that they would fail.' He said the word bitterly.

She wanted to touch him, to hold him in her arms and share his pain. She knew what it was as if she felt it herself. It was a universal grief. It stretched beyond any man or woman up to heaven itself, but there were ways in which each would taste it alone, and she was afraid to trespass. He was thinking of his sister, and she was not part of all that that meant.

He came back to the table and sat down. 'Is it in the Book?' he said at last, looking at her.

'Is what?'

'In the army,' he explained, 'especially on the frontiers, there are always sentries, men whose job it is to guard the rest of us while we clean weapons, cook, tend the wounded, plan the next attack, whatever else needs doing. We trust them, it is only the trusted men who are chosen.' He regarded her gravely.

'The watchman,' she answered. 'Yes, all peoples have him. Without him we could not eat or sleep, or turn our minds to any other thing. And if he fails his trust, he is executed, because without him we all perish. I know what you are saying. It is the watchman's duty to speak the truth. Whether the army then fights or flees has nothing to do with it. He must cry the warning whether he is believed or not.'

He nodded slowly.

'Then there isn't any question left . . . is there?' she whispered.

'No.' He sighed and rose to his feet. 'We've answered it. I'm not sure I like it, but I know it is the truth.' He rested his hand lightly on her arm for a moment, his fingers strong and warm, then he turned to the door, calling goodnight to the scribes. He did not speak to her again before he left the room, but their understanding was complete.

Chapter Twelve

When Ra-Nufis returned from his second journey to Shinabar, he came straight to see Tathea late in the evening. He looked weary as he came into the quiet room with the warm colour in the sharp spring light. Her pleasure in seeing him was great, though she noticed that he seemed older, as if the boy in him had given way to experience. But there was an energy of enthusiasm in his eyes and he came across the room in swift, easy strides, carrying a package in his hands, carefully, as if it might shatter if he dropped it.

She felt anticipation like a child. She had had other gifts, of course. Eleni was always generous. But this was from Shinabar, and Ra-Nufis held a place in her emotions which was special and apart, perhaps because in him she saw what Habi could have become.

He held the package out for her in his slender hands.

She took it slowly. It was lighter than she had expected, as if most of it was wrapping. She glanced up at him and saw the eagerness in his face. It was tied with fine twine and it took moments to undo it. She unfolded the cloth slowly, layer after layer, until her fingers felt the cool, smooth surface of a tiny Shinabari wild tortoise, carved from a single piece of lapis lazuli. It was perfect to the minutest detail, and only a little larger than the first joint of her thumb.

She looked up to see him smiling at her, anticipation of her pleasure in his eyes.

'It's . . . wonderful,' she answered, gratitude, longing for home, and the ache of exile and loneliness drowning her voice for a moment. 'It's good to see you again,' she said impulsively. 'Thank you for coming here so soon. You must be tired.'

'What else could be so important?' he asked with a little shrug, one shoulder higher than the other. It was a gesture she had seen a thousand times in Thoth-Moara, never here. She did not want to be too precipitate in asking him the news. All the time he had been gone she had waited, and now he was back she was half afraid to hear. She kept the exquisite little tortoise in her hand, turning it over and over, her fingers caressing its surface. She offered him food and wine, and only when he had refreshed himself did he speak of Shinabar.

He looked grave. 'The news is not good, Majesty. If you wanted

178

revenge, and the power to have it, then I would say the time is ripening fast, but I know you love your people, as I do, and hunger to teach them the words of the Book.' He took a breath. 'But now they dilute and moderate even the old religion. They keep the rituals because people like them, but they've forgotten what they mean, and they've lost the courage to speak the truth about anything. The differences between right and wrong are so blurred they are breeding a generation who are not even going to know what the words mean. They are already angry, disillusioned and hungry without knowing what for. They want everything immediately, and when they have it, it satisfies nothing.'

She was loth to believe it. Surely he was exaggerating. 'It is only a reaction to violent change. It won't last.'

His dark eyes were touched with pity as he looked at her, but there was no hesitation in his answer. 'No, Majesty, that is not true. It is a creeping sickness which has been rising for a long time, a decade or more. The ugliness is there. We are a weary people. The hardships of the war to the east fifteen years ago, and then the drought, tested us to—'

'We rose to it!' she interrupted him, remembering those bitter days clearly, the tension, the daily news of hunger and death. First they had feared for the lives of friends and family as the armies struggled. Then in the aftermath of victory had come the deeper terror that with drought in the mountains the underground rivers that fed the vast cisterns would dry up and whole cities would starve. For three years it had grown worse. Crops had failed, animals had had to be slaughtered. Disease spread. People whispered in the streets of plague.

At last the rains had come again. Slowly the cisterns started to fill. Hope surged back.

'I know we did,' Ra-Nufis acknowledged, but his voice dipped, as if he spoke of a tragedy, and his eyes looked at some greater defeat.

'What do you mean?' she demanded, standing up swiftly, unable to sit still as fear gripped her. 'What do you know that you are not saying? Tell me the truth – or what you know of it.'

There was silence in the room. The sands of the hourglass slipped through the funnel without a whisper and no rain beat against the window. The little black and white cat stretched and curled up again, purring gently.

'That after the misery and the fear of that time,' Ra-Nufis replied gently, 'your generation were determined your children should not suffer as you did. You protected us from reality. Life did not give us the discipline of war or of hunger, and you did not offer laws or standards that would and should have replaced them.' There was pity and anger in his eyes. 'You were tired, and you allowed your own weariness, and your desire to protect us, to give us licence beyond

179

liberty. You praised what was good in us; you also praised what was commonplace, even tawdry. Because circumstances placed too many demands on the youth of your age, you placed too few on the youth of mine. Soon we will have forgotten how to tell each other the truth, or even what it is!'

What he said was terrible, but as she heard the words she knew it was true. She did not interrupt him.

'Our armies have grown slack.' He watched her as he went on, knowing he was hurting her, and that he must. 'At heart they no longer believe in themselves, and they are right not to. We have no more heroes.' He lifted his shoulders again in the slight, rueful shrug. 'Perhaps some of the heroes we used to have were more flawed than we cared to admit, but even if we half knew that anyway, we admired what was good.' He smiled, an ironic, Shinabari smile. 'We may have painted on ordinary faces the masks of greatness, but at least we hungered for what it represented.'

He let out his breath in a sigh. 'Now we are afraid of it. We have lost . . . an innocence. Ta-Thea, you must find a way to come back and teach them the great truths of the Book. There is beauty in it which will win thousands, then tens of thousands, eventually millions. Everyone should have the right to hear. It is already beginning in Camassia, God knows, and Shinabar is perishing for lack of it. Laws cannot change a nation. It must come from within. Only the truth can bring about change.'

She stood without answering, and he was content to wait. She thought back over a dozen incidents, a score, and with each one she became more certain that he was right.

'Help me,' she said at last. 'Find me the arguments that will move Isadorus. He won't use his power to overthrow the usurpers and enable me to teach the Book. He believes that is the wrong way to spread the Word, but he would do it for the safety or the peace of Camassia. He would have to believe it would succeed, and he is a soldier, so he will not be fooled.'

Ra-Nufis rose to his feet slowly, smiling. 'I know my craft, Majesty. I have learned a great deal since I first understood that I must serve my people, and the Book, by returning you to Shinabar. I know military strengths and positions. I know the generals and their weaknesses. I know numbers, weapons and morale. I also know the governors of the provinces and which are most likely to side with the present regime. I know who owes whom debts of honour, or fear, or money.' He moved a fraction closer to her. He still carried a faint smell of salt and tar on his clothes. 'I know who can be persuaded to change allegiance, and who is only waiting for a chance with a true hope of success to turn against the weakness and corruption, and those who are behind it.'

'That won't change Isadorus's mind,' she said sadly.

'I know.' His voice was keen, full of hope. 'But the threat from the barbarians will be far worse if Shinabar falls and there is nothing left between them and Camassia. He will see then that we have no other path.'

Tathea threw herself into the work on the Book with even greater dedication. She wrote a translation into Shinabari simultaneously with the Camassian on which she worked with the scribes. As she finished each section, they made a hundred copies.

She still needed Alexius's help. Once every seven or eight days he would come and read what she had written, and argue over ambiguities and meaning.

She had not intended to tell him of her news of Shinabar. It would be unwise. But in the long hours of talking over passions and dreams, she found herself speaking also of the soul sickness of her own people.

It was by now high summer, the wind blew from the sea to the south, massing storm clouds heavy on the horizon. He had commented on it as he came in. The harbour masters would be working hard, rescuing all they could. No one could come or go.

'I'm glad I'm not at sea,' he said, pursing his lips and staring out as the first heavy drops of rain began to fall. 'I'd rather race the worst storm imaginable on land than any at all on the water.'

Another storm tugged at the corner of her memory, greater than this one, filled with a terror which was more than the elements, something personal, and primeval. A shiver of fear ran through her. Without reason, she thought of the barbarians on the borders of Shinabar, and to the east and west of Camassia, and perhaps even to the north also. They, too, were an unknown force, ungoverned and malign. She was glad Alexius was here. If she had to face an enemy, any enemy, she would rather do it beside him than anyone else alive. He would never find reasons to evade the struggle. He would never run away. Sometimes he was less subtle than Ra-Nufis, certainly less imaginative and amusing, less generous than Eleni, less wise than Isadorus. Sometimes he seemed to love the law with too little room for mercy, but there was nothing of the coward in his soul, and nothing of the liar. He could die facing the enemy, and there was a sweetness in that like sunlight.

'We must have courage,' she said as much to herself as to him. 'Without courage we can lose everything. It is the virtue on which all else may depend. It we won't face the Enemy and fight for what is good, everything will be lost, even honour.' She hesitated. 'Even love.'

The rain was beating harder on the windows and high over the City lightning flared. Several seconds later came the crack of thunder, as if the fabric of the sky was being torn apart.

'Do you think the Great Enemy will cover the face of the earth with war and ruin?' he asked, reaching to put his hand on her shoulder. She could feel his fingers through the cloth of her gown. It was as if his strength seeped into her.

'Yes,' she said quietly. 'One day.' She gazed at the sky as again lightning lit it in a wild glare, and the darkness that followed was deeper. The crash of thunder drowned her next words and she had to repeat them. 'I don't know if it will be in our time. Perhaps not, but it will come. It will be the greatest test. There will be no more peace, no more middle ground. We must choose one side or the other.'

He was standing so close beside her she could feel the warmth of his body as they watched the storm. His breath moved the fine hair at her cheek.

'Is there middle ground now?' he asked doubtfully. 'Is there not merely the illusion of it?'

'Yes. "Out of that desolation I will create a new earth, and those who have chosen life I will welcome home at last and they shall be before My face for ever, and they shall know Me as a man knows his father, and his friend." '

He tightened his grip on her shoulder. ' "But before that there will be war and the abomination of destruction," ' he quoted in a whisper. ' "Ruin will cover the face of the earth." It seems there is no way to be there at the victory without fighting the war . . . and perhaps being crippled, exhausted, bereaved . . .'

Lightning and thunder came simultaneously, a blue-white flash that touched every corner of the room, and a noise so violent it drowned out everything else. In the silence afterwards the roar of the rain seemed as nothing.

'How can we endure that, if we don't do it together?' he asked.

She turned to look at him in the yellow lamplight. His eyes were suddenly frighteningly honest, the tenderness in them unconcealed, as if in that instant he newly understood love and felt a bond of courage and vision which would outlast all others. She gazed at him for a wild moment that was sweeter than the touch of lips.

His hand moved from her shoulder to her cheek, so soft she barely felt it.

The rain stopped. The air was cold, as if the Enemy was just beyond the grass, waiting. 'I shall not forget your name.' The words came back to her like the echo of death.

She stepped back, ice knotting inside her. Ice beat against the window. She looked at Alexius's face and saw the same fear, and the same knowledge in his eyes. They had been so close to betraying Eleni – and themselves. The blood was hot in his cheeks. There was no need for words for either of them; words would be clumsy, and make irretrievable what was better merely known, never said.

'We must have courage,' she repeated, lips stiff. It was difficult to breathe. 'And never allow ourselves to forget which army we fight for. It is easy, too easy, to become separated from the—'

'I know,' he interrupted. 'Lost. I . . .' He stopped, uncertain how to go on.

She made herself smile, but there were tears thick in her throat and the ache inside her was almost intolerable. 'I think I can manage the work on my own for a while. You have given it much . . .' The words were stiff, ridiculously formal for the searing intimacy of the emotion which filled her. '. . . Form and logic,' she continued stiltedly, 'and clarity of law. That is what is needed.'

'Of course,' he agreed too quickly. 'Tathea . . .'

She shook her head and turned away. She could not bear him to go. It must be quick.

Perhaps he did it for her, perhaps for himself. She heard the door close and she stood alone and allowed herself to weep as she had not done since she had mourned Habi.

Isadorus saw Tissarel again by chance. He had not intended to, even though he had thought of her often, with memory perhaps softened and lent a gentleness and a truth she had not possessed at the time. He knew it, and had no desire to see her, in case she was far happier than he was. She was intelligent, and certainly she was beautiful. She knew how to please. He smiled self-mockingly at that memory. She would find another lover quickly enough, probably a younger one. She might even marry. He had at least provided her with enough money to do as her heart dictated, not her needs.

He met her in the evening after an excruciating new play. Every virtue had been hammered home like a nail. The wicked were irredeemable, and unexplained. The good were flawless and without humour or humanity. He ached for a little laughter amid all the well-meaning gravity, a little scarlet or even grey to soften the blacks and whites.

They were still at the theatre, attending the celebration after the final act. Barsymet was praising the playwright. But then she had never had much sense of the colour or complexity of life. But she did know her duty, and she was doing it admirably.

Isadorus wandered away, unable to look the playwright in the eye, and found himself almost alone at the top of the long flight of steps that led down to the courtyard. He caught the pale glimpse of a woman's gown.

'I'm sorry,' he apologised, thinking he had interrupted a private moment. He did not intend to leave. They could, if they wished to.

But she did not move, and he looked at her more closely. It was only then that he recognised her with a lurch of familiarity.

'Tissarel?' He wanted to say more, something casual and gracious, but his mind was blank. The great hall full of dignitaries and art lovers disappeared and the memory of her all but drowned him, her nearness, their shared laughter, the hours when even the Empire had not mattered. His mouth was dry. His physical hunger to hold her became a starvation, an aching emptiness which filled his body.

'My lord,' she replied, but she did not bow her head as anyone else would have done. She was just as beautiful as he remembered, the curve of her breast, the long line of her neck, the delicacy of her mouth, the way her hair grew. The man in him could not help seeing it, but it amazed him how trivial that was now. Hundreds of women were beautiful – thousands. One could buy beauty.

'Did you watch the play?' He asked the first thing that came to his tongue, simply for something to break the silence.

'Yes.'

'Did you enjoy it?' Would she tell him the truth? Could she afford to? Who was she here with? Now that he had thought of it, he had to know. Imagination would be worse than reality. And yet he had no right to inquire, and he wished her happiness, even love. But he would have given anything, short of love of the Book, for it to have been with him. But if he gave up honour, there would be nothing for either of them. The knowledge of that was all that kept him from her.

A smile touched her mouth, and her eyes. She was watching him carefully, as intently as he was watching her.

'No,' she answered him. 'It was terrible.' Laughter and tears were in her voice. He could hear them as he could feel them in his own throat. 'One of the actresses is my friend, or I would not have come,' she went on. 'I don't know what on earth I can say to her!'

A wave of relief swept over him. He found himself smiling idioti-cally. 'Say that she acted well,' he replied. 'Anyone who can make those lines remotely human has a touch of genius!'

She laughed, the same rippling, delightful sound it had always been. Time vanished. The past was with them again. Except that now she had no need to pretend. What he saw in her face would be the truth.

'Thank you. I'll tell her you said so,' she answered.

'Don't tell her I said the play was stiff,' he warned. 'That it was dishonest to life, that the characters spoke their thoughts and were never brushed by any of the cravings that move the heart, or the body.' He spoke from his own passion, his voice thick. 'Real virtue springs from conflict and from choices that are so terrible they cost more than you believe you have.' Would she understand? 'Goodness without the temptation to evil is an illusion, as is evil without a knowledge of good.'

'I know.' Her voice was gentle with a new tenderness, one that was not paid for in jewels, but in loneliness. And in that moment, without her finding words to frame it, he knew that their parting had also cost

184

her, not in the cheap physical loss of money or pleasure, but in the tearing of love. All the years he had known her he had taken her for granted, she was someone he had bought, a woman trading in her beauty. Now when it was in so many ways too late, he realised he had purchased nothing. Everything of worth that he had had from her had been a gift. He was ashamed of himself for the meanness of his judgement, and humbled by the grace that had extended to him something he had so little treasured or deserved.

How could he let her know, without misleading her? And he must not do that. He must betray neither of them.

'I wish I had known I loved you when I could still have told you so,' he said quietly. 'Now I cannot.'

She smiled, tears bright in her eyes. 'I know that,' she said softly. 'You don't need to explain.'

Close to them someone laughed, and a man called out a woman's name.

Tissarel turned and walked away. She looked back once, and smiled at him, then disappeared into the crowd.

Isadorus waited for several moments, seizing all the time he could to be alone. When he heard Maximian's footsteps coming across the marble towards him, he was ready to face him.

Alexius returned from the frontier of the Empire physically weary from battle and, far more than that, darkened in spirit by the knowledge of the increasing barbarian threat. There was a new nature to it, a savagery as if there was a force beyond, which was steadily growing, gathering its strength for some terrible end. The armies of the Empire had kept the barbarians at bay, but at a bitter cost. He had seen too many men die, too many friends. He could not help feeling that the light of the Book had something to do with the power of the darkness that was massing on the outer edges of the world.

Such news as filtered through from the south of Shinabar was just as harsh.

He was drawn to see Tathea again with a need so intense he did not even think to resist. He found her walking alone in the cypress garden in the evening light. She came towards him, dark as the trees and with the same fierce, slender grace. Her back was towards the dying sun and he could not read her expression, but she could see his.

'What is it?' she asked as she reached him.

'Is it so plain on my face?' he said ruefully.

'Something you find hard to say!' It was a conclusion not a question. They knew each other sometimes uncomfortably well, their understanding of even the unspoken was too quick.

He turned along the stone path beside her, between the fading scent of thyme and rosemary and the last flowers of autumn.

'The barbarians,' he began, searching for the words to explain the heaviness inside him. 'I feel as if there is a presence of evil greater than merely tribes of ignorant men who own nothing and value nothing. There is a lust to destroy, an intelligence of hate which is more than greed.'

She walked beside him in silence.

He felt foolish in the solitude of this quiet evening. The realities of war belonged to another world, unimaginable here. And yet the shadow of knowledge lay over him and he could not dismiss it.

'Thea?'

She started at the intimate use of her name, and felt a warmth fill her.

'I know,' she answered, her face golden in the light as she stared ahead. 'I have heard news from Shinabar as well. Now when we should be most united, it seems we are full of quarrelling over trivialities. There is a malaise over the land, as if we don't wish to see the truth and have no will left to save ourselves.'

'Do you think we will really fail?' he asked.

'Not individually, no.' Her voice was strong with certainty. ' "But in tribulation he will find his greatest strength and his utmost nobility," she quoted from the Book. ' "When he is persecuted there will be those who will bear it with patience and without hatred or self-pity. There will be those in flight who will return for the weaker and slower, who will comfort the terrified and the grieving, without thought for self. When there is starvation, there will be those who will give their last morsel to save another." '

He listened without interrupting. The light was reddening in the west and the shadow of the cypresses fell black across the path.

' "Where there is tyranny and war," ' she continued, ' "there will be those who will give their own lives for their fellows, and who will die rather than deny the good they believe. They will make even the greatest sacrifice of all, for love of the light they have seen. And in eternity I shall take them to My heart and their joy will be as Mine. They shall see all things, and understand, and be filled with peace which has no end." '

They stood in silence as the fire of the sunset bathed them and the sharp scent of trodden herbs was pungent in the air.

'Why now?' he said at last. 'Is there really another hand in it as well as God's?' He drew in his breath, struggling to clear his thoughts. 'I know the Great Enemy argues in the Book, but is he simply fate, and perversity in things, so that the truth may be stated, or . . .' He stopped. The sky was shot with a splendour of colours so wild and bright it burned against the earth. He was touched with the beginnings of ideas he would have laughed at only months ago, and a terrifying belief.

She gazed at him steadily, without a shadow of evasion, until he felt as if their minds had touched and the separation of their bodies was an illusion. The wind of dusk and the brightness in the air bound them together, it did not come between.

'Oh yes,' she said at last, and there was no wavering in her voice, soft and grave as it was. 'The Great Enemy is as real as God is real. Sometimes I remember him, as if I had once seen him face to face as closely as I see you.'

Everything in him rebelled against the idea. It was imagination! Ghosts in the night! Above all, it was a supernatural excuse for manmade sins. But that was not what she meant, and in his heart he knew it. She was speaking of something as powerful as death, as terrible as the end of all hope, as real as his skin. He had felt it on the barbarian edge.

He fought against knowing it, and did not win. He could never have won, because he could not doubt her. It was in her eyes, her mouth, and the breath on her lips. She had seen the Great Enemy's face as perhaps she had also seen God's.

He was seized with an ice-grip of fear for her. She was soul-rendingly vulnerable. She walked the earth alone, and Asmodeus knew her name, and knew her burden. He would never forget. Every hour of her life he was watching. She carried in her courage and belief, the spark to light the world. If she slipped even once, the darkness would consume her.

In that moment he would have offered his own soul to protect her, anything, everything, to keep her from destruction.

But it was impossible, and he knew it even as the sun slid below the horizon and the salt wind blew in from the sea with the coming night. He forced himself to remember the words of God: 'It takes all that a man has, to the height and breadth and depth of his soul, but it does not require more.'

He held out his hand and she took it for a moment, before letting go and continuing to walk along the path.

Tathea did not relax her work on the Book, going over it again and again to make sure that what she had written was not capable of misinterpretation, that there was no wavering, repetition or ambiguity. She spent much time in deep silence when her soul was still as deep water and a fierce and radiant peace settled within her. A light seemed to flood the pages.

'The creatures of the earth are Mine also,' she wrote in Shinabari. 'They are the workmanship of My hands. In beauty have I formed them, each perfect in its place. Their innocence is blameless before the laws of eternity. They have no sin for which to answer, and in the last day it will be well with them, with every bird that flies, every fish that inhabits the ocean, and every creature that runs or creeps upon the land. Not one of them is hurt without My knowledge, and My grief.

'But I know the end from the beginning, and they shall not perish from My sight. For a space the earth is lent to man, to come under his stewardship, not to be his possession, and he will answer to me for every stick and stone of it, every leaf and flower, and every living thing upon its face, for good and for ill.

'Just as there are those who will ruin and destroy, so there are those who will cherish and make beautiful, those who will love and who will heal, those who will praise, and see My hand in all things.

'All gifts, all wealth, whether it be of goods or of talents, of health or intelligence, of wit or laughter, even of time itself, are a trust, to see whether they are used with generosity or with meanness, with love or without it, with joy and with gratitude and humility, that they return to Me rich with the harvest of sharing. And I will magnify all things to them into time and eternity without end.'

All through the winter news came of the spreading of the Word, and always that it was more and more rapid across the Empire, its strength growing. Men and women in all walks of life were hearing the beauty in the Word, some a faint echo, some a thunder of music that filled their lives. Travellers carried it to the furthest provinces. Even soldiers on the frontiers met those who had heard it and repeated it.

But the incursions by the barbarians were increasing. The news grew worse, especially from the south, and Ra-Nufis warned that the Shinabari will to fight was being eaten away by indulgence and apathy. They were attacked more and more frequently, and with escalating success. There were tales of piracy at sea, traders had been sunk with all hands.

Tathea went to see Isadorus.

'I have come to ask once more for armies to retake Shinabar,' she said steadily, although she had no greater confidence than before, only the passion of urgency within her. 'Civilisation is besieged on all sides, and Shinabar is crumbling beneath a decadent rule imposed by murder. If it falls, as it seems it may, there is no one left to stand against the chaos except Camassia. We shall have to fight one day. Let us do it while we yet have allies, and on our terms, at a time of our choosing, not theirs.'

He did not answer immediately; at least this time he did not refuse without first weighing the judgement.

She knew enough not to press him with too much argument. Let what she had said be sufficient.

Ulciber stepped forward, close to the Emperor's seat. 'My lord, the Lady Ta-Thea's words are wise. Every victory of the barbarians feeds their ambition and gathers them more believers in their eventual conquest. With each raid, more people, more lands are swallowed up.

If we stand idle and allow this, I fear we are not blameless in their loss.'

Isadorus looked at him sharply, but his anger was momentary. 'You are right,' he conceded. 'Peace has become a luxury we can no longer afford. You may have your armies, Tathea. But I will send my own generals to command. The rule of Shinabar will be yours when and if I decide that it will.'

Ulciber looked at Isadorus again. 'The best general is Alexius, my lord,' he said softly. 'You can trust him as no one else, both his skill and his honour. No other man would serve you as well.'

'I know,' Isadorus agreed without looking at him. 'I shall send him.'

It was hers! She had won. She was going back to Shinabar with an army led by Alexius. They would take the Book, and when Thoth-Moara was in her hands again, at peace, with justice accomplished, they would teach the Word to every man and woman in the land. They would begin the rebirth.

'Thank you,' she accepted quietly.

And Ulciber smiled and stepped back.

Chapter Thirteen

Tathea would go with the army. Alexius had accepted command. Whatever reluctance he might have felt at leaving Camassia, and more importantly at leaving Eleni, he subordinated them to the knowledge that it was his duty. Isadorus's words to Tathea had been unyielding, but they all accepted that once the Shinabari were conquered and an alliance with Camassia sealed beyond reneging, the invading army would withdraw and leave Shinabar to Tathea, with possibly no more than a garrison to hold it, and the threat of re-invasion should the peace be broken.

So Tathea would ride with Alexius, and fight beside him. If she were to rule her country, she must be seen to have won it, not been given it after the struggle was over.

Leaving Camassia was difficult. She would miss Isadorus. She did not realise until the moment came how deep their friendship had become.

'Be careful, Tathea,' he said gravely as they stood on the balcony with the panorama of the City spread below them and the warships already gathering in the harbour, dark against the bright water. 'Power is a shadowed thing. We hunger for it, kill for it, and then too often abuse it.'

'I know,' she answered, following his gaze across the roofs, south to the sea, and Shinabar beyond. 'I only want to achieve peace, and the freedom to teach the Book.'

' "Only," ' he sighed. 'And what of others, your ministers and generals? What of their wants? There will always be envy, Tathea, the illusion that the power to control others is real, that we can hold it in our hands, exercise it and not lose ourselves.'

'I shall watch,' she answered him. 'Anyway, I have no choice now. I must go. I have the Book and they are my people.'

'Be careful,' he said again.

Parting from Eleni was even harder. There was a gulf of pain between them, and even though it had never been spoken, they both understood it too clearly to pretend innocence or denial. Neither meant to hurt, and yet the wounds were real.

'I'm sorry,' Tathea said as they stood in the cypress walk among the

190

lilies. 'The gift has cost you more than I thought. I gave you no warning.'

'You think I would have refused it?' There was an edge of challenge in Eleni's voice.

Tathea hesitated. The question she wanted to ask was intrusive, and yet if she did not ask it now, she would have no other chance. They might never meet again like this.

'Would you?' she asked.

Eleni was silent a long time, as if she considered many answers. 'Sometimes I think so,' she said at last. 'But then I would never have been fully myself. And I think I would rather have tasted it, even for a while.'

'A while?' Tathea stared at her, and for the first time read the depth of misery in her eyes.

'I lost it,' Eleni answered the question Tathea could not ask.

Tathea was stunned into silence. A terrible guilt filled her.

Eleni smiled. 'I lost it myself,' she said very quietly. 'You did not take it from me. But I know at last how to earn it back, and I will succeed, not today, not tomorrow, but one day I will.'

Tathea thought of this while she stood in the armourer's workshop. The armourer eyed her sceptically, shaking his head and blowing his breath out through his teeth. He admired the feminine form, indeed he had appreciated its aesthetic qualities since his youth, but he had never made armour for it, even ceremonial, let alone full metal-plated armour for war. She carried a lighter sword than an ordinary legionary, one such as a boy might use to learn, but much sharper.

She stood still, disdaining to look at him. It was his business to make it fit. Let him get on with it. She gazed around at the helmets, greaves, and chest plates hanging on hooks and resting on shelves like grotesquely dismembered parts of long dead warriors. Most of the armour was new, but many pieces bore dents and scars of old battles. Presumably their previous owners were dead, or too crippled to have further use for them.

The armourer clicked his tongue. 'You actually mean to come close to the fighting, lady? Wouldn't you be better as a . . . a figurehead? A mascot, if you like?'

'No, I wouldn't!' she snapped. 'Just make it the same as everyone else's, but the right shape for me. Can't you do that?'

He was insulted. 'There's no armourer in Camassia better than I am. And that means the world!'

'Good! Then I am in the right place. You are kneeling on my foot!'

He moved backwards so hastily that he overbalanced.

She laughed, and he resumed his measuring, without looking up at her face again.

When the time came for the army to embark, it was a bright, sharp day in early autumn, with winter lying ahead of them. It was the only season in which to march and fight in the Shinabari desert. The voyage would take seven days. Time was short. They must conquer before spring brought back the intolerable heat when no army could live in the open.

As Tathea stood on the quayside watching the massed ranks, thousands of men moving like a lava flow towards the boats, carrying their weapons and their bed rolls and rations with a terrible precision, she was gripped with fear for what she had done. She had been so certain of her cause. Now all these countless men were embarking for war. How many of them would return? How many lives would be marred or lost?

Each man had only one life. With his death, for him the world ended. Perhaps it ended for someone else too, someone who loved him and for whom he was unique and immeasurably precious. Perhaps each one had a mother who loved him as she had loved Habi, who had nurtured him and watched him grow, with impatience and love and hope.

The wind was cold off the water. Without realising it, Tathea was hugging her cloak around her. She had disagreed with Alexius as to what sort of cloak she should wear. He had wanted her to wear one in Shinabari blue, to mark her out so he and the other guards and centurions could see where she was and protect her. She had wished to wear red, like the rest of them, so the enemy would not see her as any different.

She wore red.

The enemy! Without even realising it, she had spoken of her own people by that name. There was no enemy in any human terms. And afterwards, would there be a victory, or only degrees of loss?

She was shivering. She should stand straight, like a soldier, not like a woman who needs someone else to shelter her. How could she expect an army to follow her if she stood here shaking? They knew the wind was cold, but they would think she was afraid. And so she was, not of battles or dangers, not of the desert, but of the enormity of what she had done.

She heard Ra-Nufis's voice at her shoulder.

'Two hundred thousand men,' he said softly. 'Not so many when you think of all the might of Shinabar against them, but they are the best. Isadorus has given you the most seasoned of his troops, veterans of the Irria-Kander wars.'

She could not stop shivering. 'What is going to happen, Ra-Nufis? What have we begun?'

There was no hesitation in him, no trepidation. 'A war, Majesty,' he answered. 'And men will fall. There will be the crippled and the blinded and the dead. In all wars there are losses.' His voice dropped and became suddenly more urgent, heavy with tragedy. 'But there are losses in peace too, if that peace is dishonourable. It is just that we do not see them so easily, because the wounds and the deaths are on the inside. It doesn't mean they hurt less, or that the deaths are not real.'

She looked at the men trooping up the ramps and on to the ships. Still they moved with perfect precision, as if there were some silent communication between them, parts of a giant whole. The boats tipped under their weight. The sun shone and glinted on their armour. Upheld spears formed a moving forest, naked as rain. There was no sound but the slurp of water against the quays and the sides of the boats, the sucking back from the shingle and the shuffle of four hundred thousand feet on stone and wood.

'But I asked for this, deliberately,' she answered. 'I made the decision. What if I am wrong? How did I dare do something so monstrous?'

'Then it would be terrible. But you are not wrong.' His voice rang with certainty. 'The barbarian incursions are not your doing, and that is why Isadorus is sending these men. He knows that if we do not make a stand here, then next time, or whatever time it is, it will be harder. If not now, when? When the south of Shinabar falls and they start coming up the coast, sinking our trading vessels? Or when they start taking the desert outposts? Or when the first Shinabari city falls? Or the first ten? Or at the walls of Thoth-Moara? Or—'

'All right!' she cut him off sharply. 'I understand Isadorus. But I am bringing Camassian armies against my own people.'

'Would it be better to stay safely in the City in the Centre of the World and do nothing while Shinabar sinks into apathy and corruption?' he challenged. 'That is a slower death, but it is death just the same. The decision is yours either way, to fight or to stay your hand. That is what it is to be leader, whether you call it general, Isarch or prophet.'

She stood for several moments without answering. She knew the truth of what he said, but it was hard, and in some ways the final loneliness.

He remained a little behind her, sheltering her from the wind with his body.

'Do you want to fight for what is true, so the wisdom and the light can belong to anyone who wants it?' he said with sharp urgency. 'Remember, there is no middle ground. We are either for God, or we are for Asmodeus. We are for the light, the beauty, the good, or we are for darkness, pain and bondage. There is no place between, only the illusion of it, and that too is a creation of the Enemy, the eternal lie, that you can win without battle, reap without cost, triumph without courage or pain.'

She reached and grasped his hand. 'All right . . . I had forgotten for a moment. I understand. I'm ready to go. I don't need to watch here any more.' She turned to look at him. He was slender and very dark here in the sunlight reflected from the water. He was dressed in Camassian armour, but he looked as Shinabari as she did. She smiled at him, holding his fingers more tightly. 'Thank you! You have always been there when I most need you. I hope you always will be.'

'I promise it,' he said fiercely. 'Now more than ever.'

The voyage was remarkably smooth, the wind just sufficient to fill the sails. Tathea spent much time on deck in the lead ship of the armada. It was the first time she had been away from Camassia since she had come from the Lost Lands. She had dreamed of returning to Shinabar, of seeing the cities again, of smelling the desert, seeing a cloudless sky blazing with stars, and smelling the herbs, hearing the silence broken only by the trickling of sand, and feel it sharp against the skin.

Alexius and Ra-Nufis spent many hours together reading and studying the maps of Shinabar and Ra-Nufis's notes about the terrain, the patterns of soft or shifting sand, scree beds, which oasis would have water at this time of the year, and which not. Ra-Nufis also spoke much about reading the weather. The dangers to watch for were sudden winds which could raise the sand and carry it in storms that would blind and choke and drown even an army. The sharp particles carried at whip-like speed would strip the skin from the face.

And there were other things to weigh and learn also, such as the names and strength of all the leaders between where the army landed and Thoth-Moara, who might turn in their favour, who might give information.

Tathea sat beside them and listened. Occasionally she added her own advice, but hers was from memory of six years ago, and she was constantly reminded how much had changed. But how much of it was change, and how much only reality unseen before?

It was strange to hear her own country discussed in this way, people whom she had ruled the greater part of her adult life. Every one of them would have known her name. Most of them would even have seen some representation of her on a coin or medallion, maybe even a painting or statue on the façade of a building. Now here she was speaking of them with a Camassian general as if they were enemies to be ravaged by an army and subjected to an alien occupation.

Often she stood on deck and watched the shifting pattern of light on the sea, brilliant, burning blue, in the distance so dark it was like ink. And as the light and shadows changed and she heard the hiss of water and the creak of wood and the wind in the canvas, she half remembered other voyages, brilliant, wind-washed skies higher and softer than these, shot with a different light. A sense of longing filled her, a loneliness for something ineffably sweet which she had once known – or dreamed. It lay just beyond reaching, aching with a wild and fearful beauty, but always on the edge of her mind, too elusive to touch.

Half the armada landed to the east of the great seaport of Tarra-Ghum, half to the west, disembarking in the water and wading ashore. The heat dried their garments within minutes. Even the leather of armour took no more than an hour. Tathea watched them, phalanx upon phalanx of them, perfectly disciplined to march at the command, ready to attack the city of Tarra-Ghum.

Her throat was dry. Her skin prickled with the heat and she had to narrow her eyes against the glare of it on the pale sand. It was six years since she had been here but it was as if the time between had disappeared in the hard, glittering reality of it. She must be ready too. She must not fail them. She must not fail the God who had entrusted her with the Book, and who had supported and sustained her ever since, laying the hand of peace on her heart.

But now that it was written out in Camassian and Shinabari, was she necessary any longer? She could be killed in battle, and the Book would still go forward. Ra-Nufis could carry it. He loved it enough. That thought rippled through her like ice, even in the Shinabari sun. It was sheer physical fear! She had not realised it so clearly before, but she had assumed that because she was the Keeper of the Book she would be preserved to teach it to her people, but perhaps this was not so.

Alexius was at her elbow. It was time for her to disembark. Aurelian had taken the western half of the armada. She was to go with Alexius to the east. She must march with him, at his side. It was the thought of being less than he believed of her that drove her to move, to pick up her sword and walk down the ramp into the sea without flinching as she sank to the waist and waded ashore.

Rank upon rank the army massed as far as she could see around her. There was a restlessness in them as if the suppressed energy of the days at sea was barely under control. They were hungering to meet the challenge for which they had come. There was a mighty stirring and rustling of movement, the clink of armour, the shuffle of feet.

The sun beat down on them with relentless brilliance. The sooner they were on the move, the better. She turned round to Alexius. She must tell him so.

But Alexius was fifty yards away, speaking to a dozen lieutenants, and even as she watched, the first column moved forward and began the steady, rhythmic march west across the sand, the leaders scarlet-plumed, the sun glinting on bronze and polished leather.

It was time she began to march too. She had chosen to come as a soldier, not a passenger. Alexius would march on foot, as his men did.

There was no horse for her to ride and no men set aside to carry her in a chair. She, of all of them, should be able to abide the heat. Only Ra-Nufis knew it better.

She had gone less than half a mile when he joined her, smiling, glancing around him at the tens of thousands of soldiers like a moving tide darkening the desert's face. He did not ask if he might walk beside her; he simply assumed the duty and behaved as if it were a privilege.

They did not speak. Desert travellers knew well enough that every ounce of strength should be guarded for the physical needs of maintaining an even speed, a pace that was slow enough not to exhaust the muscles but fast enough to reach the desired destination within the second hour after sundown before the real cold settled in. In the summer, the process was reversed. One travelled by night and found shelter within an hour of sunrise, or perished.

Ra-Nufis watched her closely, always ready in case she were exhausted, short of water, hurt, or found her weapon too heavy. To glance sideways and see him, sometimes to meet his eyes and know that he would not leave her, gave her more strength than she could have foreseen. She was able to bear the aching legs, the blistered feet, the weight of her sword, even the heat and glare of the sun she had all but forgotten in her years in Camassia. She had not realised how soft she had grown in the City. If Alexius had not made her work so strenuously in their mock battles she would have fallen by the wayside and been someone's burden by now, carried like a wounded man. Silently she blessed him for that. Her lips were too dry, her breath too like fire in her lungs to say it aloud.

They stopped in a dried-up riverbed an hour after sundown and made camp. Food was sparse, for the land provided no supplement to the rations they carried: dried meat, biscuits, dates and rough wine. It was eaten uncooked to avoid the need for fires, whose flame would be seen at night, its smoke by day. They had seen no travellers, no scouts to report their presence, but it could not be assumed Tarra-Ghum had no knowledge of them. Tathea was offered a little privacy, being the only woman, but there was no extra water for her to wash in. She had to dampen her face with wet hands, and be grateful for sufficient to take the edge from her thirst.

She took off her boots and looked grimly at her blistered feet, unused to hard marching.

'Put salve on them,' the legionary closest to her said sympathetically. 'Else you'll have them septic in a couple of days. Got any?'

'Yes,' she said quickly. 'Thank you.'

'Wrap them in clean cloth,' he added, squinting at her. 'Got that too?'

'Yes. Thank you for the advice.'

'Take it! Get sand in those blisters and you'll have to be carried.'

Carefully, wincing, she obeyed, knowing the truth of what he said. She must not let Alexius down through pride or stupidity.

Sentries were posted and every man slept rolled in his cloak, with his sword by his side. Tathea slept from exhaustion, although she had not expected to. To lie on the bare sand under the desert stars, surrounded by the myriad noises of two hundred thousand men, was a monstrous kind of loneliness. Apart from Ra-Nufis, she was the only one whose native earth this was, and she was not a travelling trader, but an Empress.

She thought of her father. He had been a desert prince. He would have understood this and been at home here. He would have known the great wheel of stars above her and named the brightest. From the stars he would have known where he was, as a mariner does at sea. But he was long since dead, buried in a rock tomb two thousand miles south of where she lay.

They ate again in the morning, then prepared to march, armed and at the ready. By noon they would reach the outskirts of Tarra-Ghum, but surely they would have encountered the enemy before that.

Tathea's back and legs ached appallingly. When she first set out she almost cried out with the pain of making her muscles stretch again. The blisters on her feet stabbed with each step as the thongs of her boots caught them. She was even softer than she had feared. But when Alexius asked her how she was, she gritted her teeth.

'Well, thank you,' she lied.

Ra-Nufis said nothing, but his concerned eye betrayed his knowledge that she was far from as well, or as sanguine, as she said. She was grateful for his silence.

The enemy struck without warning, sweeping in from the northeast, cutting them off from the sea. One moment they seemed alone on the endless waves of sand, the next there was shouting, the clatter of drawn swords, men moving hastily and then a breath-holding stillness before the charge.

The shock of the two armies meeting was a vortex like a whirlpool of the sea. Men were swept off their feet in the torrent of the attack. Dry sand was flung up, sun gleamed on Camassian bronze and Shinabari copper, red and blue plumes were tangled together, bodies and weapons spattered with blood.

Tathea held her sword ready, but all around her remained calm, men waiting, faces set, eyes steady. If they were afraid, they masked it well. There was barely a flicker, a nerve ticking in a cheek, sweat running free on the skin, knuckles white.

The waiting seemed endless. She could taste the salt of sweat when she licked her lips.

Then it came. The order was muffled at first, just a shout. It was a split second before she understood it. The men in front of her surged forward and the legionary captain beside her called something indistinct and tried to push her out of the way.

Someone near her yelled. There was a shock of steel meeting steel, a scream, and the next moment the battle was around her. The tide had switched unexpectedly, and although she had been placed in what was thought to be the safest quarter, it was no longer so. There was a Shinabari soldier in front of her, a spear's length away, an ordinary soldier, such as any one of the many who had served Mon-Allat, lined the streets at his enthronement, cheering, calling his name. He probably had a family in one of the cities or villages she knew.

He raised his sword and swung it. To him she was a Camassian, an invader. She might be unusually dark, but he took her for a boy, not a woman. In a moment he would kill her.

Instinctively she stepped sideways as Alexius had taught her. He moved also. She stepped back, and he lunged forward, off balance. The instant was enough. She struck at his arm, gashing it to the bone.

She had never drawn blood before, not streaming scarlet blood pouring out of a wound. It was terrible, sickening. She saw the horror in his face and froze.

She was knocked so hard from behind she fell forward on to her knees, for a moment unable to draw breath, her chest shot through with pain. Then her arm was grasped and she was yanked to her feet just as a Shinabari spear landed quivering in the ground where she had knelt.

A Camassian soldier, a weathered, grizzled man with a scar across his nose, shouted at her and laughed. Then he swung round and began laying into everything copper that he could see or reach, and a moment later his armour was streaked with his own blood.

There was no time to think. On every side was violence, the din of metal crashing on metal, screams and cries, the stagger and lurch of battle, the burning heat, the stench of blood and sweat and fear.

Tathea fought because she had no choice. It was instinct to swing the sword and to shout with the rest, to attack everything blue, to defend everyone wearing the bronze and red. She wounded and killed men she did not know, and risked her own life to save other strangers because they wore the same uniform she did.

She saw hideous injuries, agony, which would return to haunt her for years to come. She slipped and fell in blood as if in a slaughterhouse. The battle moved one way then another, but gradually she realised they were driving the enemy backwards. More of the bodies on the ground wore blue than red, although in the carnage it was not always easy to tell.

She ached with bruises and cuts but there was no time to think of them, far less to bind them. The Camassians were beginning to re-form their lines to press forward. The years of iron discipline were paying off. Only part of her brain was aware of it, but with a mixture of fierce, physical triumph and bitter emotional shame, she realised that the Shinabari forces had not the courage to face their foe when the few men of the old training, the old valour, were dead. And they had fallen early because their fellows were in disarray, lacking the heart and the faith in themselves and their purpose to stand firm. And so more of them fell than need have, driven by panic and lack of order and skill.

The mangled bodies of the old Guard, fallen in the van of the attack, filled Tathea with horror. Her imagination of the pain choked her with tears that she had no time to shed. Her own men were pressing forward, trampling on the slain, even on the wounded because there was no way to avoid them. Their cries filled her mind, and there was nothing she could do. Alexius would close the victory. Whatever he felt inside, and she could only imagine it, he never lost his mastery of himself or his men. No fear, physical exhaustion or pain, no pity or horror at the butchery deflected him.

By the end of the day it was over. The Shinabari had retreated towards Thoth-Moara, and Alexius had allowed them to take their wounded with them.

'That was merciful,' she said to him as they stood together beyond the encampment and stared in the wild light of sunset over the desolation of the battlefield. Men with torches were moving as far as the eye could see, flashing and glimmering against the sand and the darker mounds of bodies. They were physicians doing what they could for the wounded, ordinary men looking for friends, searching for identification of the dead, carrying water, bandages, blankets, cloaks. There was no time to bury the bodies. Already carrion birds were gathering. The groans of the injured and dying came sharp and desperate in the thin desert air. The smell of slaughter was every-where.

Tathea was too drenched with pity and choking, nauseating horror to be aware of her own physical pain.

'Not mercy,' Alexius said quietly, standing at her elbow. 'I wish I could afford it, but seldom does war allow mercy. Pity for the enemy too often means betrayal of your own who have trusted you. I let them go because I can't look after them or feed them. Also there is the very practical consideration that their wounded will slow them up. They are a civilised people and will not leave them behind, as the barbarians often do.'

She could not comprehend it. 'Just . . . to die? That's . . .' There was no word to describe her horror.

'No. They kill them themselves,' he corrected her. 'They consider it an honourable death.'

She did not answer. It was difficult to think of honour in the same breath as blinding pain, terror, and mangled, dismembered bodies. Honour was an idea; what she had just witnessed was the awful reality.

'Are you hurt?' he asked quietly.

'Hurt?' The question was preposterous. Every muscle burned, her flesh was tender everywhere with bruises, cuts, and blisters. 'No.' She was not wounded, not seriously. 'I shall never be the same again,' she added after a moment. 'I can't see anything but agony and death everywhere I look.'

He did not move to touch her, although he was so close. Too many eyes might be watching. He was the commander of this entire force, and she must maintain a dignity above the need for comfort.

'Nobody can know war who has not seen it,' he said. 'We use the word with no concept of what it means.'

'Is it always like this?'

'No, but the differences are trivial. It always has agony, loss, terror, dirt and exhaustion.'

'Why do we do it?'

He laughed abruptly, a sound which carried a world of pain. 'Do you want to go back?'

She did not answer. At this moment all she wanted was to sleep, and wake up in the palace of Camassia, warm and quiet and clean, to have people about her who were uninjured, going about their ordinary, mundane jobs in safety. She wanted not to be guilty of anyone else's pain. She wanted not even to know about it, far less be responsible and have to face it again tomorrow.

But she could not tell him that. He had seen it all before. He bore the scars of old wounds on his arms and legs, and one across his chest which she had seen when he had stripped after one of their lessons. He had not run away. He did not enjoy battle, but neither did he evade it.

'Doubts?' he said gently. It was almost dark. The sun in the west was low, casting red light across the sand and blackening the shadows. The wind was already cool. Now he did put his hand over hers. 'Even the dullest of us have doubts when we see what it costs.' His voice came out of the darkness softly. 'There's no man fit to command who doesn't hate the aftermath of a battle, won or lost, who doesn't wonder and question whether he could have done it better, whether he should have done it at all.'

She gripped his fingers tightly, feeling the blisters and the blood on them. 'And what does he answer?'

He did not hesitate. 'There are some things worth fighting for, and some things it is better to die fighting against than to submit to. There are prices of the soul, as well as of the body. He needs to weigh his cause with great care, and then decide.'

'Even all this loss?' She looked towards the field she could no longer see except for the moving torches, but she could hear the cries and smell the blood.

'Have you seen the slow death of a nation enslaved, a people losing their souls to corruption and tyranny?' he asked her. 'Or a culture with all its beauty suffocated, people destroyed by ignorance and perverted by lies until their struggle to survive draws them to use the weapons of terrorism and they become what they once fought against?'

There was no answer. If Ra-Nufis was right, that very tragedy was what she was about to see, or at least its beginning.

They questioned the Shinabari prisoners they took but learned little of tactical value except that the barbarian incursions to the south were even more serious than Ra-Nufis had known.

Alexius sent their own wounded back to the ships which were standing offshore, and ordered a quarter of the remaining troops to take and hold Tarra-Ghum, now all but defenceless. The rest of them met up with the other wing, which had landed to the west and began a forced march across the desert inland, towards Thoth-Moara, guided by Ra-Nufis.

Because of the terrain they could not avoid inhabited areas, as they would have done in a more temperate climate. They had to have water, and every oasis was inhabited. They met no resistance. It would have been futile, a few hundred unarmed villagers against the military might of Camassia. But the people anyway had no heart to fight and no will to defend something in which their belief had faded. Their houses were shabby and neglected, the streets were in need of repair.

Tathea stared at the first oasis they came to with a burning shame. She saw in Ra-Nufis's face a reflection of his understanding. He knew the confusion inside her, the anger that this should have happened to her own people who belonged to the oldest and once the proudest of all nations. Shinabari military power had ruled the world two hundred years ago, not long in their history. Their architecture was the inspiration for all other great cities from Irria-Kand to Tirilis. Their literature was translated into a score of other languages. Their artefacts were collected by lovers of beauty in every land. Scholars struggled to master their language, it was the tongue of philosophy and science as well as of literature and imagination. Now the people stood silently, helpless and sullen while a Camassian army passed by, not even considering the inhabitants worth imprisoning for they posed no danger.

Tathea stared at them in the harsh sun, and wondered whether it was her fault because she had abandoned them to the usurpers. If she had had the political skill to survive, would any of this have happened? Or had it begun long before? Was it she and Mon-Allat? Maybe it was all of Shinabar? Perhaps the whole nation was weary. This was not a venerable old age, worthy of respect and love, gratitude for the achievements of the past but the degeneration of those who no longer care.

They left the oasis in the morning. Tathea walked alone although she was surrounded by a hundred and fifty thousand marching men, moving inexorably towards the next great city, and eventually to Thoth-Moara itself. She must bring the Book to Shinabar, as she had brought it to Camassia. The difference was that the Shinabarians needed it as a desert traveller needs water. It would bring life to a soul that was dying.

The next battle was small, little more than a skirmish. Half a dozen men were killed, and some score or so seriously wounded. It seemed almost too easy.

Complacent with victory, a captain who had long served with Alexius posted an inadequate watch. It was a careless error, and his men paid for it dearly. A dozen lives were lost.

Tathea heard the men talking about it. Alexius did not tell her himself, but she saw his face, eyes distant, mouth tight with distress. He stood apart for a long time, speaking to no one unless he had to, and then his answers were curt. There was a hush over the heart of the camp as they waited to see what he would do. The captain was a friend. They had served together in the great forests of the barbarian frontier, marched through the snows, shared food and blankets, and guarded each other's sleep. They had seen the vast wind and storm-swept plains of Irria-Kand and faced the enemy who slaughtered their own wounded.

Tathea watched him and ached to help, but she knew that even to approach him would intrude. She had no part in his decision. She could give him nothing except the discretion of silence and the understanding that his pain had to be borne alone.

He made the only decision he could, to serve the law. White-faced and with a breaking voice, he ordered the captain's execution. It was done immediately and in silence, the witnesses watching with bent heads. He was buried in the sand and Alexius ordered that the marker should carry his name and rank and that he fell in the course of duty, nothing more.

That night they camped close to an oasis again. After sunset Alexius climbed the high, sharp escarpment to the west and watched the full moon rise over the desert.

Tathea debated with herself whether to go after him or not. Her whole body ached with weariness after the day's march and her feet were agony. She unwound the bandages and redressed them. She would dearly like to have bathed in the cool water under the shade of the trees, then wrapped herself up in her cloak beside one of the fires. She longed for the oblivion of sleep, when she would not have to think of Shinabar as she saw it now, so different from her dreams. It was shabby and tired. Only the desert itself still held the same beauty as before, perhaps even sharper because it cradled such despair.

But her hurt, duller and less personal than Alexius's, filled with uncertainty and fear of guilt, hungered for human sharing. To stand beside him, even without words, would be better than to be alone.

She started to walk up the scree slope, climbing slowly, her feet slipping, bruising themselves against the stones. The moonlight was brilliant. The air glowed with a radiance it held nowhere else, except perhaps across ice.

She saw his dark figure ahead of her. He had his back to her, staring out across the milk-pale sea of sand. Should she go to him, or would it be clumsy, breaking the trust they had, demonstrating that she did not understand after all? But if she did not go, it would seem as if she did not know his pain and believe in him, or as if she was too consumed by her own exhaustion and horror to care.

Her feet had made no sound and no mark on the slithering sand, but as she neared him he turned and looked towards her.

She felt a moment's sickening awareness of having committed herself. It was too late now to turn back. She would have to speak, and if her words were clumsy, they could break something of infinite value between them.

'Is something wrong?' His voice came quietly out of the night. He had his back to the moon and she could not see his face, only the outline of his head against the pale wash of the sky.

'No,' she answered. 'I only came because . . .' What could she say without intruding?

The silence prickled. He waited for her to finish.

'I had to see if you wanted not to be alone.' If grace was impossible, at least let her be honest. 'I think if I had had to make your decision, I would want to be able to look in your face and know you understood, that you were aware of my pain. Not necessarily to say so. Some things cannot be said. Just to be there, perhaps only for a moment. Some watches should be kept in silence, but not necessarily alone.'

His body relaxed, there was an easing of the shoulders. 'I knew him for twenty years.' His voice was very quiet and there was a crack in it, as if he were on the edge of weeping. 'When he was an old man, he wanted to have a garden . . . and a dog.' He turned away towards the radiance of the moon, and she did not look at him.

The minutes slipped by. The night wind stirred little flurries of sand. It was growing colder.

'Too many people sacrifice all they have for our safety and our peace,' she said at last. 'Most of us have no idea of the reality of it. I

203

wonder if there would be any wars if we did.'

'Perhaps not,' he answered. 'Knowledge might drain all our courage from us. But I would like to think not. God has told us it will be as hard as we can bear. Should we ask for less, and still expect to gain the glory at the end?' He put his arm round her, holding her by his side. 'We must bear each other up. Tell each other the truth . . . only ever the truth.'

The watch fires were red below them, scattered across the desert floor. She was glad of his body's warmth, even in the shelter of the giant slabs of rock crowning the escarpment.

'Have I done the right thing?' she said quietly. 'Would you tell me the truth about that? Should I have come to Shinabar at this cost? How many men are dead already?'

'There are bigger wars than this.' His voice was hardly louder than the wind over the sand. 'Wars of the soul. Death is neither here nor there to Asmodeus. Damnation is victory for him. Every sin or ugliness wounds us.'

She leaned even closer to him. 'And if I kill my enemy, the soldier who comes against me, because I have invaded his land, is that my victory or Asmodeus's?'

'If you do it with pleasure, it is Asmodeus's,' he answered. 'If you do it with pain, because the battle is forced upon you, it is yours. Suffering, fear, death are all the fortunes of war. Sometimes the only alternative is surrender.' He hesitated a moment, then went on, 'But I have come to hate war more and more as I grow older. I'd rather fight the battles of the spirit. Perhaps that is simply because I see the casualties less clearly. Corruption seems more like a disease than an injury. It is so much slower, it gives the illusion it can be stopped with less cost.'

'It is not an illusion!' she answered urgently. 'With the Book we can begin again. We can start to recover the honour and the strength we used to have. We can spread the truth and learn to live it.'

He laughed faintly. 'With the Book we could stop all wars, feed the hungry, teach the ignorant, heal the world! But will we?'

'I don't know.'

'I'm not sure if it is meant for worlds, Thea. I think that perhaps it is meant for individuals. Maybe God sees us one by one.'

She knew he was thinking of his friend that he had condemned today. Alexius saw his men not as an army, but each as a man like himself, each with one life, and one death. She could not have loved him so much had he not.

She rested her head against his shoulder. 'You are right. He knows us one by one, each by name, and each as precious as if there was no other. That is what love is. It is not a collective thing.'

He turned and looked at her, smiling a little. Her hair blew across her face, and he brushed it aside with his fingers. They were cool on her skin, but so gentle she barely felt him.

She had healed some of his hurt. He did not say so but it was in his touch. She did not need words, it was enough to know.

He bent his head and she raised her lips to his. The kiss was long and sweet with all the ache of waiting. His body was warm, and she was sharply aware of his strength.

She could smell his skin, his hair, the leather of his armour . . . and the bitter herbs of the desert, and the smoke of the watch fires in the wind. She was dizzy with the hunger to cling to him, to let passion and need be fulfilled.

Their lips parted and he looked into her eyes. She knew his longing was as great, the pain and the tenderness as soul-deep as hers. She also saw a shadow, the dark knowledge of the price.

She stepped back, shaking, pulling her arms from his, and it was like tearing the flesh. She did not say anything. She looked at him steadily for moments, her throat aching, the blood beating in her pulses, then she turned and walked away down the scree slope, back towards her place in the camp where her blanket was rolled by the fire. She might not sleep tonight, but at least she would not lie awake for ever, knowing she had stepped into the abyss.

The following morning they continued their march across the desert towards Thoth-Moara.. She saw Alexius only briefly and in the company of others. She was not uncomfortable with him. His knowledge had been the same as hers and there was no conflict, no failure of understanding.

It was three days later when they were travelling across a shallow range of hills, marching in close order with scouts on either wing, that Tathea encountered the old man. It was early in the morning, before they broke camp, and he came out of the dawn. She was alone by the rock pool in one of the few brief times she was granted privacy, the only concession to her gender. When she looked up he was walking towards her across the sand, a black figure with a halo of thin white hair streaming behind him, as if there was a high wind, although the air was motionless.

She rose to her feet to face him, her hand on her sword hilt.

But as he came closer he brought with him a great peace. His features were beautiful. His skin was darkened by the sun, but his eyes were wide and blue, and gentle as the sky. There was power in the curve of his nose and tenderness in the delicacy of his lips. She was not even sure if he was Shinabari, he was unlike anyone she had seen before.

'Who are you?' she asked, letting the sword go.

'My name is Iszamber,' he answered her, stopping a few feet away.

He was dressed in desert robes of faded duns and creams with a sash of opalescent turquoise, and there were sandals on his feet, worn as with much travel.

She thought of offering him food and water, but she knew he had no need of her help in anything. It was in his face, in the way he stood. This was his home, she was the guest, perhaps the intruder.

'Be at peace, Ta-Thea,' he said gently.

She was surprised. 'You know me?'

'I know all things that matter,' he replied with the ghost of a smile. His eyes did not waver from hers. 'I know that you sought the truth from the beginning of the world, and that you carry it with you. You would give it to all men, but you cannot.'

She drew breath to argue, but his look silenced her.

'You will speak all your heart in Shinabar, tell them all you know, but they will not hear you.' Pity tugged at his lips. 'Camassia has listened, and will remember for a space. It is a great nation, and will flourish in splendour over the earth. Its armies will conquer, its laws will prevail and its arts and inventions will enlarge the days of its people. But it, too, will fade, and in the end be consumed, and the light will flicker and then dim, until in the last nothing but darkness of the soul is left.'

She wanted to stop him. How could a man with such beauty in his face deny all hope even before it was born? She searched in vain for evil in his eyes.

He smiled at her and it was sweeter than the rising sun.

'In the days before the end,' he said softly, 'when the great darkness covers the earth and the nations sink in ruin and despair, when civilisation crumbles and is consumed in the last war, then the Island at the Edge of the World will still stand, and hold the light of the Word of God above the tumult and the dying.'

He held up his hand, as if to still her from interruption, and yet it was also like a sign, as if he were making a covenant, or keeping one.

'In a tower above the sea, eleven believers will keep the truth in heart and mind and deed. Sometimes they will stumble, they will ache and they will grieve, but they will never fall. From now until the end comes, they will not be less than their calling, and the end of all things will find them prepared. It is the promise of God.' He lowered his hand slowly, then turned and walked away into the sunrise, leaving her alone on the sand, her heart filled with the memory of another sage and another time when the wind across the sand had carried the scent not of bitter herbs but of sea pinks and wild lupins.

Chapter Fourteen

As they emerged from the low line of the hills, they were ambushed, not from the gullies as they expected but from a shallow riverbed invisible even from a few hundred yards away. The Shinabari knew how to mask themselves wearing grey and dun-coloured clothing, and they were indistinguishable from the light and shadows on the sand. The fighting was hard and violent, the losses severe on both sides. But the Camassians won because their discipline and morale were better, and when sorely pressed the Shinabari general made a tactical error; he failed to anticipate the regrouping of Camassian forces, and he left his charge too late.

By sundown Tathea once again looked over a blood-soaked field, littered with the wounded and dead, but this time the Shinabari forces had not retreated far and their camp was still in sight. There was nowhere for them to go, except to retreat towards Thoth-Moara.

Ra-Nufis came to stand beside her. She noticed with concern that he was limping. She glanced down at his roughly bandaged leg.

'It's nothing,' he dismissed it. 'Only a cut.' He looked at her closely.

She smiled at him. 'A few bruises. I shall be black and blue by morning.' She turned to stare across the desert again, towards the Shinabari camp dark on the horizon. 'They'll raise more soldiers from the towns, won't they,' she said. It was a statement not a question. She was voicing her anxiety simply to share it.

'Yes,' he replied gravely. 'But they'll be raw, and with no discipline and very little spirit.' His voice was heavy. 'They'll be slaughtered when they hit the battlefield, because they are ignorant of challenge or struggle. Years of over-protection have done that to them.'

She did not answer for several minutes. It was bitter knowledge. She gestured towards the Shinabari camp. 'Doesn't he know that?'

'Probably,' Ra-Nufis replied. 'Perhaps it has been so gradual it has passed him by. Sometimes one does not see such a decline. There is no steepness in the stairs to hell.'

She looked at him quickly. 'Where's Alexius?'

He pointed behind him to the left.

She thanked him and walked through the groups of soldiers scattered on the sand, close in groups around fires, huddled under blankets and with cloaks pulled tight round their shoulders. Alexius looked up as she came within the circle of the firelight. His face softened when he recognised her and he made a gesture of invitation for her to sit.

She accepted, glad of the warmth. She had not realised how sharp the air was already, and it was barely dark.

He waited for her to speak, sensing the burden in her.

'Ra-Nufis says the new men they'll get will be so callow they'll be slaughtered without even knowing how to fight,' she said quietly, not meeting his eyes. She hated having to admit this in front of a Camassian. These were her own people she was speaking of. She should have defended them, or if she could not then she should at least have kept silent about their weaknesses, but circumstances did not allow, and she resented that.

She looked up at Alexius. 'Do we have to slaughter them?'

'Not if they surrender,' he answered her. 'I've spoken to some of the prisoners we've taken. The general is Sol-Nahidri.'

She nodded. He had been one of Mon-Allat's best military leaders. Hem-Shash, realising the country's peril, had obviously had the sense to recall him. He must be over sixty. He had made his name in the great campaigns in the time of Mon-Allat's father. He was a man scarred and grown grey in desert fighting. The tactical error in the battle today would be his subordinate's, not his, but the whole army would pay the price.

'What else did the prisoners say?' she asked him.

'Not much. They are frightened and confused.' She heard the pity for them in his voice. Could he imagine the thoughts whirling in the heads of soldiers who had never tasted real defeat before, whose country had not felt the tread of a conqueror's foot in a thousand years? They still could not grasp that it was real, and that they would not awaken in an hour and discover it was merely the product of too rich a meal or an uncomfortable bed.

She looked down at her hands. 'What about the next battle?'

He was watching her. 'It will be bigger than this, and far worse. There could be ten thousand dead. God knows how many injured or maimed. Why do you ask? Do you want to turn back?' In the firelight there was no acceptance in his eyes of such a possibility.

'No.' She stared at him. 'But why do we have to fight a battle, all that rage and terror and pain, in a gesture that will make no difference to the outcome? We will still conquer, only there will be fewer left alive to start to rebuild.'

'Perhaps.'

'Why perhaps?' she said sharply, leaning forward. 'Of course!'

'Not of course,' he answered gravely. 'Surrender and defeat are not the same. Maybe on the day it seems like it, but a beaten people are different to govern from one that has yielded before it had to, and has kept its legions and its weaponry intact, even its chain of command.' He leaned fractionally towards her. One of the men put another piece of palm wood on the fire. 'You must look further than the bloodshed of the day, Thea. There are all the tomorrows to think of as well. If you are to govern Shinabar afterwards, you must make them believe you have both the right and the ability to do it. One sign of weakness, and someone will rise against you.'

She shivered. 'And if I kill ten thousand men who did not have to die, who will love me for that? Apart from the question, can I do it, and should I?'

'Sometimes it is necessary.'

She stood up quickly, holding her cloak round her, and turned away.

'Do you want to have to fight it all over again in another year or two?' he asked tartly. 'How many lives will that cost? Even presuming you win?'

She looked back at him slowly. His face was shadowed red in the light of the flames from the new wood, but she could see his eyes quite clearly. He was right, and they both knew it.

'I have sent a message to Sol-Nahidri.' He smiled slightly, little more than a softening of his mouth. 'But I doubt he will come. He knows even better than you what the battle will cost and he would avoid it if he believed he could.'

'Did you say that I was with you?' she asked curiously.

'No. But he will know that.'

That had not occurred to her, but of course he would.

'Sit down and eat,' he offered. 'The answer will come soon enough.'

She obeyed, but she was restless, starting at every footstep, turning to watch every shadow that passed, waiting.

'Why doesn't he answer?' she said, standing up to stretch her legs, unable to sit any longer. 'Are you sure the messenger got through?'

'He will talk over with his commanders what to say before he replies,' he explained. 'Just as you and I are talking.'

'You haven't asked me what to say!' she challenged.

He smiled broadly. 'Are you going forward, or back?'

'Forward! You . . .' She let out her breath in a sigh and a reluctant smile in return. 'Yes, all right.'

The answer came after midnight. Sol-Nahidri would meet them by the standing stone between the two camps. Two men should come from either side, unarmed.

The moon was high in the unclouded desert sky and they needed no torches. Their feet made no sound on the slithering sand.

Sol-Nahidri was older than Tathea remembered, and she realised with a jolt that it was eight years since she had seen him. He was greyer, the lines in his face deeper and he walked with a slight limp. Although Alexius was the general, it was at Tathea he stared when they stood a few yards apart, hands at their sides, cloaks wrapped close against the cold.

'I did not think when we last parted that when I met you again it would be on the battlefield, my lady, and beside a Camassian general,' he said grimly.

'Had I been Empress, and not an exile and a widow, you would not have.' As soon as the words were out, she despised herself for having said them. Vengeance was not the only reason she had come. She saw the bitterness in his face, and understood it was already too late to repair what he thought of her. 'If I could have come in peace, I would have.'

'So you come in war?' His grizzled face was bleak with contempt and he gestured with a heavy arm to the watch fires to north and south of them, and the sleeping legions of men darkening the sand in their tens of thousands.

This was not how she had meant it to be. What could she say now to retrieve anything?

'I came to return us to the way we used to be, to the honour and the labour and the justice we once had—'

'Under your rule?' he cut across her, his brows raised sarcastically.

'No,' she answered flatly. 'Perhaps we have not had these things in twenty years. They do not come without going back again to the principles we used to cherish, and to an understanding of paying for what we want, and labouring to build it.'

'And you are going to teach us that, those of us who are left alive?' he inquired cuttingly.

Now she was equally angry. 'Yes, I am! And there will be more killing only if you are bent upon it! We do not outnumber you, but our weapons are stronger and our men are better disciplined and have the heart and the courage to fight.'

'*Our* men?' He raised his voice now, all but shouting at her. 'Since when were Camassians "yours"?'

'Since you chose to let your own land slip into tyranny, idleness and self-pity!' she snapped back. 'There is no innate virtue in being born in any one place rather than another! Worth lies in what you are willing to fight for and believe in, what you do, not where you do it!'

Now his voice was ice-cold. 'Perhaps to you, my lady. To me, and to all my army, our land, our culture, and our people are dear, and we will lay down our lives to defend them if you force us to it.'

'Then tomorrow there will be ten thousand men dead who are alive tonight,' Alexius put in, his voice tight with the pain of having failed, even though he had expected no less.

'So be it!' Sol-Nahidri replied. 'But believe me, more of them will be Camassian than Shinabari!' And he turned on his heel and left, striding back over the hard sand in the moonlight.

The following morning, just before dawn, the Shinabari attacked. The battle raged all day and into the darkness, and with the following sunrise resumed again. Tathea fought side by side with other soldiers. They protected her perhaps more than they would a man, but in the hot blood of conflict with its roar and clash, the bruising weight of blows, the pain and the fear, and above it all the anger, she slew as many as those around her. That she was less injured than some was only in part due to their loyalty to her; mostly it was the fortunes of war.

By noon of the second day the field as far as the eye stretched was darkened with bodies living and dead, and both sides were too exhausted to struggle any further. Sol-Nahidri was forced to capitulate. His losses were enormous. The ten thousand Camassian dead were eclipsed by the slaughter of Shinabari, many of them young men force-marched from towns, soft and unused to the sword. Their fathers had learned in a harder school, but these had not known any reason to push themselves beyond the comfortable.

Tathea stood among the fallen with Alexius beside her, and gazed on a charnel house. Her body ached till every movement was pain. Her skin was raw with sweat and dried blood. Her leather armour was heavy and suffocatingly hot. She was gashed and bruised and filthy. The tears ran down her face and she could not stop them.

At her feet a Shinabari youth lay grotesque, one arm hacked off, the ground around him dark and stiff with blood. He looked no more than a boy, smooth-skinned, little muscle on his body. He was only a few years older than Habi would have been. She saw his hands were blistered where they held the unaccustomed weapon.

'He died without even having measured himself against life.' Her voice cracked as she spoke, drowned in tears. 'God knows how many more. If this is victory, what can defeat be?'

Alexius put his arm round her and pulled her gently closer to him.

'Having to do it again tomorrow,' he answered her. 'It is easy to say fight, until you see the reality. But there are some things worth paying even this much for.'

'Are there?' she questioned with terrible doubt. 'Is this not the Enemy's work . . . here?'

His arm was tight, holding her close to his body. 'This is the ruin of flesh.' He spoke every word with a terrible gravity. 'This war is only a shadow of the real war, which is for the ruin of souls. God can raise these men again, more perfect than they were before, with bodies that never corrupt. But even God cannot recreate a soul that sees light and darkness, and chooses darkness. You taught me that yourself.'

She put her arm round his waist. 'And what have we chosen . . . creating this?' she whispered.

The first carrion birds were wheeling overhead, dipping lower with each turn.

'A bulwark against the barbarian,' he replied. 'A chance to begin again, with the Book to guide us.'

She did not tell him what the old man in the desert had said. The Book had been given to her to teach all people, especially her own. She stood beside him in silence, the heat burning her skin. There was much to do, and she should go and start it, so should he, but these few moments of respite, of being at one in the enormity of emotion, was better than rest, sweeter than clean water, and necessary to make the burden bearable.

Tathea entered Thoth-Moara at the head of a triumphal army. Alexius had asked her if she wanted to ride. It would be more fitting for the Empress. She thought about it and weighed her decision with difficulty. She remembered her first sight of Isadorus on his white charger in the City in the Centre of the World, and the awe that had rippled through the crowds as he passed. Even she had felt something of it, and been sharply aware of his power. And it was the Shinabari custom to ride.

But riding would separate her from the rest of the army, the men who had fought their way from the sea on foot. No horse had carried her that distance. She had walked, as they had, slept on the ground, fought every battle, carried her own blanket and sword. Her armour was chipped and dented from use, the leather stained with blood. Her feet were bandaged still. This was not a ceremonial parade, it was the final seal of a conquering army as it took the capital city of a crumbling empire, defeated on the field.

She would march in on foot, a soldier among soldiers. She had earned the right to do that, and it would be well for Thoth-Moara not to forget it.

So wearing her gashed and blood-marked armour, her feet blistered and her legs aching, carrying her sword at her side, she walked at the front of the massed columns of the legions, but bareheaded, so she would be recognised.

They came in by the North Gate, hewn out of rose-pink sandstone, towering twice the height of the walls, and wide enough for five chariots to ride abreast. In the days of the great Isarchs it would have been defended to the last, even with enemy armies at the door. But now the people had no heart to pursue a lost cause, and certainly no will or courage to defend Thoth-Moara street by street, house by house. They stood lining the way, faces sullen, eyes angry or downcast, silent not out of respect but from fear. It was in the lines of their bodies and the way the women kept their children close to them and the men stood open-handed, as if to show themselves weaponless.

The city itself was as she remembered it, vast with soaring buildings, great flights of shallow steps one could have ridden a horse up, monolithic pillars and slabs, carvings of men and beasts twice life size, pictures in exquisite bas-relief. But it was somehow shabbier, dustier, as if those who had once loved it had grown weary and become indifferent.

It was not the triumphal procession she had once dreamed of. There was no sense of glory, no colour but the scarlet of plumes and cloaks. There were no trumpets, no cheering, just the tramp of tens of thousands of weary, aching feet moving in perfect unison.

Afterward some of the legions peeled off to various quarters of the city to make sure there was no resistance, and to find food and billets for the men. They were now an army of occupation. There were a myriad tasks to be completed; the immediate needs were only the beginning. Over time there would be a whole new administration to institute; stragglers from the defeated army to find and if necessary disarm, even imprison if they were disposed to continue to struggle in guerrilla fashion. This was only Thoth-Moara, there might be other armed factions, militia or renegade troops in the other major cities to the south who would not capitulate.

Tathea entered the palace with Alexius beside her and a thousand men behind. The great walls soared above the courtyards and fountains in cool marble and granite with a familiarity that brought her a sudden thrust of pain. The years of exile vanished as if she had left only yesterday. She forgot her beaten and bloody armour and the sword at her side. She could have been wearing purple silk as she walked under the great portal and through the lily-carved pillars.

On either side of her, copper-helmeted guards slowly lowered their spears in recognition. They wore white linen and ceremonial armour. They kept their eyes down, but there was a sharp jerk of the head as they saw Alexius's Camassian helmet with its scarlet plume, even though he carried it in his hand. The air was cool after the blistering sun and the unsheltered heat of the desert, but not even the music of falling water or the smell of damp stone and flowers could hide the tension.

In the great hall of audience Tathea stopped and gazed around her. The room was three hundred feet long, and almost as wide. The ceiling, forty feet high, was supported by immense columns hewn out of stone and carved with scenes from two thousand years of Shinabari history. But it was different from her memory of it. She stood motionless, trying to discover what had changed. The steps at the far end were the same, the great twin lapis thrones, the alabaster dogs on either side with their proud heads and pricked ears, the blue silk curtains that moved with every breath, billowing like clouds.

Then she noticed that the standing torch brackets were gold. In Mon-Allat's day they had been copper. Now there was gold everywhere, not only the torch brackets but in collars round the dogs' necks, on the clawed feet of the thrones. The anklets round the servants' legs were gold, even on the rings and hinges of the sandalwood chests by the east and west walls. Hem-Shash had not spared himself any luxury.

Alexius was staring around him. There was awe in his face as he took in the sheer scale of Shinabari magnificence, the splendour of millennia of power, the gathered treasures of the earth. It displayed the arrogance of those who never conceived that their rule could end. It made Imperial Camassia seem very new, very raw.

One of the servants moved forward nervously. He ignored Alexius and faced Tathea, very slowly sinking to his knees. It was a deliberate gesture of submission.

'Where is Hem-Shash?' she asked.

'Gone, Majesty,' he said so quietly she barely heard him. It was a moment before she realised he was terrified. He expected to be murdered.

'If you do as you are told, you have no need to fear me,' she said coolly. 'When did he go?'

'Yesterday, Majesty.'

'Where to?' It was probably a pointless question. Hem-Shash would be a fool if he had told anyone, and this man had no cause to repeat it.

'South, Majesty, that is all I know.' He waited with head bowed.

'Get up,' she ordered. 'Have rooms made ready, and food, water, clean clothes.

'Yes, Majesty.' The man jerked to stand upright then hurried away, stumbling in his fear and relief.

Tathea looked again around the huge, vacant hall and some glimpse reached her of the enormity of the task ahead in rebuilding this crumbling nation into what she would have it be. How could she satisfy even the simple needs – feeding and keeping order among a race which had not only been conquered by foreigners but had long since been defeated by its own apathy?

Instinctively she looked at Alexius.

He smiled back briefly, but it was not much more than a softening of the eyes. He had completed his part. Government was hers. She had begged for it, persuaded Isadorus to help her. She had marched across the desert, killed and conquered for it. Now it was in her hand.

Tathea had Hem-Shash's belongings removed and replaced with new items she chose. Everything she owned she had left in Camassia, except the small lapis tortoise. The only thing that hurt her to leave behind was the little black and white cat, which she had left with Isadorus. It would have been impossible to bring it.

She walked through the once familiar palace. There seemed little of Mon-Allat's left unchanged. She stood in the rooms where she had come twenty years ago as a bride, then lived as Empress. Every one was crowded with memories, some happy, too many now touched with a sadness as she realised how little she had understood. She seemed to her wiser self to have been so blind, so shallow of perception. And yet she could feel pity for the person she had been, and for those who had shared her ignorance.

Too many of them were dead now: servants whom she should have regarded as friends, guards who had pledged to give their lives to protect her, never believing they would have to. But how many of those she had regarded as friends had been among the assassins, or allies of the assassins, willing to follow the nearest paymaster?

She stood in the blue courtyard by the lily pool where the water ran down the walls in a smooth sheet, the sunlight from above shining on the mosaic-like jewels.

How much should she forgive? How much dared she? Would mercy be seen as weakness? If only Kol-Shamisha were alive to advise her. She did not know which of the old ministers from the past she could trust. She could not even consider those who had sided with the new tyranny, either in act or in sympathy. Those who had been loyal to Mon-Allat must have lacked perception, judgement, or they would have seen the rebellion before it happened, and have offered warning.

Or perhaps they had, and Mon-Allat had not listened.

She ordered a new room furnished for her. She would not return to her old one; she would never go into it again. She commanded masons to seal the room which had been Habi's. Let it rest in peace, and silence. She could not bear to go into it, and no one else should enter it as if nothing had happened there. Servants could have her room, and Mon-Allat's, unless they were afraid to occupy them. If they were, then let those remain empty also.

A superficial order was imposed on the city within days. The Camassian army patrolled the streets but the people showed little heart to fight. A few youths caused the occasional scuffle, and were subdued. No one was killed.

Ra-Nufis was invaluable. He brought word to Tathea daily, advice, ideas, news of people and events which each time proved accurate. He told her which governors and ministers in each province were loyal to the old regime and the principles of the past, and which she should not trust. As the days went by, she began fully to appreciate the magnificent work he had accomplished in the years of her absence. She relied on his judgement as she could no one else's.

He stood beside her not only as a minister in government and a disciple of the Book, he cared for her wellbeing as a brother or a son might have. He was concerned when she grew tired, and made certain that she ate, whatever the pressure of audiences, decisions or documents to be read or discussed. He was the one person with whom she could share both the past and the present.

'Is there any word of Hem-Shash?' she asked him ten days after the victory. She stood in the blue courtyard. He and Alexius were the only people she would receive here. It was her place of retreat from the formality of the great hall and the memories of the rest of the palace. Here she was herself, no longer entirely Shinabari. Here she could also speak of the Book.

'Yes, Majesty,' he said gravely, biting his lip.

She looked at him quickly. She was wearing Shinabari dress, loose-flowing trousers under a long tabard of white muslin embroidered with thread of gold, as befitted an Empress. But there were Camassian army guards posted at each door, with scarlet cloaks, not blue. She still felt a sickening tightness of fear when she saw the copper and turquoise of the Shinabari Household Guard. Memory was not quelled so easily. She did not tell Ra-Nufis so, or Alexius, but if she woke in the night to the heat and the silence and the smell of bitter herbs, the nightmare returned and she found her body rigid. The sweat stood out on her skin, her heart almost burst.

How could six years disappear like that?

'Have you found him?' she asked. She had spent many hours trying to decide what to do if Hem-Shash were brought back captive. She could see his bitter, treacherous face in her mind's eye as easily as if he stood before her. He was Mon-Allat's elder sister's son, but the throne did not pass through the female line if there was a male alive. He had always resented it, felt cheated by birth. But with Mon-Allat and Habi dead, he was the only male left in direct succession. After the assassination, he had not needed to usurp the throne, merely to allow justice to be carried out, and wait. If he were not guilty of the murder of Mon-Allat, then he was still by right the Isarch. Tathea as widow had no claim to the throne except possibly as regent were Habi alive. As a childless widow, she had no rights at all.

She dared not let Hem-Shash live, and yet she could not execute him unless she could prove he was guilty of murdering the Isarch. She was not certain it was true. He may have wished it and been eager enough to take the fruits when it was done, but the man she remembered had neither the courage nor the skill to carry it out himself.

'No, Majesty,' Ra-Nufis said softly. 'But he has been seen far to the south. It seems he is making for the barbarian borders. It is conceivable he thinks to rally the armies, but he will not succeed.' He said it with a certainty that surprised her.

'Won't he?'

He smiled in the sun, the light glinting on the blue and turquoise of his tabard, the traditional colours of the Shinabari royal house. 'No, Majesty. I know the general and the governor of the south. They will never send armies away from the frontier. They dare not, even if they wished to. They are realists. They will be happy enough to have a strong Isarch again. They, of all people, know we cannot afford a civil war.'

Without thinking, she put out her hand and took his arm. 'Thank you, Ra-Nufis. You have done more than any other man to make this succeed. I am not unaware of your loyalty, or your worth.'

'I serve my people, Majesty.' He looked straight at her, meeting her eyes without blinking, for a moment without deference. 'Above all, I serve the Book, and the beauty I see in it.'

'I know you do,' she answered him. 'That is why you will not fail, and why I trust you.'

He smiled widely, a beautiful, radiant smile. 'None of us will fail, Majesty, none of us who serve the Word of God.'

One person Tathea had put off seeing for as long as possible was the old Queen Tiyo-Mah, Mon-Allat's mother. She had never liked the old woman. Their relationship had been fragile at best, at worst discreetly hostile. Tiyo-Mah had never been beautiful, but in her youth and well into middle age she had had an allure which had tantalised and captivated many men, and an appetite to take whichever of them was profitable or entertaining to her. Above all she was clever. She traced her ancestry back to the first Isarchs through both her parents' lines, and no one guarded Shinabari power or heritage more jealously than she did.

Tathea did not need to wonder what Tiyo-Mah would think of her return at the head of a foreign army, and a Camassian one at that. Of all the old enemies, Tiyo-Mah hated Camassia the most profoundly because it presumed the highest. She referred to the City in the Centre of the World as Pellagris, the ancient name it had borne as a village a thousand years ago, when Camassia was barely civilised.

But just as Tathea had lost her husband, so Tiyo-Mah had lost her son, and also her grandson. And whatever their private feelings, she was the last of the royal line left, and morally and politically Tathea must treat her with the respect which was due her. As far as Tathea knew, Tiyo-Mah had not failed in either courage or patriotism, and had acted, as much as was in her power, in the best interests of her people.

She had her own palace in the ancient part of the city. It was far smaller, and as old as the narrow streets around it. The first Isarch had built it in time lost in the mists of memory. It was made of black basalt with fine, needle-like columns in front of it. It had none of the coloured frescoes of the later periods, only low, carved reliefs and inlays of veined agate and crystal. There were no watered walls to keep it cool – they were a later invention – only the currents of air that its shape and layout were designed to promote.

Tathea was admitted by a single, unarmed steward, and was startled to see how the inside had been renewed and embellished with breathtaking wealth. The building's design was simple, with smooth, dark walls. The doors were three times a man's height, but now as they swung open for her, she saw with a momentary shiver of awe that they were faced with beaten copper and hung with pictures inlaid with silver and gold. Ebony tables with golden claws held ewers of chrysoprase, jasper and alabaster. She saw a gold tortoise with dark green malachite studded across its shell and thought with a smile of the lapis tortoise Ra-Nufis had given her. To her left a perfume box was set with rubies.

She was led down a flight of stairs. The main rooms were three-quarters below ground level, kept cool by the earth around them, and high-windowed to let in little sun.

The last doors were opened by unseen hands before she reached them. It was unnerving, as if a steward on the far side could see through the polished metal. The room beyond was lit by candles which burned with a heavy odour.

Tiyo-Mah sat in a high-backed chair whose armrests were inlaid with copper and gold, and an expressionless slave moved a painted fan as wide as a man's outstretched arms.

She was utterly changed. Tathea was not prepared for it and the sight jolted her like a physical coldness. Tiyo-Mah was an old woman. Her black hair was thin and scraped across her skull so the shape of the bone showed through. Her cheeks were sunken, the outlines sharp. Her nose curved more cruelly. Her mouth was soft as old silk, perished at the corners. But it was her eyes that had changed most. Once they had been vivid, penetrating the mind, so dark as to seem black. Now they were filmed over with a pale opacity and she seemed to peer as if uncertain where to focus.

'Ta-Thea?' Her voice was as clear and cutting as always. The sound of it took Tathea back to their first meeting when she had been a new bride in the palace, uncertain, overawed by her new position, the honour and the duty it carried. She had been more frightened of Tiyo-Mah than of anything else in Shinabar, and Tiyo-Mah had known it.

'Tiyo-Mah. I am glad to see you well, but I grieve for your loss,' she replied formally. It was the correct way to begin, and for her own sake as well as the old woman's she must preserve the dignities.

Tiyo-Mah's face was unreadable. 'Of my son, or my grandson, Ta-Thea?' She leaned forward a fraction in her carved chair, her long hands gripping the arms. 'Or of my country and all that Shinabar has been for three millennia? Or that a foreign army has invaded and taken my freedom, and that of my people? What is it you are sorry for?'

'For the loss of your son,' Tathea answered levelly, feeling her heart beat faster and her breath tighten. The old woman always did this to her, and even now, when she was the conqueror and Tiyo-Mah beaten, the pattern died hard. 'I do not know what has happened to Hem-Shash. Word has it that he has gone south, but that he is unhurt. I grieve for our people.' She stressed the commonality. 'And our country that it has fallen into an apathy where the old virtues are no longer even admired, still less practised. The foreign army will leave, and when it does we will begin to restore the values we used to have, and others even greater.'

Tiyo-Mah's expression remained closed. Tathea wondered if the old woman could see her as anything more than a shadow. She seemed to be half blind. She blinked often and moved her head very slightly as if trying to place of the sound of her visitor's voice.

'Is that what you came to tell me?' she asked coldly, a tremor of uncertainty in her voice, as if she was still not quite decided whether or not to allow her anger to show.

'In part,' Tathea replied. 'I also came to see how you were and to know if all decencies were performed for my husband and —' even now she found it difficult to say — 'my son.'

Tiyo-Mah rose to her feet slowly, fumbling for the stick which Tathea now noticed leaning against the chair. It, too, was ebony and heavily ringed with gold. Tiyo-Mah did not quite straighten her back and hobbled across to the slit window, silent on her feet in spite of her awkwardness. She stood with her back to Tathea, hunch-shouldered, her long floor-length tabard black in the shadow, plum red under the candlelight. Tathea was snatched in memory to another underground room and an old man with a withered face who wore red, and for a blinding instant she was drowned in power, and pain. Then it was gone again, and Tiyo-Mah spoke, her voice low and grating.

'The murders stunned me. For days I was too ill with grief to rise from my couch. My only son . . . assassinated by his own people. His heir killed in his infancy. The throne that has been in my family for a thousand years stained with blood, and passed into the hands of traitors to their Isarch, and their gods.'

Tathea was moved to a moment's pity, forgetting it was Tiyo-Mah, and seeing only an old woman whose heart had been shattered in one fearful night. But the gulf between them was unbridgeable, and there was no comfort for such grief.

219

'To begin with I could do nothing,' Tiyo-Mah continued, still with her back to the room, her face to the light of the high window high up in the dark wall. 'But word came to me. There were still those who were loyal. I gathered knowledge . . . power.' Her voice caressed the word. 'And within a month I had sufficient to come out of my silence. I had the usurper overthrown and executed. His body was fed to the dogs.' She said it slowly, tasting the words with satisfaction. 'The assassins I had hunted down and killed. Their bones lie on the sand as a reminder to passers-by of what happens to those who betray the Isarchs of Shinabar.' She stood quite still. The smell of the incense in the candles was overpowering.

'And Mon-Allat's body?' Tathea asked.

'Dug up and reburied with his ancestors in the Tombs of the Isarchs, where it should be,' Tiyo-Mah answered. 'His sarcophagus is made of alabaster and gold.'

Tathea forced herself to say it: 'And Habi?'

Tiyo-Mah did not reply. The air was thick in the room, the incense clogged the throat and smoke stung the eyes. Or perhaps it was imagination. The ancient builders had known the secret of air currents and even in the height of summer it was cool down here.

Tathea would not ask again.

'Beside him,' Tiyo-Mah said at last. 'He would have been Isarch in his turn.' The tone of her voice dropped, it even shook a little, just the faintest tremor. To Tathea it was an acknowledgement of grief, and for the first time she could remember she shared something intense and fiercely personal with Tiyo-Mah. Perhaps it was a thread of hope for a rebirth here as well.

'Thank you,' she said.

Nothing more was necessary. Tathea bade Tiyo-Mah farewell, and with the smallest guard necessary for safety, rode out into the desert to the Tombs of the Isarchs. She left the others outside and entered alone. She had not been here in twenty years, since Mon-Allat's father had been buried and she had come with Mon-Allat to pay her respects.

The vast chamber was cool, half underground, like Tiyo-Mah's palace. It dated from the same period. It was simple, hewn out of the living rock and faced with plaster painted with scenes of the lives of each Isarch buried here. One could trace the dates by the changing styles of art, from the stiffly hieratic through the merely formal to the present day's almost lifelike representations. Dress had remained largely the same, and the colours were always copper and blue.

She had come not for the comfort of the familiar, or to be impressed by past splendour, but simply to grieve. She paid her respects to Mon-Allat's sarcophagus, remembering the beginning between them when there had been so much hope and trust, and certainly an innocence. She deliberately thought of everything that had been good in him and blocked out of her mind anything else. She found she was able to think of him with more gentleness than she had in many years, to recall laughter and a kind of love, not passion but at least a tenderness.

Then she moved to Habi's small, far plainer sarcophagus, una-dorned with the gold symbols and insignia of the Isarchs. There was only the good, and the hope, to remember here and she allowed herself to weep again, until a deep peace settled over her, a warmth that came from within.

When she left, the tomb was no longer a place of death, simply one of many remembrances, and the least important.

Before she could begin to teach the Book to anyone in Shinabar she must restore peace and make her authority sure. Camassian soldiers should not patrol the streets longer than necessary for her immediate safety. Every passing day she was here by their military strength and not by her own right or power, she was undermining the future.

It was Ra-Nufis who pointed this out to her most forcefully. They were in the blue lily courtyard again. It was mid-afternoon and the winter sun was already low at this hour, hazy and gold in the air, glittering on the water falling over the wall.

'Majesty, you should not hesitate longer.' He was speaking increasingly bluntly to her as urgency and the volume of matters he brought to her mounted. There was no time for the prevarications of courtly language.

'Hesitate?' she asked.

'You must take the throne,' he answered frankly. 'Only the mantle of Isarch will give you the strength to bring peace to Shinabar and set the foundations upon which we can teach the Book to the people, and begin the rebirth.'

Isarch? She had thought of it, of course she had, but to hear it in words from another's lips was still momentous, a leap of power she had only played with at the edge of her mind. From a Camassian it might have been rooted in a failure to understand Shinabar's ancient law of heritage and the weight of prejudice it embodied. But from Ra-Nufis it was different, he knew the law as well as she did.

'Isarch.' She tasted the word without meeting his eyes, a flutter of nervousness inside her, amazement at her own temerity, and then a surge of excitement like a shiver of music.

'Of course,' Ra-Nufis replied steadily. 'It has to be.'

'There has never been a woman Isarch in all our history.' She kept it at bay a few moments longer, but she was already past the point of refusing.

'There is no man left.' He smiled very slightly, a flash of humour in

221

his eyes as well as on his lips. 'And the Isarch must be seen to love the Book, above all things, to know and understand it, to be the leader of the people in keeping its commandments.'

She said nothing. The magnitude of the thought was already settling in her mind. It was true. The Book was the reason for it all, and whatever served the ends of teaching it must be right.

'Isarch!' The High Priest Tugomir stared at her with a mixture of derision and incredulity. He was dressed in the magnificent robes of his office, a floor-length tabard of turquoise embroidered with gold, over skirts of white silk and gold muslin. He was a small, lean man with narrow shoulders who walked ungracefully. His long face with its square-cut beard was fierce, and he had a crooked mouth and dark, brilliant eyes.

'Yes.' Tathea had made her decision and no one was now going to dissuade her. She had asked to see the High Priest in order to inform him, not to persuade him.

'There has never been a woman Isarch!' he protested.

'Then I shall be the first,' she replied smoothly. 'There are going to be a lot of new beginnings.'

His expression hardened, his body was rigid with barely suppressed anger. He was the religious leader of the nation. He was passionate, ascetic, a man full of burning conviction and the courage to fight anyone who blasphemed his faith. There was no self-doubt in him and, unfortunately, little humour.

'We have a great deal to learn,' she continued briskly. 'Much that we have allowed ourselves to believe recently must be done away with and truth put in its place.'

'From this . . . creation of yours?' he asked with ill-concealed sarcasm. 'This . . . Book?' He said the word with scalding disdain.

'It is not a creation of mine, or anyone else's,' she said sharply. 'It is the Word of God. I brought it here, I did not write it.'

'From where?' he asked. His voice was grating, ugly, and yet commanding. It remained in the memory – like his face. She did not know him – he had been appointed since the coup – and yet there was something about him that was familiar, an echo in the mind.

'From the Lost Lands,' she answered. 'From a region of the spirit, and life before this where we all chose our paths . . .' She stopped, startled at what she had said. It had come from some depth of her mind below conscious level, as if seeing Tugomir had recalled it. 'Just as there is resurrection after death,' she went on more slowly, 'so there was a life in the spirit before birth, but we have forgotten it.'

'All except you, it would seem!' he said trenchantly.

'I have forgotten it too. I simply know it exists.'

'It makes no sense.' He was looking at her now with contempt. 'If we have forgotten it, what was its purpose? If we learned anything, it is all gone. Your god is a fool!'

'It is not wasted,' she said with calm certainty. 'Then we could see the choice, and the good evil was clearer, and the worth of the prize was understood.'

'So why forget?' he demanded, his mouth twisted. 'Now we have nothing. Why should we obey this god of yours if we have forgotten the reason?'

Again the answer was swift to her lips. 'There is no worth in virtue practised for reward. In the end it is not what you do but what you are.'

'Sophistry!' he spat. 'What is a man except the accumulation of what he has done?'

'What he feels, what he wishes,' she said. 'Your soul must become as God's, not for fear or reward, or even obedience, but because you have understood, and above all because you love.'

His eyes widened. His voice sank to a whisper, shivering with rage. 'You think to become as God is? That is blasphemy! That is the supreme arrogance – and absurdity.'

She did not waver. 'I don't want it just for me, I want it for everyone.'

The blood was dark in his face. 'Then it is hardly an exclusive prize! All gods? You and the court jester, the cook, the vagabond and the thief! You are depraved. I will have no part in it, and I shall fight you every step of the way.' His narrow chest swelled. 'As long as I have breath in my body, you will not lead the people down into the darkness of your insanity.'

'I will not lead anyone,' she rejoined. 'I shall tell them the truth, and those who will may accept it. It is here for everyone, every man and woman who ever lived, or will live. How many will climb to the height of heaven I don't know. Perhaps only a few. The reward will be the light or the darkness in their souls when they face God and see themselves as they are.'

'And hell?' he asked gratingly. 'The fires of damnation for the wicked?'

'Would not the knowledge of chances lost burn inside you for ever? To know what you could have been, and were not! Is that not hell enough?'

'If it were true, yes.' His face was pinched tight, his eyes blazing. 'But it is lies. You deny all the old virtues, the things our forefathers have believed from the beginning, and which made us great.' There was a panic of horror in him. 'You promise magic, forgiveness for sin, power no man has the right or virtue to hold. Your ideas are born of arrogance and in the end you will reap the dust.' He slashed his hand in the air furiously. 'I care not if you eat ashes to eternity, but I weep for the innocent you will take with you!'

'I can't make you see the vision of what is in the Book,' she said quietly. 'I wish I could – although perhaps I shouldn't.'

He looked startled.

She laughed. 'No one can make you believe. Even God can't do that for you; only grieve for you if you choose the dark.'

He turned on his heel and strode out. Only the High Priest would have dared leave her in such a way. Tugomir feared nothing except evil of the soul. She had heard it said of him. Now she believed it.

Ta-Thea was crowned Isarch of Shinabar with all the ancient power and splendour of a hundred generations of kings before her. She walked alone, wearing the blue and white robes and the golden helmet, carrying the sword and the staff of the first Isarch, now crusted with gold and gems, but still symbols of the warrior who protects and the shepherd who leads. Behind her, courtiers carried the shield set with red jasper symbolising blood shed for sacrifice, her life for her people's. Then they brought the cup containing water, the source of life for all things, man, bird, beast and plant, all things that fly or crawl or grow, the unity of all the earth.

She proclaimed her sacred oath of office in a steady, clear voice. She promised to guide and defend her people, to place their wellbeing before all else. She could not speak the names of her Shinabari ancestors as if they were deities, nor allow it to be believed of her that she did. She had covenanted with the God of time and eternity to serve Him and none else.

She gave her word simply, without embellishment of any kind.

The trumpets shrilled out a single, high note, splitting the air. The copper cymbals clashed in a shimmering collision all down the solemn rows of priests and courtiers, a hundred men long, fifty men deep. Everyone bowed their heads, except Tathea. The copper crown with its single carved jewel must never be lowered.

Five thousand throats hailed her as Isarch. The noise swirled around her like a roaring sea, a blue and white sea of linen and lapis and purple dye, dark faces . . . her own people.

She had stood behind Mon-Allat when he was crowned, a few yards from where she stood now. It had been overwhelming then, giddy, stupendous. Today she was Isarch, supreme ruler of a fading nation, a people stumbling into the dark, and she held the only light. She must hold it high. Nothing must bar her way from sharing it. It was the trust for which she had been born.

As the weeks became months and winter passed into spring, a kind of peace settled over Shinabar. Alexius commanded the army over the entire country. Ra-Nufis's network of allies and informants were a strong foundation. Many courtiers returned from the places to which they had fled at Mon-Allat's murder, seven years earlier. They were keen to claim old loyalties, and Tathea knew the wisdom of forgetting as well as of remembering. Sufficient justice had been done in Tiyo-Mah's punishment of the assassins, and Hem-Shash could not come back. Word came occasionally of Hem-Shash's exile and then, in the summer, of his death. Such resistance as existed was sporadic, disorganised, and met with little support. There was no heart for war and greater loss.

The only voice raised against Tathea was from the High Priest Tugomir, and that was directed at the blasphemous teachings of the new religion, not the Isarch in person.

She rewarded Ra-Nufis as he merited, and she needed, by making him her First Minister. His knowledge far exceeded her own, and his love of the Book made him trustworthy as no other Shinabari could be.

A new peace treaty was signed with Camassia. Eight Camassian legions were to remain in Shinabari, the rest of the army would withdraw. A new commander, Beel-Habak, was appointed to lead and re-inspire the Shinabari army. He was from the southern outposts, a desert man as Tathea's father had been. He had fought the barbarian and he knew battle and hardship; his courage was tested. He understood the reality of the danger which ever threatened the idle and the unwatchful. Tathea had no need to warn him of the price of internal disunity.

It was time for her to turn her mind to teaching the words of the Book to her own people. Politically, and militarily, it was also time for Alexius to return to the City in the Centre of the World. Tathea had toyed with the idea of asking him to remain in Shinabar, but it was only a dream, a desire she lingered over in the hours of the night when she lay awake and stared at the bright square of moonlight in the window.

She must teach the Book. She could not keep Alexius here. His task was completed. If she indulged in loneliness, or wishes, imagination of what might have been, or could be, she had but to place her hand on the warm gold of the Book, not even to open its pages, and she knew the price would be terrible, and eternal. She looked in the glass, and saw not her own face but Eleni's.

She received Alexius in the blue court of the lilies. She wanted it to be there. Then she could remember him every time she was here alone. It was ten days since she had seen him last and that had been in Beel-Habak's company as he reported on the latest military situation.

As always he wore Camassian uniform and his old leather armour. He kept his red cloak, even in the heat, but no helmet. The servant withdrew and left them alone.

225

He stood just inside the entrance, respectfully. He was the general of a vast army, but she was Empress of a nation. Could she force herself to preserve that barrier between them? To her they would always be a man and a woman; everything else was superficial, temporary. Eternity would wash away such differences.

'Thank you for coming,' she began. How could she express herself so that he understood all she meant without saying the words which should never be spoken between them?

He said nothing, standing to attention and looking at her.

'You have done all that was needful,' she said quietly. Her voice was a little husky, as though her mouth were dry. It was terribly difficult to look at him, and worse to look away. 'And you have done it with courage and honour, as I knew you would. Neither my people nor I can repay you, except by using well the gift you have given us. I shall never cease from striving to teach the Book to every man and woman who will listen.'

'It was my privilege to serve, Majesty,' he replied. 'The cause is mine as well as yours.' His words were stiff and formal, a general answering a queen. His eyes were tender, wrought with pain, and his lips were touched with grief.

There were no tears in her eyes, no tightness in her throat. She would weep later. She would have years in which to weep.

'You return to your own country with honour, and with our gratitude. We shall not forget.' She swallowed. 'I shall not forget . . .' she added. 'Not anything.'

He stood silently, spinning out the moment. His next words would be their last, and they both knew it. There would be nothing more to add. She looked at him intently. She could never forget his eyes, the light on the slant of his cheeks, the curve of his nose, his lips. She would see his brow, the way his hair grew, every time she closed her eyes, years from now.

He was staring at her with the same fierce intensity, making this moment live for ever.

'Nor I,' he said at last. Then he bowed, and turned and walked out, not looking back, and the door closed behind him.

Chapter Fifteen

Tathea threw herself into teaching the Book with all her strength, but nothing could dull the sharp stab of knowing that Alexius had gone, back to Camassia and a life she knew so well. She could picture him at any time of the day, knowing what he would be doing, knowing the places, the people, hearing their voices in her mind. Even when he returned to the barbarian frontiers, she could now be with him in spirit better than Eleni or Xanthica could, better than anyone who had not fought, marched and kept the still watches of the night, or wept for the slain as the carrion birds wheeled.

And yet she missed Eleni also. There was no one in Shinabar to whom she could turn for that same warm, generous friendship, with whom to laugh and share beautiful things, as they had in the past, to speak openly of her feelings, to joke about the trivial or ridiculous.

She was surrounded by serving women, courtiers, the wives of nobles, but she was Isarch and there was always a gulf between them. She would see them together, at ease with one another, and then when they noticed her their behaviour changed. They were respectful, they muted their voices. They waited for her to speak first. They laughed at her jokes, but politely. She never knew if they were genuinely amused or not. In fact she never knew if they were sincere about anything. Everyone said what they thought she wished to hear. It was like living in a hall of mirrors, all distorting a fraction, according to their own perception.

Only Ra-Nufis was honest, but he spent almost every waking hour working to spread the teachings of the Book. A hall full of scribes copied the original, and each copy was read by four people to make certain it was exact, letter for letter. It began in Thoth-Moara, but two by two those who believed the Book were sent out to begin teaching others, a body of adventurers of the heart and pilgrims of the spirit. Every inquiry, whether made with good will or ill, was met with an answer. The labour was immense.

Tathea had much else to demand her attention. She was Isarch. She must meet foreign emissaries and ambassadors. She must consult with ministers and stewards about every aspect of the nation's wellbeing. To sow the seeds of the rebirth of a new morality was an all-consuming labour. There was little sign that the ground was fertile and no way of knowing whether the seeds would grow, let alone yield a harvest.

Tathea kept the day of remembrance for her mother, as she always did, and for Habi. The summer passed. She found the heat difficult to bear, she had grown unused to it in Camassia. And all the time the voice of the High Priest Tugomir praised honesty and diligence, and cursed the Book and all who touched it.

Tathea thought often of the City in the Centre of the World. She stood in the courts and gardens of Thoth-Moara in the blistering late-summer sun and thought of rain with a sense of longing, as for some remembered dream.

She also thought of Barsymet and Tissarel, and as she did so her mind turned to Mon-Allat, and Arimaspis. She had made no inquiry about what had happened to her husband's mistress, not even whether she had survived the assassinations. Now suddenly it was important to her.

It took three days to find her. She was living in a small house in the old quarter of the city, and Tathea chose to go to her rather than send for her to come to the palace. Such a move might be unwise for many reasons. Arimaspis might fear vengeance and disappear, and it would seem to others that she was the victim of a jealous woman who harboured betrayals long and fatally.

Also Tathea wanted to keep their meeting unknown to those in the palace, and certainly to the public. She had to be very careful of her reputation, not only as the first woman in four thousand years of history to dare ascend the throne, but as the bearer of the Book. Any personal sin, however small or understandable, would stain her.

She dressed in a plain brown tabard and white trousers and took a single guard, Yattu-Shia, whom she had learned to trust. They travelled into the old quarter of the city to the narrow, rose-red stone building where Arimaspis now lived. Tathea climbed the stairs and Yattu-Shia knocked with his sword hilt on the weathered door.

It was answered by a woman in a plain sea-blue tabard and trousers which were faded to gentle tones and clung to her body. The very simplicity of her clothes was beautiful. Her hair was russet fair, unlike any Shinabari, and her eyes were blue. She was lovelier than Tathea had ever been, and it was not a face without strength or character. The hardships of the years since her fall from favour had marked her features softly. Even searching, Tathea could see no bitterness reflected in her.

Arimaspis might have recognised Tathea had they met in the palace. They had seen each other in Mon-Allat's time, even if seldom and by accident. But the last thing she expected was the Isarch on her doorstep here in this shabby area, as simply dressed as she was herself, and accompanied by only one man.

228

'Yes?' she said curiously. 'Are you looking for someone? The jeweller lives below, and the spice merchant opposite.'

'Arimaspis?'

'Yes?' Her face paled and she took a step backward. Tathea's voice was distinctive, it had a timbre unlike anyone else's. The sound of it had awoken memory. Arimaspis swallowed, fear in her eyes. 'Majesty?'

'May I come in?'

Refusal was impossible. Arimaspis, white-lipped, led her inside. The place was cramped and sparsely decorated, but there was a simplicity to it which was restful and the bleached cotton rugs were beautiful, their colours the washed tones of sand and sky. There was a single scroll on the wall, a painting of marsh birds at dawn. A water lily bloomed in a green earthen bowl. The noise of the street outside was calmed by the steady drip of water into the bowl. It would be hard work, and heavy, carrying the pails of water to refill the cistern, but obviously it mattered to Arimaspis. Tathea knew instantly she would have done the same.

Yattu-Shia, ever tactful, waited outside the door.

Arimaspis said nothing. One did not speak before the Isarch.

This was not how Tathea would have wished it. She would rather they had met as equals, but in Shinabar she had no equal. It was one of the prices of power.

'I am glad you were not killed,' she began, coming further in but not sitting.

A flicker of pain crossed Arimaspis's face. Tathea had wondered if she had loved Mon-Allat. Could she have seen in him what Tissarel had seen in Isadorus? Had she brought out in him a better man than she herself had? After all, Barsymet had shrivelled all that was best in Isadorus.

Tathea needed to be rid of the ghosts of doubt that haunted her, but she could hardly ask if they had loved one another.

'I have no wine,' Arimaspis said tentatively. 'But I have good water, and honey cakes.'

Tathea accepted and sat down on one of the wide, low seats.

Arimaspis disappeared and returned a few minutes later with the water in a blue jug and the cakes on a dish.

It was an absurd situation. Tathea must break it. Arimaspis could not. All the things she had planned to say were cast aside. There was a dignity in this woman which made old rivalries or resentments a pettiness she did not want. She began obliquely.

'Much has changed in Shinabar in the last seven years. I thought at first it was sudden, but now on deeper consideration I think perhaps it was happening for a long time. I simply did not see it.'

Arimaspis understood her. 'I used to live by the sea,' she responded. 'The waves gather far out in the ocean, but they only break when they

229

reach the shore. It seems sudden, but that is an illusion.' She was watching Tathea as she spoke.

Tathea chose her next words very carefully. 'I lived in the court of Camassia for several years, most of the time I was away. I came to know the Emperor Isadorus quite well.'

Arimaspis was silent.

'Have you heard of the Book? I taught him many of its precepts. He learned quickly, and believed. He was a man of great strength and integrity.' She looked at Arimaspis, searching her eyes for emotion, understanding, and was not certain what she saw – passion, intelligence . . . 'To accept it cost him very dearly,' she continued, 'because he had a mistress he loved. I don't think he realised how much until after he had told her to leave him so that he might live according to the laws of purity of both heart and body.'

The colour burned slowly up Arimaspis's cheeks, but she did not look away.

'She understood,' Tathea went on. 'I think she was a more generous woman than his wife. She certainly loved him more truly.'

'Did his wife not love him?' Arimaspis asked, her voice hesitant. She knew what she was asking.

Tathea was momentarily confounded. Should she answer for Barsymet or for herself? For herself. That was what mattered. Arimaspis knew nothing of Camassia; it was irrelevant.

'After a manner,' she said softly. 'She was loyal to him. But she did not laugh with him, or share his dreams.'

'Perhaps he did not bring out the best in her,' Arimaspis answered equally carefully. Her fingers were knotted together in her lap, knuckles white. 'He may not have seen in her the courage or passion she possessed. He may even have been a little afraid of her. After all, she was almost his equal in rank, whereas a mistress could never challenge him. She would always know her place. That was in a way more comfortable . . .'

'He was . . . more . . . at ease with her?' Tathea was fumbling towards light, and it was painful.

Arimaspis smiled. 'No, not as you are saying. I mean perhaps his wife had a vision he had not, even a strength he guessed at but did not understand. One can be afraid of having to stretch, to meet the expectations of someone who will not lower their beliefs.'

'Do you think that was the case?' Tathea was surprised. Was this woman really prepared to tell her such a thing? She hurried on before Arimaspis could answer her. 'Or was it simply that his mistress was kinder?'

'She could hardly afford to be anything else,' Arimaspis pointed out. Then she bit her lip. 'But I dare say she did love him, even if she could sometimes see his flaws.'

'Then she was a good woman,' Tathea answered gravely. 'I hope things go well with her, even though she is no longer at court.'

Arimaspis looked down at the wheaten honey cakes on the table. 'Did the mistress accept the teaching of the Book also?'

'Yes.'

'And it did not matter that she was – had been – a courtesan?'

'Not at all. She was more honest than the Empress.'

'What?' Arimaspis was startled, her blue eyes wide with disbelief.

'Than the Empress Barsymet,' Tathea said quietly.

'Oh . . . of course.'

'Would you like to study the Book?' It was an impulsive question, and the last thing Tathea had intended to do when she came.

'Yes,' Arimaspis said in a low, clear voice. 'I would.'

'Then Yattu-Shia will bring you a copy,' Tathea promised, wondering what she had done, and yet knowing it was right.

Half an hour later, with a lighter step and a sweetness inside her, she found herself smiling as she walked through the narrow streets and out into the burning sun of the wide and spacious squares.

But Arimaspis was one of the very few to desire the Book. As the summer passed into autumn and the dark blue skies and desert winds of winter approached, Tathea began to realise how deep was the malaise in Shinabar. Again and again Ra-Nufis returned with stories of excuses why the leaders of other cities would not teach the Book or espouse its precepts themselves.

'It's everywhere!' he said exasperatedly, pacing back and forth in the blue lily courtyard, his fists clenched at his sides. He was wearing a long, pale desert cloak and riding boots scuffed at the heels and abraded by sand. 'One governor told me he could not teach mastery of the appetites because at least half his lieutenants had mistresses, or might have in the future. He would lose their loyalty. Some would be offended because he would be criticising their way of life.' He turned and stared furiously at Tathea, his brows drawn down, his eyes blazing.

'Can you believe it? He even said that if he were to give up his mistress, she would tell his wife, and since her father is a banker to whom he owes money, he could not possibly do that.' His voice was harsh with contempt. 'Excuses – always some reason why the way of God is too difficult. Not now, not here, not me!' He flung his arms out. 'My brother would object! My father would object! My children will not love me if I curtail their freedom! They will think I am pompous, no fun. I will crush their spirit if I tell them this or that is wrong!' His face twisted with the pain of his own disgust and the loss he could taste for them.

'It is always someone else's fault. We must not ask too much of them because of the famine, the occupation! He is old! He is young!

He has just got married! His father died! He witnessed an accident, a riot, an execution!' He slashed the air again. 'He has a stomach ache, a headache, someone was rude to him! Nobody is willing to take responsibility for anything. They fear man more than God!' He stared at Tathea with desperation in his face, the softness of youth already gone. 'I have tried everything I know to show them the beauty of the truth, but they lie! Lying to me doesn't matter but lying to themselves is death!'

She could see the weariness in his face, but it was due to anger, not discouragement. There was nothing in him which allowed defeat.

'It is worse than that,' she said quietly, looking at him as he stopped pacing and faced her, listening. 'Tugomir's enmity to the Book is absolute.'

'Tugomir!' he exploded, his body clenching tight again, his shoulders rigid under the sweep of his cloak. 'If only we could silence him, how they might listen then. That man does more harm in one day than any other hundred you could name!' He stood motionless, his eyes dark. 'Is he an emissary of the Great Enemy?'

'I don't know,' she said honestly, but there was a coldness inside her. Tugomir seemed to her inexplicably familiar, as if she had known him in some time before memory. 'But I know he hates the Book and all it teaches,' she said with a deep shudder. 'And he is taking with him many good people who would be honest enough to try the teachings had not Tugomir convinced them that they are blasphemers against the old faith, and are betraying their ancestors even to open the Book.'

'That's not the reason!' Ra-Nufis snapped. 'He is a High Priest, and the more people turn to the truth, the fewer disciples he will have. He will lose power, and he knows it!'

As autumn passed and the relative coolness of winter descended on Shinabar, Tathea found herself drawn more to Arimaspis, who had accepted the Book wholeheartedly and before witnesses made her covenants with God. Their past relationship was not mentioned again. Neither spoke of Mon-Allat, even obliquely, and Tathea felt at ease in Arimaspis's company. They shared a similar amusement at the absurd and sometimes burst into laughter until they gasped for breath and the tears were wet on their faces. Sometimes the same trifles made them angry, or impatient. It was good to be with another woman. There were so many things Arimaspis understood without the need for explanations; a glance, a meeting of eyes, and the knowledge was there.

'Tugomir was preaching again in the great square,' Arimaspis said as they sat together in one of the outer courts of the palace, a quiet tree-shaded place of falling pools, green water into blue. 'Hundreds of people were listening to him.'

'I know.' Tathea sighed. 'But I can't stop him or I deny my own beliefs. And he would be the first to point that out.'

'And he can win, can't he?' Arimaspis asked, frowning. She had read the Book many times and she understood much of the nature of light and darkness. 'He can deceive people, even the most elect.'

'Yes.' It was a truth Tathea struggled with and found hard to accept. 'If they permit it. But I am not sure that he is an evil man . . . I don't know.' She pictured the High Priest's ugly, passionate face, trying to be subjective and dismiss from her mind the uneasy sense that she had seen him before. 'I think that he truly believes the old faith. And there is much good in it, honour and courage, devotion to duty and care for the poor in body and heart. There is a reverence for all that is beautiful or of use, for learning and labour.' The growing oppression inside her clarified as she tried to frame it in words. 'In the old way there was not the superstition there is now. That is recent, an escape from the responsibility for one's own decisions, and mistakes. If you can believe in fate, the stars or the sands, then it excuses you from trying. Why rail against destiny? Only a fool wastes his energy and substance on that. It is the easiest escape of all.'

'Then to teach it is evil!' Arimaspis said fiercely.

'Tugomir doesn't teach it.' Tathea stared at the light rippling on the water. She did not find it as restful as she once had. 'He is a man of fantastic energy, who is blind to the truth in the Book. I never listened to anyone with less of the hypocrite in him, or of the coward. The mass of people reject the Book because it demands sacrifice, obedience and the acceptance of responsibility. Ultimately you must become the keeper, and the lover, of all things. It also demands that you learn how to make your own decisions, but it is so much easier to be told exactly what to do, and what not to do. You can obey, and feel justified. It is measurable.' She smiled bitterly. 'You can even establish a hierarchy of righteousness and feel proud, and safe.'

There was silence but for the water and the lazy humming of bees in the flowers. A gardener walked by carrying a hoe and a knife for pruning. His feet made no sound on the stone.

'Tugomir sees the Book as a force which will overthrow the order which once made Shinabar great,' Tathea went on gravely. 'He sees it as death, not life. He thinks it is magic, an offer of escape from this world's realities. He sees the growth of superstition, and its corruption terrifies him. It is a rejection of work, justice, even order. It springs from chaos, and would lead us back into it. The whole concept is irredeemably corrupt. It makes nonsense of the nature of choice, and of growth, which is the core of good and evil. He should hate it, and he is right to be afraid.'

Arimaspis moved closer to Tathea. She did not touch her – that would have been impertinence – but her closeness held the warmth of friendship, her silence and her smile conveyed her understanding.

Tathea turned to her and smiled back.

Tathea returned from a long ride in the desert with no one but Yattu-Shia beside her, and the Household Guard at a distance. She dismounted in the same yard from which nearly eight years ago Kol-Shamisha had helped her escape the assassins. She had barely set her foot inside the stables when she became aware of a presence other than the horses and her own men who were dispersing.

She looked around. At first she saw no one. Then as she became used to the shadows she found him: a dwarf, squat and powerful, huge headed. The dim light caught on his glittering, diamond-patterned tunic and his white hands fluttered as if picking at the air. His eyes were brilliant amber with black slit pupils, like a goat's. He looked at Tathea with recognition as ancient as time and she felt a cold fear crowd her heart. Without thought her hand moved to her dagger, then dropped again. This battle was of the spirit.

'Who are you?' she asked him, touching her horse's neck to still it, feeling it shake with fear – did it sense her own? Or was this its own innate recognition of evil?

'My name is Azrub, Majesty.' He bowed, the gesture intended as mockery.

'What do you want?' she asked.

Azrub was smiling. 'No, Majesty, what do you want?'

'Nothing from you!' she said tartly. She was more unnerved by him than she could mask. It startled her.

'Ah, but you do not know what I can give you.' His voice was curiously sibilant, very soft but it penetrated as if he could lay his white fingers on her mind. 'I have power you cannot imagine.'

She wanted to move, to leave the stable and get out into the sunlight, but he was standing in the doorway and she would have to brush past him. She might even touch him, and the thought made her skin crawl. Her horse was beginning to sweat, its eyes were rolling.

'You have nothing I could want,' she repeated, but her voice trembled.

'Look down, Majesty,' he whispered, licking his lips.

'What?'

'Look down,' he repeated. 'Look at the dust by your feet. Tell me what you see.'

She did not mean to obey him, but against her will her gaze dropped. A flurry of wind blew in through the open door and the dust shifted. Gradually it took a distinct form, a picture, people, faces. She could see a man holding the Book in his arms, opening it and beginning to preach. There was a transfiguring beauty in his narrow features, and everyone who heard his voice believed because of the passion of his conviction. It was the High Priest Tugomir.

234

If only it could be!

The wind blew again, covering the scene, and as it moved it formed a spreading map of Shinabar, as if she was watching the light of faith cover the entire country.

The breeze stirred again, and she saw herself on the lapis throne, surrounded by a sea of faces alight with joy, all turned towards her in gratitude. A deep peace had spread over them. Man, woman and child alike shone with an inner knowledge. She looked up to the golden goat eyes of the dwarf.

He pursed his lips and blew the faintest of breaths. The picture in the dust vanished.

'It can be yours, Majesty.' The words slid over his tongue close to silence but they were imprinted on her heart as if carved by fire.

All Shinabar believing the Book! Even Tugomir. Peace, not enforced by armies or laws, but sprung from the heart! A whole nation who loved honour, compassion and purity! A race walking in the light!

An echo sounded in her spirit: 'I will bring back every soul as perfect as I received it – let me have the dominion over them, and the glory.' And then another voice, like music in the soul. 'Let man choose. Prove to him that he may work his own salvation and inherit glory and dominion and everlasting joy, for this is indeed why he was born.'

'No!' Her voice was low and fierce. She kicked the dust roughly with her feet. 'No! That is the denial of everything! Get out! I know who you are . . .' Without understanding why, she held her hand high, palm towards him. 'In the name of God, leave here!'

His lips drew back from his stumps of teeth. His yellow eyes glittered with a hundred thousand years of hate. 'And I know who you are, woman. I know your name from eternity past through all time to come, and I shall not forget you. You were offered all. Now you shall have nothing! I will fight you over every soul, and those you lose will become the armies of hell for ever. I curse the ground you walk on, that it perishes at your touch!' And he spat on to the sand, his saliva spawning maggots in the dust and a stench which caught in her throat.

She fought to overcome the giddiness which engulfed her, and the sickening revulsion. She was swaying. The ground hit her hard, and she found herself on her hands and knees. She looked up at him, her voice choking in her throat. 'You cannot curse the earth God made. You have no power over the innocent.' She stretched out her hands in the air, over the writhing maggots, and as she watched them they shrivelled up and disappeared in smoke, and where they had been the stone floor shone opal with a fire of blue and green and pearl.

The dwarf let out his breath in a hiss between his flat, worn teeth, and turned on his heel and left.

Tathea staggered to her feet, clinging to her horse to hold herself up. Her body was shaking, her legs so weak that without the animal she would have fallen.

When the groom came he found her still like that, and he walked on the opal in the floor without seeing it, unknowingly covering it with straw.

It was spring when Ra-Nufis brought her the final information about the coup. She was in the room where she did most of her work. It was full of tables and papers. Scribes came and went regularly. The sun was sharp on the marble patterns on the floor. He was dressed formally in blue and white. She stared at him in disbelief.

'Tiyo-Mah? Afterwards, of course . . . but . . .'

'No,' Ra-Nufis said levelly, his eyes unwavering. 'Before also. It was she who planned it, she who bribed and corrupted the Household Guard, who found the ones who hated Camassia as much as she did and persuaded them that in making an alliance with the ancient enemy the Isarch was betraying his country . . .' His lips curled in a bitter smile. 'Which is a marvellous irony, if you think of it! She colluded with the Great Enemy, and in so doing drove you to seek the Book.'

She could feel the anger, the black laughter and the amazement in him as if he had touched her. Or perhaps it was because she felt the same vortex of emotions tearing at her.

'But Mon-Allat was her son!' she protested. 'Her own child . . .' She tried to force the pictures of Habi out of her mind, and could not. They crowded in on her. She could feel the warmth of him as a baby lying in her arms. She remembered his first wobbly steps, the sound of his laughter, the smell of his skin. And Tiyo-Mah had murdered him as well as her own son!

Ra-Nufis was holding her arms. She realised it suddenly and with a sense of shock. His grip was strong, iron-fingered. He was staring into her face.

'Ta-Thea!' There was fear in him; fear for her.

'Yes . . .'

'She has already destroyed herself. Don't let her destroy you too.' His voice was urgent, pleading.

She knew what he meant. She was rigid, every muscle clenched. Deliberately she made herself relax, and at last he let go of her.

'I will face her,' she said. 'I will have her arrested and imprisoned, not here in Thoth-Moara but out in one of the far desert fortresses, and with no more than she needs to survive, no servants she can corrupt. Let the desert princes guard her – my father's people. They won't forgive her my son's death.'

Ra-Nufis stepped back, satisfied.

'Come with me.' It was a request, not an order. 'We'll take

236

Yattu-Shia, and the best of the Guard, in case she has men and tries to resist.'

They posted twenty men discreetly in the streets around Tiyo-Mah's ancient palace, and Tathea, Ra-Nufis and Yattu-Shia went in alone. Tathea carried a dagger from habit. For past Isarchs it had been symbolic only. Hers was razor sharp and not at all symbolic.

She found Tiyo-Mah alone in the same incense-filled room as before, sitting in the same high-backed ebony chair. Her face was more deeply sunken, and her claw-like hands gripped the arms. But it was her eyes which shocked. They were now totally sightless, milk-white across the pupils, like stones.

'Returned to savour victory, Ta-Thea?' she said, leaning forward a little, her ears straining to catch the slap of sandals on marble.

Tathea shivered. She had permitted no servant to warn Tiyo-Mah, and yet the old woman knew who stood in the room. She could not have remembered the step after so long.

Tiyo-Mah smiled mirthlessly. 'Drink it deep,' she whispered, her voice dry with disuse, her sightless eyes fixed on Tathea's face. 'It will not last; a few weeks, a few months, no more. Long before you are my age it will be dust in your mouth. Nothing you build will last. Believe me, I know.' There was no rage in her, no squeal of hysteria, just the quiet jubilation of certainty. It was sickening, like laughter in a graveyard, infinitely malicious.

Tathea summoned all her strength, every memory of goodness she could recall, the gleaming Book, the feel of its warmth under her fingers, the white radiance of peace that settled in her heart when she caught memories of a voice that was sublime, and hands upon her head.

'The future is not predestined that anyone could know it.' She found it hard to clear her throat and form the words. 'We have it in our own power. You may wish, or guess, but you don't know.'

Tiyo-Mah broke into a dry laugh, a sound like the rustle of rags falling from old bones. She lifted her arm, and out of the shadowed hangings of cloth of gold and black and bronze silks behind her slid the dwarf Azrub, his yellow eyes gleaming in the candlelight.

Tathea froze, horror crawling on her skin.

'Do you still believe I cannot see the future?' Tiyo-Mah said softly. 'And the past! Remember, Ta-Thea, what it will cost you if you lie!'

Tathea looked into the blind, milk-opaque eyes, and then at the dwarf beyond her.

'The future is not yet cast . . .' she repeated, but her voice faltered. There was a vast power in the chamber and it filled the air like a giant pulse, beating against her, seeking a way inside.

'No prophecy?' Tiyo-Mah raised her arched eyebrows. 'No seers, no revelators of God?'

'Of God, yes—'

'Then if God knows the future, it must be certain, at least in part!' Tiyo-Mah reasoned.

Tathea drew in her breath to argue, and the weight of the evil in the room all but crushed her.

'Tell her, Azrub,' Tiyo-Mah said gently, smiling with inward pleasure.

The dwarf faced Tathea and his goat eyes seemed to look into her mind. His voice when he spoke was whispering soft and as pervasive as the sound of the sea, and yet every word fell clearly in her head like rung crystal.

'God knows the future, because he knows your heart.' His white fingers wove in the air and the light from the candles glittered on his arms. 'He knows what you will do, where you will fail, and where you will succeed. Nothing is predestined. But if you know enough, as God knows enough, then you can prophesy.' His fearful mouth widened in a smile. 'And of course there are others who know you also, know your dreams and your sins.' He rolled his tongue over the words. 'Knows the things you would hide from God, the places in your soul where even you do not tread; the passions, the hatreds and the desires you dare not name. And the fears that haunt you in the darkness when you meet yourself in the night, and at last you are alone . . . we know those also.'

Tathea was paralysed. She tried to move, but her limbs would not obey her.

'Yes, there is a life before this one,' Azrub went on. 'Just as there is a life after. I saw you there. I know you, as in your soul you know me!'

It was a shock so violent it was as if the whole room had turned over, buffeting her from floor to ceiling, wall to wall, before it righted her and cast her up, grasping for support. This fearful creature beside Tiyo-Mah knew the truth she had only half recollected in bursts of light from deep in the mind: a great concourse of people, a number-less host awaiting the plan of life, a promise of everlasting joy, a knowledge that superseded all.

She stared from the dwarf to the old woman. How could they know? It was not possible.

Tiyo-Mah laughed, a low, gurgling sound, as if relishing some obscene appetite. It came as a surprise that she did not lick her dry, soft lips.

'Not so clever, Ta-Thea!' She leaned far forward. 'Did you think you were the only one with knowledge? When you brought light into the world, you brought darkness also. I know what is in your heart infinitely better than you do, child, and you will never escape me.'

Tathea stared into the sightless eyes. 'You can't!'

'Oh, but I can,' Tiyo-Mah assured her. 'Through the arts Azrub has taught me, the secrets of the dead are mine.' She stopped speaking suddenly, her head to one side, listening, as if her ears, pulled out of shape by the gems suspended from them, would read Tathea's face for her. She strained to hear the slightest movement, the sigh of a breath.

'There are many powers, Ta-Thea.' Now it was the hissing voice of Azrub intruding in her mind. 'If you are with the Man of Holiness and His angels, then you are against Asmodeus and all we who serve him. And we are many against you. Far more than you know. A third part of all the hosts of heaven.'

'I know.' It was a whisper through her stiff lips. 'But however strong you are, I don't want to be part of you.' She breathed in and out shakily. 'Your rewards are misery and the eternal loneliness of those who cannot love.'

'And what is yours, Ta-Thea?' Tiyo-Mah asked, clutching the armrests of her chair, the light glistening on the rings on her thin fingers. 'Power? The time when you can tell all Shinabar what to believe, and they will tell the world?' Her voice dropped even lower. 'You will take our rewards in the end. Believe me, I conjure the dead, and they tell me secrets you cannot conceive.'

Necromancy!

Tathea was suffocated, as if the dead thronged the room with her. The sweet smell of decay filled her nose and throat.

It could only be imagination! She must control it!

Yet the evil was real. To deny it was also to deny the good. She was not strong enough. She despised her cowardice, but she knew her own vulnerability. She wanted to flee the chamber with its candles and silks and odours, the old woman with her smiling lips and the glittering dwarf beside her. But she felt crowded in on every side, as though hot bodies were pressing against her, taking the air she would breathe, holding her down, draining her strength so her feet would not move.

The candles burned lower and the incense grew thicker in her nose, sweeter, till she could taste it.

I will not!

But the words were in her mind, not on her tongue. The silence in the room was unbroken.

She stared into Azrub's goat eyes and heard his voice in her mind. 'Ah, but you will! You will pay my price in the end. You will want the power, and you will take it!'

I will not!

The smiling eyes seemed to grow brighter, and his voice was as clear in her head as speech. 'You may not think so, but in the end you will.'

'Prove me! Let me choose, and I will not!'

The eyes wavered. She drew in her breath and there was strength in it, the sickly sweetness was less. She moved her hands, then one foot, and the other.

She turned and walked, heavily, as though she dragged herself through water, and made her way across the terrible chamber, through the doors and back to where Ra-Nufis and Yattu-Shia waited. They saw her face and Ra-Nufis started towards her. Yattu-Shia's hand went to his sword.

The sweat stood out on Tathea's skin and she was cold, as if a fever had broken. The power of the Great Enemy had touched her like a sheet of ice from an eternal chaos, a darkness beyond the reach of the furthest stars, where all light is consumed and lost.

'What is it?' Ra-Nufis demanded. 'What happened? Did she deny her part in the assassinations?'

Tathea realised with surprise that she had not even mentioned it. It was no longer any act of Tiyo-Mah's that appalled her, it was what she had become.

'We must take her,' she said huskily, her lips dry. 'I need all your power to help me. She is not alone. She has an emissary of the dark with her. We shall need all the spiritual power we have, but I will not let her get away!' Tathea looked at their white faces, the sheen of fear on their skins. They, too, had felt the power.

'We must pray,' she whispered. 'Pray together. Give me your hands.'

Yattu-Shia hesitated, unwilling to sheath his sword.

'Your hand!' she commanded. 'We are not fighting men, only God can help us in this.'

Reluctantly he put the sword back and took her hand. They stood together, gripping each other, heads bent.

'Father of eternity,' Tathea said softly, 'we have no weapons against the darkness except those you give us. Azrub's power is very great. Please walk with us.'

'So be it,' Ra-Nufis and Yattu-Shia murmured together.

Tathea let go of their hands. 'Remain here,' she said to Yattu-Shia.

He started forward.

'That is an order!' she snapped.

He stood still, his face flushed, but he obeyed.

Ra-Nufis followed Tathea back down the passage. The air was motionless and heavy. Nothing moved. The silence swallowed their footsteps, and the cloying smell thickened the air. No servant was visible.

They reached the room where Tiyo-Mah had been and it was deserted. Sunlight filtered in from the high, narrow windows. The heavy curtains were illusory in the light and shadow.

They stared at one another for a moment, then turned to leave. But their way was barred by the squat, powerful figure of the dwarf. His arms were folded, his diamond-paned sleeves hanging, and his eyes were brilliant with malevolence.

'She has gone to see her treasures.' Again, his voice was soft and sibilant, like rain on dead leaves, but every word was hideously clear. 'For the last time,' he added. 'At least, for the last time as they are.' There was a moment's silence, thick as water. 'She is ready to depart.' He moved past them and disappeared into a high-ceilinged passage behind the ebony chair as if he knew they would follow, his tunic glittering even in the dim light from the high windows.

He led the way further downward, at first shallow steps in the black basalt, then narrower and steeper stairs lit by low, burning torches. Hidden vents took the smoke away and kept the air sweet, but they were below the earth, and the weight of the building seemed to press down on them.

Ra-Nufis followed close behind Tathea, almost touching her. If he also felt the oppression and the choking fear, he gave no sign of it, and not once did he hesitate.

Azrub's golden feet made no sound whatever on the floor, as though his massive body had no substance, and not once did he look round to see if they were with him.

He led them through chamber after chamber, each with one entrance, and, at the far end, one exit. In all of them the floor was thick with dust, and there was one set of footprints across it ahead of him, two after he had passed. The first were narrow, sharp-toed, and the left foot dragged a little. Tiyo-Mah. His were broad and smooth, with no arch to the foot, as if he was so heavy his own weight flattened his flesh.

In the last room, a rounded place like a cave, its walls hewn from the desert rock beneath the city, the old woman stood facing them, surrounded by ornaments of gold, jasper, beryl, chrysolite and alabaster, workmanship stretching back three thousand years, the greatest and most exquisite pieces Shinabar had produced. It was a world's ransom of treasure.

She ignored Ra-Nufis as if he were not there and faced Tathea.

'There are those who say you are like me,' she said, leaning forward a little. Her adorned black tabard made her look like some scrawny bird of prey, beak-nosed beneath her high forehead. 'They are fools! You have a surface strength, but it is shallow. You have not the courage to grasp the real power. You will always give it up in the end, because you want to be loved!'

'I don't want power,' Tathea said.

Tiyo-Mah laughed, not the dry cackle one would have expected, but a soft, ugly sound which penetrated the ears and was totally human.

'Yes you do, daughter-in-law. Oh, yes you do! Perhaps you will realise it too late. I shall know. I shall taste it on my tongue with pleasure.' She took a step back. 'I must go. You have left me no alternative.' Her blind eyes flickered to the dwarf, then back to Tathea. 'But Azrub will wait here, and watch for me. He will guard my interests, and you will never defeat him.' She bent her thin shoulders a little. 'But you know that. I have no need to tell you. You understand eternity, and the times of all things.' And she turned and walked away from them towards the far wall. When she reached it she hesitated a moment, then continued forward. The solid rock seemed to waver, melt, then close around her, and she was gone. The chamber was empty but for Ra-Nufis and Tathea, and Azrub standing in the entrance, his goat eyes golden in the torchlight.

'She was wrong,' he said with a gurgle of dry mirth. 'You don't understand time at all. There are doorways, places where we have weakened the fabric . . .'

'We?' Tathea demanded.

'We who serve your Great Enemy,' he answered, smiling more widely, showing his gums. 'She has stepped into the past. You will not find her. But she will return, now . . . or later . . . or earlier! When the time is right.' He stepped aside. 'Go your ways. There is nothing you can do. The future may be yours, or it may not, but the past is safe, and Tiyo-Mah with it!' Then he turned and walked away, and when Ra-Nufis and Tathea went into the passage he had disappeared.

It was not until they were outside in the sun that Ra-Nufis looked at Tathea with blazing eyes, sweat glistening on his skin.

She answered his unspoken question. 'They can remember the existence before this, things we have forgotten. They know all truth.'

His eyes narrowed and his body stiffened. 'How is it they remember and we don't? Why would God allow them such an advantage?'

Yattu-Shia stood in silent confusion, looking from one to the other.

'Advantage?' she said slowly. 'Is it?'

'Yes, of course it is!' There was certainty in Ra-Nufis's face, the attitude of his slender body. 'Knowledge is always an advantage. If they have retained what they learned there, and we have lost it, then they have weapons we have not! It is unjust, and I cannot believe that God is unjust.'

'Nor can I.' A tiny spark of light kindled within her. 'Which is one of the reasons I believe it is no advantage. Recalling what we knew there is not a weapon. If we did know, then the choice is already made. To think otherwise is to mistake the purpose of life. We must make our decisions for good or ill with no knowledge of the reward, simply because we love. No other choice has any value, it would be merely self-interest.'

'That is a contradiction,' he pointed out, squinting a little into the sun. It was suffocating in the street, shadowed by the high old

242

buildings, the air motionless. 'If it were true, then the emissaries of darkness would have chosen light, because it is the only decision which carries a reward.' He shook his head. 'You have misunderstood something.'

The light inside her was absolute certainty. 'It is not the knowing that matters, it is the loving,' she answered. 'You can know all things, indeed the Great Enemy does know.' She was willing Ra-Nufis to understand. 'But he has no belief in goodness. He has no love for man, or for anything else, not for anything in creation. Knowledge is good, and from it may spring wisdom, but it is love that is the power.'

'You may be right . . .' he said slowly, following her thought. 'He taught Tiyo-Mah, that . . . dwarf?'

'Azrub? Yes. All manner of things, even necromancy.'

Yattu-Shia shivered in the heat, his hands clenching.

'Necromancy?' Ra-Nufis's voice was high and a little hoarse. 'Is such a thing possible?'

'Yes. I felt . . .' It sounded hysterical out here in the street but it was true. 'I felt the weight of the dead, the unforgiving and unforgiven, there in the room with her. I smelled the decay of it. The rot clung in my throat and filled my nose.'

Ra-Nufis shuddered, moving his head from side to side in denial. 'I didn't know such things were more than nightmares.'

'The power for evil walks hand in hand with the power for good,' she said quietly. 'When I brought the light, I also opened the doors for darkness. That is what choice is about.'

He did not speak, but let out his breath in a sigh of understanding.

In spite of the fact that the vast majority of the people of Shinabar did not believe in the teachings of the Isarch's Book, the High Priest Tugomir was still deeply concerned that it was being preached at all. It was worse than misguided, it was a dangerous disease in the heart of the nation which desperately needed to rebuild its morality after the ravages of first war, then famine, and now, the worst of all, conquest by Camassia. The philosophy in the Book ate away at strength of character, it corroded virtue and propounded magic and reliance on mystical beings where there ought to be courage, self-mastery, honour and devotion to duty.

He had spoken and taught against it with every skill of reason and oratory he knew, and with great success, but still the Isarch persisted, and too many believers remained like a dark current in the core of the city, and even out in the desert.

He was wearing a single tabard instead of his usual regalia because he had been visiting an elderly friend. They had spoken in civilised and cultured terms of the days before Mon-Allat's overthrow, long before Ta-Thea had returned no more a Shinabari but a foreigner, determined to destroy all that was unique and precious in her people. They had taken a little wine, well-matured, and eaten honey cakes in the shade by the cool, watered walls.

Passing close to the tower above the great cisterns, the vast underground chambers hewn from the rock by primeval rains, where the water was stored for the entire city, he heard ugly shouts and a note of raucous laughter. He quickened his pace to see what the disturbance was and put an end to it.

He came round the corner into a small square. On one side stood an ancient temple with a carved façade, and on its shallow, sandstone steps a woman was defying a mob. They were closing in to attack an old man with a crippled arm. They crowded round the two figures, fists raised, faces red with fury.

'Stop it!' the woman commanded. 'What is the matter with your wits? Do you think one old man's words are going to change what you are? He has no power. Leave him alone!' She put her arms round his scrawny, misshapen shoulders. She was a handsome woman with a fair skin and bright auburn hair tied loosely back, wound in a turquoise rope of silk. Tugomir knew her, she was the courtesan Arimaspis who used to be Mon-Allat's mistress and was now one of the few who openly espoused the Book.

The crowd was quieter but no less menacing.

'He cursed us!' a thin-faced woman cried out. 'He said one day Shinabar would fall and become a wilderness. If he lives, the curse lives!' She flung out her arms dramatically. 'That's what you want, you and your Book! The priests know that.' She swung round to the others, her face mottled and ugly with rage. 'Haven't you heard Tugomir, the greatest priest of all, warn us that its filth would weaken and pollute us all till we are no longer acceptable to our ancestors and we will be cut off from the gods – alone in eternity.'

'Yes!' came back the cry. 'Stone him! Stone them both!'

'Yes, stone her too!' yelled a man in blue and grey. 'Get rid of the Book. Send it back to Camassia with the witch who brought it!'

'Get rid of the obscenity!' echoed the shouts. 'Stone the blasphemers!'

'You're wrong!' Arimaspis tried to raise her voice above them. 'No one has the power to curse you! Your soul is your own. You can be whatever you want!'

'I want to be rich!' a voice hooted shrilly. 'What about that, eh?'

'I did not say you could have what you like,' Arimaspis replied, still holding the old man and half protecting him with her own body. 'I said you could be what you wanted. You can be good or evil, cowardly or brave . . .'

She did not finish. A stone flew past her, hit the wall behind and clattered to the ground. She flinched but did not step back.

'You can't always choose what happens to you,' she tried again. Her body was shaking and her blue eyes were wide with fear. 'But you can choose what you do about it, what you feel, whether you love or hate.' She swallowed, facing them with her anger and her belief. 'Shinabar will stand or fall on the strength of her people, not on an old man's words!'

Tugomir was half aware of a strange figure standing shadowed by one of the temple pillars, a heavy, squat man with a huge head and hands that were always moving, but Tugomir's attention was on the woman in the crowd. He pushed his way forward, forcing people aside with his sharp elbows till he stood next to her, facing the mob. He saw the hate in their mouths and their eyes with a rush of coldness that caught him by surprise. These were his own followers.

'The Book is a mistaken and wicked teaching!' he said loudly.

They knew him, and a shiver of excitement passed through them. They fell silent to listen.

'But this is not the way to oppose it!' he cried, the fire in his voice burning across their emotions. 'Screaming in the streets like animals dishonours your ancestors and brings shame on your families! That is what will tear Shinabar down. Forget the old man!' He flung out his arm dismissively. 'Whether he speaks true or false, you cannot change it by beating him, only by changing yourselves.' His face burned. It was what the woman Arimaspis had said. The last thing he had meant was to echo her.

'Yes, we can!' a woman shrieked. 'Stone the curser and the curse will be undone!' She stooped to pick up a smooth piece of rock and hurled it at them. It caught Arimaspis on the shoulder and she staggered back, tripping on the step and gasping with pain. Another stone struck the old man, drawing blood. A third landed with a sharp crack on the wall beyond them.

Tugomir was horrified. Had his people degenerated so far? And they were his people, mirroring his hatred of the Book, repeating his words against it, but twisted, with a violence he had never meant.

He shouted, but this time he was barely heard above the din. They were not listening any more. Unthinking rage possessed them, born of the fear he had taught. They pressed forward, fists raised, hurling punches and blows, stones flying. It was hideous and bloody. Arimaspis fell to the ground.

Choked with horror, buffeted and knocked to the ground, Tugomir tried to cover his head as the stones thudded into him, tearing his skin. He shouted, and no one heard him. Another stone struck Arimaspis, and another. There was blood on her head, on her face. A stone hit Tugomir's shoulder. Another broke the bones of his thin arm and pain shot through him. The old fortune-teller was a trampled heap, unable to resist the blows raining on him. Everywhere was the din of screaming and cursing, the thrashing of bodies, the smell of sweat and fear and sticky, sweet blood.

Then suddenly the crowd was silent and they stood motionless, staring at the bodies crumpled on the steps, blood running over the stone.

One by one they moved back, shuffling in the dust, and Tugomir leaned awkwardly to lift Arimaspis's head with his unbroken arm, sick with pain and misery. She was covered in blood and disfigured by terrible injuries.

'Why?' he sobbed, holding her with desperate gentleness. 'Why? You don't believe in fortune telling. Why did you defend the old fool?'

Her voice was less than a whisper as she fought darkness and pain. 'I wanted them to see . . . that God gave them the right to choose.'

He attempted to raise her, wipe some of the blood from her face, her tangled hair, but his broken arm was useless and he was dizzy with pain.

She was trying to speak. He bent closer to her.

'No power of heaven or hell can take it from them,' she whispered, 'only themselves. I wanted . . .' For a moment she struggled and her breath caught, stopped for a while, and a slow trickle of blood stained her lips. He held her tenderly, fiercely with his one arm, as if he could will his own life into her, as if his horror and his grief could give her strength. A drenching guilt racked him, worse than any physical anguish. He saw himself as if until this moment he had had his back to the sun.

'I wanted to . . .' she began again, very low, '. . . all their promise.' Her eyes met his and saw his pain. The faintest smile touched her mouth. She moved agonisingly slowly and put her fingers on his shattered arm. 'That is what love is . . .' But she had no more breath left, no more life. Her heart stopped, her hand slipped away. Where it had been, his flesh was whole.

He stared at it in disbelief. There was not even a scar. He would have doubted that the splintered bone, the pain, the uselessness had ever existed, but his pale tabard was soaked with his own blood.

He looked up. A man near him was staring where the wound had been, his skin ashen. He put his hands up to his face slowly, smearing himself unknowingly with dust. Then he took them away again, his eyes filled with wonder and terror.

'Oh God! What have we done?' he said hoarsely.

Another began to weep.

No one looked at anyone else, all were shocked and suddenly afraid.

They parted, stepping aside. The uniforms of the Imperial Guards showed blue and white against the dust colours. Yattu-Shia pressed the crowd back, sword drawn. The Isarch Ta-Thea came forward, her face dark with fury and grief. She knelt beside Arimaspis, so close

Tugomir could smell the perfume of her hair.

'She's dead,' Tugomir said with tears choking his voice. 'I couldn't save her! I tried.. I . . . I was to blame in the beginning.'

Tathea glared at him, then straightened to her feet and swung round to face the stoners.

'Is this your faith?' she demanded with scalding contempt, tears running down her face. 'Is this what you believe in, murdering women in the street and stoning old men to death because you don't like what they say? Is that what you admire, what you want to be?'

There was a sullen silence. They shifted uncomfortably.

'A hundred of you to kill one old man?' she went on. 'I see courage is also one of your virtues . . .' Her sarcasm was acid. 'Tolerance, nobility of thought and act, and honesty!'

They began muttering under their breath. Several moved forward, ugly with rage.

She stood facing them, her fury and pain mounting. 'You are cowards, all of you, vicious, corrupt and despicable. If this is what your creed has brought you to, then it is a doctrine of damnation . . .'

She got no further. A huge man with a protruding belly snarled a curse and bent to pick up another stone. Others surged forward roughly.

Tugomir tried to rise, but he was held down by the weight of Arimaspis's body, and he could not bear to let her go, even to save himself, or the Isarch.

The Imperial Guards drew their swords. Another moment and there would be a massacre in the streets.

It was then that the dwarf spoke almost at Tathea's elbow. He stood in the shadows half behind the nearest pillar, barely distinguishable from the bars of sunlight and shadow on the stone.

'Choice!' he whispered in his soft, hissing tone. 'You have choice, Ta-Thea! Blood in the streets. Your people's, your guards', Yattu-Shia's for certain . . . Tugomir's . . . perhaps even your own. Is that how you want it to end, your bringing the Book to your people?' He let his breath out in a sigh between his teeth. 'And more than that. I can crumble the tower into the cistern below, and poison the whole city's water, and I will. The dead will choke the streets, and they will blame you and your Book for it. You have just promised them damnation. We all heard you. Never doubt I can do it. You know well enough . . .'

She made herself turn to look at him, to meet the dreadful goat eyes.

'Or?' she whispered.

A spark of triumph lit inside him. 'Or denounce the Book, say it is a lie, a device you used to gain the throne, to dupe the Camassian Emperor into helping you, and you can have the crown of Shinabar, keep it all your life, and I will see that that is long, far longer than you can know.'

'No!' Her body was tight, as if she had been struck. She was holding her hands up to defend herself. 'No, I can't . . .' She seemed to have forgotten the crowd, the heat, the danger, even Tugomir crouched on the steps, with Arimaspis in his arms. She saw only the dwarf. 'No!'

'The cistern?' he whispered. 'I will!'

'No!' She moved forward, then stopped.

'There is one other choice.' His voice caressed the words.

She said nothing.

'Leave Shinabar for ever. Never set foot on this land again. Then I will stay my hand, the crowd will let you pass. Go, as you are, without returning to the palace, without the Book – and Thoth-Moara will live.'

It was monstrous! Everything in her rebelled against it . . . except a tiny heart of stillness inside her, so far inside it was like another age, Iszamber's voice in the desert, his wide blue eyes, which looked beyond the known into ages undreamed. He had said Shinabar would not believe, but the Island at the Edge of the World would, even after the ruin of the earth.

'I will go,' she said clearly. 'I will leave Shinabar.'

Azrub's eyes flickered, and in that instant she knew with amazement and a shock of joy that he was disappointed. It was not what he had wanted, not what he meant to happen. He turned away from her, to Tugomir.

'There you are, priest,' he said softly. 'Now you can rule your people's faith again.'

At last Tugomir let Arimaspis's body rest and rose to his feet stiffly. He stood very straight, a narrow, ugly little man with a great nose and burning eyes.

'I have seen a terrible beauty today.' His voice was harsh with passion. 'And I must follow it. I will go with Ta-Thea. Where she goes, there I will go also. Now, whatever heaven or hell bids you, let us pass and begin our journey.' He turned to Yattu-Shia. 'Bury the woman, and the old man also. God will preserve the light of their souls.' He raised his hand in parting, then followed Tathea out of the square.

Chapter Sixteen

They left from Tarra-Ghum. They passed unrecognised through the city and took a ship westwards towards the Island at the Edge of the World. Tugomir had never left Shinabar before, but if he were afraid, or the immensity of the shifting, turbulent ocean troubled him, he was too proud to show it even by a clenched jaw or a shaking hand. His mind was consumed by the desire to learn from Tathea all she could teach him of the true meaning of the Book, not the mangled fragments he had heard. The darkness of his misconceptions caused him constant anxiety and he spoke of it every time they were alone.

The Book itself was in Thoth-Moara where she had left it. It was the first time it had been out of her keeping since she had awoken in the skiff on the shores of the Lost Lands. It was a bereavement that hurt with an almost physical pain, but worse than her own sense of loss was her fear of what would become of it.

What would happen to Ra-Nufis, perhaps the only true, passionate believer left in Shinabar? He knew where it was, and would surely take it and guard it – if Azrub left him alive to do so!

The knowledge of defeat was overwhelming. It was only Tugomir's constant demands, and the obligation to answer him, which drove the heartsickness from her mind.

They sailed across the vivid cobalt seas off the coast of Shinabar, then on into the harder, cooler blue waters westward past the mountains and to the north of the wild coast of Tirilis. She remembered all she could of what was written in the Book, explaining it to Tugomir from the beginning. She could recite the first pages as if they were written on her heart. Then she told him of the conversation between God and the Great Enemy, Asmodeus, and how God had answered each argument, showing how the plan met every need of the purpose of life, and how the Adversary still would not accept it.

'But it does!' Tugomir said eagerly, grasping the essence of the meaning almost before she had said the words. It was as if all his life he had been searching for this, and now that he has found it he could not drink deeply enough of it. 'We have it all!'

They were almost beyond Tirilis, in seas even colder and wilder green, before she realised with a surge of surprise how deeply, in

249

teaching him, she had confirmed her own faith. It had begun with her love of the words in the Book, knowing that they were true. Now, standing on the deck in the haze of dawn, watching the arch of heaven pale in the east behind them, spreading light across the face of the water, white on the wave crests, there was a new strength in her heart. Failure lay behind and darkness ahead, and yet her grief lifted. She felt a confidence that had no origin in reason.

The words rested with a great peace inside her. 'I am the beginning and the end. Your name is before My eyes, and I shall not forget you.'

But the sea was not at peace. The further west they travelled, the more troubled the wind and water became, until as they turned northwards towards the Island, the air grew heavy with the presage of storm. By nightfall the captain was pacing the deck, eyes on the sky, his face tight and anxious. The mariners stood together in twos and threes, muttering and then silent. The wind grew more shrill in the rigging till it was a high whine, and with darkness came the first jagged bursts of lightning. The current beneath the ship was fast, the water leaden but still unbroken by spume.

Tugomir stood on deck, gazing at the gathering violence. In the blue-white glare of the flashes, his face was filled with awe. The fear all around him did not seem to disturb his certainty. He knew the Word of God, and nothing was stronger.

Tathea understood. Some deep well of memory within her knew of another storm so terrible it threatened an entire people as the forces of destruction combined, the elements of air and water, and chaos of barbarism within men, and the eternal hatred of the Great Enemy who would corrupt creation itself. And yet with the knowledge came a white pinpoint of certainty, a memory of love that was worth any price, brighter than the darkness of all the spaces between the stars.

The storm struck them with a fury that hurled the seas in torrents about them, tearing the tight-reefed sails as if they were rags and hurling the ship like a ball thrown at random. They were drenched with water on deck, then bruised by being battered against the wooden walls of the cabin, knocked to the floor again and again. In the darkness they knew nothing of what was happening about them except the tumult and the incessant, deafening noise. They clung together, wrapped in each other's strength.

When at last it was over, they were too shaken and exhausted and pressed by the need to mend all that could be salvaged to have time to speak of it.

They limped into the port of Sylum, grateful to make harbour and set foot on land, any land. It was the following day before they even looked around them to observe its nature. A glance showed it was far newer than the City in the Centre of the World, but of the same style of architecture, adapted to suit a cooler clime. Here the stone was more mixed with grey, and most of it was still clean from the mason's knife.

There were Camassian warships and merchantmen lying in the harbour, native ships built for rough seas rather than great distances, and graceful skiffs with rust and saffron sails from the Lost Lands. Tathea recognised them, and the pull of memory was sharp. There was something in the movement of light across the water, wind-streaked cloud over a vast sky, which brought back snatches of something else, sweeter and further away, but gone again too swiftly to capture.

'This is a Camassian province now,' Tugomir said with an edge of disgust to his voice. 'Conquered about forty years ago, in the time of Baradeus. If Isadorus has been true to his beliefs, they will at least have heard of you. We should make ourselves known to the Governor.'

Ortelios had indeed heard of Tathea and had some knowledge of the teaching of the Book. He made them most welcome, eager to listen and to learn from the source of his belief. He had become a follower and made his covenants only recently, and knew that his understanding was in its infancy.

'We have many who inquire after the Book,' he told them earnestly the first evening they sat together around the great hearth where half a tree burned to keep at bay the chill of the spring night. The stone-flagged floors were covered with hides and the walls were hung with tapestries, which at least moderated the worst of the draughts. Several large dogs lay half asleep, close to the fire, and a striped cat washed itself thoroughly.

Tathea glanced across at Tugomir and saw his clenched hands and fixed gaze. She knew he was cold and frightened. This barbarous culture horrified him. He had given up everything he loved, everything safe and familiar, and he had no idea what lay ahead of him, except that it was dark and seemed always chill, and apart from herself he was alone among strangers. It must have taken all the courage he possessed to endure it, and she loved him for his faith.

'I hope you will teach many more,' Ortelios was saying, throwing more wood on the fire. One of the dogs stirred and stretched, then went back to sleep again. Outside, the wind was rising, rattling the windows. 'But the old belief is strong, especially away from the cities,' he went on with an apologetic smile. 'Most of the land is covered in forests, except for the mountains to the west where the Empire's armies have never been. And to the north, of course.'

Tugomir shuddered. Forests were a misery he had not even contemplated. 'What brought the Empire here?' he asked incredulously. It was beyond his imagination why anyone should come to such a place of their own volition.

Ortelios smiled and leaned back in his chair, making himself more

251

comfortable. 'It is a very rich land. It has the best timber I've seen. One can grow all manner of crops here.'

'Crops?' Tugomir scowled at the darkness beyond the window.

'Oh, yes,' Ortelios said enthusiastically. 'Wheat, rye, barley, oats, all sorts of vegetables because of the regular rains, and of course fruit and some nuts. Also there is always plentiful grass, so the animals are excellent. The wool here is the best in the world.'

'No doubt it is needed!' Tugomir responded drily.

Ortelios smiled. 'And cattle and swine,' he added. 'And very good horses indeed. We have crossed some of the Island breeds with Shinabari, and they are superb.'

Tugomir gritted his teeth. 'Indeed?'

'And there are other resources as well,' Ortelios continued. 'Fish, of course, any amount or variety . . .'

Tugomir showed the first sign of interest. Good food was a part of civilised culture he assumed he had left behind.

'And pearls,' Ortelios added. 'And various metals, especially tin.'

'Is that why they came?' Tathea asked him.

'In part.' He turned to her. 'The first expedition was largely exploratory, when Baradeus was making his name as a general, before he had aspirations towards the throne of Camassia. It proved a most fruitful investment. To begin with the conquest was hard fought. Some of the tribes are fine warriors, but of course the Camassians had superior weaponry, and in the end they won. It took ten or twelve years. They began to build cities, roads, and harbours. Many soldiers settled here, my grandfather among them. He married an Island woman.' He said it with pride.

'And gradually they taught the Islanders a new way of government. Peace spread among the tribes who had previously warred with one another more or less all the time. The country began to prosper. Now many Islanders are quite proud to have a Camassian heritage. Most of us speak both languages.'

Tugomir said nothing. Tathea looked across at his sombre features in the firelight and knew as plainly as if he had spoken it that he was thinking of the subtlety and beauty he had left behind him, the long philosophical discussions with friends late into the desert night. He would never again wander through great libraries with their tens of thousands of scrolls where he could choose any at random and explore the great minds of the past, the history and legend, the poetry and the dreams. The loss was marked deep in the lines of his face, and she saw loneliness there, and the fear of the dark and unknown ahead.

She smiled at him, but he did not see her.

The following evening Ortelios held a great feast in their honour, welcoming them to Sylum and the Island. There were above seventy guests, all powerful by virtue of either office or influence.

Tathea noticed one man above the others. He sat at the great oak dining table three places to the left of Tugomir. He was of ordinary build and height with a lean face, fair-skinned and faintly freckled, as if he had stood too near when some craftsman had been grinding gold, and the dust had settled on him. His eyes were blue, light as clear glass. In his movements, and the way he watched before he spoke, there was something faintly vulpine. His name was Nastemah, and he was lord of lands rich in silver and iron ore.

Next to him was his wife. Her cloud of dark hair framed a face of unusual beauty. Whenever Nastemah spoke, she listened intently, her eyes wide, as though she would memorise every expression of his face and each word would be graven in her mind. When anyone addressed her, she deferred to Nastemah before replying.

Tathea assumed they were very recently married, and said as much later to Ortelios.

'Oh no.' He shook his head and there was a curious regret in his face for which there seemed no cause. 'They have been married for many years. Verrani is gentler and more obedient now than she was when I first knew her.'

'Then she loves him the more,' Tathea deduced.

Ortelios looked away. 'Perhaps.'

'Does she owe him some debt?' Tathea searched for explanations other than love. 'Has her family committed some wrong against him? Or did he rescue them from war, or bondage?'

'Nothing, as far as I know,' Ortelios answered, but the unhappiness in him lingered. Possibly it was envy. Verrani was not only beautiful, there was a haunting quality to her loveliness, a fragility which was almost childlike. Tathea noticed how several men seemed eager to protect her, to see her smile, as if they wished her safe from some fear or pain.

Tathea and Tugomir began to teach as many people as wished to learn more deeply of the Book. The foundations had already been laid in words and letters from Camassia. It was a matter of adding, refining and explaining, of answering questions and attempting to instil obedience to the discipline as well as conveying the joy of the promise. To make covenants willingly, even eagerly, was one thing, but again and again they found themselves having to urge the necessity of keeping them, that the penalty for breaking them was harsh and real.

Tugomir learned as he taught. Tathea watched with ever increasing pleasure as his mind expanded to grasp the full meaning behind everything she could tell him of the Book's teachings.

Spring passed into summer, and then into autumn. The glory of it faded in wood smoke, scarlet berries in the hedges and a sharp, clean light with the tingle of frost. Tathea and Tugomir had been teaching in an outlying area and the sun was sinking as they drove together in a chariot along one of the few great Camassian-built roads back towards Sylum. Tugomir sat in silence. He had never enjoyed chariot riding even on the smooth desert roads of home. This rougher vehicle with its unpadded seats and the cold edge of the wind stinging his face was something to be endured with fortitude.

Tathea gazed with a strange, burning joy at the flaming red of a tree, the late sun gold on a shaved field, stubble gleaming where the scythes had cut the stalks low. She found its beauty almost overwhelming, as if it touched a chord of memory in her of another age too good to bear recalling because its loss was unendurable.

They were almost at the walls of Sylum when she spoke.

'It is time for us to teach in the other regions,' she said, glancing sideways to see his face.

His body stiffened. 'South,' he said immediately. 'Perhaps we should start in the south.' There was a tiny thread of hope in his voice, but he did not betray himself by looking at her.

She smiled. 'A good idea,' she said gently. 'We can begin at Kyeelan-Iss.' She was referring to the long peninsula to the far south-west which jutted out towards the Lost Lands, a natural fortress of rock cliffs pounded by seas that stretched to the edge of the last ocean known to man.

She saw the answering smile on his face before he pulled his cloak up round his ears and nodded.

They laboured hard all through the winter; it was a season unlike anything either of them had ever imagined before, let alone experienced. Driving winds howled in off the sea, carrying torrential rain. Winds screamed on the wings of storms that seemed to tear the ocean off its floor and hurl it at the cliffs. But the hospitality was warm. The harshness of nature seemed to make men cling closer together. Hunger, weariness, cold, even the rain which Tugomir loathed with intensity, did not stop their work. Soaked to the skin, shaking with chill, wind-chapped and with a streaming nose, he still spoke, between coughing fits, with an enthusiasm which touched his hearers. Some hated him, but most held him in a kind of awe, whether they believed his words or not.

They travelled from one town to another, huddled together under blankets and skins, telling each other wry, Shinabari jokes and trying to remember the words of old songs. Sometimes the hills were mantled with snow and the skies bleak and blue, sharp as dawn over the sea. The days were short. At night the blackness seemed solid, as if they were in a pit. Sometimes the dazzling clarity of the stars shed a faint glimmer over the snow. Sunset, flaming wild and splendid across the wash of ice crystals, shone like fire.

They heard many tales of the other parts of the Island. In the far west, beyond the mountains of Horvellyn, was the fortress of Dinath Aurer, where no Imperial soldier had ever set foot. Of the last shore to the west, beyond the fortress and the cliffs of Kharkheryll, no man had returned to tell. Nor had any travelled to Lantrif of the River, lying low to the west.

The great central forest of Hirioth, full of ancient gnarled trees and sudden glades, where the very air seemed green and gold, was the land of the Flamens, the old religion of the Island, and no Camassian trespassed into its primeval sanctity.

Tathea and Tugomir went up the eastern coast to the city of Yba, and beyond to the ruins of Layamon. Eventually perhaps they would even go to the north. Tathea kept that in her heart, treasuring the promises of Iszamber. She would not tell Tugomir yet. He had more than enough to bear with what he already knew. The Waste Lands stretched up towards the last shore before the lands of ice. She heard tales of their beauty, the high, wide moorlands beaten and scoured by mighty winds, bright with secret tarns whose waters reflected the sky and lay peat-dark in hollows of the hills. In autumn the land was covered with purple flowers and bracken the shade of old bronze worn smooth on warriors' shields.

The renewal of the year was slow and sweet as they rode east, a season of glancing rainstorms, birdsong so throbbing with ecstasy it seemed as if throats would burst with the sheer, blazing joy of it. Tiny flowers appeared in the shelter of southern hillsides, pale and delicate as a scattering of petals. And as they skirted Sylum and passed the outermost edges of Hirioth, Tathea saw the tree buds swelling and breaking into green one by one, as if the life in them were too delicious to be taken hastily but must be savoured every moment, each translucent leaf carefully unfolded and set against the sun.

They taught everyone who would listen. By the time the hedges were rich with flowers and the banks danced with gold and misty, fragile blues beneath the ancient woodlands, a thousand people had covenanted to follow the Book and five thousand more were on the brink.

The Eastern Shore was a place of great sand dunes scented with yellow sea lupins, washed by harsh tides and mighty winds, a salt-tasting land of wide skies and crying seabirds. Here, too, there were people who listened, and Tathea and Tugomir spent much time talking, explaining. Spring became summer, and autumn. They moved north again and spent the winter in the city of Yba, then turned and came back inland past the edges of Hirioth towards the south.

By high summer when the trees were green, towering over the land, and the apple and plum boughs hung so heavy they leaned to the ground, the teaching had spread through every city, village and hamlet of the Imperial occupation.

Then it was time to go north. It could no longer be put off. All had been accomplished here, and Tathea felt pulled by the memory of Iszamber's words about the darkness to come at a time no man knew of, when the only ones to stand would be eleven priests on the Western Shore, the last stronghold of the light.

She told Tugomir of it in a quiet garden overhung with plum trees where the sunlight fell through the boughs in half-tones, dappled on the grass.

'North?' he said warily. He could not refuse anything that served the Book, but she could see in his face the dread of what it would mean. 'Further than we've been already?'

'Yes. Through the forest.'

He blanched. 'The forest? Are there any people there?'

'Oh yes, quite a few.'

He stood silently for several moments in the glancing sunlight. A bird sang in one of the plum trees. A hedgehog ambled through the grass, all spines and black toes.

'How do we travel?' he said at last.

She knew what he was thinking. She had seen his expression every time circumstances forced him to pass close to a horse. Fear was written deep in his eyes, the angle of his body and the haste and clumsiness of his movements. But there was no other answer. The forest tracks were not wide enough for even the smallest cart, and they could not carry on their backs all they would need, let alone copies of the Book. Apart from that, she doubted Tugomir's narrow chest and spindly legs would carry him the thousand miles or so they needed to travel.

He anticipated her answer. Perhaps he read it in her eyes. 'Horse-back,' he said quietly. 'I suppose God will preserve me.' He did not sound as if he believed it.

And indeed it proved even more difficult for him than he had imagined. He hated his horse because it terrified him. Although it was normally a good-natured beast, it seemed to sense his dislike and reacted accordingly. It fidgeted, started at sudden sounds or move-ments, shied at the running of a rabbit or the flight of a bird across its path. Once, to Tugomir's outrage, it twisted its head round and actually bit his foot.

The horse Tathea chose for herself was a long-legged creature, largely grey but with fine black speckles and patches across its back. She named it Casper. It was not especially beautiful, but it was swift and intelligent and of a gentle temperament. She grew fond of it very quickly.

On the second morning, having slept in a blanket on the ground, Tugomir was so stiff he could not rise to his feet. Pain shot through every joint and he sank back again. Tathea was standing by the horses and saw his predicament. She came over quickly and offered her hand to help him. He took it because he had no choice, but it was humiliating and he was acutely embarrassed.

'Thank you!' he snapped. She wanted to offer to anoint his feet, but before she could he hobbled away to find a private place to perform his morning ablutions.

Two days later they left the open woodland and entered Hirioth itself, where ancient tree roots twisted deep into the earth like gnarled hands clinging on. Tugomir had a painful sense that the forest was alive and sentient. Branches spread above them in towering layers so dense the very light between seemed green, like deep water, and the sun penetrated only in glancing shafts in clearings and glades where suddenly all was gold. The sounds of the human world, all that meant sanity and reason to Tugomir, were closed out. Yet there was never silence. He was uneasily aware of constant movement around him: leaves, birds, small animals about their business, night and day. Always something was whistling, or snuffling, rustling leaves or snapping a twig. The forest itself seemed to breathe.

And of course the days were growing shorter, the nights longer, and it was incessantly damp. He ached for the burning heat of Shinabar. He remembered its clear, dazzling sunlight as some lost heaven from which he had been for ever cast out. This was a form of slow torture.

He rode hunched up in the saddle, jiggled around like a sack of grain. Every bone hurt. The trees closed in on him, and he shut his eyes and imagined the great open sweep of the desert skies and the sharp smell of bitter herbs. Even the endless shift and abrasion of sand would be infinitely preferable to the cold trickle of rain, dripping from leaf to leaf, and the ceaseless, hidden, whispering movement all about him.

He did not complain. He knew Tathea was aware of the depth of his misery, and that if she could have relieved it she would have, but it was the nature of the forest and there was nothing for him but to endure it. But it did not help that she seemed to find it beautiful. It was incomprehensible to him; she was as Shinabari as he was, but glancing sideways at her face when they stopped, he thought from her expression that she even felt strangely comforted by it, as if in its own way it were familiar from some other age or time.

She tried to show him the beauty, to make him laugh, even to teach him to like his horse, and he tried to respond, to please her, but it was an alien world to him. He missed the civilised conversation of his old friends whose experiences and tastes matched his own. Above all he missed the sweetness and safety of being known and respected for a lifetime's devotion to his priesthood. He knew that was gone for ever. Now he was a follower of the Book of God.

This was a hideously uncomfortable way to travel. He spent the

257

entire day being constantly jolted around on the back of a creature that disliked him and seemed as nervous of the forest as he was. He was wet at least half the time. The leaves around him were turning brown and gold and red; soon they would fall off, and stark branches like withered limbs, the grotesque bones of dead giants, would surround them. It would be worse.

Their first meeting with the forest people came on the eleventh day. They rode into a wide clearing within which wooden houses were set so close under the trees they were almost hidden. A man was standing in the sunlight. He was stocky, fair-haired and dressed in browns and greens. He showed no surprise at seeing two travellers on horseback and Tugomir assumed the man had been alerted to their approach by some system of vigil. Perhaps that explained why he always felt watched in the forest.

'Welcome,' said the man courteously, but with the wariness of one who is unused to strangers. 'I am Garran. The hospitality of my house is yours. Where do you travel?' He looked puzzled.

Well he might, Tugomir thought. He must answer! He must do something to make this whole abominable journey have meaning. He dismounted with embarrassing awkwardness. For all Tathea's teaching and encouragement, he had never mastered it satisfactorily. This time he all but fell at Garran's feet, jarring his aching bones so sharply he knew his face must reflect his pain. He gritted his teeth and straightened up.

'My name is Tugomir,' he announced. 'And this is the Lady Tathea. We have come to bring you good news, the word of a great love that the hosts of heaven bear for you and all your people.' He had learned not to speak of a single God to those who revered many.

Garran looked surprised, but not resentful. He regarded Tugomir as the leader, probably because he had spoken first. Tugomir had not done it to usurp Tathea, but to remind himself why he had journeyed into this version of hell, and perhaps make it bearable.

Garran offered them food and water, care for their animals, and shelter for as long as they chose to remain. Tugomir was grateful at least to hand over his horse and go inside one of the forest houses and sit on a stationary and well-cushioned seat.

He looked around with more pleasure than he had expected. The small room was constructed with great skill and needed no ornamentation to make it beautiful. This excellent use of timber somehow justified the endless legions of trees. In the coming winter, which he dreaded, they would at least be warm. He noticed the logs already piled against the outer walls in anticipation. There were also bins, presumably to store food, and he had noticed fowls outside. Maybe there would be eggs.

Garran invited them to take the evening meal with him, and it turned out to be very agreeable, composed mostly of root vegetables and something that looked like stalks. Tugomir was careful not to ask what it was, but murmured a silent prayer over it, and ate. It was delicious. The texture was firm and the taste delicate.

The meal was finished with fruit and berries as full of sweetness and juice as any he had ever tasted.

Afterwards they went outside into the clearing and found about forty people gathered in great expectancy. Word had travelled of the stranger who brought good news, and they had all come to hear him.

He rose to speak in the hazy gold of the late sunlight amid the shimmer of leaves and sudden liquid birdsong.

'I have so much to tell you,' he began. His voice with its hard edges caressed the words and rang with a certainty of truth no listener could deny. 'It will take me a long time, but I shall begin with what is most important of all, and that is who you are!'

They stared at him. No one moved.

'You are the children of God! He created all things, worlds beyond your imagining, or mine, worlds beyond counting, more numerous than the leaves of all the trees in Hirioth. And yet He knows your name, each of you, and your face, and He loves you as if you were the only one.'

There was a sigh of breath. A bright weasel darted out of the shadow, its coat gleaming like bronze, stood motionless a moment, then shot away.

'Your spirits have existed from eternity, and shall continue for ever more. In an age before this one, which you cannot recall, you walked beside God and spoke to Him face to face, as one man with another. God has loved you with a power and a truth beyond imagining. He wishes us all to grow up, not to remain like little children, unknowing and unfulfilled, just as all of us wish it for our sons and daughters. So He has created a plan whereby we can do so, and one day become heirs to all the glory and the joy which He possesses.'

The sunlight was lengthening on the grass and the air cooled, but no one moved.

'To achieve this will naturally be long and difficult,' Tugomir went on. 'As men of the forest, you will know that the great prizes come only to the brave, the diligent, those who are prepared to labour and to learn. You are free to accept this challenge, or to pass it by. To take it up will be dangerous. Just as there is God, so also there is an Enemy, one who hates you and has done so from the beginning, who burns with jealousy because he has forfeited his chance of what may be yours. Above all things he hates the thought that one day you will pass beyond all the griefs and pains of the world and into a region so blessed that the darkness can touch you no more, and once again you will walk with God, only this time not as a child, but as a man!'

He looked at them and saw reflected in their shining faces his own passion, but with an innocence that moved him to a strange sadness, and a love for them which caught him by surprise, bringing a sting to his throat.

The following day it was the same. More people came and word spread of the wonderful teachers who brought a new way of life, and of a God who loved all men.

By day he and Tathea taught them from the words of the Book, and they learned eagerly. In the evening they lingered, keen to hear anything they might say, and Tugomir started to tell them stories. He invented as he spoke, not Shinabari legends, but something else; tales of a land of his imagination, a beautiful city by the sea where an old and exquisite culture created great works of art, and a far greater form of government where all played a part in discussion and decision. He invented characters, and a tale of one man who seized an unrighteous power and began a tyranny, and of brave men who stood against him, and a great civil war.

It was only a tale, something with which to end the day, but in its people he showed the passions of good and evil, and he saw in the faces of those who listened that they understood his deeper message.

Tathea listened to his stories as well, and they rang in her heart with a strange echo of familiarity, although she knew they were only a way of showing greater truths. But watching Tugomir's strange, ugly face and seeing the fire in it, the gentleness and the softening of his eyes, she knew that he was strong enough to remain here without her. She must press on alone, north and westwards towards the further edge of Hirioth and the mountains of Kharkheryll where the Flamens still kept the ancient faith of the Island people, and from there to Celidon and the Waste Lands.

Parting from Tugomir would be hard after nearly a year and a half in his company, sharing so many things, sad and joyous, funny, harsh and wretched. But she had only to look at his face and hear the passion in his voice to know that he would be too enthralled in his work to miss her more than now and again, perhaps in the darkness of the night, and when there was no one else to understand his terror of the forest, no one with whom to speak his own tongue. But even when they had been enemies in Shinabar, which seemed now like another life, she had known he was no coward.

The day she departed, he stood in the open glade in the morning light, staring at her with slight surprise, as if he had not truly realised that the parting must come.

'Going? So soon?'

'I must,' she answered. 'Before the winter. I must reach the people of the Western Shore.'

260

'Alone? Should you not wait until we have taught these people, and I can come with you?'

'You do not need me,' she replied with certainty, smiling at him.

He flushed faintly. 'Have I assumed too much?'

'No!' she assured him with a quick touch to his arm. 'This is as it should be. I shall leave for Kharkheryll.'

'But should I not go with you? Will you be safe alone?' He looked anxious, his narrow face filled with concern.

'I don't think two of us will be any safer than one,' she replied truthfully. 'As long as I walk in the pathways of God, He will preserve me, until the work is done. And He will be with you also, Tugomir. I shall miss your company.' And she kissed him lightly on the cheek and turned to mount Casper. She rode into the forest, disappearing into the green shadows among the trees.

Chapter Seventeen

She rode alone for many days, always north and west, as far as she could judge, although under the trees it was not easy to be certain.

The forest was thinning, the open spaces wider and more frequent, when she met the first people of the old faith. She knew a little of it from Ortelios. It seemed an animistic cult, a worshipping of trees and stones; something left over from a more barbaric age. Yet the man who stood in the glade before her was possessed of an extraordinary dignity. His face was powerful with a curved nose and broad brow. His grey hair stood out in a mane and his beard melted into it in one magnificent sweep. He wore a cloak whose colour was neither blue nor green, and yet was both.

'What do you here, woman?' His voice was deep and held a startling music, in spite of the challenge of his words.

She could not answer with the simplicity Tugomir had used to Garran. This man was more sophisticated and far more deeply rooted in his own certainties. She saw it in his eyes, in the stance of his body as he stood before her, spiritually if not literally barring her way.

'To speak with you,' she answered him. 'To learn of your beliefs and tell you of mine.'

'You are the one who brought a Book to tell us who we are, and how we should live,' he said grimly. It was almost an accusation.

She kept her voice level. 'It is for all people to take, or to leave, as they choose. Hear what I have to say, then search your heart and do as it bids you.'

'And you, woman, will you listen to me, and the beliefs of the Flamens who have lived in this land since long before you or the Camassian Empire were born?' There was a note of anger in his voice, a deep, shivering timbre of outrage. 'You and your kind come here with marching legions and swords of steel. You build mighty roads across the land as far west as Lantrif of the River, south to Kyeelan-Iss, and north to the borders of Celidon and the Waste Lands. The fortress of Layamon is like a city graven in a mountain's form. Ten million bricks stand witness to your holding of our land. Am I really free to take or to leave this Book of yours?'

It was so easy to force without meaning to. Freedom was delicate; it

262

could be marred by a word, or the omission of one. When given by a conquering race, an inflection of the voice might unintentionally imply punishment or reward.

'There is no prize except life in the eternity ahead,' she answered. 'And no penalty except its loss.'

He smiled slowly, the sad, bitter smile of a man who has been cheated often. 'Then I too may speak to my people, and remind them of their fathers dead on the battlefield, of the land which gave them birth?' he asked. 'I may bid them stand here in Hirioth and touch the bark of these trees –' he held his arms wide – 'listen to the boughs murmuring and see the leaves move in the sun, and say aloud that they have taken a new faith from our conquerors? I may bid them go to the mountains of Kharkheryll where the bare cliffs brush the sky and the wind blows clean and hard from the edge of the world, and tell the earth that has nourished and fostered them that they are heirs to some new god, and have no need of their old faith any more? That they are lords of another hope now, and the past has no more meaning?'

She did not know how to answer him. She must not fail, and she could feel his anger and his pain like a living thing in the air.

'Then I will learn from you.' She heard her own words as if from a stranger, and was filled with doubt as to whether she should have said them.

It was a reply he had not expected. It was written plain in his face. He drew breath to respond, and then also found he did not know how to.

'I am Immerith,' he said slowly. 'High Priest of the Flamens. If you will, in truth, listen, then I shall take you west, to Kharkheryll, and teach you our laws, and you must do with them what you will.'

Tathea dismounted and from then on led Casper behind her, going with Immerith on foot, in the old way of the Flamens. For some time they travelled in silence, and Tathea observed how this strange man seemed to watch and listen to the forest, even in his own fashion to commune with it. When he stopped to eat he knew without hesitation which leaves or fruit to take. It was a long, slow autumn. The last flowers of summer still entwined in long, fantastical golden trumpets, sweet-scented at evening, which climbed in vines spreading over the fallen branches in the rare glades where sunlight pierced the canopy. He looked at them long, and in deep satisfaction. He shared his food with small animals – squirrels, weasels, a badger. Even the wide-eyed deer did not run at his coming.

It was the second day before he began to tell her of his faith. It was unlike anything she had heard in either Shinabar or Camassia. Some echo of it seemed to sound from legend, but too primeval to be written.

263

'You Camassians trample through the world as if it were without life or meaning, other than that with which you invest it,' he said grimly as they set out in the morning. He walked beside her with Casper behind. 'You are blind and arrogant beyond the mind to grasp.'

She drew breath to deny being Camassian, then realised it was irrelevant. She waited for Immerith to continue.

'The birds and beasts have souls, just as we do,' he said fiercely, his voice ringing with certainty. 'You rode here on a horse. Look into its eyes, and then into a man's, and tell me why you conceive in your heart that you have some immortal spirit which he does not! Speech? Because you understand your own words and not his, you think that gives you some divinity? Because he carries you patiently, lends you his strength to perform your labours? Because he carries your kind to war, and is prepared to die for you, that makes you a better creature?'

'No,' she said quickly. 'It makes us cleverer . . . and therefore gives us the greater responsibility not to abuse our power.'

He looked at her curiously, a quickening in his face. 'All beasts? Or merely horses?'

She did not know the answer. She had not considered beyond the beasts she knew – horses, dogs, cats.

'You hesitate!' he charged.

The assumptions of pride would be ridiculous here in this murmuring forest with the wild depth of green above them. A million million leaves whispered and turned in the air. Sunlight reached the earth only in glancing shafts now and then. Gnarled roots writhed like curled snakes. In their protected hollows mosses lay in sudden pools of emerald.

'Because I don't know the answer,' she admitted.

'All beasts, all birds,' he replied gravely. 'Everything that lives. And more, the trees, the flowers, the green plants, the rocks themselves are possessed of a form of intelligence which must be revered. Nothing must be wasted, or wilfully broken or abused, spent for no cause.'

They continued moving westwards through Hirioth, sometimes under trees crowded so close the dense shadow was like deep water. Then gradually the glades became more frequent. Sunlight glanced bright on grasses still starred with late flowers and the same blossoming vines cascaded down, filling the evening air with sweet, heavy perfume.

Immerith walked often in silence, but when he did speak it was to recount some of the old legends of his people, stories that mingled man and beast in a time when they were not divided, when there was no death, when man and beast ate only fruit and grain, and each creature communicated with all others and there was innocence upon the earth.

Both knew they were fables, but as they passed into evening, and then day again, Tathea began to see a new vision of all things. Words in the Book which she had not understood were lit with a clarity that now seemed so plain she hardly knew how she could have failed to see it before.

Miracles no longer seemed a manifestation of the power of God to move nature against its will, but nature itself responding to the will of the God it, too, loved and obeyed with a spirit purer than man's. The greatest gift of all, the right to choose, had been given to the children of God, and with it went the terrible burden of knowledge of the law, and the power to keep or break it. The rest of creation kept the order for which it was designed, and bore no guilt.

They left the edge of the forest and climbed upward into a bare, steep land where the mountains were jagged against the sky, and great rivers plunged from cliff edges and disappeared into a roaring void. The wind was harsh and clean, and when it blew from the west it carried a dark, bitter aroma of salt and weed. This was Kharkheryll, one of the last strongholds left to the Flamens, where Imperial power had never reached.

Immerith continued to teach Tathea and she learned a new kind of respect for him, unlike anything she had felt for anyone else. He lived close to the earth and loved it as if it too were a living thing, capable of passion and pain, and its beauty was not accidental but full of purpose and intense, fragile joy which must be nurtured by those who would share it.

Still she had not spoken of her own beliefs, and he had not asked her. Once or twice over the fire in the evenings she had caught his dark eyes watching her, and he had seemed on the edge of speech, then the moment had died, and she had said nothing. She had promised that she would listen to him, and she had been abundantly rewarded, not with a new faith, but with an immeasurably deeper understanding of her own.

'What about the law?' she asked him as they walked together up a steep path over the rise of one of the great, bare mountains of Kharkheryll. The wind was colder here and the heather was dark amid the burning bronze of the bracken. It was a land of merciless and terrible beauty, like a great truth, scouring the soul.

He looked at her once, turning his face to the light, then strode forward again, answering her. 'The greater law is kept by eternity. We do not administer it. If a man or woman commits sin, they step out of unity with the earth. That is punishment greater than any pain man could inflict upon them, and we cannot save them from it.'

As the words came from his lips, she knew it was truth. It was in the heart of the Book; she simply had not understood it.

They walked in silence for a while, feeling the spring of the turf beneath their feet and watching an eagle soar into the great sweep of the wind-dragged sky.

'What of the lesser law?' she asked him at last.

'That we must answer to upon earth,' he replied. 'If a man wrongs his neighbour, or his neighbour's beasts or his lands, or that which is common to all, then he must answer to the Council of the Priests, who will judge him. If it were not so then the weak would have no protection from those who would abuse the strength or the skill they have been given. The ignorant or thoughtless would not learn,' and mistakes would serve no purpose.'

'That sounds like the law of the Book!' The words were out before she thought, or remembered her promise.

Immerith stopped and turned to look at her, surprise in his face. 'Does it? Is not man the master of the earth in your faith?'

'He should not be,' she answered instantly. 'To be truly Lord means to be protector and lover of the earth, to guard it from violation, to nurture its vulnerability and take joy in its beauty.' She dropped her voice in amazement at the understanding illuminating her mind. 'Truly to be in the keeping of God is to serve. Nothing gives you the right to hurt needlessly. Why should you wish to, unless there is a darkness inside you where there should be light? How could one ever imagine holiness while thinking of pleasure in any creature's pain?'

'One could not,' he answered softly. 'Perhaps there is something of God in you after all.'

She kept her peace as they walked eastwards again, but her mind was filled with thoughts, and she knew that in time he would ask her.

They were in the open, rolling land beyond Hirioth when at last he did. 'I, too, keep my word,' he said. 'Tell me of this Book.' He did not look at her, but she knew he was listening and his heart was open to hear.

They walked steadily, Casper still a step behind at her shoulder, and she told him of Asmodeus's argument with God, and all that was planned for the soul of man.

Sometimes he debated with her, requiring her to clarify, to explain, and as she did so she found her own understanding enlarged. She saw quite dazzlingly, as if in a shaft of light, how one thing enhanced another, how every law was magnified by its reflection in others.

'Yet it is unreconciled,' he said at last as they passed into the wide sweep of lowlands towards the eastern shore. 'The workmanship of God's hands –' he gestured at the broad earth and the sweeping skies around them – 'has been violated, ignored or abused by His children and His heirs. How can those who have kept their first estate abide the injustice of the greatest of all glories, the blazing stars of joy, being given to the one creature who has broken commandment after commandment? It defies all you have said, and I cannot believe it.' At last he looked at her and his eyes were fierce and searching, and she knew in that moment that he hungered for an answer of truth, a right and pure answer, more than for the breath of life.

'They could not,' she said quietly. There was no sound but the wind whispering and shivering in the grass and the far crying of birds overhead. 'God Himself has said He cannot break the law, He cannot defy justice or He would cease to be God.' She hesitated, then spoke with a certainty like a white fire inside her.

'An atonement must be made for the outrage of worlds. If it were not, then Asmodeus would challenge God and chaos would reign. The universe of spirit would crumble into darkness. Light itself would be dead, light of the mind, the heart, the soul. Unruled by law, the fabric of creation would decay, and life cease. In his fall into oblivion, Asmodeus would take all existence with him.'

Immerith nodded slowly, the wind tugging at his hair, the sweet smell of grass around them. He waited, such hope in his eyes as kindles the stars.

'There was a beloved Son, of whom God spoke,' she said, 'who lived on another world from ours, in such a way that he might answer the law and redeem worlds without number. I do not know how He did it, only that He did. I cannot touch such a thing with the furthest reaches of my imagination, but I know that it is so.' She looked into his eyes. 'I cannot give you my certainty. But if you ask God yourself, He will cause you to know it. You will feel a fire of warmth inside your heart, a radiance and a great peace, and it will be the voice of God.'

'I will do it,' he said, then started to walk again, and he spoke no more all that day.

The day after, they reached the Eastern Shore. They stood above the long, low sea-line, the sunlight and the salt wind in their hair. Great cloud racks stretched across the endless sky. The breakers roared white up the sand, the scent of late lupins was almost gone. Birds wheeled and plunged above them, their cries clear above the thunder of the sea.

Immerith turned from the horizon and looked at her. 'What you have told me is the greatest of all truths,' he said softly. 'Greater than this world. It is for all creatures, everything that moves and breathes and has life, for every rock and star in worlds beyond all the stars we can see or dream of. I shall keep it, and teach it to as many as will listen to me.' He hesitated. 'I would wish you well, but you walk the path of God, there is nothing for me to add or to give.'

'You have given me much,' she answered him truthfully. 'Wisdom and love of the earth, and the knowledge how to live with it in peace. And you have given me friendship.'

'I return to my people,' he said. 'I must tell them they are the heirs of God, and if we are just and faithful to His way, then He will answer

267

all our hopes, and fill the emptiness we have not dared name.' He held out his hand, his eyes never leaving hers.

She took it, held it for a moment, felt the warmth of him, then before the parting could gouge too deep or leave a silence for words that were not needed, she turned and mounted Casper and rode west again and south, to find Tugomir. She would share with him the higher law of stewardship of the earth, and perhaps also a glimpse she had seen of an act at the heart of time and space upon which all things rested.

She found Tugomir in high spirits. News of her coming had travelled ahead of her and he was waiting for her where the track widened towards the village. He still looked at odds with the forest, dressed in clothes of Island fabric but worn as if they were Shinabari.

Tathea smiled. She had been gone two months, and he still hated the forest just as much. It was there in his tight muscles, the way his narrow body hunched, the little grunt he gave and the startled look of distaste as a bright weasel ran across the path.

'Tugomir!'

He swivelled round to see her and his face lit with joy.

'Ta-Thea!' He came forward, his dark eyes bright. 'Are you well? Did you find the Flamens? How are you? Did they listen? Here . . .' He held up his hand to help her dismount, even though they were five hundred yards from the village yet.

She slid down. 'I am well, and so are you, I can see it. Yes, I found the Flamens, and I have much to tell you, all of it good. Tell me of the people here. Are they progressing? They must be, from your face!'

'Oh yes!' he said eagerly, falling in step beside her, but carefully keeping her between himself and the horse. 'They are most excellent people – diligent, quick to learn, and obedient to the commandments as soon as they understand them. I can easily see why the desert prophet spoke of them as those who would believe the Word and carry the light even when all other nations are plunged in darkness.' Unconsciously he was increasing his pace, waving his hands in his enthusiasm. 'They have a most noble spirit.' He smiled with a rare flash of self-deprecating humour. 'I can even say in honesty that I am glad I came here!'

Tathea laughed at him and clasped his arm. 'You have done excellently well, my friend. I am very glad you came too. And I have much to tell you myself.'

He coloured fiercely, and stared straight ahead, flinching as a small animal stirred in the undergrowth close by.

That evening Tathea sat with Garran and the other men and women of the village and listened to them talk. The change in the pattern of their lives was apparent in their obedience to the laws and teachings of

268

the Book, their reverence for all they grasped of it. There was a dignity in them which was greater than before, a decorum in the young women, a lack of violence or hasty and ugly language among the younger men, a greater respect for each other. Now there was a willingness to share one man's plenty with another's need. But overshadowing and exceeding everything else was their love of Tugomir. His words were repeated with reverence as if they were holy. He was obeyed to the letter.

She sat up late by lamp and firelight, wrapped in warm blankets of fleece, and told Tugomir something of Immerith, and the beginning of what he had taught her. He listened avidly, seeking to understand it all.

Long after midnight she went to her bed happy and deeply at peace in the certainty of their striving, and for Tugomir in his labour and his success.

The following day she observed the same. It was not until the third day when a sudden crisis emerged, a moral decision between two men who differed over the weighing of a crop, that her joy slipped away like water between her fingers.

It was Garran's judgement to make, and he stood confused.

One of the disputants glared at him. 'He weighted the scale!' he charged, jerking his elbow at his neighbour.

'He said the gleanings were mine!' the other responded furiously. 'That was our agreement when I lent him my ox.'

'Gleanings!' the first shouted at him. 'You have half the crop there!'

Garran looked from one to the other, apparently unable to make a decision as to what he should do.

'I must ask Tugomir,' he said resolutely, then turned to see where he was.

Tathea realised with horror that because Tugomir had not told him what to do, he was at a loss. The forest people had been taught rules, and they were obedient. They did not understand the principles which governed them. It was Tugomir they loved, and Tugomir they were following. No spark had been lit within them that would burn if he left. The true fire of the Book would remain alight even if heaven and earth were washed away and a man stood alone against the darkness.

She must resolve Garran's distress, and without humiliating him. She walked forward.

'Do you know both those men well?' she asked him.

'Oh yes!' he said quickly.

'Perhaps if you consider their stewardship of the land, the needs of their families and what has been shared in years past, you will know for yourself what judgement is wise and just. Maybe a surplus from the crop could be kept in a storehouse against the needs of the old or the sick.'

Garran's face cleared with relief. 'That is excellent! Yes, yes, I'll do that. Thank you!'

The other two men looked at her, ill-satisfied but recognising a finality in her voice and aware that Garran was set to obey her.

How could she tell Tugomir? She sat by the evening fire and watched the tenderness and the pride in his face as he listened to a young man express his belief in the Book and his commitment to live by its precepts all his life. 'I know it is the truth!' he said passionately. 'I covenant with God to seek His way in all I say or do, in all I think and all I am. What I possess in His, lent to me to share and to magnify in the service of all life, and above all in the love of my fellows.' He looked at Tugomir, and Tugomir smiled and nodded his approval and his joy.

Another stood up and also promised all he was or should be in the love of God, again turning to Tugomir before he sat down, his eyes wide and clear, his face burning with innocence.

Tathea sat among them and yet apart, the ache inside her growing till it blotted out all else. They seemed strangers and this was an alien place. She was far from home. Her legs were singed before the heat, and her back cold. She was not one of them. They believed she was. Their eyes looked at her with friendliness, no suspicion that in an hour she was going to shatter their comfort.

She could not look at Tugomir. She remembered his instant loyalty in front of Azrub, his unquestioning courage. He had sacrificed everything he possessed, which was a great deal, and endured physical hardship, which had cost him dear. He was uncomfortable and afraid most of the time, and yet he did not complain. Even when she had laughed at him, he had borne it with stoic graciousness. If she closed her eyes she could see his hunched shoulders in the rain and cold.

After the others were gone and she and Tugomir were alone by the fire, she told him of Garran's indecision.

'I should have been there,' he said immediately. Then he looked at her with furrowed brow. 'They are not evil men, just quick-tempered, and afraid of the hardships of winter. Fuel and grain are vital to them. Without sufficient they will die.' His own face in the firelight reflected his horror of the season to come. His voice was raw with the dread of it.

'I know.' She looked away from him, down at her hands. 'It is not like Shinabar, except perhaps that we would have been as afraid of the heat. We might have fought over shade, and water.' She stopped. How could she say it without hurting him?

There was no way.

'Garran waited for you to tell him . . .'

'He is eager not to do wrong!'

She looked up. 'You have taught them obedience, Tugomir, and they love you. It shines in their faces. They want to please you, and that is a mark of their respect for all that you say and do. You are like a father to them.'

'Thank you,' he said gravely.

She closed her eyes. She could not bear to look at him. 'They should not be children!' she said so softly she barely heard herself. 'We should teach them not to need us! They are beautiful, but they are not growing.' Slowly she looked up and saw the dawning understanding in his eyes, and then the horror . . . and at last despair.

'Then I have achieved nothing!' he whispered. 'I've created them in my own image! They've learned nothing but to obey.'

She reached out and touched him. He was not a physical man. Even after so long his arm felt bony and strange under her hand, but she needed to express something that words alone could not.

'That is the beginning,' she said gently. 'Build from there.'

His eyes were full of panic. 'I don't know how to! I don't know where and how I have gone wrong now. I don't understand!'

'Neither do I,' she admitted. 'We must go back to the beginning and start again.'

He pulled away, closing his eyes and putting his hands over his face. 'No.' His voice was muffled. 'It is my failure. You must go north to find the eleven priests who will hold the light. They are not here. We both know that. I will pray to the Father of us all that He will show me the way, and I will keep on trying.'

She knew what it cost him to say that, the sacrifice to remain alone in the forest that terrified him, with no one to speak to in his own language, no one with whom to share his dreams of old cities and subtle and delicate ideas refined over the years, never to speak of the sweet and familiar, of home.

She leaned forward and touched her lips to his cheek, then sat back and remained silent.

The firelight flickered and faded, and neither of them broke the peace of understanding.

After Tathea had gone, a loneliness settled over Tugomir so deep he all but drowned in it. He had no idea when she would come back, or even if she would. The forest people were good, generous, eager to please him, but their very admiration for him was a burden that crushed him. He was always cold, and with winter it grew darker every day, the nights longer. The chill seemed to eat into his flesh and wrap itself round his bones. Even in his bed he was chilled and he woke from sleep with cramp in his muscles.

Now that Tathea was gone, the trees seemed to close in on him even more. People spoke of ice and snow, and the dread of them crowded his thoughts. Sunset was ever earlier and dawn later. In the lengthening darkness, every sound was a terror he dared not even imagine – hungry beasts prowling, great ones that would eat him whole, small ones with sharp, rodent teeth, which were almost worse. He felt as if the world had abandoned him. This was surely the curse of the Great Enemy!

Garran came to him one bitter morning, his expression grave. He seemed embarrassed, and yet there was a determination in him. His face was a little flushed, his eyes cautious, but his shoulders were set square. He was about Tugomir's height, but twice his muscle and strength.

'Yes?' Tugomir said quickly.

'The winter is come,' Garran began awkwardly.

It was something of which Tugomir was bitterly aware. He hoped with a feeling close to desperation that Garran was not expecting that the great God of whom he had taught them would somehow change that.

'Hard times are for us to learn strength,' he said wretchedly. He must believe his own words. 'To teach us courage, and compassion for others, and to use our intelligence to overcome, to invent, to build upon experience so that we may be masters of ourselves.' That was easy to say but a world of fear, discomfort and loneliness to do.

'Oh, I know,' Garran agreed instantly. 'But I was thinking not of the spirit, but of the body. Of course you are welcome to stay in my house for ever.'

Tugomir kept the horror from his face with a mighty effort. The thought of remaining for ever here in this barbarous forest was worse than death. When he tried to speak his voice would not come.

'It will be my honour to look after you,' Garran went on. 'You will always have food and warmth and clothing.' His brow furrowed. 'But that is not enough. The forest is not safe when it becomes colder. If you were lost you could freeze. Food is more difficult to find.'

Tugomir stared at him. The fleeting thought ran through his mind that perhaps freezing would be better than living on here.

Garran was flushed with self-consciousness, but he would not retreat. He had not the faintest idea what was in Tugomir's head. The forest was the only place he knew, the idea of longing for something different had not occurred to him.

'It is time I taught you how to care for yourself,' he said determinedly. 'In the forest no man should depend for his life on the skills or knowledge of another. I will show you how to find the dry places, how to make fire, which are the roots you can eat and where to find honey and how to get it without being stung, and where to find nuts. I will teach you how to avoid the wolves and not to waken the sleeping bears – they sleep all winter – and how to find your way again when it is daylight.'

Tugomir was paralysed with dread. It was his worst nightmare realised. Garran stood in front of him smiling and gentle, refusing to give way a step, and unable to understand a shred of Tugomir's emotion. His blue eyes looked back unwaveringly. 'I'm sorry,' he said without moving from the doorway. He was already dressed in boots and a heavy, green, wool coat, ready to go. He held another over his arm. 'It is necessary.'

Tugomir gave in; he had no choice. He went like a lamb to the slaughter.

It was the worst month of his life. He lived in a state of physical pain and mental terror. Coldness developed an entire new world of meaning.

Garran walked ahead of him cheerfully, pointing out small facts of forest lore. 'Here,' he said helpfully. 'You must learn how to make fire, and where to find dry wood.'

'Nothing is dry!' Tugomir retorted. 'Nothing in this whole Island is dry!'

Garran smiled patiently. 'Oh yes it is. The beasts know where to find food and warmth. You must learn to notice them, make them your friends.'

Tugomir shuddered. The idea was obscene, and ridiculous.

Garran kept his temper; as with any recalcitrant pupil, one needs time. 'Be careful when you explore a hollow tree. You will almost certainly not be the first one to have noticed it. Water falls downward.'

That was such an idiotic remark Tugomir did not dignify it with an answer.

'Higher places will be drier,' Garran added. 'Look.' He moved a pile of dead leaves from the leeward side of a tree trunk and found several dry twigs.

Tugomir bit his lip.

Garran showed him how to use flints to strike a spark, then he collected rain water in a tin bowl which he carried, mixed the water with roots which he had dug up, and boiled them over the fire.

'Or you could bake them,' he said enthusiastically. 'Wrap them in leaves and put them in the ashes.'

Tugomir tried to be civil, even to sound as if the idea pleased him, but he found it disgusting. His body ached in every joint and each movement he saw threatened to be some creature larger and hungrier than he was, and possessed of teeth and claws to rend his flesh. He slept little and badly, and then it was full of nightmares. He woke so stiff he was afraid he might never walk properly again. But Garran was relentless.

'Come,' he said cheerfully. 'Today I shall show you where to find honey. You'll like that. Just watch for the bees.'

Tugomir got stung. It was acutely painful, but it did him no lasting harm, and the honey was indeed delicious. Actually he felt a certain sense of achievement, and the oatcakes they ate after that were a great deal less unpalatable.

The rains passed and were replaced by sharp, tingling frost. It crackled underfoot and formed exquisite, jewel-like stars on the leaf edges, like millions of diamonds in the sun.

Garran showed him which leaves were good to eat, and which were poisonous, how to find the small, sweet apples and the wild plums. He also showed him how to find nuts, and tell the ripe from the unripe, and which wild grain was fit to eat.

Once they discovered a bear, a huge beast like a mound of earth and leaves, fast asleep in a cave. Garran treated it with immense respect, and tiptoed away with his fingers to his lips. Tugomir would have been delighted to run, had his legs been willing to carry him.

The time passed in a haze of long, cold journeys with numb, squelching feet, meals of unmentionable foodstuffs eaten over a miserable fire, perishing nights filled with sounds, creaks, footsteps and more cold. But Tugomir did learn, and without realising it felt a fierce sense of having endured hell and survived it with something like honour.

When they returned to the village, the frost was sharp on the skin and the earth was hard. Dead leaves lay in bright drifts that crackled underfoot. Scarlet berries blazed on the vines, and they smelled wood smoke in the air before they reached the village.

Tugomir had seen beauty in the forest and developed a respect for it. Garran was pleased with his pupil, and he said so, only once, his eyes bright with pleasure. He had shared his own gifts with the man who was more than mere mortal to him.

And Tugomir's joy ran over, not for his own mastery of his fears and his physical inadequacy, his ignorance and defeat, but because Garran had learned that just as a man cannot live in the forest on another's skills, so in the spirit he cannot grow on obedience alone. He must understand the purpose of the law, and see behind it the reason and the love.

They came into the village together, cold and wet, but side by side and smiling broadly.

Chapter Eighteen

Tathea rode north alone, thinking of Tugomir left behind in the forest, but she was impelled forward by the knowledge that her purpose was still ahead. She had learned much of survival on the land from Immerith and felt confident in her ability to find food for herself and sufficient warmth.

Beyond Hirioth she came out into open uplands, vast skies mackerel flaked with cloud, wind sweet off heather already dark as the year began its slow, splendid waning.

As she rode she thought more and more deeply of what Immerith had taught her, and as the days passed she became in a new way at one with the sky and the earth around her. She drank in the physical loveliness of it; the great sweep of the moors, the shallow tarns bright with reeds spearing the water where the wind, hard and clean, ruffled the surface in silver ripples. Far overhead an eagle soared in blue, unimaginable heights.

As she pressed further northwards she perceived also the splendour of the greater plan, the unity of a brotherhood in the universe where nothing was wasted, nothing despised or cast out. The entirety was not merely the creation of God; from the beginning it was formed of intelligence that was willing and obedient to the law. The beauty of it became overpowering, an endless miracle too vast to comprehend, only to wonder at with an awful joy.

Beyond Celidon she came to the wilder, cleaner hills of the Waste Lands. With a shock so great it caught in her throat, she saw burned roofs in a small hamlet, then the corpses of beasts and the blood and devastation of battle.

It was deserted now, the people fled. She could not help. There was nothing left living, and she passed by sick with misery and sorrow, and began to travel only by night, by secret ways and hidden valleys away from the high roads. She found shelter in dry caves or clefts in the rock. This was the land where the legions of the Camassian Empire still fought against the barbarian Yaltabaoth of whom Immerith had once spoken, and no man had victory.

It took her three nights more of careful travelling, avoiding all human habitation, before she found Merdic, the last legionary general in the north, and two hundred of his soldiers, all that were left alive.

The camp was in a valley facing west, and well outposted with guards. Tathea stopped when the first one barred her way. She saw his outline against the dawn sky and the glint of light on the scarlet of his cloak and the bronze of his armour. It brought a wave of memory over her so deep and so powerful she swayed in the saddle and grasped Casper's mane with sudden dizziness. The soldier was tall, broad-shouldered, beaten and weary with battle, his cloak torn. He could have been Alexius. For a moment in the light against the sky, he was.

Then she recovered her wits and straightened in the saddle.

'I am Tathea,' she said huskily. 'I have come from Sylum, and before that from Shinabar, and the City in the Centre of the World. Immerith of the Flamens has told me of Merdic, and I would speak with him.'

The sentry looked beyond her, then up. 'Alone?' he said sceptically.

'Alone since Hirioth,' she replied. 'How long have you been without news of Camassia?'

He shrugged bitterly. 'Nine years. Eleven years since we came north from Sylum.'

His answer should not have surprised her – nine years ago she had left the Lost Lands for Camassia. When she had brought the Book into the world, Azrub had come to Shinabar, the Lord Nastemah to Sylum, and Yaltabaoth had stirred out of the west and driven down from Dinath Aurer, into the Waste Lands, destroying all before him. Now he led his forces against Merdic and the Lost Legion and they fought not for land; Merdic fought to survive, and Yaltabaoth to destroy.

'There is a new faith in Camassia,' she said quietly. 'I have come to tell you of it. Take me to Merdic.'

Perhaps it was the authority in her voice, or more likely the fact that she travelled alone, but after only a moment's hesitation he did as she bade him, turning to lead the way down the incline. As soon as she was gone, another took his place.

It was a small camp, a fraction of the size of those she had known in the desert, but the pattern was the same the world over. They found Merdic at the fire in the centre, kindling it to make a hot gruel for the first meal of the day. He was dressed in full armour and ragged cloak, a lean man with a face at once powerful and lonely, though he was little beyond his youth.

'This is Tathea,' the sentry told him. 'She has come from the City in the Centre of the World to tell us of a new teaching there.'

'A teaching from whom?' Merdic asked, straightening up. 'If Camassia still remembers us, then it is men we need, not beliefs.'

'When I return I shall tell them so,' she answered, puzzled by the neglect of this outpost. Ortelios had not seemed to know it existed. Certainly their distress had not reached him. All the south believed the Island secure as far as Yba and the fortress of Layamon, and beyond it no longer concerned them.

'If you return,' Merdic said with a bitter smile. 'It is not as easy to leave as it is to arrive. Yaltabaoth's men are everywhere in the land. If we could ride south, do you not think we would?' He barely glanced at the great hills around them, stark, cloud shadowed, and the wind-scoured arch of sky above. The knife-edge of snow was in the air already and the long winter lay ahead.

Merdic turned to the fire and set another piece of twisted heather root on it. 'You should ride back as soon as you are rested and have eaten. We will give you a fresh horse. Yaltabaoth's quarrel is with us. He may let you pass. Certainly you will fare no worse alone than you would in our company.'

'Thank you, but I will remain,' Tathea answered him.

He swivelled around, his face bleak, almost angry. 'We are at war, lady! We cannot protect you. We are harried from battle to battle. We have no certain camp, no shelter to offer you, and sometimes no food. Only death lies ahead of us.'

'I must remain with you.' Tathea had no doubt as she stood in the broadening light, silver as it never was in the gentler south. All might seem to the mind purposeless in teaching this lost band, hard pressed by the enemy and driven ever northward, but there was a peace within her which was greater than all arguments of reason. A warmth filled her body and a sense of radiance that did not dazzle or shadow, and made arguments of logic irrelevant. She had felt it before and knew it was the light of God. 'I shall not ask for rest or protection,' she answered. 'I shall travel with you and fight at your side.'

'Fight?' he said with disbelief that edged on derision.

'Yes, fight,' she answered quite calmly. 'I marched with the Camassian army from the sea to Thoth-Moara, and fought battles on the way.'

He frowned, puzzled. 'Thoth-Moara? Is that not in Shinabar? Are we at war with Shinabar now?'

'No. It is conquered.' It still hurt to say that. 'There was a coup ten years ago. The Isarch was murdered. A new, corrupt order took his place. It was the Camassian army who overthrew it – at least for a while.'

He looked at her more closely, his eyes narrowed, sudden perception in his face. 'You are Shinabari!'

'I am the Isarch's widow.'

'Ta-Thea . . .' He gave the name its Shinabari lilt. 'If you overthrew the usurper, what in the name of the gods are you doing here?'

'It was temporary. The corruption was to the soul.'

'I'm sorry.' He said it instinctively, but his sincerity was plain in his face. 'But we have no time for new teachings, lady.' His candour

277

robbed his words of rudeness. She saw too clearly in it experience of past battles and deaths and the knowledge that the future held only final defeat. The hour could be altered, but not the fact.

'Then if time is short,' she answered him softly and with equal gravity, 'it would be best to spend it well and learn the truth while we yet have life to do so.'

He stood facing her for only a moment longer, then accepted her decision.

After a brief meal shared over the camp fire, she prepared to travel with them and share their life as she had promised. She would face the hard winter of the north, open camps on the windswept moors and fells, already feeling the first frost and then the bite of ice. Soon a blanket of snow would smother the mountains.

She braided her hair back and cut her skirts to form a more suitable garment. She bound the spare fabric round her legs with thongs to protect them from the cold and the scarring branches of the heather. She was given armour made hastily from odd pieces left from the most recent dead, and the lightest sword they could find. There was chest armour and leg greaves for Casper too. He found it strange at first, stamping and shaking his feet.

She was ready to travel when they broke camp.

They moved steadily, always watching, waiting for attack. Around the fires at night she learned their history, how they had marched north at the command of the Governor before Ortelios, and secured the borders beyond Yba and subdued the last of the warring tribes. Then they had been cut off and lived from the land, their numbers dwindling with each battle and each bitter winter. No relief had come.

Then nine years ago the whole pattern had changed. The last fire-haired chieftain had been killed, and in his place with fresh troops from the west had come Yaltabaoth, fiercer than any before him, bloodier, and with a rage in his soul that allowed nothing to live.

She pondered long in the silence of the wide, star-burning night what she should say to them. Speech of ordinary life was purposeless, a denial of all that was their reality. They had no homes, no families, no posterity, and no hope. They had no trade in which to be honest or dishonest. They struggled to survive, and knew even that was doomed in the end.

The only teaching was the bare truth: the murder of her family, her own journey to the Lost Lands; her return from Orimiasse with the Book; and how one people after another had learned it, and taken or rejected its words.

She told them how she had struggled with the original language to translate it into Camassian, and then Shinabari, so that all might read it easily and find the depth and the beauty of its meaning. She told them how Alexius had clarified the passages that spoke of the law and how the perfect order of it had touched his soul with an understanding of God, and how Ra-Nufis had loved its beauty above all things. She told them one evening in the soft, cold rain as they sat huddled by a dying fire, of her own failure in Shinabar. Isadorus had told her she could not teach truth on the heels of an army, and she had not believed him. But Shinabar did not want to know.

She told them of the prophet Iszamber who had met her in the desert and spoken of the Island at the Edge of the World and the eleven priests who would stand at the last days, when all else was overtaken by darkness, and the clashing of ignorance and evil in the ruin of nations.

'You marched on foot, all the way across the desert?' one named Drusus asked her with amazement.

'I wanted to be part of the army,' she answered wrily, remembering how she had felt then: the terror and exhilaration of it, the sense of overwhelming power, the horror of wounds and death, the unity, the strange, fierce and tragic fellowship, the laughter that was half pain. 'I wanted to go back to my own country in a way that would show I had fought to be where I was, and earned it.'

'But it didn't work.' Merdic looked at her in the firelight.

She turned away. 'No. At the time I didn't know why. I thought it was their fault, that I could change it if I tried harder. I thought I had failed God.'

'Did you not say His purpose cannot be thwarted?' Drusus frowned. 'That was what you said, wasn't it? How could He be God if mere human folly could spoil His plan?'

She looked up and smiled at him. 'You are right. It can't. I don't think Shinabar was ever going to believe the Book, except a person here or there, like Tugomir, and Arimaspis. In the end it is all individuals, not nations. I still did not understand choice. I thought I could lead Shinabar somewhere it did not wish to go, because I wanted it so much.'

'Perhaps it was for your learning,' Merdic suggested, his eyes searching her face. 'Perhaps it was never Shinabar that was the purpose. If Iszamber spoke truly, then it was something else, something yet to be.'

He was right, and she could see glimpses of a far greater pattern even as she sat, rain-soaked in the firelight. She could not see the whole, not even the hour ahead, but looking at the past with a greater wisdom, she found a new perception of how what had seemed to be darkness was now light, what had seemed loss was a different kind of gain. The most terrifying dangers had come not from external events, but from within herself. The greatest power for destruction had been her own loneliness and temptation as she had stood on the desert scree with Alexius. It was Ulciber who had wanted her to go to

Shinabar! And Alexius to lead the army! Should she have seen evil in his eyes and recognised it?

She had been weakest when she had placed the crown of the Isarchs on her own head, and imagined she could save her people.

Now she sat in the rain with two hundred lost soldiers on the edge of the world, and waited for yet another emissary of the darkness to attack, and felt through the chill of her flesh the burning peace inside her that God had promised He would never leave or forget her, and would not ask of her anything that was not possible.

She did not need to tell them that this was why she chose to ride with them, even though word had come that Yaltabaoth was now on their heels, and in another day or two he would attack again. She saw the understanding in their faces. They smiled with pity for her because she was a woman and Yaltabaoth would not spare her any more than he would them.

Two days later they knew with sinking hearts that the enemy was at hand. Birds fell silent. The wind dropped and ceased to whine in the heather. The sky was streamered with cloud like flying mares' tails as they stood together, two hundred horsemen in a close phalanx, swords drawn, waiting.

Suddenly there was a scream, high, unearthly, like a demon's song, and Yaltabaoth galloped over the crest of the moor, his spear raised aloft. His black hair streamed behind him and his cloak swung wide and flapped like the wings of some terrible bat. Behind him teemed three hundred horsemen, hooves pounding the earth, gouging out clods and sending them flying. Their black armour was without glint or gleam in the cold light.

The battle was fierce, desperate and without quarter to the injured or respect for the dead. There were no prisoners.

Tathea fought even more desperately than she had in the desert. The horror of it was almost beyond belief. The black warriors seemed possessed by a hatred that drove them, screaming, to hack at enemies already fallen. And even when they themselves were crippled, staggering and streaming blood, they still slashed at everything they could see, drowning in their own gore.

Tathea went beyond exhaustion into a state like a hellish dream, but she could not stop. Men fell beside her, and there was no time to help.

As the light faded and darkness dragged its pall across the east, Yaltabaoth was driven off, for a little space. Merdic, his sleeves torn and soaked with blood, his sword scarlet, ordered the legion to retreat further north. There was no time to bury the dead, only to stand for a brief moment in silence and grieve for brave men perished, and commend their souls to the God who had made them. Then the wounded must be lifted and carried, food and tents loaded, and the bitter journey begun again.

Casper was cut across the shoulder. Tathea dressed the wound with balm and walked beside him.

All night they travelled, weary of heart and flesh. The darkness and the ache of muscles seemed interminable, like an evil that has no ending. The horses were bruised and wounded from the battle, and close to collapse from exhaustion when finally before dawn they stopped in a deep gully between two buttresses of rock. They had walked along the bed of a stream, so no tracks would be visible for the enemy to trace.

They had little wood for fires, and what heat they could raise must be used to warm the injured. All others must make the best they could of blankets and cloaks and one another's weary and battered bodies. There was hot gruel of grain and herbs, nothing else. The dawn came pale and cold across the eastern horizon, hard followed by a thin rain.

Tathea lay huddled on the ground in a blanket, too tired to weep, too racked with pity for the suffering she had seen, and the courage which knew no hope of victory, the selfless sacrifice of one man for another, and the white-faced, ever patient ministering of the surgeons. If this was the path that God had planned, it was bitter beyond imagining.

She thought of Alexius, and wondered if she could ever have told him of this different, inhuman war. It was beyond her power to describe. Words only convey the known, or imaginable. And he was not here.

When she could rest no longer she sat up and found the sun low in the south, a watery light filtering pale and clean from the high rocks. The noise of the stream sounded sharp above the careful movement of men, and the muffled whimpering of those in pain. Beside the remains of the fire, Merdic stood gaunt-faced, his left leg bound in worn linen and the blood already seeping through.

She rose, shaking with cold and stabbed with pain. She went over to him, walking awkwardly. There was nothing she could say, but she felt a great need simply to meet his eyes, to be sure that he knew she was with him, not only in body but in heart. When she reached him, without thought she put her hand on his arm. She meant it as a gesture of warmth, though her fingers were like ice.

He smiled bleakly. 'I hope your God is right, and all pain has purpose,' he said too softly for anyone else to hear. 'I confess I see none in this. One more such attack and we will all die, and this land will fall to the barbarian. He puts everything to fire and the knife. There will be no one left to be your eleven priests.'

'The purposes of God are not frustrated,' she answered him, her voice steady. 'He knows the end from the beginning.' She spoke to

281

comfort him, to ease the terrible burden of love and grief for his men that he bore. But even as she heard her own words, a warmth was opening up like a spreading sweetness inside her, a memory or a vision of someone she had loved with a wild and terrible wholeness, who had led another lost army through a cold greater than this, against an enemy he could not defeat. He had made mistakes and walked the bitter night of the soul alone, as all must. He had trusted God when there was no hope. He had remembered the light of the star he had once seen, and kept its path in the darkness.

She would do the same, in the blind knowledge that God existed, and her name was written on His hands.

Higher up the gully a sword hilt rapped sharply on the rock, and a second later an answering rap returned. Merdic stiffened and all through the camp heads followed the sound, hands went to sides. Slowly each man staggered to his feet and stood ready.

Down beside the stream bed, fantastic in the light, a solitary figure in parti-coloured jerkin and breeches was walking with a light step. The left diagonal quarterings of his garb were in purple like the heather, the right in a shade that was one moment gold as the gorse of summer, another bronze like the dying bracken. He wore a cloak over his shoulders, and his shoes were dark as peat, the toes curled up at the ends. There were ridiculous tiny bells on them. He carried a staff in his hand, and from his waist hung a leather pouch. He was smiling.

'Who are you?' Merdic asked wearily. 'This is no land in which to wander alone. Have you not seen the signs of battle, the bodies of the dead? Carrion birds darken the sky.'

'It is my land,' the man answered simply. 'My name is Menath-Dur. I am a healer. I will treat your wounded.'

'We have our own surgeons.' Merdic barred his way, suspicion hardening in him. This man most assuredly was not of martial discipline. His features were mercurial, neither Camassian nor Islander. If he walked alone, why should he help this desperate legion lost here in the Waste Lands with its back to the sea? And if he was an ally of Yaltabaoth, he wrought nothing but evil.

Menath-Dur was not disconcerted. His eyes moved to rest on Tathea.

'Ah, so you came north so soon!' he said softly. 'I feared you would leave it late, and there would be few left.'

She stood up slowly and came towards him. 'How do you know me? Are you of the Flamens?'

'No.' The thought seemed to amuse him. 'I am far older than the Flamens – immeasurably older. Have you tended the sick?'

'As we can. Their wounds are grave.' She was puzzled at his sudden change from one subject to another. His name meant nothing and his words were strange. Yet there was that in his face which held her, like sun on a far landscape, and his absurd shoes with their upturned toes woke a memory of hope in her, sweeter than reason, older than the death of Habi, or loneliness, or war and loss in Shinabar, older even than Azrub. It was a memory of light in a great darkness, swift, and then gone again.

'Of course they are,' Menath-Dur agreed. 'It is the bitterest of wars, the hardest in all a man's life. Come, let me pour ointment and balm in the wounds, that they may heal.'

Merdic did not move. He was afraid and confused, uncertain how best to protect his men, or which danger threatened them most.

Menath-Dur stood motionless in front of him, smiling very slightly, meeting his eyes in a long, steady gaze. 'It is for you to choose,' he said at last. 'Shall I leave, or remain?'

Merdic searched his face yet again, then his body eased and he stepped aside. 'Stay.' He was too tired to argue. 'Heal us, if you can!'

For twelve days Menath-Dur remained with them. They travelled through the darkened, winter land north and west till the first snows fell and suddenly the moors glimmered white in the dawn light as far as the eye could see. He was as skilled a physician as he had said. Wounds healed with amazing rapidity, even scars disappeared. There were no fevers and no infection. He treated men and horses alike, and when he left them suddenly and without warning on the thirteenth day at noon, walking along the track between the pale mounds of snow, they were touched with an extraordinary sense of loss. But they were again a force of one hundred and seventy men ready to face an enemy, and armed in body and heart to fight.

The second battle against Yaltabaoth came as the first had, when the air was edged with ice and the sky filled with a mist of gathering chill. There was the thin, high, wailing scream on the wind, then the charge with Yaltabaoth in the van, black hair wild about his head. He rose in his stirrups, spear whirling about him and his black cloak flapping.

The fighting was harder than before. Merdic stood his ground. Three spears splintered in his hand and the enemy fell around him. Then he fought with sword, hand to hand, on foot in the old manner, before the legions took to the Island horses.

The wounded were dragged away. Physicians tended, bound and padded gashes and staunched bleeding. The dead piled up. Tathea fought in a nightmare of pain and dying, of courage, sacrifice and the fellowship of those who have faced agony together and not found each other wanting.

When it was over, once again Yaltabaoth retreated. The remnants of the legion – a hundred whole men, forty wounded, many sorely so – stood before the walls of a ravine. Its rock faces were such that no man could climb them. They hung sheer and overwhelming, patched with moss and bracken and thin, silver threads of water. There was no escape except past the blood-drenched army of Yaltabaoth, wounded, enraged, and waiting.

'We will die,' Merdic said plainly and soberly to them around the glitter of the fire. 'But we will cost them dearly. We first came north to protect the settlements from the fire-haired tribes who looted and burned. That, at least, we have done. It is better that we die with honour than that we should have lived in ease by the hearths of our homes, and not have fought for the right. Tonight I shall listen to the words of Tathea, and I will covenant to serve the God of her Book. You may all keep this last watch however your heart chooses. Tomorrow we die.' He looked at Tathea a moment, then added very quietly, 'We shall not let you fall into his hands, I swear.'

She smiled bleakly, knowing what he meant, and grateful for it.

All evening she taught from the Book: the law of love, its beauty, and the compassion in it for everything in all the worlds within and beyond the knowledge of man. She spoke of the redemption wrought by the pain of God, known only by the power of the spirit, of eternal brotherhood for all who wished it, of the long, marvellous, terrible climb to the glory of the stars and the light which never fades.

All of them covenanted to keep the word in their hearts, and on the morrow to die in the law of God, without hatred, arrogance or any shadow of deceit. When the moon set, they rested, and a sleep of utter peace descended upon them.

Even the watchmen did not hear the soft, strangely shod feet of Menath-Dur, nor see the shadow of his form as he stepped silently among them and poked the embers of the fire. It sparked upward, catching the last of the wood, and from no apparent place he put dark lumps of what seemed like stone upon it, but miraculously it burned with a wild, glorious warmth.

When the cauldron boiled, he woke Tathea, finger to his lips, his eyes brilliant.

'Waken Merdic,' he commanded. 'Have the men drink. There is hot gruel in the cauldron, with herbs that will give them strength. Then come. I will show you the way to the Western Shore.'

'We cannot leave,' she whispered back. 'Yaltabaoth is camped behind us, and there is no pass south of this ravine.'

'Trust God, and hope in all things,' he said quietly. 'Never lose hope! When you cannot see the light, walk in the path your heart remembers – and hope.'

'Who are you?' she asked him insistently, sure that in some forgotten corner of her mind she must already know.

'My name if Menath-Dur,' he replied.

'I know that, it means nothing. Who are you?'

'A servant of God,' he answered lightly, as if it were an easy thing to say, and nothing strange. 'A companion through the journey.'

She opened her mouth to ask more, but words eluded her, the questions slipped through her mind without form.

'Do not forget,' he said softly. 'When there is no hope – still hope! Now do as I bid, time is short!'

There was no purpose in arguing with him. There was nothing to lose, except sleep, and the ease of abandoning herself to accept death. It hurt to begin again when she had let go of hope and its labour and risk, but she did as he commanded.

Merdic awoke to the same pain, disbelief, and struggle to force life back after surrender.

When they had all eaten the thin gruel, which was surprisingly refreshing, Menath-Dur started, a strange spring in his step and the bells on his ridiculous shoes like some insect singing in the night.

No one spoke; the flutter of hope came achingly slowly. The ravine had seemed a blind alley beyond escape, sheer walls where weary eyes had searched in vain for the smallest crevice that would allow a man, if not a horse, through, or for footholds to enable them to climb the walls.

But Menath-Dur did not hesitate. He walked a narrow, twisted path through the fronded bracken that seemed to cover nothing but wet rock, and led them to hidden caverns leading to open gullies.

They travelled slowly, on foot and leading their animals, boots slipping on the scree and loose stones rattling and falling away. In the darkness there was little to see except the occasional reflection of starlight on a wet surface, a momentary gleam of water, or a fretwork of bracken against the dusting of a faint wheel of stars across the sky.

Still no one spoke. The sound of horses breathing was close, familiar, the creak of leather and clink of harness muted; now and then someone gasped as he stubbed a foot against rock.

The sun rose slowly, pale and dim in the south-east. Once Menath-Dur seemed to step straight into a waterfall, only to emerge beyond it, wet, chilled, but in a deep chasm slanting upward towards a valley. A dead tree leaned over a shattered, stony buttress and in its shelter he stood smiling, his hair plastered to his head and his absurd clothes bright like flowers in bloom.

'Cut the tree,' he said to Merdic. 'Build a fire and dry yourselves. Tend to your horses. Rub them down. Eat. Rest. Beyond there –' he pointed with an outstretched arm – 'is the Western Shore. Yaltabaoth will find you – but not yet, and he will be weary when he does. You have time to heal, to rebuild your strength.'

They stared at him as he stood in the sun, joy surging up within them, rising like a white bird with dawn on its wings. Then one by one they set about obeying, reaching for axes, caring for the beasts, then unrolling blankets and unpacking grain.

Menath-Dur jumped down from the rock and came over to Tathea. He undid his satchel and took out dried powders and oils and gave them to her.

'For wounds,' he said softly. 'For fevers and agues, and to prevent infection.' He smiled, an odd, lopsided smile. 'Keep hope – keep hope for ever. We shall meet again!' And then without another word he turned and loped away so swiftly that in a matter of seconds he was gone, and there was nothing left but the winter light on the grass, and the smoke of the beginning fire, pungent and sharp.

The worst of the winter raged in white torrents, crowning the high moors in shining armour of ice, and filling the valleys with drifting snow. Under the moonlight it shone like a living jewel, the very air seemed to glimmer and the night tingled on the skin like the touch of cold water.

The season for grain and berries was long past, but they knew which roots to dig and eat. Mostly they lived from the sea. Many of the weeds washed up in the shallow pools at low tide were edible, and they grew accustomed to their taste. And there was an abundance of fish which necessity taught them to catch.

As the year turned and the days began to stretch again, the coldness ate into flesh and bone, and snow turned to ragged slush. The earth was dark, stained with death. The light itself was grey, but they grew rapidly stronger in both body and spirit. They drank so deeply of the words of the Book they became of one heart and mind in purpose and every man sought his fellows' wellbeing.

Before the first frail blossom or the first spear of new grass appeared, Yaltabaoth attacked. It was noon on a day when a pall of cloud had shredded in the gale to show thin banners of ice-blue sky, and the wind keening in the heather all but swallowed the high, thin scream of the demon war cry. Merdic and his last warriors, a hundred and thirty men, were camped on the plains by the Western Shore that looks on to the sea which bounds the world. Here they must stand and fight.

The fearful sound came to them as they sat by the camp fire, burning peat cut from the moor and dried seaweed. Suddenly their blood was chilled and fear struck as a blow to the heart, stopping the breath in their throats.

Merdic spun round, for a single instant hoping it was a delusion, a sound born of memory. But even as he faced the wind, he knew the truth.

'To arms!' he called, and every man obeyed, reaching for sword or spear, springing for his horse.

He turned to Tathea. 'There is nowhere to fly,' he said quickly, his eyes narrowed to the wind. 'We will do all we can, but this is our last stand. If we are beaten, it would be better for you to be dead than for Yaltabaoth to take you. God would count it no shame that you did not suffer yourself to come into his hands. I would that you could be saved, but it is too late now to regret, and my soul rejoices that you taught us the word of truth. May God's will be done.' And he raised his hand in the old Imperial salute, then mounted his horse and moved to lead the charge.

In a clash of arms Yaltabaoth's dark force came over the brow of the last rise and met Merdic's legion at full gallop. There was a splintering of spears. Shields flew awry and at the first shock many fell dead to be trampled by flying hooves. The scream of horses, the clang of metal on metal, the cries of men filled the ears. Birds left the air, even the carrion crows flew away to wait. The small beasts in the heather scattered and burrowed for their holes. Only the vast, icy sky and the endless sea beyond the Western Shore remained as they were.

Back and forth they fought, lunged and struck. Wounds went unheeded, every man was in the saddle with his sword, surgeons, armourers and farriers alike – there was no future beyond this battle for which to guard or prepare. Tathea rode with them, dagger at her side, sword in her hand.

The sun began its short descent and still the battle was neither lost nor won. Casper was wounded and Tathea dismounted and fought on foot, slashing hand to hand, stumbling over the fallen. But the dead were more of Yaltabaoth's force than of the legion. Still the small animals cowered away and the carrion birds dared not come, for all the dying and dead that lay amid the darkened heather.

There were not more than fifty alive on either side, although unknown numbers of Yaltabaoth's forces lay beyond, men he could draw on in another season.

In the centre of the battle, Merdic faced the black figure with the streaming hair and the bloodied sword. They were both on foot now with only the naked blades of their swords to fight with. For an instant's silence their eyes met and Yaltabaoth's lips drew back from yellow teeth in a smile, victory in his nostrils and on his tongue.

Merdic swung his sword, and Yaltabaoth met it with his own. The clash and scrape of steel came again and again. Merdic was wounded. Blood gushed from his side, his thigh, his arms. Seldom did he strike flesh himself and Yaltabaoth seemed to feel no pain even when the sword point pierced him.

No one came to Merdic's aid; all his men were fighting their own desperate battles. Tathea was freed from her struggle by a legionary as Merdic fell to his knees and Yaltabaoth plunged the sword home to his opponent's heart with a thin scream of exultancy.

He drew the sword out and whirled it about his head, eyes blazing, mouth wide in a cry of victory. Merdic did not move again.

Tathea stood as if alone. The clamour of battle, the icy wind and the withered heath seemed to recede as she stared at the black figure of despair before her, his jubilation clear in his face.

She thought of Menath-Dur, the fantastical man with the parti-coloured costume and the bells like birdsong on his feet, who had told her to hope when there was no hope, and when the darkness was complete still to follow the light of the star she remembered.

She stepped forward with her sword in her hand, and gazed for a moment into those terrible eyes. Then she lunged forward, head down, and drove the sword not into his heart, or his throat, but into the side of his belly.

Black blood spurted out in a jet and his shriek of anguish tore the air, rocketing upwards in jagged sound till the very clouds were rent, and fragile as the wings of dawn the sunlight came through.

All other fighting ceased. As if stricken, the dark warriors stood with weapons useless in their hands. Merdic's legion were exhausted, wounded not only with swords but with grief. They had loved Merdic, he had been their leader and friend since youth. His loss could not be borne without a numbing pain.

Tathea looked down at Yaltabaoth where he lay writhing on the ground, not dead, not even mortally injured. But the sunlight fell not on the dark lord who had ridden over the hill with his demon wail, but on an old man, hair blasted white like the down of a thistle, his face gaunt, the flesh sunken, gums shrunk back from his teeth, limbs wasted. Only his eyes were unchanged, still burning with the fire of hatred and lust for the night of the soul.

Slowly he rose to his knees, clutching his sword in his gnarled hand.

Tathea backed away, fear in her throat, her body shaking. She had struck her blow. She had nothing left.

Yaltabaoth leaned on his sword, and as he did so it became a spear, then a staff, but his eyes never glanced towards it although his hand must have known the change. His smile was mirthless, and he did not move, even when he was upright, a wild figure, white hair flying in the wind, clothes bloody and ragged.

'You have not escaped,' he said to her softly, his voice sibilant and penetrating, reminding her of the dwarf Azrub, far away in Shinabar. And suddenly she knew Yaltabaoth. He was the Lord of Despair – as Menath-Dur was the Lord of Hope.

'You have wounded me!' he hissed. 'But I shall not die. I shall wander this land for ever, and my staff is the Staff of Broken Dreams. I am still the Lord of Disillusion, and my reign will last as long as the earth!' And he swung round, glaring at the remnants of the weary and wounded legions. Then he started off into the heather and the dark bracken and in moments was gone, and his forces after him.

Chapter Nineteen

They buried Merdic and the other dead with legionary honours, after the old fashion of Camassia, with plumed battle standards upright and spears aloft as they stood on the Western Shore in the evening light. The waves beat grey and silver on the long stretch of sand and hissed white foam up to the weed-strewn tideline, translucent as the sun set scarlet and spilled fire over the sea.

Birds wheeled and called in the air above, their underwings flashing as they turned. There was no sound but their cries, the wind in the reeds and the roar and boom of the water. It was a place of peace, and when they had said their last farewells, they turned and walked to where their horses stood waiting.

'Where shall we go?' Drusus asked. 'Yaltabaoth is changed. We have defeated him, but his forces still hold all the Waste Lands and there is no path back for us.'

'We must remain here,' Tathea answered unhesitatingly. 'We will build a fortress on this headland, where the tide will protect us. There is much stone here, and we have tools. We can make all that is necessary. The sea will feed us. In time we can find trees, and seeds. There is fresh water and peat for the fires.'

Drusus stood with the wind tugging at his hair, his cloak flapping around him.

'Until one by one we die,' he answered.

For a moment she did not understand. Then she looked at the last fifty alive. They were all men. For a moment, ice-like, despair flickered at the edge of her mind, then knowledge returned to her that to those who have faith, nothing is lost, and the purposes of God are never defeated.

'God never abandons any creature who trusts in Him and walks in his commandments,' she replied. 'There will be a way.'

One by one they dropped to their knees, the wounded, the weary, the bereaved, and each prayed to the God who had begotten him in the world before this, and whose love never died.

They tended the injured, man and horse, and gradually they recovered. But it was thirty-nine grim and toiling days before they had hewn from the ground with adzes and chisels enough rock, split and cut to size, to lay just the foundations of a shelter to house them from the sleet driving over the moor. There was no mortar and on the wind-racked shore only driftwood. Their spirits sank and they grew silent as they laboured, failed, and laboured again.

Casper recovered, and Tathea rode alone up over the dark moor, still patched with white in the hollows and the lee side of the valleys, the far mountains brilliant in reflected sun against louring clouds. The wind had dropped and the air was clean and prickling sharp, laden with the smell of wet bracken and earth, and the bitter pungency of wild herbs.

For a long time she rode, not quickly, merely needing to be alone. Then as the sun sank in brilliant colour across the south-west, she dismounted, leaving Casper to graze, and hunched down in a hollow where the earth was sheltered and dry, and wrapped her cloak round her. She bowed her head and spoke her heart to the God who had called her upon this mighty purpose which she could see no way to fulfil. Darkness was everywhere against her, across the relentless earth as far as she could see, and in the ruin of despair Yaltabaoth had woven in heart and mind.

Then as she sat, the shadow across her vision cleared and she saw a garden where there was no death and no birth. Every creature under heaven dwelt there without enmity, and there was perfect peace.

And in the garden dwelt also a man and a woman who knew no sin. Their faces were fair and smooth, time had not begun, and age had no meaning for them. Their eyes had never seen grief and their innocence had no blemish. They had freedom to do anything they pleased. Nothing was barred from them except one thing only; of all the fruit of all the trees, there was one of which they might not taste, and they refrained from it, having no wish to do other than obey.

For aeons without name or number they dressed the garden and took joy in the beauty of it.

Then Tathea saw another person standing under a shining tree, and his face was terrible, as if he carried with his soul a darkness so great it would crush the stars and consume all life. And he spoke to the woman.

She knew him not, and asked his name.

'I am Asmodeus,' he answered. 'I am your brother.'

She had never beheld evil, and she knew no lie. She looked upon him without fear, and without understanding.

'Eat of the fruit,' he said to her. 'It will give you the knowledge of good and evil.'

She shook her head, puzzled. 'But my Father commanded me not to. It is the only thing I may not do. If I should, then I would also taste death.'

In his eyes cunning, corruption and truth were twisted to snare and destroy.

'You are a babe unborn. You know nothing! If you do not know bitter from sweet, light from darkness, then you are a child damned never to grow up. Would anyone who loved you wish such a thing? Life, and knowledge of good and evil is how your Father became God! Take the risk. Take life . . . and become like Him.'

She hesitated. 'There must be another way.'

'Without knowledge of good and evil, there can be nothing,' he replied softly. 'It is God's way – how could it be wrong?'

The leaves rustled in the shining tree. Still the woman was uncertain.

Tathea could see into the heart of Asmodeus and the black exultancy that waited there, the triumph already sickly sweet on his lips. If the woman ate, then all mankind would take mortal flesh. Because they knew good and evil they would be accountable for sin. The path upward to God would be open before them, but so would the descent to the mouth of hell and beyond.

Asmodeus already possessed in his dominion one-third of the hosts of heaven, fallen as he had fallen. If the woman did not eat, then that was the extent of his dominion, less than half that of God! But if the woman did eat, then he might have them all, every last one of them, because as surely as they gained knowledge, they would also gain corruption and death, because they would sin, be it ever so slight, even a lapse of watchfulness, a chance missed, an indifference.

It all depended upon one man, in the meridian of time, who had offered to live without stain, and at the appointed hour to face Asmodeus in another garden. He would be alone, with all the frailty of human heart and flesh, and Asmodeus would have his immortal powers and the hosts of hell, all the pain and terror of eternity in his hands. That man would fail! Asmodeus would crush him slowly, destroy him with the collected evil and suffering of all life. Then every human soul would be his, every living thing that had ever drawn breath or put forth leaf, even the rocks and clay of the earth itself. His dominion would be boundless. His fingers grasped it, his eyes beheld it and the smell of victory was in his nostrils. He believed it with a fearful triumph.

Creation held its breath. Eternity stood still.

The woman reached out her hand and plucked the fruit. She put it to her lips and ate.

Asmodeus smiled, satisfied. Now all he had to do was wait until that white centre of time and the ultimate conflict, and then all life would lie within his grasp.

The woman looked at him steadily, not yet afraid, but there was already the beginning of knowledge in her eyes.

'I know who you are,' she said slowly. 'And I know that I have eaten death, as well as life. But it is better so. Without knowledge of good and evil I cannot become like my Father. I know that I walk a knife blade between life and darkness.'

Asmodeus smiled, and was content.

Tathea watched the woman go, and knew that she was leaving the garden for ever, and that the man would choose to go with her into the exile of the great journey, with all its trials and pain, its labour and grief. Together they would travel the path to its end, understanding its meaning, and believing that they would find the light.

And she loved them with all her heart.

Then as she watched Asmodeus, a suffocating weight descended upon her so that she could not move. Her mind was crushed by it. She saw inside his soul and knew the world as he beheld it. All was vanity, appetite and rage. He saw love, he felt its hand in his own and its breath upon his cheek. It whispered his name and he did not hear. He thought it a deceit, a thing that would disappear in the face of test. He did not understand it. In his vanity and cowardice he would not even try.

Then she saw that the man and the woman had children. Birth and death were in the world, not only for them but also for beasts and herbs. All things were subject to it. The number of people grew and they covered the face of all the earth. The multitudes of them seemed endless, and they had a wealth of crops and beasts, trees of the forest, rich metals of the ground.

Slowly righteousness became corrupted and turned into such evil that God opened the heavens and let loose the floods, and the waters beneath broke their bounds also and swelled up and roared and swallowed the dry land until it was no more. Tathea watched in horror as all living things were drowned, save only one family and its creatures, the cargo of a single great ship.

The waters receded, and from that handful the earth was again peopled and covered with animals and herbs. And again there were both the just and the unjust. There was passion and pain, laughter and weeping, anger and joy.

Great men sought to walk in the footsteps of God. They offered all they had in His service, and loved the unlovely without condition or reward. They kept faith that in that white instant at the centre of time, one man would come who would stand alone in a garden and look upon hell, and he would not turn his face away from it.

She saw nations rise and fall, heroism and cruelty, splendour and ruin. She saw war sweep over cities, and plagues decimate lands. Prophecy was mocked by the many, and still the few kept a bright hope. The heart of time grew closer. Signs were fulfilled and nations saw them not.

And all the while Asmodeus waited in a black laughter, certain of his victory, and creation watched with him. A million worlds kept the light of hope across the stars of eternity – and waited.

The moment came, the day and the hour. The man was born. He became a child, and then a youth.

Asmodeus prepared. He whispered in the ears of kings and priests, common men and leaders of nations.

And the man came to maturity with a pure heart and clean hands, and began to preach the Word of God with power. Some listened to Him, many did not. His teaching was a sword to divide the true from the false, the coward from the brave, and those who loved God from those who would not. And because He shed light about him, those who feared the light conspired against Him, and the weak, the cruel and the self-seeking cast in their lot with them. They hated Him with a terror, because He showed them the truth, and they could no abide it.

It was the moment. They sought to put Him to death, and He prayed alone in the garden, His soul trembled for what He knew must come, and He longed to step aside, but He knew at last what weighed in the balance. Eternity before and after hung upon this one battle.

Armed only with love, He stood forward. 'I will . . .'

And Asmodeus faced Him as one man faces another, but with all the legions of hell beside him. He opened up the pit of damnation and showed Him all the torment of sin, guilt and terror, all perversion and madness. He saw disease and lingering death, loneliness and failure, all mockery and corruption of innocence. He saw famine and slaughter, the beauty of the earth wasted, its creatures hunted and tortured. He saw His own truth twisted into monstrous shapes and used to justify abomination, until in body's agony and soul's despair His spirit was poured out like water.

But He did not turn away. He let the pain roar through Him, and the darkness of hell cover His face, and still He did not cry out for Himself, or let go of love for even the weakest and ugliest and smallest of them.

Creation held its breath.

Perdition raged against Him, and was confounded, because it did not understand the power, the magnitude and the endlessness of love. And the darkness shrivelled and returned to its place, and Asmodeus knew that the centre of time was over, and he had not won.

And they took the man and killed him, and He died in the flesh. But His spirit was whole and perfect and living, and all creation rejoiced. The dead of all ages past who had kept faith with Him awoke and were restored, and those who had died in ignorance were taught in accordance with the promises of God.

And the man returned to the earth to tell those who loved Him of

His victory, and they believed and were filled with a hope which no darkness could crush or devour.

They taught in His name, and some believed and some did not. And when they passed from mortality into immortality their words became perverted, even as the man had foreseen in the face of hell. Evil things were done in His name and twisted doctrines spread a new kind of darkness over the world. But even while there was ignorance, war, corruption and tyranny, there was also love, courage and sacrifice, and a hope which never quite faded away. Again men waited and watched and prayed.

And after a great time, truth was given anew out of heaven, and the old powers were restored, and the old persecutions, because as ever the Word of God was a sword which divided the people, and a mirror which showed a man his face as it truly was.

A darkness of evil troubled the earth as never before, even when God had cleansed it with many waters. Whole races of men perished in holocausts of slaughter, and there was famine and new and fearful pestilences. Greed starved and polluted the land itself until the voice of the earth cried out in anguish, 'How long must I suffer? Oh Lord, how long?' And God reached out His hand and cleansed it again and it was restored, and the harvest of men was gathered, and then it was made perfect, and its joy was greater than Tathea could behold.

The vision melted from before her eyes, and she awoke to see the dawn pale in the eastern sky, spreading wide and clean and pure as the breath of heaven.

She stood up slowly, her stiff body cold, and found Casper, then began the long ride back to the fortress on the shore.

Tathea told Drusus what she had seen, hesitantly, in words of awe, and then afterwards she engraved it painstakingly on thin, metal plates which the farrier made for her, because they had no paper. But she knew the knights of the Western Shore must never forget.

They continued with building, and in the spring they began to plough the earth and plant the seeds they had gathered from the wild verges of the woodland, and the roots which they had learned to eat over the years in the north. In time they would domesticate beasts.

But there were still no women, and they were bitterly aware that all the labour and the dreams would end with their own mortality, and there was no one to whom they could leave the blazing light of their knowledge.

'We must do everything we can,' Tathea told them with a certainty that rested inside her with a piercing sweetness. 'And then the Man of Holiness will do all else that is needed.'

Iszamber had said that there would be eleven priests who would keep the light of truth, and she prayed day after day to know which of the legionaries should be chosen. And no matter how hard she struggled, she was certain of only nine names. She called those nine, and each accepted with surprise, humility and gratitude, at first overwhelmed by the magnitude of the call and uncertain of their ability to meet it. Then as time passed they learned faith in the unseen, and mistakes became fewer, knowledge widened, and hope became a staff to lean upon in the moments of loneliness as the seasons changed. Life became more certain, they gathered seeds of grain, crops grew and beasts multiplied; but still they were alone.

It was winter, two years since the defeat of Yaltabaoth, when under a sickle moon a great boat was washed ashore from the sea. The outrider of the night watch found it as dawn whitened the east. He went down to it quickly, his horse leaving deep prints in the wet sand as he approached, curious and afraid of what he might find. He splashed through the shallow foam and peered over the high gunwale into the boat. What he saw huddled inside, half insensible with weariness and cold, sent his heart soaring. They were women, old and young, at least fifty of them. One stirred, seeing the shadow above her, and opened her eyes.

'Don't be afraid!' he said urgently. 'You are safe. God has brought you here.' He reached out slowly and touched her, smiling to let her know he meant no harm. Her clothes were wet and she was rigid with cold. 'I'll get help,' he promised. 'We'll make you warm . . . and find you food . . . and dry clothes. Wait here!'

He turned and spurred his horse back, galloping along the hard strand by the waves' edge, then swinging round and clattering up across the stones to where the first men were beginning to collect the cattle for milking.

'Fetch Drusus!' he shouted excitedly. 'Tell Tathea! There is a boat washed ashore with women in it! They are perishing of cold and hunger! Fetch blankets, prepare food. God has answered us!'

Everyone set aside their usual tasks and in overwhelming thanksgiving offered the best of what they had to make the women welcome and revive them. The best food, the warmest blankets, the most comfortable rooms were given.

When they were dressed in dry clothes and wrapped in wool blankets to warm them while they ate hot gruel, Tathea spoke to the dark-eyed woman to whom the night watchman had held out his hand.

'My name is Tathea.'

The woman gazed at her. 'Where are we? Why do you care for us in this way? Do you know who we are?'

'You are on the Western Shore of the Waste Lands. We care for you because you are in need. Do you not care for those who are cold or injured or lost?'

The woman gave a brief smile, then it vanished and was replaced by fear in her eyes. 'My people would not care for the outcast. I would, because I am one of them. I know what it is to be exiled from your own place.'

'So do I,' Tathea said with more feeling than the woman could know, but no longer any bitterness. The end of comfort had also been the beginning of growth, and that she would not have forfeited for anything. 'What is your name?'

'Sefaris.' The woman laughed abruptly, and then shivered, drawing her borrowed blanket tighter round her. Her face was still ashen pale. 'Do you not want to know why we are exiled from our people?'

'If you wish to tell us,' Tathea answered. 'But it does not need to be today, or even tomorrow.'

'We blasphemed against the gods of our race,' Sefaris said challengingly, her eyes wide and angry. 'I can see you have given us not of your spare but of your best, and you have gone without, but grateful as we are to you for generosity, we will not forego our beliefs for you.'

'Our help does not rest upon your belief,' Tathea replied, 'but upon our own.'

Sefaris smiled, the shadow of both humour and apology in it. 'I should have known that. Thank you.'

Over the next few days Tathea learned something of the faith of Sefaris and why she and the women of her household had been driven from their place. Sefaris was the daughter of the High Chief of Lantrif of the River whose beliefs were alien even to the Flamens.

'They are in many ways good,' she said defensively, as if still she would protect her own. 'But their power did not seem to me to rest in morality. I spent much time alone, and one night I was meditating upon good and evil, and man's course between the two, when I heard a voice command me to seek wisdom in the love of all mankind, and of all the earth and everything in it, which is the workmanship of one God.' Her eyes dared Tathea to challenge her.

'And did you?' Tathea asked.

'Of course! Only a madwoman, or a coward, ignores the voice of heaven.'

'And what did you learn?'

'That you must love God before all else, before all men, ideas, places or dreams, and that you must learn to long for the wellbeing of the souls of all people, friend and enemy alike,' Sefaris answered. Her gaze did not waver from Tathea's face and there was no moderation or evasion in her.

'Then it was indeed the voice of heaven you heard,' Tathea responded. 'And whoever tries to change you from that is either blind or evil. Remain with us as long as you wish. Make your home with us, and be welcome.'

'Perhaps,' Sefaris said guardedly. 'But we are in your debt for your compassion and your honour.'

The days grew into weeks and winter gave way to spring. It was no preaching of words which wrought the acceptance of the Word by Sefaris and her women, but the slow lessons of kindness, of watching men who kept an order larger than any one of them, who held all goods in common and who loved the least as much as the greatest, and who spoke of God as one who above all loved the world.

Sefaris came to Tathea and asked if she might make her covenants to live in the way of the Book, and if it would be good in her sight if her women were to give themselves in marriage to those legionaries whom they loved.

By late summer Tathea knew which two legionaries were pleasing to God and should be chosen to make up the eleven priests; to heal not by the laying on of hands, but by that gentleness of heart which listens to another's grief and failures, who loves when the sufferer is at their weakest, their ugliest, their most lost, and casts out no one; who has the strength to tell the truth when it is hardest to hear, even to be hated for it, and not to turn aside. She had learned to love them in a way she had loved no one since Arimaspis, or Eleni.

Then one day the following spring, as the orb of the sun sank in a blaze of fire across the sea and wild clouds flew like a witch's hair, Menath-Dur returned. He came over the heather and down to the shore on foot, and his step was as airy as ever, the tiny bells on his ridiculous shoes singing, the sunset colouring his clothes till they shone as if the gold in them was alight from within, and the purple like amethyst and twilight.

The tide was running fast and the pale waves crashed further and further up the sand. He moved swiftly to the portcullis and the watchman saluted him and let him pass.

Inside the great hall he found seventy people sitting at the tables, men and women. He had passed ten more on watch. As he entered, the noise of speech and laughter stilled and everyone turned to gaze at him.

He saluted Drusus, then with a smile that embraced them all he walked over to Tathea and stood in front of her. It was one of those moments which is held in the heart and towards which history looks, both before and after.

'The time has come, lady. The light of the Western Shore is safe. It shall not dim nor the torch fall from the hand from this time forth, until the last war is fought and won, and the world reborn of God. Now you must leave here and return to the path, which calls you. Your journey is not yet completed.'

Tathea was startled and dismayed. She had not foreseen this. She had become certain that she would live out her life here, leading these people with whom she had faced the darkness, fought and won such terrible battles, and built a fortress of the heart as well as of the hand. She had imagined herself growing old here among them, loving and loved, and in the end passing on the torch.

She looked at Menath-Dur's strange, gentle face, and saw no wavering in his eyes.

'How can she cross the Waste Lands?' It was Drusus who spoke, his face dark with doubt. 'The forces of Yaltabaoth are still waiting in the hills and valleys, and the Wanderer with the Spear of Broken Dreams will hunt for her with enmity deeper than for anyone else. He swore it!'

'She has all the weapons she needs to fight the Enemy,' Menath-Dur answered him softly. 'What she will do with them, and with her armour, rests with her. But they cannot wound her unless she permits it. And the forces of darkness that will come against her are such that no man or angel can fight them for her. There are parts of the journey upward that each of us must travel alone; in the beginning because the choice must be free, in the end because there comes a time when the spirit has known the light well enough to stand in its own power and become the warrior, no longer the defended.'

Drusus bowed his head in acceptance. He had watched Tathea and he understood.

Menath-Dur gave her only one night in which to prepare, and to grieve for what she must leave behind. She had shared terror and pain with these people, she had been part of their labour and had tasted keenly their joy. Now she would not see the children born. This wild shore with its pale sand and booming sea had become dear to her. She loved the cry of the birds and the light on the water. The bitter winter had a clean beauty, which blessed even as it hurt.

In the morning she stood in the courtyard with Menath-Dur and stared upward at the walls she had helped build, the people she had taught and loved, the beasts she knew by name. Farewells had a unique pain, but when there is no cry of denial inside, there is a dignity which allows friends to part without the need for tears or promises.

They stood to attention, like legionaries before a commanding general, heads high. They had dressed in their tattered uniforms and full armour, scarlet-crested helmets and ragged cloaks blowing in the wind. Drusus raised his sword in the old Imperial salute, a single bright blade in the light. No one spoke. Everything had already been said.

Tathea stood still for a moment, imprinting on her heart their faces so that she could never forget. Then she turned, leading Casper by the rein, and followed Menath-Dur under the portcullis and out on to the sand.

All day they travelled inland and southward over the wide sweep in the Waste Lands, its reed-speared tarns bright in the pale sun, wind-rippled. In the sheltered valleys the new grass was filled with flowers, golds and blues like fragments of a fallen sky.

At the border of Celidon, Menath-Dur left her.

'The enemy lies in wait for you, in many forms,' he said gravely, touching her face with his long, gentle fingers. 'Some you will expect, some you will not. Some will be very terrible, and will test your soul. But you are known unto God, and He will not suffer you to be tried beyond your bearing. Remember hope. Always hope. I cannot tell you more. It is forbidden me. If I were to help you now, I should rob you of eternity. Farewell.'

And before she could answer him he turned and strode over the heather, the sun glinting on the gold at his shoulder.

An intense loneliness settled over her as soon as she lost sight of him. Celidon was a beautiful land and the spring had filled it with an abundance of life. Saplings in the hollows were veiled with translucent leaves. Streams chattered down the gullies, leaves and flowers sprang from the earth and beasts came forth from winter sleep. Yet she pressed forth with urgency as if there were no time to bask in its loveliness.

She rode past the fortress of Layamon, a million Imperial bricks in the vast buttresses black against the eastern skyline, and travelled on towards Yba and then the outskirts of Hirioth, where the trees stood knee-deep in drifts of bluebells. She saw no demon on her heels, but she felt a shadow behind her. White plumes on the wind reminded her of the Wanderer, and gold buttercups in the sun of Azrub's glittering arms.

But under the giant trees of the forest itself, when she had made camp for the night, the Enemy showed a face that she knew instantly. The first being appeared in the precise likeness of a bald-headed man, naked but for a cloak about his loins. His oiled flesh gleamed in the red light of her camp fire. Then there was a rustle behind her, and swinging round she saw another, exactly the same as the first, shaven, glistening, his eyes sunken pits in his skull. He crept towards her, low to the ground as if he would use his hands to balance himself, like paws. There was a third, out to the right, also coming slowly closer, eye sockets turned toward her, broad nostrils quivering as he sniffed her scent.

Casper rolled his eyes in fear and reared back, snapping his tethering rein. Cold terror took hold of Tathea. She scrambled to her feet and backed against the trunk of the giant oak behind her.

'Run!' she cried to Casper, as terrified for him as for herself.

As the creatures came closer in slow, weaving steps, she felt the rough bark under her hands. There was no escape except upward, and even to try was instinct not reason. They were probably far better able to climb than she was. Yet the cold breath and smell of decay that came from them filled her with such horror that she swivelled round and climbed the trunk. She hauled herself up a twig, a branch, a bark hole at a time, careless of torn skin and nails, until she was astride the first great bough. The three creatures were crouched below, their hands reaching upwards, clawing at her feet, arms outstretched, sightless eyes searching for her.

They were reaching higher, their hands closer to her, less than a span away and nearer with every leap, their mouths open, leering with jubilation.

What were they? Creatures of the abyss, hell-begotten, or fallen men, once human, but now so lost to all light that they had become thus? Had they any conception of truth? Was even the faintest spark known to them?

There was no escape. She could not climb any further up the tree, and her strength was sapped, draining away moment by moment like blood gushing from a wound. And they smelled it, their faces avid, mouths open, tongues questing.

She was slipping towards them, too weak to fight. One almost touched her; another leap and the fearful hands would close over her feet.

Then a wild thought came to her, born of despair. She could not escape them, she was so weak she could feel herself sliding, the bark of the tree scraping her skin. Nothing could save her from them. But what if they had souls? What if there was still something left in them that had once been human, and capable of light?

She began to speak to them. 'It is not too late for you. There is no corner of earth or hell so forgotten that God cannot see it and reach out his hand to you, if you will take it . . . and live.' She gulped, her heart hammering. 'Only learn to love, even the smallest fraction, and you can be loved. Forgive something, anything, and you can begin to be forgiven. The road is open, take it. I will come with you.'

As she heard her own words, her terror of their obscenity faded. A moment of pity stirred inside her, a glimpse of their loss. Very slowly she stretched out a trembling hand, downwards towards them.

'Come with me,' she whispered. 'Come with the light.'

But like darkness before the sun, they shrank away, shrivelling to small, misshapen things, their power vanished.

By the time she was back on the ground, she was alone. The glade was filled with moonlight. There was nothing there but the smell of damp loam and the night air, and Casper, head down, blowing through his nostrils, waiting for her. Suddenly, far above her, came the piercing song of a bird, an exquisite cascade of sound, and then silence again.

She stood with her face to the stars, knowing that she held in her spirit the weapon and the shield against the Enemy, and the light to guide her steps through every storm that earth or hell could send, if she would but use no other.

She stopped at the forest village to see Tugomir and found him much changed. There was a deep heart of calm within him, which embraced the million trees of Hirioth with love. She did not need to ask him if he had succeeded at last, it was written in his dark face and his eyes burned with it.

It was there in Garran and his people also. They wished Tugomir to remain with them not because they leaned upon him or needed his command, but because they loved him, as he now loved them, knowing the strengths and the weaknesses of each, the laughter and the pain.

She lingered there three days, telling him of all that had passed on the Western Shore, or Merdic and Yaltabaoth, of Drusus and his fortress, of Menath-Dur, and of the vision she had seen of the centre of time, and the redemption of all things.

When they parted, she travelled south again, in the direction of the open lands beyond which lay Sylum, and whatever awaited her there.

On the wide forest path she saw a man coming towards her on horseback, a tall man, riding easily as if he were well used to the saddle. When he saw her he reined in his animal for a moment, then leaned and urged it forward almost to a gallop until it stopped in a flurry of mud and grass a yard from her and he leaped from it. Only then did she recognise Alexius.

It had been over seven years. He was changed, older, there was a leanness to his face and grey in his hair, but his eyes and his mouth were the same.

Happiness surged up inside her without thought of anything beyond the joy of seeing him. She leaped from the saddle and threw herself into his arms in a wild embrace and clung to him as fiercely as he to her. She touched the roughness of his tunic, smelled the familiar tang of leather armour, felt the warmth of his body and the strength of him. Her heart beat so savagely she was shaking. When at last she let go, there were tears on her cheeks, and on his.

'I have everything in the world to tell you!' she said breathlessly, searching his eyes to know how he was, if he suffered any loss or grief, any cloud of the spirit.

'And I you,' he said gently. 'But you tell me first.' He gathered his horse's reins and swung up into the saddle, holding out his hand to lift her to join him. Together they rode gently along the path, Casper following behind, and with the warmth of his arms round her she told him all that had happened since they had parted in Shinabar.

301

The shadows lengthened into night and at moonrise they made camp, and still they talked. In the morning they rose and continued on their way. Again she told him of what she had seen and heard and of the battles on the Waste Lands. She recounted to him the vision she had seen, and how all the creations of the earth, even the trees and herbs, had watched and waited as the man and Asmodeus moved towards the centre of time, knowing their soul's light or darkness was won or lost in that hour. She felt Alexius's arms grow rigid and sensed an agony of pain in him as if it were in her own body.

She twisted round to stare at him, pulling his horse to a stop. 'What is it?' she said hoarsely. 'What has happened?' The look in his face terrified her, as if he himself had seen hell. 'What is it?'

His voice was dreadful when he answered. 'There was a rebellion in the east. An evil man arose and killed many villagers because they stood in his path. I fought for Ortelios.'

She waited, knowing that was not what tortured him.

'He fled with his men into Hirioth, east of here. I followed him. I knew he would hide where I could not find him, and then when I was gone come out again and harry the villages.'

She reached to put her hand on his wrist, and then withdrew it. This was beyond her power to touch and she knew it.

'I burned him out,' he whispered. 'I burned the living forest, and the trees and beasts in it. I did not know then what it was I did, but I know now. I have wounded the earth, and I have separated myself from it.'

She understood his horror. She shared it with him as if it had been her own. She could see the terror and destruction, the pain, the charred bodies and the ruined stumps with an agony he was only just beginning to know, but she saw the path he would walk.

Gently she slid her arms round him and buried her head against his neck, but she could not comfort him. There was no comfort to give.

She did not know how long it was before she let go of him and he dismounted, leaving her in the saddle. He needed to walk, to feel his feet on the earth. They travelled steadily and in silence. He was alone in a darkness where she could not be with him. He spoke only once.

'I shall go and find the Flamen priests. I have broken the Higher Law and I will answer to it.'

She did not argue. He had lived all his life with reverence for the laws of men, and then of God. It was not in him to breach them and not pay. To do so would be a greater price than anything they could exact from him.

They went in silence but for the song of birds, the movement of the wind in the leaves and the creak of the saddle. She looked at his bowed shoulders, but there was nothing she could say or do. He was alone in a night of his own making.

302

It was she who first saw the figure of Immerith ahead of them on the path, his green cloak like the forest leaves. There were two others with him, standing back, their faces grave and filled with fierce pain of loss.

Alexius looked up and knew who they were. He hesitated in his step only a moment, a faltering, no more. Then he straightened his shoulders and walked towards them.

'I am Alexius,' he said quietly. 'It was I who ordered the burning of the trees. I did not understand then, but now I know what I have done. I have murdered a part of the forest, and I am here to answer the law.' He took his sword from his belt and held it out, hilt towards Immerith, then stood bareheaded in the sun.

Immerith took the sword and let it fall to the ground where it lay.

'You would answer to the Flamen law?' he said slowly. 'Even if it takes your life?'

Alexius looked at him. 'Without the law, creation perishes. Even God cannot and will not break it. What I have done is terrible. I wish with all my soul that I had not, but I have. I will answer for it.'

Immerith looked beyond him to Tathea only once, then he nodded his head slowly. He did not glance at his companions, as if he had no need to question their countenance in what he would say.

'You understand that you have murdered the forest, and that is against the law of God. Your hand was that of the destroyer.'

'I know.' Alexius spoke so softly his words were barely audible.

Tathea sat in an anguish of helplessness.

'Yes,' Immerith nodded slowly, 'I perceive that you do indeed understand what you have done, and it is hideous to your soul. There is a law in the universe, which cannot be broken. But it is satisfied by repentance and fulfilled by mercy, which is the bond of heaven and earth. You have sinned, and you have been pardoned.' He held up his right hand. 'You are again one with all the creatures that God has loved, the birds and the beasts and the stars, and you are one with the forest – and with me, because we have seen darkness and light together, and we have understood both. Go in peace.'

Tathea felt the radiance blossom inside her and the fire of joy blaze up in her spirit.

Alexius stared at Immerith. He was dazed with wonder. He sought for words but there were none that could express what he wanted to say.

Immerith stooped and picked up the sword from the ground and offered it back, this time with the hilt towards Alexius.

Very slowly, still in awe, Alexius accepted it.

Immerith bowed. 'Thank you,' he said solemnly. 'A miracle has happened here, and we are both enlarged by it, I because I have given freely, and my soul is blessed, you because you have received in humility, and you have seen something more beautiful than justice, and thus you are blessed also.' He glanced at Tathea once more and his eyes were filled with tenderness, then without speaking again he turned and walked back into the shelter of the trees, and his companions with him, and the green shadows swallowed them.

Alexius raised his eyes to Tathea, and they were bright with wonder. He had been given a larger gift than he could grasp, but a sense of the magnitude of it was in him already.

She smiled at him, and urged the horses forward. She knew he needed to walk alone for a space longer. He was too drenched in emotion to touch or share yet, and she was content.

The following day they came into Sylum and were welcomed by Ortelios and given shelter and food and fresh clothing. He listened with great excitement to the news Tathea brought of the Lost Legion and how they had built a mighty fortress on the Western Shore.

The day after that there was a great feast held in the castle. Soldiers, landowners and merchants were there, including the Lord Nastemah and the beautiful Verrani. At least three score men and women were seated round the tables. Torches burned on the walls, shields and armour and tapestries decorated them. Fires burned in huge hearths at either end, dogs lying sprawled before them, waiting for scraps to be thrown.

Alexius sat at one end of the hall, Tathea at the other. He had had no time to speak to her alone since their arrival. He had been too stunned and amazed with the mercy of the Flamens even to think of telling her why he had come to the Island at the Edge of the World, except that it was to seek her and to ask her to return to the City in the Centre of the World. Word of her had drifted back from mariners sailing the northern seas, rumour only. He had come in a wild hope, knowing what had befallen her in Shinabar. He had wanted to see her again. The hunger in him had never died. There was a soul-deep loneliness when he could not speak to her, see her, touch her mind with his dreams. But the more urgent reason concerned her return to Camassia, and this he had barely mentioned.

Now he made trivial conversation with Islanders and watched Verrani's fragile beauty and the sadness in her eyes. Always she looked to Nastemah, but there was no joy in her. It was not the gaze of a woman in love, rather of one who was bound by ties of need, and fear. When she spoke to another man, the will to please and the expectation of hurt flickered across her face, giving her a vulnerability which stirred his heart with pity.

Why should she suffer so? The laws of neither the Empire nor of the Island compelled a woman to remain with a husband who frightened her. Surely the measure of a nation's civilisation was the way in which it treated its weak, its troubled, those who were different by chance or birth. A race still sunk in barbarism put to death its outsiders, one that was in decline ignored them and allowed them to suffer and to die. Camassia was at the high tide of its power.

He looked across the table and caught the gaze of Nastemah's golden, vulpine eyes.

The evening grew late and still the guests laughed and talked and drank. The other women were full of eagerness, quick and natural to speak, but Verrani dared offer no opinions contrary to her husband's. No one seemed to address her directly except on the utmost trivia, such as to pass something across the table, or thank her when she did. On anything deeper they deferred to Nastemah, as if Verrani could have no friends other than those he approved. When she was hesitant, he belittled her, and laughed at her expense.

Alexius watched with mounting anger. As the evening passed, she grew paler and now her eyes brimmed with tears she dared not shed. He could only imagine her loneliness and her fear. He would have intervened, defended her swiftly and hard, but he knew it would be only momentary, and as soon as they left this hall with its warmth and company, Nastemah could take a terrible revenge upon her for any crossing of his will, let alone a public humiliation.

So he kept silent, but inside he was burning with anger.

When the final sweetmeats were eaten and the last of the wine drunk, the guests rose to leave. Alexius saw Tathea go with Ortelios. They had much to discuss before she sailed from the Island back to the Centre of the World. When he told her why she must return there, she had not questioned the need, and Alexius wondered if some vision or prophecy had told her. Perhaps the words of the strange man named Menath-Dur had been sufficient. Explanations could wait until the voyage. Right now it was Verrani's white face which filled his mind, and her desperate misery.

Alexius found her in one of the antechambers, standing alone, shivering as if she were cold. There was no one else within sight. He walked over towards her.

She smiled at him hesitantly and came a step closer. It seemed she wished to speak to him if she could find the courage. Perhaps she had sensed his compassion and his will to protect her.

'There is no need for you to be afraid,' he said very gently, his voice little more than a whisper. 'Imperial law will protect you if you want to leave the Lord Nastemah. There would be no disgrace, no slur on your honour or your name. You need not be kept in any bond that has become repugnant to you.'

She looked at him in amazement, her eyes so wide and clear she seemed like an astonished child, willing herself to believe the incredible.

From the room beyond the door curtains came the sound of

laughter. The light flickered in the torch brackets, making the stone seem golden.

'Are you sure?' she asked, fear and hope alternating in her eyes, shadows he could not read, memories of pain and dreams from long ago. As she turned her head, the angle of her cheek and the dark coil of her hair could have been Xanthica's. She was a thousand miles away in a different world, and yet his sense of anger and urgency to protect was the same. He had failed Xanthica. He had been unable to help her see the light that could have been hers, to give her the courage to test faith and prove it. She had denied herself rather than risk losing some part of Maximian's love. It was never too late, but the cost was higher now, the path immeasurably harder to find, and she had no faith in herself to try, and no hope that she deserved it.

But he could save Verrani.

'Yes, I am sure,' he answered her.

'I'm afraid,' she whispered, her voice catching. 'If I defy him he'll hurt me. He might even kill me! You don't know how strong he is.'

'I'll protect you,' he promised. 'I have power also, both physical and spiritual. If it is what you want, I can take you away from the Island altogether. When we sail, you may come too, to Camassia, if you like, or anywhere else.'

She shook her head, but her eyes still pleaded with him. He saw a strange mixture of honesty and despair in her.

'Do you want the freedom to choose for yourself what you will do, to follow your own beliefs and answer honestly to your own spirit, to befriend whom you will?' he pressed.

She bit her lip and her voice was no more than a whisper. 'Yes, of course I do!'

'Then you can,' he said fervently.

She stiffened, fear gripping her. She swallowed convulsively. 'I must go to Nastemah now. But come for me!'

'I will gather soldiers I can trust, and follow you,' he promised.

'Tonight?'

'Yes, within the hour.'

'Do you swear it?'

'I do.'

She nodded, the rigidity easing out of her. With the shadow of a smile she turned and walked away, glancing back at him once, a tumult of emotions in her face, a darkness and a terror he meant to free her from for ever.

He went immediately to the legionary captain who had fought beside him suppressing the rebellion on the Eastern Shore. He was willing to bring ten men and come that moment; indeed he was eager. He had no love for Nastemah and believed him to be the dark hand behind many of the Island's troubles. Alexius left a written message for Tathea, and rode out to keep his promise to Verrani, his last act on the Island before he sailed for Camassia in the morning.

They travelled east and south along the Imperial road. It was not far, no more than two or three miles. The lights were still blazing in Nastemah's great house although it was not long till morning. Alexius posted the soldiers in the grounds and went alone to the great iron-studded door.

The servants admitted him without showing more than slight surprise. Inside the hall, fires leaped in the hearth, crackling bright. The walls were hung with tapestries and the gold of ornaments reflected the flames. Verrani stood slender as a sapling, still dressed in silver with a dark rope of silk round her waist. Behind her Nastemah smiled and stared with his fox eyes at Alexius.

'You have ridden far, my lord,' he said softly. 'Let us offer you wine. Verrani! Fill the goblet for the Lord Alexius.' He gestured with his arm towards a ewer of blue enamel chased in gold, and a crimson goblet beside it.

Meekly Verrani obeyed and brought the goblet over, offering it to Alexius with averted eyes. Then she poured another and gave it to Nastemah.

For Alexius to decline would have been rude to Verrani, and he was thirsty from the ride in the chill night air.

'Thank you.' He looked beyond her at Nastemah, knowing his enemy, seeing the evil in his face. 'The Lady Verrani does not wish to remain with you.' He would not deceive by evasion. 'Your acts and your thoughts are repellent to her. I have come to give her safe escort to wherever she pleases. I have soldiers outside, and you would be unwise to offer violence.' He sipped the wine, it was delicious.

Nastemah's eyebrows rose in surprise, not in anger. 'Indeed! How little you understand. But Camassia is so young.' He shrugged. 'So very young. And your wisdom is wrought with much foolishness, my lord.' He was standing by the mantel, the firelight bright on his head and shoulders. 'A lovely face, a seeming victim – and you rush in where wiser men pass by. You think I hold Verrani here against her will?'

'Not any longer,' Alexius answered firmly. 'I have made provision for her. I will be her guardian until she is able to choose for herself another husband, and what manner of life she will.' He would not mention the ship or any voyage. Let Nastemah think she would remain here.

'Oh, brave!' Nastemah was smiling, there was no outrage in his face at all, only mockery. 'But such a fool!' He spat the last word and turned his goblet over and poured its contents on the floor. 'You know nothing of me! My power is not that of the sword. I do not keep Verrani – or anyone!' He laughed, a cold, ugly sound. 'You think I have her in thrall? I do, but it is of her own choosing. I serve the darkness. I am a son of Asmodeus, the Great Angel of the Pit. But I hold no one against their will.' His voice dropped to a whisper. 'The darkness has no force, only seduction.'

Alexius swung round to Verrani, and for the first time he saw shadows in her face. Under the fair skin there was greyness; the eyes were hollower, the lips had petulance and a sourness invisible before. It might have been no more than a change in the light, and yet suddenly she was repellent. He felt cold inside.

'Verrani is with me because in her soul she chooses to be,' Nastemah said softly, and with infinite pleasure. 'It is not I who make her miserable, it is the war within her. She wants the light, and yet she had not the courage to take it.'

Alexius stared at him. The slim, golden, vulpine figure seemed to sway in the hard flamelight, the eyes and the hair to become richer, more obvious.

'She has chosen the dark,' Nastemah said again.

Alexius tried to say 'No' but his lips would not form the word.

'Ah, yes!' Nastemah spoke as if he had heard the cry of his mind. 'That is why she herself offered you the poisoned goblet. She betrayed you, Alexius, Lord of the Book, as she betrayed herself. That is why she will remain with me. I spoke the truth: darkness has no power over light. Those in bondage to me have chosen it. And you have not seen the least part of their number!'

Poison. The room wavered and blurred and drifted into a haze as Alexius sank to his knees. The floor rose to meet him, not with violence as he had expected, but with a softness as if it were a bed; and he knew no more.

Nastemah walked over and stood above him, looking down at his body where it lay, and at the peace which was even now smoothing out his features, laying a grace upon them as if the weariness and the conflicts of the years had slipped away and were resolved in understanding of such beauty it consumed all pain and transfigured it.

Suddenly Nastemah's features twisted in a paroxysm of envy so violent it seemed it must destroy him. His body shook as if with an ague. His teeth bit his lips till they bled and his nails gouged the flesh from his palms. He let out a wail of fury and despair that so filled the night that in the far fields even the beasts in their burrows fell silent, huddling together. In the trees all birdsong ceased.

Chapter Twenty

The soldiers carried the body of Alexius back to Sylum. It was the ashen-faced legionary captain who brought the news to Tathea.

Horror gripped her even before he spoke. He stood in the doorway to her rooms in the early morning light, haggard and wretched.

His voice was very low, rough with the strain of his emotions. 'The Lord Alexius is dead, my lady. Nastemah slew him . . . with poison.'

She could not grasp what he had said. It could not be true.

'Dead?' she repeated.

'Yes, my lady. He went in alone. It was poison in a goblet of wine.'

She stood motionless. In a few sentences the whole world had changed. Suddenly it was colder. Something immeasurably sweet had been taken away. She was hardly aware of the room around her, or that she was shaking and the legionary captain had come to her side and was guiding her to a seat.

He stayed with her, silently. There was nothing to say. At last she gathered her thoughts and, leaning on his arm, rose to her feet again.

'Where is he? What have you done with his body?' It was her duty to see that he was buried properly. His wife – his widow – was the Emperor's sister.

'I'll take you to him,' he offered.

She stopped, pulling against him. 'I – I don't want to see . . .' She could not bear to look at his dead face, especially if the poison had disfigured him. She wanted to remember him alive, as he had been.

'You should, my lady,' he said, for the first time without awkwardness. 'There is a peace in him perhaps you will understand. You should carry that back to his family.'

She looked at him. She had not even thought of that. He was right, it was she who should go and tell Eleni. Everything in her rebelled at the thought, but there was no argument, there could be none. The last thing she could do for Alexius was to tell his widow, and she owed Eleni that and more – debts she could not pay.

'Of course,' she agreed, following him as he led the way out of the room and along the stone passage down to the main stairs and the great hall. Ortelios was there, white-faced and grim. He bowed his head, but he did not go with her. The moment was one on which he

309

would not intrude. He did not know what lay between Alexius and Tathea, but his perception told him it was more than a common faith or purpose.

She went past the guard and entered the room. Alexius was lying on a simple table. He was dressed in the same robes as the evening before but his sword was by his side and he had simple chest armour over his shirt and breeches. Someone, perhaps Ortelios, had laid his scarlet-crested Imperial helmet by his side and his cloak was folded neatly at his feet.

None of that mattered. She saw them only on the edge of her vision. His face was so familiar it tore at her with a pain that made her gasp for breath, and yet it was also different. Peace spread around him like a light, enfolding her as well, smoothing away the sharp knife edge of grief. He had left her, and nothing would be the same again knowing that he was no longer somewhere in the world, thinking of her as she was of him, remembering. But his spirit was in a brighter place, beyond the reach of the Great Enemy. His battle was over, and won. She could not doubt that, the victory was in his face. She could not weep for him, only for herself.

She looked at him for a long time. She would not see him again and when she left, it would be the last goodbye. She must remember every line, every part of him, his mouth, his cheek, his hands. She must never find she could not picture him in her mind.

Finally she knew it was enough. Alexius was no longer here, and she should leave also. It was time to thank Ortelios for all he had said and done during her long years on the Island. Alexius's ship was waiting and she must go. He had come to take her back to Camassia for some reason he had not told her, but that did not change her mission. Menath-Dur had warned her there was a greater conflict ahead and she knew she had not fought it yet.

She arrived in the City in the Centre of the World in early summer. It was thirteen years since she had first come here, carrying the Book in her arms. She had forgotten how bright the sun was, how strong the heat of it on the stones. Once again she was alone. There were no courtiers, no army, not even Tugomir as companion. And now there were none of Kol-Shamisha's jewels left.

It had been hard to leave the Island. She had loved the people, and in a deep and unexplained way she had loved the land itself. Hardest of all to part with had been her home. It was the one farewell she had not been able to make without weeping.

She passed unnoticed in the teeming streets, a woman darker skinned than Camassians but with a scattering of silver at the temples of her black hair, and a certainty in the way she held her head which was more than pride, more even than courage. She was only fleetingly aware of those she passed, or the changes in the City, subtle to the eye. All her mind was inward.

Ortelios had given her the money Alexius had had, and she used what was necessary to pay her way to Eleni's house. There was a strange servant at the door who asked her name.

'Ta-Thea, of Shinabar,' she answered. 'Tell the Lady Eleni that I have news from the Island at the Edge of the World, and have her maids wait upon her.'

There must have been something in her face or her voice, some knowledge of grief, because the man obeyed without argument or question.

She was conducted to the same quiet, earth-toned room overlooking the cypress garden which she and Eleni had shared so many years ago, before Shinabar, when the Book was new and exciting. They had had a kind of innocence then, which was gone, and now they had new losses to share, or to separate them. Alexius had gone to the Island to bring her back. If he had not, he would still be alive.

Eleni came in quietly. She, too, had changed. There was grey in her hair and she was not so slender as in the past, but the gentleness was still there, and the warmth in her skin, her eyes. The lines in her face were good ones, born of laughter and time. If there had been anger, it had been resolved, if bitterness, it had been overcome. She looked pleased to see Tathea and walked towards her eagerly, until she saw her face more closely, then she stopped.

'What is it?' Her voice was rough-edged, catching in her throat. 'Where is Alexius?'

There was no answer that would not hurt. It was ridiculous, Tathea reflected, that even now, with all her knowledge, it was so hard to say.

'He met an emissary of the Great Enemy,' she answered softly. 'They fought a battle and Alexius won, but it cost him his life. I saw him afterwards. The peace of God was in his face. You could not weep for him, if you had seen him, only for those who loved him and are left behind. I . . . I wish I did not have to tell you this . . .' That sounded like an excuse, and it was not what she had meant.

Eleni was staring at her. Anger, confusion and grief showed in her face. 'Why?' she said, shaking her head in denial. 'There's no war there! How could he be killed?'

'There is war everywhere,' Tathea answered, aching to be able to cross the gulf between them, and prevented by her own guilt, not only that Alexius had gone to the Island to find her, but for all the things they had shared which had excluded Eleni: the marches and the battles in Shinabar, the horror of victory and the slaughter of the dead, the comradeship which was like nothing else, the silence of the desert night and the moment when they had resisted temptation. Perhaps they had been closer then than at any other moment in all

311

their years of sharing. And she had seen his darkest moment also, when he understood how he had broken the higher law, and then seen a greater mercy, and understood that too. She had seen him after death and known something of his spirit's peace, and that also should have been Eleni's, not hers. None of it could she give to Alexius's widow, or even speak of. To do so would be an injury in itself.

'What do you mean?' Eleni was angry. It was her denial of loss. 'There isn't war everywhere!' Her voice was sharp.

'A war of the spirit,' Tathea answered. Eleni had been a warrior in that as much as anyone, with her own courage and her own wounds.

'Thank you for coming to tell me,' Eleni said stiffly. 'It must have been difficult for you.'

Tathea flinched. The coldness in Eleni's eyes was undisguised. The words were oblique, polite, but their meaning was not lost. How should she answer?

'There was no one else who could have told you . . .' she fumbled for the right way to phrase it, '. . . of the peace in him, that it was greater than that of most men who die in battle, that—'

'That you knew him better than I did?' Eleni's eyebrows rose.

Tathea felt the heat surge up her face. 'Of course not. I had not seen him for seven years. It is simply that it happened where I was.'

Eleni's expression did not change or soften. 'And you could not help?' She gave an abrupt little laugh. 'I used to think you could always defeat the Enemy.' Now there were tears in her eyes. She blinked rapidly. 'How did you let him take Alexius?'

The question was absurd in a dozen ways. She had not been in Nastemah's house, she had not even known Alexius's intention to go there. She had no power over the ability of the Enemy to cause physical death. She had proved fallible all too often even to avoid his corruption of the spirit or his power to deceive. She had the same path to walk as everyone else. But Alexius had gone to the Island for her. And he had loved her. They had never spoken it between them but they had known it far more surely than any word could have expressed. In that she was guilty. To argue over any of the lesser issues was a dishonesty neither of them deserved.

'I wasn't there,' she answered. 'Alexius went to help a woman who seemed to be held against her will. He took soldiers with him, but he went into the house alone. No one knows what happened, except that the Enemy lost the battle of the spirit, and in his rage he killed Alexius.'

'How do you know he won?' Eleni asked. 'Don't lie to comfort me.' Her voice was hard, full of warning and fear.

'We used to know each other better than that!' Tathea accused. 'I haven't changed. Have you, that you could forget?'

Eleni turned away and walked over to the long window, staring at the sun on the cypresses. A golden-flowering vine trailed over the steps.

'I am not lying,' Tathea said more gently. 'I saw his face afterwards, and that was why I came rather than anyone else. I wish I had the words to let you see his expression. The peace of God was in him. I grieve for his loss, but the pain I feel is for myself, not for him. To feel pain for him would be to deny that what I have seen is true. You cannot wish to hold anyone back from the great journey upwards, if you . . . if you love them.'

There was silence in the room. It was hot. The sunlight fell in bright patterns on the smooth floor. There was a perfume of cedarwood and flowers in the air. The breeze from the open windows carried the smell of cypresses. It was a world away from the Island, a beauty almost from another creation, no rain-wet blossoms, no full-throated bird-song, no wild, dark heaths and wind-ragged skies. And yet love and loss were the same.

At last Eleni turned to face Tathea. There were tears on her cheeks. 'You did love him, didn't you?' It was half a question, half a statement. She wanted an answer, but she knew what it must be if it were honest.

'Yes,' Tathea said softly. 'And I loved you also. But most of all I love the light I have seen, and I never forgot that.'

Eleni took a quick breath and closed her eyes. She walked over towards the windows, her back to Tathea. 'I did. I forgot for a season . . . then I remembered again.' She took a long, shaky breath. This time when she spoke her voice was gentle, the anger was gone. 'I remembered who I am, and who I must be, if I am to keep my gift. It can be held only with love, when it is hardest as well as when it is easiest. I thought I had lost it . . . but it has returned, stronger and sweeter because of my knowledge.'

Silence settled in the room, but it was softer now. A fountain played somewhere just beyond sight. The murmur of falling water drifted on the air.

'Did Alexius tell you why he came for you?' Eleni asked.

'No. There was too little opportunity.' Tathea hesitated, wondering for a moment if she should tell her of the Higher Law and Alexius's breaking of it, and his mercy at the Flamens' hands, and how suddenly he had understood so much. And as soon as the question arose, she knew she should not. It was perhaps the greatest single moment in Alexius's life, the vision of the love of God, not in the word but in the brilliant white light of reality. Tathea had been there, and Eleni had not. There was time in the future for her to learn. Now the moment was too fragile and grief too raw.

Eleni looked down at her hands. 'A great deal has changed since you left. You didn't even see it in the streets as you passed, did you?'

'No . . .'

Eleni's face shadowed. 'Isadorus is dead. Did he not even tell you that?'

'No.' It was another grief, but she should not have been surprised. 'Is Tiberian Emperor?'

'Yes. But that is not why we need you back.' Now Eleni's voice was edged with harshness, a deeper, angrier pain than anything before. 'The only way you will understand it is if I tell you from the beginning.' She stood up and went over to the table and poured wine from a turquoise and gold painted jug. She returned with two goblets and gave one to Tathea.

'After you left Shinabar, Ra-Nufis returned here, with the Book . . .'

Tathea had not even dared to ask where it was. She had made herself believe God would protect it, and refused to torture herself further. Now relief flooded through her and she found she was smiling.

Eleni put her hand up and pushed a strand of hair off her brow. It was a simple gesture, and yet there was soul weariness in it, as of the revisiting of some familiar tragedy.

'What is it?' Tathea demanded sharply.

Eleni sighed. 'He brought it here and within a few days, perhaps because he had been with you, more probably because he actually had the Book, he resumed leadership of all the believers. At first it strengthened us greatly. Just to have the Book itself in Camassia again was wonderful.' She smiled as she said it, but it pulled her lips at the corners as if she had tasted something that burnt.

'It was very slow,' she went on, 'so gradual nobody noticed. I didn't myself, so I can blame no one else.'

Now Tathea was afraid. 'Noticed what?'

'He was marvellous!' Eleni's face was pinched. 'He preached with such fire and passion, such a love of the beauty of it. His whole countenance used to be alight—'

'Used to be?' Tathea said hoarsely, remembering with an ache of loss all that Ra-Nufis had been, his loyalty, his courage, his skill. He had loved the Book above all else. Nothing was too much for him to give in its service, no sacrifice too great. 'Is he dead too?'

'Dead?' Eleni bit her lip, and this time it was she who reached to touch Tathea, holding her hand with all the old warmth, so gently Tathea felt a terror grip her.

Even so it did not prepare her for what Eleni had to say.

'Dead? Only in a manner of speaking.'

'What do you mean?' She did not want to hear the answer, but there was no way to evade it.

Eleni leaned back and sipped the wine, her face shadowed with anger and pity. 'He loved the beauty in it above everything,' she replied. 'Even above the truth. On his lips, little by little, it grew softer in the telling. The hard edges of price became blurred and finally so dim as to be ignored.' Her voice was lower as the pain in her increased. 'In time they disappeared altogether. Of course more and more people joined the faith, people who understood the teachings only a little, a fragment of an idea that was beautiful to them, but not the whole. We were so eager to welcome them we feared teaching them the pain of truth as well as the joy.' She was watching Tathea intently, her face lined with concentration.

'We twisted mercy into a softness of the soul that denied the existence of sin,' she said so quietly her words were barely audible. 'We made too few demands. We did not want to exclude anyone or drive them away because we asked more than they wanted to give. We thought they would be unwilling to let go of their old pleasures, so we changed the faith to accommodate them.'

'Ra-Nufis wouldn't do that!' Tathea said hotly. 'What have they done to him? Who is it? Is he imprisoned?'

Eleni looked as if she were consumed by inner misery. She shook her head, a tiny movement. 'Not in the way you mean. It was very slow, the relaxing of the law for a sin one understood and could have committed oneself; the lifting of a rule for a person whose potential we could see, only one weakness held them away. It was very slow. The followers grew. There are millions! Perhaps all are a little better for being members even in name. I have pondered that so long, and still I don't know the answer. It is an argument used by many philosophers . . . the saving of all the world. Surely God is not a respecter of persons, wanting only a few, casting out the many.'

'That is twisted thinking,' Tathea said angrily. 'God loves us all, but to think He can alter the laws of light and darkness is to misunderstand everything. Your reward lies in what you are. If you do not become like Him, loving good above all else – if you cannot at the last touch holiness, He cannot give you the power and joy that are His, and nor could you receive it. If you would have heaven there for everyone, whether they would climb or not, then you must lower heaven, and that would be the greatest of all tragedies. What more terrible could even the mind of hell conceive than to soil the ultimate light?'

Eleni stared at her with the beginning of a horror deeper than any grief she had felt before, as if a pit had opened in front of her. She did not need to say she understood, it was written in her eyes.

'Ra-Nufis has the mantle of leadership now.' She breathed the words in horror. 'I don't know how we can stop him. No one does. If we speak against him, we are made to seem as if we are condemning others to be shut out of a glory we want only for ourselves. He says he loves all men, and would have the joys of heaven for all, and that that is the will of God. He has tasted a terrible power, greater even than that of Tiberian, and God knows that is great enough, but Ra-Nufis's is greater because it is of the hearts and the minds, not the temporal laws. Nothing in the world is stronger than a dream people want to believe.'

'But Alexius was prepared to fight it?' Tathea said.

Eleni nodded fractionally. 'When he heard word of where you were, yes. He believed if anyone could succeed, you could. And there is a small group who resist the new way, but they are very few and it calls for much courage. Ra-Nufis has the Book itself. It is the symbol of the power of God. No one can defy that openly. It is seen as a blasphemy.' She leaned forward, her eyes searching, bright with the beginning of a thread of hope. 'But together perhaps we can begin, and God will help us. I hesitate to use my power. Miracles and signs are publicised now and are used to whip up great storms of emotion.'

Tathea stood up slowly. She was shaking and she felt dizzy and sick with misery. The darkness seemed to be closing all around her, as if the stars themselves were going out. Ra-Nufis! Only an hour ago she would have believed that impossible. Part of her still clung to a hope that somehow Eleni had made a mistake, misunderstood something – anything. Not Ra-Nufis! She had loved him as she might have loved Habi, had he lived. She had believed in him without shadow! How could it have happened?

And as she said it, she knew. The seduction of beauty, the rationalisation, and then the greatest of all cancers of the soul, the whisper, as soft as hell, of power, the last temptation of man.

'I'm sorry,' Eleni said with tears in her voice. 'Perhaps what I had to tell you was even harder than the news you brought me. Alexius won the light.'

'Yes, he did,' Tathea said with certainty. 'But we must still battle in the darkness.'

Eleni touched her. 'How can I help?' she asked. 'At least let me begin with the practical. You will have nowhere to live, no means. Let me deal with that.'

'Thank you,' Tathea accepted with twisted laughter. 'You are right. I have nothing . . . less than when I first came.'

Eleni fulfilled her promise quickly and installed Tathea in quiet and elegant apartments in the old quarter of the City near the Imperial Hill, where Baradeus had lived before he became Emperor. Eleni had inherited the house and it was still maintained and kept with servants. The loan of it was generous and Tathea was profoundly grateful to find herself so well cared for, and in such a discreet manner.

The day after she moved in she went walking in the City streets. She was dressed in a Camassian gown of comfort and grace, but no obvious wealth. She was merely a woman alone, in her middle years, and unless one looked at her face carefully, there was nothing remarkable about her. If anyone noticed the great dignity in her bearing, there was no sign that they recognised an Empress, let alone the bringer of the Book.

On the street of clockmakers she stopped an elderly merchant. 'Excuse me, sir, where might I find the nearest meeting of believers in the Book?'

His benign face showed surprise. 'You are a stranger in the City?'

'I have not been here for some years,' she replied truthfully.

'The Light Bearers meet every sixth day, in halls all around. But the best, of course, is the Great Hall in the square beside the Hall of Archons. Do you know where that is?'

She smiled. 'Yes, thank you. Every sixth day?'

'Yes, lady. That will be the day after tomorrow, at noon.'

'Thank you.' She inclined her head in gratitude, and went on her way.

On the appointed day she arrived at the Great Hall just before midday. The building was vast, like something transplanted from the deserts of Shinabar. It dwarfed the buildings around it, even the Hall of Archons. At first she thought it was newly built, then she realised it was the old library and justice courts which had been given a new façade and a higher roof.

People were approaching from all directions, singly and in groups, talking together, smiling. Every now and then she heard a burst of laughter. There were hundreds of them. They were well dressed, as if they wore their best for the occasion. Many robes were trimmed with borders of vivid colour, muslins fluttered in the slight breeze, jewels winked in the sun. The Empire had widened its borders. She noticed Tirilisi, mostly by their embroidered tunics and hot, earth shades with fringes of silk that swayed and rippled. There were men from the north with pale skins and hair, in cotton of cold greens, and Irria-Kanders with breeches and fine leather boots, and a few dark Shinabari. She even saw with a lurch of memory flashes of copper and blue.

She walked up the steps behind them and in through the vast portals.

The interior took her breath away. The huge vaulted ceiling was supported by pillars so vast a chariot and horses could have hidden behind each one. The whole interior was carved of golden Camassian stone and lit by bars of sunlight shining in brilliant colours through stained-glass circular windows fifty feet up, making the air above shimmer in a haze of blues and golds and rose-red. It was a work of genius, dazzling the senses and filling the mind with awe. One could not help but look upward and the glory of light caught the imagination and stilled all thought of the clamour outside, of the trivialities of daily life.

She had to force herself to look downwards. The floor was marbled in dark greys and greens, beautiful, intricate, but sombre. One lifted the eyes again instinctively.

All around her people were pressing in, silent now, faces calm, attention on the platform at the far end, raised at least ten feet above the body of the hall. On it was a table spread with white linen embroidered with silks and decorated with pearls, their pale sheen visible even from where Tathea was, halfway towards the back.

Set upon golden plinths at either side of the table were two artefacts. To the left was a wheel whose radius was the height of a man. It was wrought in gold and set with hundreds of jewels along the spokes and round the rim. At the right was an abacus of similar size, and all the counting beads were gems, blue lapis, green malachite, red jasper, white and golden agate, rose crystals that caught the fire of light. Obviously they had some symbolic meaning to be set so, as if to decorate an altar, but they were not from the Book.

She thought of asking someone, then was suddenly wary of drawing attention to her ignorance. She felt a stranger here. She had seen no one she could remember from the past, there was no familiar sweetness here at all.

There was a hush. All talking ceased and everyone stood gazing at the great beaten copper doors to the side of the platform. Slowly the doors swung wide and a procession wound its way out, traversing the width of the hall before climbing the steps of the platform. At the head was a man of magnificent aspect whose white robes drifted like silk as he walked. His mane of black hair was crowned with a triple circlet of gold and round his waist was a blood-red apron whose edges were encrusted with agate, crystal and corundum.

Behind him came forty others, all moving with a strange, hesitant, rhythmic step. They were also clad in white, but less rich, and they had not the brilliant apron. They carried tall, bronze tapers of light in their hands and they were singing in unison. As they crossed in front of the platform and mounted the steps, the singing changed to become harmony, exquisitely skilled, the bass voices resonant and rich, the tenors mounting the scale, the tempo increasing, and altos soaring above with brilliant descant.

There was a rising excitement in the huge hall. It was not a congregation but an audience, watching a choreographed ballet of movement and sound. Not one of those around Tathea stirred and no one raised their own voice.

The music became subtler. The underlying rhythms altered and the volume increased. The complexity was almost more than the ear could hold. It was a glory of sound battering the walls, dizzying the senses, a wave of tumultuous beauty which when at last it faded left the hearers drained.

Tathea stared around her at the rapt, almost hypnotised faces, and felt a cold hand of fear grasp her.

The leader in the crimson apron stepped forward and spoke to the assembly. His figure was superb, his voice smooth as warm honey.

'Let us give praise to God who is above all worlds, all men and all imaginings,' he cried. 'Let us ponder God who is immortal, who governs the universe with almighty power. Let us think upon our own unworthiness, our inferiority in every respect, our frailty, sin and inherent weakness. Let us acknowledge that we, and all men, are dependent upon God for life and breath, for grace to proceed from day to day, as we will be throughout time immeasurable.'

Around Tathea the people began to chant a slow, beautiful response, pulsating with the perfect diction and cadence of long familiarity.

'We worship Thee, oh unimaginable, ineffable, omnipotent God for whom nothing is impossible.'

She stared at them in amazement. This was no part of the Book. Did they even know what they were saying?

The leader spoke again, his voice ringing out in the silence of the huge hall above the heads of the multitude up into the swirling shafts of coloured sunlight above.

'We give praise to Thee, and acknowledge Thee beyond our comprehension, who are without form or passions and a mystery to our finite minds. Thy glory and power are boundless and without end.'

'Boundless and without end!' the crowd echoed. 'We praise Thee, oh infinite God.'

There was more music, and this time everyone sang and the volume of it filled the air, echoing back from the walls. It was a lovely, joyous sound, and when it was over, happiness washed around them like a tide. The leader stepped forward again, and a whisper went round. 'Zulperion is going to speak to us! Hush for Zulperion.'

'My friends!' he began, raising his hands in the air as if in a blessing. 'My fellow travellers on this journey of life! What can I say to you but what I have already said – the words of the Book of God. Be just and obedient, be humble and keep in the way of love, and you may pass through the veil of mortality without fear or pain.' His voice caressed the words and their faces stared back, lost in rapturous emotion.

'Walk meekly and righteously before God,' he continued, his voice intoning more than speaking, 'and you will come to the end of your days unmarred by the stains of the world, and you will be acceptable to Him. Great will be your reward then, unimaginable in richness, peace beyond your dreams, the end of all toil and misery. God has prepared a place for you, and if you will but give up the sins of the world, it will be yours. That is His promise to you, in the name of His love, who cannot be denied and to whom all things are possible.'

319

Tathea was raging. She was hearing principles put forth which were such a distortion of the truth that she beheld the subtlety of darkness as never before. In a flash of terrible vision she remembered a vast concourse of people, infinitely larger than this, and a figure so nearly beautiful and yet with cruel eyes and twisted, hungry mouth, speaking of a plan wherein every soul should be kept to the narrow course of righteous acts, not for the love of good, but because there was no other way. The growth of man stopped there, the glory of the love of good was murdered in a single blow. He would return every soul to its primal innocence, a thing stillborn, and he would possess the dominion and the kingdom and the glory for ever.

She moved from her place, pushing forward between the crowds, permitting no one to bar her way until she stood on the platform before the startled Zulperion.

'Sister,' he said gently. 'You are welcome to be among us but your action here is inappropriate. Return to your place and I will speak with you afterwards.'

'I am Tathea,' she said clearly and without flinching from his gaze.

Zulperion faltered. 'Tathea?'

One of the other priests stepped forward and drew breath to speak, but something in her face silenced him.

'I am Tathea,' she repeated. 'It was I who brought the Book from the world before this.' She half turned towards the congregation but continued to address Zulperion. 'You have perverted the doctrines of God, perhaps in innocence, but you are preaching untruth. You are promising life without pain.' Her voice rang out, gathering power. 'Don't you know that such a life would also be without learning, which is the whole purpose of mortal life? It would be without terror or pity, humility or the remorse which teaches us to forgive. That is the Great Enemy's lie, that abstaining from life, and risk, will end in your being praised for your purity above those who have the courage to love, with all its perils, and who have magnified life!'

Zulperion made to interrupt her, but she overrode him, her voice passionate with anger. 'Yes, you did! You told these people that suffering is unnecessary!' She flung her hand out towards them. 'You told them that if they make covenants with God and strive to keep them, then He will remove all afflictions from them. If that were really so, wouldn't all people of any sense obey God?' she demanded. 'It would be madness to do anything less!' She almost laughed. 'And we can only pity the mad for their suffering, but they are not accountable. God is their judge, we are only their watchmen and their shepherds.'

There was total silence among the massed crowd, uncomfortable and embarrassed. Nothing like this had ever happened before.

'Is it virtue to do that which you know will be rewarded, or is it well-informed self-interest?' Her contempt was scalding. 'Do you wish to be loved by someone who does so only as long as you pay him? Is that anything more than purchase?'

One or two people moved uncomfortably. For the first time there was doubt in their faces, the beginning of uncertainty.

'There is nothing noble in an equal trade!' she went on. 'There is no courage without the knowledge that there may be pain, loss, even death. What is brave in those who know they cannot be hurt?' She glared at Zulperion, then back at the throng. 'He has offered you a life without pain. What for? What would you learn? What more would you be at the end than you were at the beginning? There is no pity without the understanding of what it is to suffer. No forgiveness without a knowledge of temptation and frailty, and your own need for pardon. There is no growth without anguish which must be borne well and without bitterness, self-pity or anger; there is no love without the ache of loneliness which must never tire of giving, never surrender to indifference or despair. There can be no victory if there is no battle!'

There was a slow murmur of amazement from the throng, then a new light in their faces. Not an eye moved from her.

She lowered her voice. 'There is nothing beautiful, no praise of God or love of man written on an empty page. Affliction is not a punishment from God. Most of it we bring upon ourselves, but it is the fire which burns the dross out of our souls.' She leaned forward and her voice became intimate, urgent. Such were the acoustics that even in that vast hall every man, woman and child heard her. 'Do you want to walk with God – or with the Enemy?

'The reward may be long in coming. God does not reap his harvest each day. The seeds you sow now may not ripen until you rise from the dead. That is the requirement of faith, to know that God is, and that He is just. No pain will be lost, no sacrifice unaccepted if it is given in love. The harvest is sure. What you have cast into the ground in love will yield a hundredfold, in God's time.'

Zulperion made as if to move towards her, then saw the faces of the throng, and knew better.

Tathea spoke gently now, tenderly, as if she was with close and dear friends. 'Prove your love of the good because it is good, whether you profit or lose by it. And afterwards will come the glory and the splendour and the everlasting joy. Then your eyes will be clear enough to see God, and your soul large enough to abide His presence, and to hold the things He has prepared for you from the beginning.'

Quietly she stepped back and turned for a moment to look at Zulperion. He was mute, numbed by a confusion so great it clawed his heart. Talons of darkness entered his soul and he saw only his own power slipping away, eroding like sand towers before the tide.

'We will be ever grateful to you for bringing the Book, Tathea,' he said loudly, so that his voice, suddenly harsh, carried over the murmuring, disturbed crowd, speaking more to them than to her. 'But we have moved on since you left. You cannot cling on to power now, and arrogance will not serve.' His confidence began to return. 'We have learned more. Ra-Nufis has understood what you did not, which is why you failed. We have seen a greater vision. God is kinder and immeasurably more powerful than the limited being you had supposed.' He smiled with a cold, careful movement of his lips, and Tathea saw the ice in his eyes.

'You measured God in the likeness of men.' There was derision in him now, even an aping of pity. 'You do not mean to blaspheme, nevertheless you do. You are frightening people. Come away from here and we will discuss this in a quieter place.' He put his hand on her arm and his grasp was so hard it dug into her flesh, bruising her. She tried to protest, but the fingers tightened and she gasped.

His mirthless smile widened. 'Come.' His voice still dripped honey. 'Let us conduct the resolution of our differences somewhere more discreet. I'm sure you do not wish to discomfort or confuse these people.'

It is exactly what she wished to do, but to admit it would destroy her purpose. And his sheer physical power overwhelmed her. Short of screaming for help, which would make her seem hysterical, exactly as he wished, she had no choice but to allow him to lead her from the platform, back down the steps and through the great beaten copper doors. She heard the music swell again as the doors closed behind her.

He let go of her arm at last. The pain shot through her and without thinking she clasped it with her other hand.

'You should have stayed on the Island at the Edge of the World,' he said viciously, the hatred in his face no longer masked. 'There is no place for you here. Speak those views again in public and you will be lucky not to be attacked.' It was a naked threat. 'We have great happiness now, people know a virtue and believe in hope. I will allow no one to mar that!'

The door opened and another two priests came in, their faces hard, full of anger and fear. They looked to Zulperion.

'What is it?' he demanded.

'People are disturbed,' one of them answered. 'Some wonder if what she says could be true. Others are angry.'

Zulperion looked quickly at Tathea, then back again. 'Take her out by the back door,' he ordered. 'I'll go and calm the people. There is nothing to worry about. She is confused. I will apologise for her. You know what to do?' His eyes were steady and hard.

One of them swallowed and nodded, the other looked less certain, glancing unhappily at Tathea, then at Zulperion.

Zulperion strode through the great doors back into the hall in a swirl of white silk. The doors closed behind him.

The priests moved to Tathea and took her by the arms, leading her the other way, towards the back of the building.

'This way. You have upset the people. They find what you have said to be blasphemous. You cannot attack people's faith like that and promise them pain, you know, and then expect to be liked for it.'

'I don't care about being liked!' she said incredulously, half dragged along by them. 'I care about speaking the truth! Is that what you want, to be liked?'

'Love is the greatest power in the universe,' the other replied with ringing certainty.

Tathea tried to snatch her arm away from him, but his grip was tight and hard, and he was a young man, with twice her strength.

'For pity's sake!' she spat out. 'There is all the difference in creation between love and saying whatever people want to hear so they will like you! You don't care a whit about those people! You don't care whether their souls grow or perish! All you want is their adoration in order to feed your own appetites!'

One of them hit her sharply.

Suddenly the outer door flew open and two men in street clothes stood there, one carrying a knife, the other a short club.

The priests stopped abruptly.

'I won't kill you,' the man with the knife said very slowly. 'But I will certainly hurt you very badly if you do not let the woman go.'

Both priests stepped back as if burned. Tathea stood frozen.

'Come!' the man with the knife ordered peremptorily. Then seeing her dismay, he said, 'We won't hurt you, lady. We know what you say is true. We believe the old way.'

She made up her mind. She moved instantly and the three of them went out of the door and ran along the alley past startled onlookers and into another narrow side street. There were shouts behind them, the sound of running feet. One of the men grasped Tathea by the hand and pulled her faster. They swung round a corner into a small square just as three men entered the side street.

Tathea and her rescuers crossed to a wooden door. One banged with his knife hilt in a staccato rhythm while the other watched the square behind them.

'Who are you?' Tathea demanded, gasping to catch her breath, her heart pounding. 'Why did you come for me?'

'Because Zulperion would have had you killed,' the man with the dagger answered. 'It would have looked like an accident.' He beat on the door again, more urgently. 'I am afraid you have more courage than sense.'

The door opened and they scrambled inside, closing it sharply behind them. It was a very ordinary house like those of thousands of artisans in the City, with plaster walls washed in pale colours, a tile floor and plain wooden furniture. The woman who stood in the centre of the small room was obviously in the middle of a domestic chore. She regarded Tathea with wary curiosity.

'Best you don't know,' the other man warned her. 'Safer for you.' He turned to Tathea. 'We'll go out of the back way.'

'Where to?'

'The leader,' he answered. 'We are a resistance to the new perversions of the Book. Come.'

Tathea followed obediently. Perhaps this was why Alexius had come for her, to begin again. It would be a difficult battle without him, harder, lonelier, but now she understood more of the Enemy than she had before, and more of herself. And she understood also why Nastemah had lured Alexius to his death. It was not just a solitary victory, it was part of the war, more than she had understood until now.

She was led through a warren of alleys and passages in the old part of the City, built before the days of the Emperors, and at last down a flight of steps into an underground room. The door closed behind her.

There was one man inside. He was slender and dark with a poet's face, and yet there were lines of courage and endurance in it, and wisdom in his eyes greater than dreams.

'I am Sanobiel,' he said with a smile, a little uncertain, as if he knew who she was and it touched him with awe. 'I'm sorry,' he said quietly. 'I wish you had not returned to this. You should not have spoken so openly. Did Alexius not warn you? Where is he?'

There was something familiar in his voice, and for an instant she remembered music, glory and terror, and moonlight over the ice. Then it was gone and she was alone in the room with a man she had only just met.

'He died on the Island,' she answered. 'It happened before he told me about this.' She saw the shock and grief in Sanobiel. 'He died well,' she said gently. 'He faced an emissary of the Great Enemy, and beat him. It cost him his life, but he won certainty of the soul. If you had seen his face afterwards you would know that as I do.'

'I'm glad.' But his voice was thick with pain. 'And you?' He looked at her closely, searching her eyes.

'I have learned many things which I must share with you,' she answered. 'I have seen what happened at the centre of time, and I know that at last it will all be well. Any victory of the Enemy's is only for a short time. Individuals may fall, but the world will not.'

Sanobiel sat down on one of the wooden seats and offered her the only one with cushions on it. He poured wine from an earthen goblet and unwrapped a loaf of bread. 'Tell me, please.'

For hours she told him of her years in Shinabar, not the physical truth but the spiritual, her knowledge of Tiyo-Mah and the dwarf

Azrub, of Arimaspis's death and then of Tugomir. She remembered almost word for word Iszamber's prophecy. She told him of the Island at the Edge of the World, describing its wild beauty, at once gentle and terrible. She made him laugh at Tugomir's hatred of the forest, then weep for his failure, and for Merdic and the Lost Legion.

She recounted something of Yaltabaoth, and of Menath-Dur, and their victory and the building of the fortress on the Western Shore, and how the women had come, and of Tugomir's triumph in the end. And she told him of her vision of the beginning of time and the woman in the garden, her choice of the man who faced hell and whose love was stronger than darkness, then of the terror and the glory when time should end and eternity begin.

Sanobiel told her in return of his crossing to Camassia in search of truth, and his discovery of the Book, touching only lightly, and by omission, on the cost it had been to him. His love for the Book had brought him courage and disaster to leadership of the resistance against the new apostasy.

'Tell me of Ra-Nufis,' she asked. She was deliberately walking into pain, but she thought now that she was strong enough to face it. She must face it.

His face shadowed. 'We watched it,' he said slowly, seeking for the words. 'We saw it happen, without recognising what it was.' He looked at Tathea to see if she could understand and believe what he said. 'When he first came back from Shinabar with the Book, and told us what had happened, we were devastated that the whole nation had been offered such light, and had turned away.' He frowned. 'It was difficult to believe, but as he recounted it detail by detail, we realised how it could be so. There will always be those who will not accept the Word, and the changes it must bring. And the more there are of them, the easier it is for them to blind themselves to the good.' He gave a wry little smile. 'I can see it far more plainly now than when he told us. And of course he had the Book. It was returned to us, and that was a joy. We had a sort of revolutionary zeal then, as if we could redouble our efforts. We thought we could be the light of the world.'

'He did not tell you of Azrub, and the stoning of Arimaspis?' she asked with surprise.

Sanobiel bit his lip. 'He told us you had been driven out by a great evil, and that the High Priest Tugomir had been at the head of it, and something terrible had happened in the streets, but accounts were garbled and he did not know the truth of it.'

There was nothing for her to say.

'We grieved for you,' Sanobiel went on. 'I especially, but in my heart I believed that God would preserve you, even if we had no idea where you were. It was only a month or two ago that word came that you were still on the Island at the Edge of the World. We had heard earlier

325

that you had been there, but had left – some said to the Lost Lands again.'

'I was always on the Island, but I went north. Tell me more about Ra-Nufis.'

He stared downwards. 'We redoubled our preaching under Ra-Nufis's leadership. Of course there were more converts all the time, but some found certain laws hard to keep, the austerity of it was less appealing than the old ceremonies, so Ra-Nufis introduced a little of the pomp.' His lip puckered and his voice dropped a little. 'It seemed harmless then, an outward manifestation of the inward beauty which he so loved. The abacus was introduced as a symbol of the exactness of the law.' He looked up quickly. 'That's a nice touch of irony, isn't it? And the wheel symbolised eternity. We started carrying tapers of light. They liked that. It happened so slowly we didn't even see it at the time, like a glacier creeping.'

'A what?'

'A glacier.' He frowned as he said it. 'A river of ice that moves only inches in a whole season. They have them in the far north, so I hear.' He looked puzzled. 'I don't know why I thought of that, except it was a slow, terrible coldness, a kind of death, though it had an outward semblance of beauty. That's what it was, I think, in Ra-Nufis's mind, an outward beauty to win more people over, a relaxing of laws an inch at a time, so as not to drive people away because the discipline was hard for them.'

She could see it with a hideous clarity. It was so easy to do, and could seem like kindness, even love.

'And it did grow,' he went on. 'He was very skilled. He even wooed Barsymet with flattery and deference to her opinion. He made her important again, and she loves it.' He sighed and shifted his position in the chair. 'Through her he won many of the old noble families, even those of the Archons. It has become perfectly respectable now, even among them, to be a believer of the Light. Only a few like Maximian still will not yield.

'People flooded in, whole towns at a time. The beauty and the promises drew them. It is hard to understand the Book, and they want something immediate.' He looked at her intently. 'So Ra-Nufis began to appoint special priests to explain it to the people. Within a year they became a profession. They interpreted the Book. They saved people the labour of studying for themselves. They could go to meetings once every six days, and be told what to think and what to believe.' He bit his lip, a terrible weariness in his voice, as if he had seen something old and very ugly. 'They wanted quick answers, not the miracles which come after faith but the magic which comes before; answers unrelated to keeping commandments and seeking God with a whole heart.'

She nodded but did not interrupt. The candle flickered on the table. She was barely aware of it.

His face hardened. 'Grace became stronger than works. And of course the less knowledge the people had, the more power lay with the priests. That was it in the end – power. They loved Ra-Nufis. I have seen meetings of twenty thousand people all crying praise be to God! But in their heart it was Ra-Nufis's name they were saying, and I think he knew that. Twenty thousand became two hundred thousand, two million, and then twenty million.' He took a long, deep breath and let it out in a sigh. 'Now, spiritually, the priests do not lead the people, they follow them because they are prepared to say what they know the greatest number wish to hear.'

She could see it, the intoxication of beauty, the desire to share it, the shallow stairs of the descent to darkness, each act only a single candle going out. Gradually the power became a habit, and then an addiction, and finally a kind of madness.

'You have spoken to him, of course?' she said.

'I have tried.' He laughed abruptly. 'He won't even receive me now.' He gestured to the room around him. 'As you can see, I am a fugitive.'

'Is the resistance strong?'

'Strong, yes, but still small, and secret. But now you are here, you must lead us. We can begin again.'

'You have led them so far, you are the founder of the movement and I am perfectly content to follow you,' she answered.

'No.' He shook his head quickly. 'You are the bringer of the Book, and much more important than that, you have a vision and a certainty that we shall need. Your knowledge is more than faith now. That is why you left, and why you have returned. I can see it, even if you cannot yet.'

'But a leader must be by common consent,' she argued.

'It will be.' There was no doubt in his voice. 'I was only the beginning, now you must take it up.'

She did not protest further. 'If it is agreed, I shall do as the people will.'

Chapter Twenty-One

Sanobiel had told her that it was useless trying to plead with Ra-Nufis, but there was a part of Tathea that remembered too vividly his old loyalty to her and the goodness in him. He had been gentle with her when she was tired. In the desert he had not rested until he was certain she had food and water, a blanket, and a place to lie. When she had doubted herself, his faith in her had never wavered, either in her calling to God, or her strength and courage to carry it through. He had worked unceasingly and often at great personal risk to pave the way for her return to Shinabar. It was his labour, his gathering of information with such skill and accuracy that had secured the invasion.

She could not believe he was beyond reaching. So in spite of Sanobiel's advice she went to the palace on the Hill of Cypresses where he now lived when he was not travelling to other cities and to the provinces.

She presented herself at the hall where he customarily held audiences, and waited her turn, giving her name to the steward. He took it without any apparent recognition. She waited into the late afternoon until finally, as the sun was lowering, she was admitted.

Double doors of cedarwood were opened by two servants in white linen. She went in without looking at either of them, and the doors closed behind her. The room was magnificent with a high, coffered ceiling of pale plaster, and western light gleamed gold through the windows. The furniture was gilded wood, and a life-sized alabaster hunting dog sat on an ebony plinth. She remembered with sharp misery the tiny lapis tortoise he had given her.

Ra-Nufis was standing in the centre of the room. He was robed in white and gold with a blood-red apron around his waist, the ties falling to the floor on either side. It was embroidered with the abacus and wheel in gold thread. He was a little heavier, his face fuller, the youth gone from it.

He smiled when he saw her, and she realised that until that moment she had been hoping that somehow when they met all the ugliness would prove to be an illusion, a mistake, the old friendship would still be there. One glance shattered the hope.

'I wondered if you would come,' he said with slight amusement. 'You are too late. Your day is past. You have no place in the Empire, Ta-Thea. You have proved that – twice. Go back to the Island at the Edge of the World. There is nothing for you here except disappointment –' he looked at her very steadily – 'and perhaps humiliation.'

'They told me you had changed,' she said slowly, still searching his face for the man she had loved. 'I found it hard to believe, but I see they were right. What happened to you?'

'Not changed, Ta-Thea, grown,' he corrected. 'My perception is larger than it was when we were together in Shinabar, and before.' He moved at last, walking easily, still gracefully, towards the windows. 'My understanding was only beginning then. I had barely caught the vision. I thought only of my own people.' He glanced at her. 'As you did.' He turned back to the windows. 'Now I realise all people are mine, there are no outsiders to God. The Book is for every man on earth.'

She challenged without thinking, her words born of the anger and the loss within her. 'Is it? Or has it become for you, for your power and your glory?'

'Jealous, Ta-Thea?' His voice was mocking, no anxiety in it. He did not even bother to look at her. 'You had your thousands of followers, I have my millions. I shall see that the Book reaches across the face of the world, as it was meant to do. You should rejoice.'

'It is not the Book which is spreading!' she retorted, moving towards him. 'You have adulterated it until it is only what people want to hear, not what is true!'

He swung round to face her. It was a momentary violence, a swirling of skirts, but she was overwhelmed by a sense of his physical power.

'It is what they can take,' he replied easily. He was very much at home in this magnificent room. His voice remained soft, infinitely reasonable. 'There is no good in giving people a doctrine they will not accept. You of all people should know that! What did you achieve in Shinabar? Nothing, except to get yourself exiled – again. What I am doing is different, because I have learned. The people love me.' He said it with immeasurable satisfaction, rolling the words on his tongue. 'They listen to what I say, and they believe me. I can lead them to goodness, even to God. You had your chance, Ta-Thea, and you failed. I can do it, and you will not stop me. For your own sake, don't try.'

'And you will save them all . . .' Tathea said softly, ice-cold inside. The words were an ache of something so dreadful it was beyond memory to recall, and yet it was on her lips with certainty.

'Not all,' he answered, still smiling. 'But most of them, yes. Does that displease you?' His black eyebrows rose. 'Do you want salvation to be exclusive, just for you and those few you choose? Do you want to see some people damned?'

Was there any point in arguing? Had she not already said it all?

'No,' she answered him. 'But what you or I want doesn't matter. What anyone wants, even God, has nothing to do with the truth. You are teaching that God can do anything, and that is a lie. Wickedness cannot be joy. Even God cannot make it so.'

'That is blasphemy!' Ra-Nufis's face darkened dangerously, and he took half a step towards her, then stopped.

She did not flinch. 'No it isn't. Go back and read the Book. They are His own words. If the indifferent, the cowardly, the unclean or unloving were to enter heaven, it would no longer be heaven.'

'Heaven is a mystery!' he said between clenched teeth. 'Would you dare to stand here, one puny woman who failed in every task she was given, and tell God what heaven should be?'

'I haven't failed yet, because I haven't finished trying!' she returned hotly, and knew the instant the words were out of her mouth that she should have let him think her beaten. Alexius had taught her better tactics than this. 'And I am not telling God, I am telling you.' She saw the rage in his face, and at last she was afraid. The man she knew in the past, and had loved so dearly, was gone. The person who stood in front of her was beyond her reach. He reminded her for an instant of someone else, precious and close, bound by blood and heritage, in another room in a tower above water, and another betrayal. And then it was gone again.

'It was a mistake to come,' she said quickly, catching her breath, her heart beating hard and fast.

'You have made a lot of mistakes,' he replied, taking a further step towards her, now only a yard away.

She whirled round and walked out of the room, too hastily for dignity, swinging the doors open and seeing the hall full of people with a surge of relief.

Outside in the sun and noise of the street she was ashamed. She had run away from him! But she continued on her way and did not slow her pace until she was back in the old quarter and within sight of the house where Sanobiel lived and had prepared a room for her.

'We must be better organised,' he said urgently, sitting in the same chair where he had told her of the changes in the City. 'So far we have done little more than encourage people who wish to follow the old, true faith, and given them a place to gather together and worship. We cannot read the Book, because it is available only to the priests, and they re-interpret it in different ways. But we discuss the principles we remember clearly, and give each other comfort and whatever help we can to those who are in need.'

330

'How many people are there? Do you know?' she asked, sitting opposite him.

He shook his head. 'I prefer to know as little as possible. It is safer.'

A flicker of fear moved across her mind, like a cold wind. 'Is that necessary?'

'Perhaps not. But I think maybe the Great Enemy matches his stride to ours.' He looked at her searchingly to see what she thought. 'I believe that as we lengthen ours, so he will lengthen his also.'

She would have liked to deny it, but the instant his words fell into the still air of the room, she knew they were true.

He saw it in her eyes and a deep sadness filled him. 'It is war, isn't it?' he asked.

She nodded, tightening her lips. 'I suppose it always was. If the Enemy were not concerned with us, perhaps that would be the surest sign that we were achieving nothing.' She stood up and began to pace back and forth. 'In this battle, and I know from Ra-Nufis it is close, there will be no bystanders. Everyone will eventually be on one side or the other. We need to be very well armoured in the spirit. We can make no allowances for false teaching, for error or any kind of lie.'

'We need the Book,' he said simply, looking up at her. 'And Ra-Nufis has it. Only priests are allowed to read it, and we have none in our number. They have too many vested interests to leave the Light Bearers, as they call themselves. We have been trying to convert some of them, but it is becoming too dangerous. Even so, much of what they think they know of the Book is false anyway. Shall we keep on trying? We have those who are prepared to risk their lives.'

'No,' she said without hesitation. There was no doubt in her mind. 'I will write it again. With God's help I can. Give me a room where I can work, ink and paper, and I shall do it.'

He watched her for a moment, his eyes soft and bright, filled with hope at last. Then he rose to his feet and took her arm gently. 'Thank the heavens you are back! We will start again. If God is for us, what can it matter who is against?'

Through the heat of summer she worked. Often she slept by day and sat at the plain wooden table all night, working by candlelight. Many times she would stop and fall to her knees to pray, and the brilliance of memory returned so sharply it was almost as if she was hearing the words spoken in her head. Their meaning was so utterly clear that she understood them anew with a depth and a love that filled her till there was no room for anything else. She was unaware of time passing as she wrote. The teeming City only a few yards away did not impinge on her consciousness. Sanobiel brought her all she needed, but he did not interrupt her with news or conversation.

When her task was completed it was both a triumph and a parting.

The time for study was over. Now she must use the weapon of knowledge in battle. It could not be put off any longer.

She gave the papers to Sanobiel, watching his face.

He took them, his delicate hands holding the sheets as if the heart of the world was in them.

'I have scribes ready,' he said quietly. 'We shall have it copied as many times as we can, and given out to believers.'

She nodded. 'And when we have sufficient for all of us, we will leave pages in places where people can find them, and some will know they are the truth. It will spread.'

And it did indeed spread. By the waning of the year there were over twenty-five individual cells of believers in the City, with up to a score of people in each. Pages with quotes from the Book were being left in all sorts of places. Any scrap of paper blowing about or lying on a table, a chair, in the folds of a scroll might have neatly copied on it some discussion between God and Asmodeus, from Tathea's hand, not the altered version Ra-Nufis had given to his priests.

It could not go unnoticed. By midwinter the first warning came with a young man called Timmaron. He raced along the street, his sandals slapping hard on the dusty pavement, and swung round the corner to the doorway. He banged with the urgency of fear, and the moment it was opened he all but fell in.

'We've got to move! They're coming! Zulperion's men. Get the scribes out – quickly. I'll carry the ink and paper. Hurry!'

After a single frozen moment, Saspia, who was in charge of the work, turned and slammed the door closed, then ran ahead of Timmaron to warn the scribes, collect the finished work and hide the supplies.

'Run!' she ordered. 'Out of here, and don't come back! We'll meet again in the street of the basket weavers. Don't sit there! Go!'

From then on the scribes never stayed in any house more than six or eight days, moving carefully, one at a time, and at night. But the pieces of paper kept on appearing. Zulperion's priests might rail against them from the platform and say they were blasphemous, but more people read them and kept them, and the cells of believers continued to grow.

Tathea and Sanobiel worked tirelessly, helped by people like Saspia and the young man Timmaron.

It was a few days into the spring, and raining hard with the wind behind it, when Lindor, a middle-aged man who worked in the tax office of the Archons, came one day to Tathea as she walked from the marketplace past the weavers' shops. She saw him, and respected the courage and power of conviction that even in his position he dared espouse the old faith. He had much to lose and the risk of discovery was greater for him than for most.

He fell in step beside her, his face grave, his voice low. He was dressed very plainly, and must have hoped that no one in this quarter would recognise him.

'I have very bad news, lady,' he said breathlessly. 'I overheard it. I came as soon as I could, and I fear I may not be able to come again.'

'What is it?' She only glanced at him. They must not draw attention to themselves even here where they were safest. A chill settled inside her, greater than the wind or the rain.

'A new law,' Lindor answered. 'I have friends among some of the priests, but don't ask me who. One comes to me in the dark. I know him only as a shadow on the steps down by the old road to the harbour. But he has never told me less than the truth.'

'What new law?' She did not want to know the name of the informer. It was safer not to know. Silently she blessed his courage.

'Ra-Nufis's interpretation of the Book is the only correct one,' Lindor answered. 'Anyone who deviates from it will be guilty of the crime of heresy.'

She stopped, swinging round to face him. 'What?' she demanded. 'What do you mean, a crime? Camassians have always allowed people to believe whatever they liked! You can worship a pile of stones if you want to! The Hall of Archons will never pass it.'

'The majority will,' he answered, taking her by the arm and impelling her forward again. He glanced from side to side as they crossed a busy street, wary in case she had drawn attention to them. 'The new law does not deny freedom to pagans. You can still worship a pile of stones if you want to. What you cannot do is teach or practise a different version of the Book. Any other faith is free. But the Book is the official religion of the Empire, and it must be kept pure from adulteration. That is considered different from ignorance.'

'You mean it is against us.'

'Yes,' he agreed, his head down, eyes straight ahead. 'There is from now on no room for differences of opinion. What Ra-Nufis has taught is holy, and to question it is heresy and the law will punish offenders appropriately. They are a danger to the welfare of the state, to the peace and prosperity of their neighbours.'

'That's absurd!'

'Of course it's absurd.' He nodded to a group of women gossiping, cloaks drawn tightly round them. 'But if you frighten people, you can make them do all kinds of things. They are saying we are seditious and undermine morality and that you in particular will do anything for power.'

'That's monstrous!' She was furious. 'Ra-Nufis knows that is untrue!'

'Perhaps he doesn't,' Lindor said quickly.

'Of course he does!' She tried to stop but he pulled her forward, hurting her arm.

333

'You forget, lady, or perhaps you don't know,' he answered, his face set in sad, angry lines, 'we tend to judge people by our own standards. If a man says all people are liars or thieves, you may be sure of one thing, that he is himself. Ra-Nufis is obsessed with power, consumed by it. The love of power has eaten his soul. He has forgotten what it is like to be able to let it go, to love another's welfare more than your own. Perhaps he has even forgotten how to love at all.'

She was unaware of the people around her, even the street dimmed to a shadow beyond the rain. She was conscious only of Lindor's fingers tight round her arm, and her wet feet stumbling on the cobbles. He was right. Ra-Nufis saw her as driven by the lust for power because that was the mission of his own soul and he knew no other.

'I must go,' Lindor said as they came into a small square. 'I dare not stay in case I am recognised. Then I would be of no more use. I will do all I can.' His voice caught. 'God protect you.' And before she could answer, he had let go of her and turned away. A moment later he was hidden by a cart carrying hides.

She went back to the rooms they occupied this week and knelt alone in prayer, racked with a terrible knowledge of loss for Ra-Nufis. Without meaning to, she had invested in him the tenderness and the hope she would have placed in Habi.

He could not have betrayed her more totally.

She poured out her grief before God, not seeking an answer, simply the knowledge that He understood. Gradually a great peace descended upon her and a warmth, as if she was encircled by His arms. A still, small voice spoke to her soul, 'Asmodeus too was My son,' and she knew the anguish of God.

What Lindor had said was true. The doctrine of the Light Bearers was now very closely defined, and to alter it or question it became a crime before the law, punishable by confiscation of property. Quoting from the Book, even Ra-Nufis's version, became a crime for anyone except the ordained priests. Those suspected of heresy were excluded from public office or preferment in the army. No one would lend them money. They were forbidden to plead in the law courts or teach in the academies. The guild of architects refused them membership, as did the goldsmiths, the stone masons and the apothecaries.

By summer it was not unknown for those accused of heresy to be driven from their homes, their belongings vandalised, even for them to be openly attacked in the streets. Youths set on an old man and his heart stopped in fright. Everyone knew who they were, but they were not prosecuted. A woman was stoned to death. It was barely investigated. Yet the number of believers in the old faith continued to rise in spite of persecution and injustice.

By autumn it became a crime punishable by death to hold a copy of Tathea's re-writing of the Book. It was Eleni who told her so, brought by Saspia to the rooms they currently occupied. Eleni looked tired, as if she had been awake many nights, but there was peace in her face. To Tathea's great joy, she brought with her the little black and white cat.

'I have come to join you,' she said simply, looking at Tathea. 'I can no longer stand apart. The time has come when we must choose which side we are on. Those who are not with you are against you.'

'Not with me,' Tathea corrected gently, 'with God. It may cost you your life.' She knew it would make no difference to her. The very way Eleni stood, head high, eyes clear and sad, made her knowledge plain, and her commitment.

'I know,' she agreed. 'I also know it will cost me my soul if I do not.' She set the cat down. 'I want to be part of the battle, I must be, and I would far sooner do it with you than alone.'

Tathea held out her hand, and Eleni clasped it. Their friendship could not be as it had been before. It must be different after Alexius, but it was just as deep.

The days grew cooler and the old quarter of the City was a hard place to live. There were none of the luxuries Eleni had been accustomed to all her adult life. She was an Emperor's daughter and an Emperor's sister, and now she walked up and down flights of steps carrying pails of water from the street well. She ate coarse bread and wore plain linen and simple sandals, even in the rain. She could not afford to be different. Word would fly back to Ra-Nufis. She would be asked to deny the Book, publicly, and she would have to refuse. He could not then spare her without losing his authority.

And Tathea who had been Empress, and then Isarch, also carried water, washed her own clothes and shopped in the market for bread, cheese and fruit. But she had been a soldier, and for her the hardship came more easily.

At night they often sat long into the darkness and talked of all manner of things, occasionally matters of no importance, simply to share. They told jokes or long, funny and trivial stories. The only way to make things bearable was to laugh. The net was growing tighter all the time. Every few days news came of some follower losing his work or his home. People were being robbed without recourse to the law to help or avenge them. No one was safe. Old men, women, even children were injured in property and in person. The number of those found in possession of Tathea's new translation of the Book and executed for heresy and treason grew steadily.

The winter passed. Every twenty or thirty days they were obliged to take their few possessions and move, in case some careless word or prying eye, some too observant watcher, should betray them.

Zulperion's spies were everywhere and there were thousands willing to do his bidding.

Fear settled over the City. 'Zulperion of the Honeyed Throat' convinced even Tiberian not to threaten him. Devotion became rigidly orthodox. The voices of the established faith grew louder and more strident. People vied with each other in proclaiming their adherence to the letter of the law, and were ever quicker to accuse those they imagined were deviating. No one dared differ with his neighbour. The frightened, the simple-minded or inarticulate became victims of those who judged before they could themselves fall under suspicion.

It was Eleni who brought Tathea news of the death she found hardest to bear. Eleni had been out to buy bread and had heard the talk at the baker's, and then in the street. She came in white-faced, and closed the door behind her, shutting out the noise. Then she stood motionless, not putting the bread down.

It was her stillness which caught Tathea's attention. She looked up from the table where she was writing, the cat beside her. 'What is it?' She had become accustomed to hearing of injustice and loss, but it never ceased to hurt, or to amaze that Zulperion's golden tongue could persuade so many that it was right, even that it was the work of God.

'Lindor,' Eleni answered, her mouth pinched, her voice catching. 'He had a copy of the Book. I don't know whether someone informed on him or if he grew careless. It doesn't take much these days. Zulperion's men came at night and forced their way in – that's legal now if there has been an accusation. They searched the house. They found his Book, and there was no denial. Not that denial is ever any good.' She moved from the door and put the bread on the table. The cat went to it immediately, smelling the warm crust. 'It only prolongs the whole wretched pain and farce of it,' Eleni went on. 'Lindor didn't try. He's seen too many others dispossessed to imagine escape. He wouldn't denounce the Book.' Her eyes filled with tears. 'Hardly anyone does. Almost all of them go to their deaths branded fanatics and enemies of the people with their heads high.' She took a deep, shuddering breath. 'I'm so sorry!'

It was one senseless injustice too many. Tathea sat numb for minutes, then rose slowly to her feet, feeling stiff and suddenly old. She excused herself and went to her own room. She sat on the cot which served as a bed. She had the cat in her arms and the hot tears trickled down her face and she allowed herself to weep as she had not done for years. It was not for Lindor, good man as he had been and a friend to the cause, who had never counted the cost, but for all the brave, loving and honourable people who had believed her words and gone to their deaths.

Was she doing the right thing? Or was this really only a slow descent, step by shallow step, down into the very destruction she thought she was avoiding?

She missed Alexius! That was the one thing she could not tell Eleni. And it would hurt Sanobiel to tell him. He would feel he was being measured and found wanting, that somehow he should have made this decision for her. And that was false. It was hers alone.

Eventually she sat up and washed her face in the dish of water, then dried it on the rough cloth. She could not ask Alexius. He was gone. Anyway, there was only one person who knew all things.

First she must still the clamour of confusion within herself, drive out the sense of guilt for all the pain.

She knelt to pray. She asked first for clear-headedness enough to hear God's answer and know it was truth, and not her own wishes or fears. Gradually, a stillness descended upon her. With pure clarity she remembered what Alexius had said about the watchman on the tower, and the cry of warning. Those who see have the burden of speaking the truth whether they are heeded or not, whether they are loved or hated for their words.

And she saw, as if in vision, Merdic and the Lost Legion, fighting without hope in the Waste Lands, battling the Lord of Despair, willing to die but not to surrender. Then she saw Menath-Dur, and heard the tinkling bells on his shoes. He had taught her the meaning of hope and, without ever saying so, of faith also.

Above all she remembered in her soul the great vision which had shown the plan of all things and the purpose of God. She knew the answer to her prayer. The war with the Great Enemy was for souls, not for lives. This news was bitter and hard to bear, but it was not a defeat, unless she allowed it to be. For Lindor it was the final victory.

She straightened her skirt and pushed her hair back off her face.

She found Eleni sitting copying in her careful, beautiful hand. She looked up when she saw Tathea, her face puckered with concern.

'It's all right,' Tathea said gently, going to sit beside her. 'It hurts, but it is not a destroying pain. This is as it has to be.'

Eleni looked at her steadily, seeking to read the deeper heart behind her eyes.

Tathea put her hands on Eleni's shoulders, holding her gently. 'It is,' she repeated. 'You told me this is a time of choice, there is no more middle ground. You are right. Lindor chose, and that was his victory. It is our burden and our blessing to be the watchmen on the tower, and to speak the words which warn and also divide.'

'And Ra-Nufis?' Eleni asked. 'And all those who go downward?'

Tathea slid her arms round her and held her close. 'They are God's children as well. He loves them more than we know how to, but they are free.' Her voice dropped to a whisper. 'Asmodeus himself was God's son too.'

Eleni clung to her in silent, overwhelming knowledge.

Tathea did not realise how deeply Zulperion hated her, or how greatly the steadily growing number of men and women who defied him and chose her Book threatened everything he had built with such care. He punished more and more people with confiscation of goods, expulsion from labour or homes, loss of position in the community, even with death. But far from frightening them off, it seemed to feed their rebellion, until they seemed now to endanger the very fabric of the faith in the City. If he did not put an end to it, in time it would spread throughout the Empire. The core of treachery and unreason, as he saw it, was deeper than he had at first believed. Ra-Nufis had warned him, and then gone to the provinces to forestall rebellion there, leaving him with the responsibility for settling the issue in the City. He must do it before Ra-Nufis returned, or his own position might be at risk. Ra-Nufis was no easy master to serve. One needed a position of power to rest in one's bed at night.

The woman Tathea was the heart of the problem. Without her, the rest of them would soon wither away. It was unfortunate that Isadorus's sister, the Lady Eleni, had joined her. It would have been a great deal better if they could have somehow prevented that. He should have worked harder at wooing her to his cause, as he had with Barsymet, although Eleni had not the same vulnerabilities. But it had been a clumsy omission. Her gift of healing was a superb tool. It was exactly the kind of miracle that produced awe in people. Word of that kind of thing passed like fire. It did not need to happen often, the tales grew in the telling, and could always be nurtured a little.

He stared out of the window of his palace at the gardens and fountains below.

And Eleni was not the sort of woman to try to make personal capital out of her gift, not like Tathea. Eleni had no hunger for power, and now that she was a widow, she had largely retired from public life. Still, she was loved by the people and held in good respect. He was angry with himself for having ignored her.

But the real problem was Tathea. Ra-Nufis had been very angry indeed at her return from the Island. He had warned she was unpredictable. Zulperion had made the mistake of assuming that her defeat in Shinabar had shown her the futility of her goals. Apparently she did not learn.

He left the window and crossed to an ebony table on which stood a jug of wine. He poured himself a goblet full. It was excellent, but he barely tasted it.

She would have to be got rid of. She had forced the issue by persisting in this heresy to the point where it threatened to destabilise the whole of society. She could blame no one else. She had engineered her own destruction.

He finished his wine and poured more. It slid down his throat with a soothing fire. It would have to be done discreetly, of course, made to look like an accident. She had provided plenty of legal cause to have her executed, but one never knew which way public opinion would go. She certainly could not be tried. Only a complete lunatic would allow her such a platform for speech, and heaven knew the woman would take it! She had demonstrated that. And then she would look like a martyr. There were always gullible fools who would be persuaded to excuse her heresy and undermining of the truths he and Ra-Nufis had laboured so hard to build, and to teach.

No, there could be no question about it. She must meet with an accident at the moment of arrest. She must resist, offer violence. After all, she had marched across half Shinabar with the army, fighting side by side with soldiers. And what sane and decent woman would do that? It would be easy enough to believe she tried to fight when she was cornered and knew she was guilty of heresy – and, yes, sedition!

He took another long draught of the wine. She might very well be planning to overthrow the Emperor and set herself on the throne of Camassia! That was not in the least difficult to believe. After all, she had done it in Shinabar. The more he considered it, the more he thought it might be true. There was no end to her ambition.

The more swiftly he acted, the better. He strode over to the golden bell on the stand by the door, and rang it sharply.

It was answered within moments by his private clerk.

'Yes, my lord?'

'Fetch the Lord Mynoth.'

'Yes, my lord.' He withdrew to obey.

Mynoth came immediately, a dark man with quick, intelligent eyes and a sense of waiting power in him. Like Zulperion, he was dressed in a long brocaded silk robe with embroidered crimson and gold borders.

'I have delayed too long in dealing with the seditious heresy of the woman Tathea,' Zulperion said, watching Mynoth carefully to see if he understood the intent behind the words.

'Indeed,' Mynoth agreed. 'Your forbearance borders upon the dangerous. A little mercy is virtuous, too much may be an evil thing.'

Zulperion smiled coldly. 'Do you consider me evil, Mynoth?'

'I consider you have taken leniency to its ultimate degree, my lord,' Mynoth replied. 'But you will not take it beyond, unless I am much mistaken in you.'

'You are not! The time has come. To hesitate longer would be irresponsible. I have stayed my hand as long as I can. Take a suitable force of men whose discretion you can trust absolutely. Do I make myself clear?'

'You do.' Mynoth nodded. 'It would be most unwise to take any whose judgement might be suspect, or whose loyalty could be swayed – under pressure.'

'Precisely. Go and arrest her. A certain person has told us where she may be found. He required a little persuasion.' He shrugged. 'But it is done.'

Mynoth pursed his lips. 'Are you sure it is wise to bring her to trial, my lord? She will not go quietly. She will cause as big a public furore as she can.'

'I am aware of that!' Zulperion snapped. Mynoth irritated him acutely at times. He knew very well what was necessary but he was demanding to have it spelt out. 'It would be most unfortunate, even dangerous to public good,' Zulperion went on. 'But then I doubt she will come without a struggle.' He watched Mynoth closely. 'She is a soldier – of all things. I think it extremely likely she will be carrying a knife or dagger of some sort, and will attack you. You must take great care she does not injure any of you – or even kill you. She knows what lies ahead of her if she is tried, because she is most assuredly guilty. She can hardly afford to recant.'

'Yes,' Mynoth agreed with a curl of his lip. 'I imagine she will fight. An extraordinary woman. I look forward to meeting her.'

'Then go and do it!' Zulperion said tartly. 'And bring me word.'

Mynoth withdrew. He did not like Zulperion and he coveted his position. He was not pleased to be doing this particular piece of work for him either. Killing women, even this one, was not a priest's job.

He picked four of his most trusted men and went discreetly to the old quarter, armed only with daggers.

They broke in and found the woman. She was alone, sitting reading. It was one of her own copies of the Book, the evidence of her damnation was there in her hands. She was a very handsome woman, thought Mynoth, noting the auburn hair streaked with grey, and the broad brow. She did not look foreign. In fact she looked vaguely reminiscent of the Emperor Isadorus. Perhaps there was something about a crown that stamped itself in the features.

She admitted who she was, almost as if she was proud of it, and she came with them surprisingly willingly. It was awkward, because she made not the slightest effort to fight, and she certainly was not armed. It was all very unpleasant. He wished she had fought; then at least they could have killed her in hot blood. As it was, they murdered her in an alley, coldly and deliberately, and then two of them had to fight each other to make it seem there had been some resistance. They carried the body out into the marketplace and demanded a way through the crowds.

'We caught her in the act,' one of the men said boldly. 'She had the Book in her hands. We only wished to question her, but she attacked us. Now make way, we must carry her back to the High Priest Zulperion. Stand aside!'

But the people did not move. They stood ashen-faced, huddled together and strangely angry.

'What do you care?' Mynoth demanded. 'She was a foreigner, a Shinabari, and she brought nothing but trouble!'

'She was Baradeus's daughter!' one old man said with tears in his voice. 'She was more Camassian than you are! She was Isadorus's sister, and she healed us of all our ills, in the name of God!'

'Nonsense, you old sod!' Mynoth snapped. 'It is Tathea, the Shinabari!'

'It is the Lady Eleni, the Emperor's aunt!' a young woman said with withering contempt. 'She lived here because she believed in the old way. She is no more Shinabari than I am!'

Mynoth felt the coldness wash over him, filling his body and dragging him down, drowning him.

The crowd moved closer, angry and unforgiving. This time the priests had gone too far. They had ceased to be merely part of the general oppression of life and become acutely, personally responsible for a violation in their midst. They knew Eleni. They knew she had not fought these men. She had lived here. She had talked to them and laughed at their jokes, played with their children. Above all, she had healed their sick. Her death was a trespass which stirred a deep, primal anger in them; they would not back away, and they could not forgive.

Mynoth held up his dagger warningly.

They looked at him with cold disgust.

'Want to murder some more of us, do you, priest?' one old woman said scathingly. 'Now we see what you really are!'

'Tell Zulperion to go back to his master the devil!' a man in grey shouted. 'We want none of him here!'

His cry was echoed in the crowd till the noise grew to a roar, and Mynoth and the priests dropped Eleni's body and fled.

Tathea heard what had happened as she was returning from delivering the latest copies of the Book. The crowds in the streets were still clustered in groups, talking. They fell silent as she approached. It was a very young woman with a child who told her, tears still wet on her face.

'Zulperion's men came for you. They took the Lady Eleni.' She swallowed and her eyes brimmed over. She was not ashamed to weep. 'She let them think she was you. They murdered her. She didn't resist them, but they murdered her anyway. I think they always meant to.'

She was very pale and there was fear in her voice. 'You can't go back there, or they'll get you too. I have an uncle with a house near the arena where they train the horses. My brother will take you. Go now! And God speed!'

Tathea stood still in the shadowed alley, sick at heart. She should have foreseen this, and yet it caught her with numbing shock. These past months Eleni had been her sister and her friend. Now she had died to save her. She knew that absolutely. It came from some memory within her, of sunlight on golden stone, steps, bright water, another betrayal and another sacrifice.

'Go!' the woman repeated urgently, her voice growing louder. 'I'll tell Sanobiel where you are, and Saspia, and Timmaron. Run, while you can!'

Tathea turned and obeyed, her feet stumbling, her eyes blind with tears.

News of Eleni's death spread through the City and was carried by word of mouth to other cities, and with surprising rapidity even into the provinces. There was no softening of the truth. She had gone unresistingly, a quiet woman with grey in her hair and peace in her eyes, who had taught the word of God and healed the sick . . . and she had been murdered by the priests of Zulperion. It was the beginning of the end of his power. In order to preserve his own, Ra-Nufis charged him with instigating the crime. Zulperion took his own life before he could be tried. Mynoth claimed he was merely following orders, and was executed anyway. Ra-Nufis felt it was safer to show no leniency, and he did not want Mynoth left alive anyway. His tongue was too ready to excuse himself at his master's expense.

The Emperor Tiberian was not satisfied, but he was powerless to take matters further. Ra-Nufis had expressed horror and grief, and separated himself from the act. The people wanted reassurance and he gave it to them. 'All is well,' he told them. 'We had one rogue and he has been dealt with – he has paid the price. The illness of the soul is past. Now all is as it was before. Go your ways in peace.'

But in Ra-Nufis's heart there was anything but peace. Measures were needed to stop this happening again. Priests must be chosen with greater care, and even more highly rewarded. Their power must be seen to be beyond the ordinary laws that governed the rest of society.

'From now on there will be no discussion of doctrine,' he told the Light Bearers newly invested with the authority to forgive human sin at their discretion, in exchange for a suitable penance to be paid in money according to the means of the sinner. They sat before him, gowned in white, edges embroidered in gold and blood-red. 'The people must be protected from confusion and deception. They are children in spirit, and it is our charge to lead them along the paths of righteousness. In eternity they will thank us and bless our names that we have kept their feet from straying.' Ra-Nufis gazed at the eager, upturned faces before him.

'Preserve their innocence before heaven. Command them, teach them in all things, step by step,' he preached. 'Cut out all contention and dispute as if it was a rotting limb. Remind them of the briefness of their lives. Tell them the hope of eternity is all, that their body of flesh is worthless, a temporary house of dust, here today, and tomorrow consigned to the earth again. Innocence and obedience will give them a body which will be immortal. They shall inherit everlasting peace.'

His voice reverberated around the walls and not a soul looked away from him.

'Go now, and be shepherds to your people,' he commanded. 'Never use violence of the hand! It is not necessary. You have all the power you need in the teachings of the Book. You know the secrets of salvation, and they do not. You have the knowledge of miracles and, above all, I am behind you, and I have the great Book which Tathea brought from God. She could have been where I stand, but she lost the Book through sin. Thus God gave it to me. If anyone dares question you, tell them that.' He held it up before them, shining gold and warm in the light, and there was a sigh of breath around the hall and hearts beat faster, dizzy with wonder.

Then he took the Book and locked it in a mighty room, with guards posted at the door, so no one but he should ever touch it. It was the ultimate symbol of power, greater than any laurel or crown, because it was the pathway to heaven. It could not be shared with anyone.

Chapter Twenty-Two

Not very long after this, as the season turned, Saspia came to Tathea in the narrow stable where she now lived. Her face was anxious.

Tathea looked up from her copying. Her fingers were stained with ink, there were straws in her hair and her clothes, prickling through the coarse-woven linen. The candle flickered in the breeze from the door. The smell of horses was sharp and warm in the air.

'The Archon Maximian wants to speak to you,' Saspia said in a hushed voice.

Tathea felt a sharp stab of fear. 'Where?'

'Not here,' Saspia answered quickly. 'He does not know any of us, even if he may suspect one or two. He has simply said so, discreetly. One of those to whom he spoke is a member.' A tiny flash of wry humour touched her eyes, although it frightened her also that Maximian should guess so rightly. 'He will know to be more careful from now on, or go underground.' She shrugged slightly. 'Timmaron thinks there are probably about five or six thousand people now who have left their homes and disappeared in hiding because they are followers of the true Book. The poor quarters are teeming with them. Do you want to see the Archon Maximian? We can find a safe place, if you do.'

Tathea hesitated. What could Maximian want? He had believed the Book was an evil teaching even in Isadorus's time. How infinitely worse he must think it now. Would he come as a representative of the Hall of Archons to ask her to withdraw her teachings, for the sake of peace?

She could not do that. She could not leave Ra-Nufis unchallenged to spread his great apostasy throughout the world. As long as she lived, she would defend the truth.

Saspia was waiting, watching her.

Maximian as she had known him in the past was a man of strict honour. He had an unshakeable love of the old, austere ways of Camassia before the Emperors, stoic, self-reliant, brave, kind but unforgiving.

'Yes, I'll see him,' she answered.

Saspia smiled, then turned and went out.

★ ★ ★

They met in the fish market in the old quarter down by the docks. It was noisy, salt-smelling, the sharp wind blew cold off the water. People came and went. Since her return from the Island, Tathea had made her home here among those who laboured all the daylight hours and were still poor. She felt safe here, as much as she could anywhere. She might hide from men, but the Great Enemy would always know where she was, and his emissaries would find her if they wished.

Maximian came alone, dressed like a merchant, not an Archon. There were no purple borders to his robes.

He looked much older than when she had seen him last, his face was deeply lined and his hair almost white, but he still walked with a straight back and a graceful step. It was grief which had marked his face, not age or illness. The decline of his country from its old stoicism into self-indulgence had hurt him deeply.

He looked at her with a slight smile. She realised how much she, too, had changed. The last time he had seen her she had been dressed in scarlet beneath her armour, ready to sail for Shinabar and take the throne of the Isarchs. Now she must look like any of the other women who gutted fish on the wharf. And there was white in her hair too.

'I would not have known you, but for your eyes, and the way you hold your head,' he said ruefully. He did not use her name, and perhaps that was wise.

'Much has happened,' she replied, smiling back. 'Through all the world.'

'I only know about Camassia.' He moved closer to her. He wanted them to seem like a merchant and a fishwife bargaining. A flash of sympathy crossed his face. 'I am sorry about Shinabar . . .'

'Don't be.' She bit her lip. 'I thought it was failure at the time, but I know better now.'

He was surprised, curious. His brows puckered. 'If this is not failure, for both of us, then what would be?'

'To join with Ra-Nufis,' she answered him. 'To cease to fight for what is good. I know your perception of that differs from mine, but we can only seek what we believe the truth to be, and then fight to preserve it, to carry it high and show it to all who will see.'

He smiled. For all his austerity, there was a softness in his face, a great kindness. His eyes never wavered. It was not hard to know why Xanthica loved him, only tragic that she had placed him before God, and would thus lose them both.

'You haven't changed much, have you?' he observed. 'Yes, my truth is still different from yours. But your Book was a beautiful thing compared with this mystical blasphemy we have now.' His mouth pinched. 'Ritual is everything – music and tapers of light, incense that dulls the mind, chanting until the wits are half alive, buying forgiveness with money, and no understanding of the sin.'

Two women passed by, arguing vociferously.

'The priests have become wizards,' Maximian continued grimly, 'able to grant all kinds of dreams regardless of virtue or vice. Innocence and ignorance are held to be the same. The priests get more power every day, and the love of it corrupts their souls.'

'I know,' she said bitterly. 'I had hoped the evil of it would be so apparent that people would turn away.'

He laughed abruptly. 'Ever an optimist!' He shivered although the wind was not cold. 'Some do, but far too many love it. The velvet of sin is easy compared to the hard reality you teach.'

A flock of gulls swooped low, their cries filling the air. A man waved his arms at them and they ignored him, diving for the fish heads.

'Strangely, in the perversion of it, I can see something of the virtue of what you teach.' Maximian's voice was soft with regret. 'But that is not why I have come.'

'Why have you?' she asked.

He hesitated, looking beyond her to the light on the waves. 'Is the Book really of God? I don't mean the words in it, I mean the Book itself. Or is it manmade, the dictation of some spirit?'

'The Book itself is of God,' she answered. 'I did not write it or craft it. I journeyed in some world beyond this. I remember only moments of it, like a dream re-visited, but the Book was in the skiff with me when I touched the shore.' She did not press him why he asked, she knew he would tell her when he found the words, and was ready to say them.

A bird swooped and took the entrails of a fish from the wooden boards of the wharf, then it soared up on the wind, away over the blue water.

'Ra-Nufis has made it the symbol of his power,' Maximian said. 'It is more than a sceptre or a crown.'

She took his arm and began to walk along the quayside. They must not seem different from the other people working, arguing, haggling over prices. No one had time to stand long in conversation.

'If it is truly what you say,' Maximian went on, 'then it does not belong to him. It belongs to everyone, or no one. Without it he will fall – by his own words.'

'Will he?' She was not sure, but even as she questioned it, the doubts were shredding like mist before the sun.

'Yes.' He turned to her, his gaze steady. 'I see more of it than you do, now. It is a long time since you have been at court, or in the Hall of Archons.'

'The Book is locked away,' she replied softly, waiting for his next words.

'I know,' he answered. They were close to the sea wall. The tide slurped noisily under the stones. 'But not in his own palace,' he pointed out. 'That would be impolitic, and he has learned from Zulperion's downfall. It is in a special vault in the Imperial Palace, with its own entrance. It is very magnificent, and very secure. It used to be the place where Baradeus met his generals. I know it well, and I know the old entranceway. After that we would have to overpower the guards who are there night and day.' Without even giving it words, he had assumed she understood his intent.

It was a momentous thought: take the Book back. But not for her own power, not to challenge Ra-Nufis. That would only precipitate civil war and turn the oppressed into oppressors. It was time to end this dispensation of knowledge. The world was not ready for the great truths; only the lesser commands could survive, the laws that were innate in men of good will, of charity and honour everywhere. She must take the Book back to the Lost Lands where it would be safe from the lusts of power until this madness was forgotten and a new generation arose who could begin again.

As soon as the idea had formed in her mind she felt the certainty that it was right. She had no need to hesitate, to ask for time to go away and think more deeply, or to pray. If the Book remained here, in their hands, they would destroy themselves with its power.

'Yes,' she said firmly. 'If you are offering to help me take back the Book and return it to the Lost Lands, then I accept.'

His eyes narrowed. 'You will take it from here?'

'I will.'

He did not ask her to swear it. Implicit in his coming to her was the understanding that she would not keep it in Camassia.

'Then we must plan,' he said very quietly. 'It will require the greatest care. You must tell no one except those who have to know, and then as little as possible.'

She agreed. She did not mention the Great Enemy. Maximian did not believe in him. 'I will have to make plans to leave the City.'

'Have someone else hire a ship for you,' he urged. 'Trust no one you do not have to. We are all fallible.'

She sighed very slightly. 'I won't. Meet me here in three days.'

'Two,' Maximian insisted. 'I have my reasons.'

'Two,' she agreed.

He nodded briefly, half smiled, then turned and left, swallowed up almost immediately by the crowd of merchants heading towards the square.

She sat in the small room where they copied the Book, only Sanobiel, Saspia and Timmaron with her. A single candle was lit against the gathering dusk, its yellow light illuminating their tense faces.

'Back to the Lost Lands?' Saspia said quietly. 'Yes, perhaps that is

347

best. What a terrible thing for the world. We have been offered the light, and we will not accept it.'

'We must be practical.' Timmaron leaned forward. 'How will you do it? Do you really trust this Archon Maximian?'

'Yes,' Tathea answered without hesitation. 'Better you know as little as possible. Your task is to warn all the other cell leaders so everyone understands what has happened. Ra-Nufis's retribution will be terrible.'

Sanobiel frowned. 'Without the Book, his power to govern will be diminished. He may even be too busy with his own priests to bother with us.'

Saspia laughed abruptly and her face showed all too clearly what she thought of that hope.

'Warn everyone,' Tathea said urgently, looking from Saspia to Timmaron and back again. 'Give no reason. Speak only to those you trust absolutely, and say no more than that they must go further into the ancient quarters and become invisible. Trust no one, however close, however honourable you think them, unless they are proven believers whose lives would be forfeit also. Break all the chains of command, so no one can trace back, no one can betray even accidentally.'

Timmaron was very pale. He sat motionless, his shoulders hunched. He was not yet twenty. 'It is war, isn't it?' he said softly.

'Yes,' Sanobiel answered. 'And some will die, but we must save all we can.' His voice cracked a little. 'We shall not see each other again after tonight.'

Timmaron looked as if he had been struck. Suddenly it was real. The secrecy, the whisper of danger, even of torture and death, in the end it all came down to one truth, a final parting. He took a deep, shaky breath, and looked at Saspia.

She smiled at him and put her hand on his shoulder. 'We shall get word to everyone,' she promised. 'There will be no carelessness, no thoughtless trust.'

Timmaron forced himself to smile. 'That's right. We'll do it.'

They said no goodbyes, just wished each other God's speed, then turned and parted as if it were just as always, and they would meet again at the end of the day. There was no time for tears.

Tathea left the little cat with Saspia, and took with her only the blue silk cloak from the Lost Lands. She and Sanobiel set out just after sunset, dressed darkly and with daggers concealed. They met Maximian under the cypresses near the palace. He had four men of the old Imperial Guard of Isadorus's time with him. No one spoke. Maximian led the way under the trees towards the huge outline of the palace buildings and Baradeus's old battle headquarters where the Book was now housed.

The rising moon was palely reflected on the polished black marble and the guards posted showed only as dense shadows against the gleam.

One of them turned, hand to his sword as the first of Maximian's men stepped forward, came to a halt and saluted.

'The Archon Maximian,' he said firmly.

The guard was unperturbed. Like everyone else in the City, he knew who Maximian was, and his views on the Book.

'What does the Archon want here?' he asked curiously. 'There is no one inside, except the watch.'

Maximian stepped forward, his face clearly visible in the moonlight. The gold glistened on his Archon's robes.

'I have a message for Captain Ramus. It concerns a matter of importance, and secrecy. Please tell him I am here.' The name of the captain convinced the guard. He saluted and obeyed.

Tathea and Sanobiel waited, shivering a little.

The guard returned. He had no premonition of trouble. He conducted Maximian up the broad steps and made no objection when Tathea and Sanobiel followed. The others remained outside.

The doors closed behind them and Maximian walked forward as if he had no fear. There were three men in front of the great bronze inner doors carved with scenes of battles and victories of long ago. Two of them stood motionless and awkward, a little sideways, and it was a moment before Tathea realised they were asleep, or drugged.

The third man came forward and clasped Maximian's hand.

'Ramus,' Maximian said simply. 'Thank you.' He gripped him hard.

'Be quick!' Ramus said softly. 'Ra-Nufis has the only key.'

Maximian said nothing. He led Sanobiel and Tathea along a narrow passage to the side, under a heavy curtain and through a small door. Behind this was a narrow stair leading downward into the dark.

'Follow me,' he whispered, and started down, step by step, fingers on the stone wall. At the bottom they went along a tunnel. It was completely lightless. They were deep underground. Tathea could feel the damp in the air. There was no sound whatever except that of their breathing, and her own heart.

Maximian came to halt, feeling along the wall with his hand. Then he gave a little sigh of satisfaction and moved forward again. 'Stairs up,' he warned, and they began to climb. At the top he found a door, and they were inside the painted chamber where Baradeus had planned his strategies. And in front of them, on a pedestal under a single torch, was the Book.

Tathea felt a surge of joy so powerful she was dizzy with it. Whatever it had cost, however long or hard the path, just to see it again was worth anything she could have paid. She found she was trembling as she walked towards it. It was as if the Book gave off the light and the torch merely reflected the fire.

She put out her hand and her fingers touched the gold surface. It was warm, as it had always been, and the power of it sang through her veins, filling her heart. She picked it up and turned to Maximian.

He was looking at the Book, curiosity in his face, and a slowly awakening surprise. 'It's beautiful.' He let out his breath. 'It is hard to believe it is the cause of so much . . . war.'

'It is the truth,' she answered him. 'It will always divide.'

Sanobiel interrupted them. 'We must hurry,' he urged. 'We must catch the tide. The boat cannot wait. And the other guards will waken.'

'Of course.' Maximian turned. Tathea wrapped the Book in the blue cloak and followed, holding it in her arms. Carefully they made their way back down the ancient passage, up the steps again and into the outer chamber.

But it was not Ramus who awaited them, but Ra-Nufis, with the two guards from outside the doors, and another, slender and fair-skinned, smooth-featured. He was as young as when Tathea had last seen him all those years ago, and with a chill of ice she recognised Ulciber. His lips curled back in a smile, and it was as if she had known him always.

Ra-Nufis looked at the silk cloak in Tathea's arms, as if he could see through it to the Book.

'I knew you would come for it, one day,' he said softly. 'I always knew the power of it would call you. I didn't want to kill you, Ta-Thea, but you leave me no choice.' His hand dropped to his sword hilt and tightened over it.

Ulciber leaned gracefully against the wall, watching.

The two guards drew their swords. Maximian drew his also, and Sanobiel his dagger.

Tathea put down the Book, drew her dagger and faced Ra-Nufis. He came towards her smiling, the torchlight gleaming gold and red on his blade. It was more than twice the length of hers, and he was taller, his reach longer.

Maximian backed away from the guard facing him, over towards Tathea, ignoring Ra-Nufis.

She thought he was going to fight back to back with her, so they could protect each other. It was not what she wanted. She needed room to move easily, to duck and feint.

But when he was close enough he held out his sword, hilt towards her. 'Take it!' he commanded, reaching for her dagger.

As she turned, Ra-Nufis lunged. He only just missed her.

Maximian snatched the dagger from Tathea's hand and forced the sword on her. She took it and parried Ra-Nufis's next blow. There was no time to think of Sanobiel or Maximian. She needed all her wits to fight. And all the time Ulciber leaned against the wall, smiling in the torchlight.

They swung back and forth, blades clashing. She watched Ra-Nufis's hand, his shoulders and the balance of his body shifting, as Alexius had taught her. She thought of all the battles she had fought across the Shinabari desert. Ra-Nufis had fought just as many, and probably just as skilfully. He had survived them all with few wounds. But after that his warfare had been of the intellect and the spirit. She had marched and fought with Merdic and the Lost Legion. She had faced the dark warriors of Yaltabaoth in that last, terrible battle on the Western Shore.

She thought of it as she faced Ra-Nufis now.

His blade passed close to her head. She stepped sideways and dropped back, then lunged low. The tip of her sword ripped open the flesh across his ribs. She saw the anger and surprise in his face. He redoubled his efforts. His blade scarred her left arm, drawing blood. He smiled with vicious pleasure.

Ra-Nufis was far stronger than she was, but his magnificent robes hampered his movement. She did not want to kill him. Once he parried clumsily, a misjudgement, and the chance was there, a clean strike through the heart – and she hesitated.

He saw her lose the moment, and smiled, showing his teeth.

'Kill her . . .' Ulciber said softly, but his voice was as clear as a shout in the room where there was no sound but the slap of boots and sandals on the marble floor, the clash of blades and the hiss of breath.

Ra-Nufis lunged forward, sure of himself.

She had expected it. He had thought she would move sideways again, but she stepped back, and then to the other side, bringing her sword down hard on his, as close to the hilt as she could reach.

It fell from his hand and slid across the floor. In a moment Maximian was on it, substituting it for his dagger. He was hard pressed and it saved him from the soldier's finishing blow.

Ra-Nufis stood for an instant, his face slack with terror. Then jubilation as he remembered her hesitation. She could not kill him. She could not bring herself to strike the final blow. He whirled round to Ulciber.

Ulciber took one of the torches from its wall bracket and threw it to him. He caught it perfectly and came forward towards Tathea, waving it in front of her, the flames and smoke weaving back and forth. It was a different but equally deadly weapon. If she were to strike it with her sword, her blade would chip or break against its iron, spilling fire over both of them, and she would be left all but disarmed.

She backed away, unsure how to fight. He came after her, triumph in his eyes.

To her right Sanobiel was struggling, blood on his clothes, his dagger too short to outreach the soldier he fought. To her left Maximian was doing better, armed with Ra-Nufis's sword. He was moving towards Sanobiel, ready to help him.

Ra-Nufis swung the torch. She could smell the smoke and feel the heat of it scorching her face. She must win! She must take the Book back to the Lost Lands, and give it again to God. Men were not ready for its power. They twisted and perverted it into a weapon to oppress and it became the Enemy's tool.

Ra-Nufis swung the torch again. The flame burnt her arm. She thought of Yaltabaoth. She dropped to her knee and drove forward, catching him low on the thigh, feeling her blade strike flesh.

He cried out in sudden pain and fell forward, hard on to the blazing torch in his hand. The flame caught his robes and flared upward in a sheet of fire. His screams filled the chamber. The other fighters froze.

Ulciber lurched forward, his face aghast, but there was nothing he could do. There was no water, no sand. The flame roared upward in furnace heat, the contents of the torch held in the cloth of Ra-Nufis's robes.

The screams stopped. A blackened body lay smoking, wound in a smouldering shroud, hairless, skin charred.

Maximian was the first to move.

'Run!' he commanded, looking at Tathea, then at Sanobiel.

Sanobiel hesitated, knowing as Tathea did that if they left Maximian it must cost his life.

'Run!' Maximian repeated, his voice rising high and sharp. 'While you can! Take the Book! It is God's, not man's!'

Sanobiel thrust his dagger back in his belt and stooped to pick up the Book. He almost pushed Tathea, his arm round her, as he made for the doors.

She turned to look a last time at Maximian, sword in his hand as he strove to hold off both the soldiers. He could not do it for long. She saluted him, the old Imperial salute that Drusus had raised to her as she left the Western Shore, then swivelled on her foot and ran after Sanobiel.

As she went down the steps she heard a terrible sound behind her, high, thin, jubilant laughter. It was Ulciber's laughter, as unmistakable as the darkness itself.

They passed through the columns into the open space of the square, then into the shelter of the streets, going as fast as they could, stopping only to catch their breath.

The moon was high and the tide full when they reached the wharves, black against the sharp, glittering sea and a sky so clear the very air seemed vibrant with the light.

The ship was waiting for them and they boarded quickly. They went below into the cabins already prepared for them before any casual watcher might see them and wonder at a man and a woman huddled together, carrying some object close to their bodies, and putting to sea at midnight.

The crew raised the sails and loosed the moorings. Silently, like a ship in a dream, they pulled away on the silver, shifting tide and set the bow towards the harbour bar and the open water.

They treated their wounds the best they were able with clean water, and bound them with strips torn from linen in the cabin.

Afterwards Tathea lay alone on her bed. She had made one of the most momentous decisions of her life. She still did not doubt it was the right one. It was not the Book that had failed, but men. They were not ready for the light. And yet it must have been possible, or else why would God have given it?

But there were the few: Alexius, Eleni, Tugomir, the knights of the Western Shore . . . Sanobiel. Even one would have been enough, one soul to climb upwards and at last see the face of God.

The pain was there too. How could Ra-Nufis who had known so much yet choose the darkness? Why had the great counterfeit been so beautiful to him? Why had the distortion of truth lit within him such a hunger that he had in the end consented to evil which would have horrified him only a few years before!

Or had the seeds of damnation always been in him? She stared into the night, remembering. She thought of all the times they had spent together, of his loyalty and courage, his untiring energy and how he had given all of himself to the work. Nothing had been too much to ask of him. All for what? She could not believe he had planned to overthrow her even then. The shadow had come slowly, a step at a time. The love of beauty had turned into the love of power. He had seen how people grasped after that which promised hope, order out of confusion, redemption out of guilt. And then he had tasted their gratitude and the supreme power of being loved. He had allowed them to think it was he who had given the gift, and not God; and in time he had come to believe it himself.

She turned over at last and fell asleep, exhausted and grieving, but no longer filled with confusion.

When she woke, the sun was high. She was stiff and every movement ached with bruises and the unaccustomed exertion of muscles she had not used in nearly two years. The cuts from Ra-Nufis's sword blade needed to be re-dressed and it hurt to wash away the dried blood.

When she finally went on deck, it was noon and the City had long since vanished below the horizon. She looked up at the great sails bellying above her, white against a cobalt sky. It was a swift ship, elegant and keen through the water, leaving a long white wake behind.

There were few men on deck. She saw one at the ship's oar in the stern, his skill apparent in the ease and lightness of his hand. Another man stood forward, gazing at the water ahead. A third was lashing a rope to the rail, and a fourth bent his head over some weaving or splicing task. Sanobiel must be still below. She would not disturb him.

She went back to her cabin and shortly afterwards Sanobiel knocked gently on the door. He looked tired and anxious and he stood awkwardly as if his body ached. He was holding bread and fruit in one hand.

'Come in,' she said quickly, moving aside for him.

They ate with hunger, then sat talking of things of the past, people they needed to or wanted to remember. Foremost in both their minds was Maximian, who had never believed the Book and yet who at the end had been willing to give his life so that it could be returned to God.

'They will have killed him,' Sanobiel said quietly, staring at the close, wooden walls of the tiny cabin. 'He must have known that when he first offered.'

'He was a good man,' Tathea answered, eating the last of the bread. 'Was it our fault that we never managed to show him the Book in such a way that he could believe it? Did we do something wrong, or omit something?'

'I don't think so.' Sanobiel poured more water for her. 'He heard it all but he chose another way – a good way, but incomplete. Perhaps in the end he will know the Book is true.' A smile flickered across his tired face. 'Of all the gifts of God, the one I am most grateful for is that He did not give us the right or the power to judge each other. That is His alone.'

Tathea smiled back at him, touching his hand lightly where it lay on the small table between them. He reached out quickly and placed his other hand over hers.

They talked of people they had loved, whose faith, honesty and courage had lit their path. They remembered some in sadness, others only with joy.

The following day was the same, and the day after. They occupied their time talking. He told her of some of the events in the beginning of the resistance, before she had returned, and she told him of the beauty of the Island and the people she had known there.

Lastly she told him of the Maelstrom and how they would smell it in the air, feel the shivering on the skin as they drew close to it, how they would hear the roar from over the horizon, dull at first, only a difference in the pitch of the wind in the rigging, before the ear detected the steady, sullen rumble of everlasting tumult.

On the fourth day they went up on deck into clear sunlight, the water burning blue around them. Tathea looked south towards the expanse of the horizon, Sanobiel west where he expected to see the haze of the Maelstrom in the distance.

Tathea felt his grip on her arm, so hard it made her gasp with pain. She swung round and saw what he was staring at, his face bleached with horror: the shore of some low-lying land, sharp and clear, on whose slopes a great city nestled, its stones rose-pink and ochre.

'Tirilis!' he said between stiff lips.

She turned and moved from the side of the ship towards where the helmsman stood bent over the oar, his back to her.

'Why are we going to Tirilis?' she demanded.

He neither moved nor made a sound.

'Why are we going to Tirilis?' she shouted at him, fear rising sharply in her voice. When he still made no response, she put her hand on his shoulder to force his attention.

Slowly he swung round, and the face she saw was so fearful it was as if hell had opened in front of her. In the hollows of his eyes she saw corruption and the descent into chaos and the darkness which had no end. The face had the sunken cheeks and gaping mouth, the high Shinabari bones of a man who had been a thousand years dead.

'Oh, God!' The words formed in her heart, but her lips were frozen, her pulse motionless.

Sanobiel strode to the forward watchman and caught at his arm. As the watchman looked up, words gagged in Sanobiel's throat also. The visage he beheld was so terrible, nothing could have prepared him for it. The eyes far back in the hooded sockets had given no mercy in life, and in five centuries of death had not learned to find it.

Sanobiel fell back, his heart beating wildly and a sick terror twisting within him.

Another gaunt figure risen from the spirit prison descended from the mast and went about its careful business of lashing ropes and steadying the sail.

Tathea crossed over towards Sanobiel slowly, her body lurching, her legs weak. The salt wind blew about them, clean on the skin. The sails billowed against the sky and the sweet, bright water rushed past the white hull as they sped towards Tirilis.

'Tiyo-Mah,' Tathea said hoarsely, remembering the suffocating oppression and the terrible weight of the dead in the underground room in Thoth-Moara. 'She has learned from Asmodeus how to raise the unrepentant dead . . .'

'Unrepentant?' Sanobiel grasped the halyards to steady himself. The earth seemed to reel as if they had already entered the Maelstrom, though the sea was as calm as midsummer.

'Those who even after death reject the light and turn their backs on God,' Tathea answered. 'They will have until the end of the world, then if they still choose darkness, darkness they shall have. Somehow she knows the Book has gone from Ra-Nufis's power, and she has raised these creatures and sent them to take us to Tirilis.'

'Can we not bribe them?' he asked.

'How?'

'Offer them something?'

'What?' Her voice was rough-edged with pain. 'God has already offered them everlasting joy, the glory of love and laughter and worlds without end, and they have rejected it. What in heaven's dreams could we offer them?'

He clasped her hand. 'Then can we not fight them? Is there no weapon, some sword of the spirit?'

'To do what?' she whispered, her mind filled with a brilliance of almost unendurable clarity. 'They are already in an unending night without love or hope. They have seen light and chosen darkness. What could we do to them?' She searched his face. 'What could even God, or the Great Enemy, do which would touch what they have done to themselves?'

'Nothing,' Sanobiel answered softly, putting his arms round her and holding her closely. The sea shone in a streaming tide. Gulls circled the mast against the dazzling sky. The wind was sharp, stinging the skin. He drew in a deep breath, searching his soul. 'Nothing,' he said again, a pure flame of certainty inside him.

Then he let her go, kissing her once, softly, on the cheek.

'God keep you.' He smiled, then walked over to the mast and stood in front of it. He lifted his face to heaven and closed his eyes in a mighty prayer. Living flesh had no power over the damned, nor had they over him. But there was one way in which he could join battle with them, and his soul knew it. He hesitated only a moment, and then asked of God the one gift he needed, not for himself, but for those creatures of hell around him.

The light brightened across the water.

As one man the mariners advanced toward him, their arms raised. Each struck him a terrible blow. It was the last which killed him. But he did not fall, he seemed to burn with a radiance as if in an instant he had passed from mortality to immortality. With a fearful majesty he raised his right arm and spoke.

'In the name of Him who faced the powers of hell and overcame them, I command you to depart!'

The mariners staggered back, stumbled and fell. They lay like dark stains on the deck, their robes empty of substance, and a wind arose and carried them away over the side where they sank into the water and the sea consumed them.

When Tathea looked again at the place where Sanobiel had been, there was only a brightness in the air. She was alone, without friend or enemy of any kind. Alexius, Arimaspis and Eleni were dead. Kol-Shamisha had given his life to save her. Maximian had too. And now

356

Sanobiel. Each had been a victory of the soul, but the loss was vast, the hollowness unfillable.

She stared seaward. Somewhere beyond that shimmering water lay the Maelstrom and the Lost Lands where she must take the Book and give it back to God again. There it would be safe, beyond the reach of man or devil.

The sails were flapping loose, the ship beginning to jib and yaw in the water.

She went to the stern and lashed the helm, not even certain when or how she had learned to do such a thing, then reached to tighten the ropes on the sails and reel them in. The wind seemed to be rising. The ship heeled and the canvas tightened. The bow cut through the water sending up white spume.

She did not know how long she worked. The sun set in scarlet, dripping fire over the sea, and she sat in the dark, drifting in and out of sleep. She awoke to a slate-blue morning with the high fin of dawn pale in the east, light spilling across the ruffled crests of the waves.

All day she travelled without smelling the Maelstrom in the air. Strangely she did not feel alone. The memories of those she had loved filled her mind as if they stood about her, and the Book itself was like a living flame, a compass in the trackless paths of the ocean, a fire in the empty spaces between the stars.

On the sixth morning she awoke and saw land ahead of her. It was not the bright harbour of Orimiasse as she had hoped, but the long shoreline with the low hills of the eastlands of the Island at the Edge of the World. When the boat was carried high and beached, she clasped the Book in her arms, stepped over into the white water and waded ashore on to the hard strand, picking her way through the bands of weed and the tiny shells. The scent of wild lupins hung heavy in the air and the birds wheeled and cried overhead. The sky was a softer blue here, wide and ragged with mares' tail clouds.

She walked up the wind-combed grass on to the headland. Skylarks hovered in the sun, pouring out cascading trills of sound, piercingly sweet. She would travel south. Perhaps in Kyeelan-Iss she would find a mariner who would take her past the Maelstrom to the Lost Lands.

The country was even lovelier than her memory of it. Trees huge as clouds whispered and rustled in a breeze sweet with the breath of flowers. Wild roses climbed the hedges, daisies tangled beneath them. She passed workers on the land, shepherds, woodsmen, swineherds under the trees, a few travellers like herself. She ate apples and wild berries from the hedge.

The sun was high and warm on her face when she saw a lean figure coming towards her along the narrow path through the grass. There was something familiar in his gait, and the flying hair fluttered a wing of fear in her heart, but it was not until he was within a few yards of her that she knew his face. It was haggard, the eyes blazing, and the gaunt body leaned on a great staff as if he needed it to support his weight. It was the Wanderer with the Staff of Broken Dreams who had once been Yaltabaoth, Lord of Despair, until she had wounded him on the Western Shore.

Now he stood in front of her barring the way, his eyes brilliant with glee, his gnarled hands clenched.

'I told you we would meet again,' he said softly. 'I keep my promises.'

She had no weapon, nothing with which to fight him.

The Wanderer's lips drew back from his yellow teeth. 'You fear for your life, Woman of the Book? You have no need. I cannot kill you, I can only wound you, but that wound will never heal. The ache of it will be with you night and day for the rest of your life.' He moved so rapidly she was startled, barely seeing what he did, only the great spear whirling round his head, missing her shoulder by so little it actually brushed her garments.

But for the Book she would rather he killed her than deal her such a wound. All those she loved were gone. But she was the only one who could take the Book back to the shore of Orimiasse. She had brought it into the world, and she could not now abandon it to be used and misused by men.

The Wanderer had no care for the Book. All he wanted was revenge, to leave the pain of disillusion that endures for ever, the gall of bitterness which eats away everything, and the life that knows no hope.

They stood facing each other in the silent sunlight. Then just as he stepped forward to strike his blow, there came a faint tinkling of bells, tiny bells on outlandish shoes.

The Wanderer froze.

Tathea swung round and away, hope singing wildly inside her.

Menath-Dur came through the grass and the flowers, but his face was set and his eyes never left the Wanderer's. In his hand he carried a long staff and his fingers round it were tight, ready to lift it and strike.

But there was no battle. The Wanderer had time, and all mortal flesh were his victims. Menath-Dur would not be everywhere. He strode away, slashing at the grass, breaking its slender reeds, destroying the flowers in it, and where his feet had trodden the earth was left black.

Menath-Dur stared at the blackened earth, his grey eyes sad. He lifted his strange staff, and as he did so the dead earth quickened. The green grass of life returned and the Wanderer's footsteps were no longer visible.

He turned to Tathea. 'Come,' he said simply. 'We must go to Hirioth.'

'No,' she refused. 'I am going to Kyeelan-Iss, where I can find mariners and a ship who will take me to the Lost Lands . . .'

He shook his head, smiling gently at her. 'You will not go to the Lost Lands. It is not time. You must come to Hirioth.'

'You don't understand . . .'

He took her arm gently, but his hands were strong. 'Yes I do. Come. There is no time to waste. There are other enemies who will soon know you are here.'

'I must take the Book back to the Lost Lands.' She would not move. 'It can no longer remain in the world. If you knew what—'

'I do know.' He let go of her arm and took her hand instead. She felt a ripple of warmth incredibly sweet. 'I have been from the beginning, and I shall be until all things are restored. Your path lies in Hirioth.'

Could it be so? God could take back the Book anywhere, the whole earth was His. It was only memory that told her it should be Orimiasse, because she could see so clearly the sky and the water and the vast spread of light. But perhaps the forest was the way.

Menath-Dur waited while she pondered it in her heart, allowing the peace to grow inside her and the knowledge of truth.

'Yes,' she said at last. 'We will go to Hirioth.'

'Good. Come quickly. There are many forces abroad, and I can battle some of them, but not all.' And he set off with his rapid, easy step through the grass and under the shadow of great trees, out into the sunlight again and along hedgerows tangled and bright with flowers. She had to walk as fast as she could to keep up with him. When he stopped at last to pick wild fruit for her to eat, she was aching with tiredness and the Book had grown heavy and awkward to carry.

But he allowed her little respite. The sun was sinking and the air took on a patina of gold. Poplars shimmered like columns of satin, every leaf stirring in the sunset breeze. The daisies in the grass caught the light and became a million fragile stars. Homing birds swirled across the sky like a shower of leaves thrown up.

They were on the edge of the great forest, its outer saplings lissom, silver-trunked, leaves whispering and turning. The great-skirted oaks leaned towards the earth. Under them, as they trod the first path inward, the very air was green.

Menath-Dur stopped, his face grave. 'I can go no further. The rest of your journey you must walk alone. Go with the light of God . . .' He hesitated, as if he would say more, but all that his heart meant was in those few words. After touching her hand once, he turned rapidly and without looking back walked away, the bells on his shoes tinkling until they were swallowed in silence.

She was left alone to follow the earthen path into the deepening shade. Far above her the wind murmured in leaves bright in a luminous sky, but the way before her was as calm as deep water. The ancient trunks were beautiful in their motionless writhing. Vivid moss crusted their roots and ferns spread delicately against the numberless shades of brown.

She had walked for some time and the gentle evening was still glowing across the sky and shedding enough light for her to see quite clearly when she met a man leaning against a giant oak, as if he was waiting there for her. He straightened up and came forward, slender, graceful, his face marvellous in the perfection of its bones, his black hair springing from a fine brow.

She stopped, her heart racing. There was something familiar about him, a memory stirred from some deep recess in her heart. He smiled and when he spoke his voice was soft.

'So you are ready to give up the Book for which you paid such a price. The world has beaten you!' There was no anger in him, only sorrow.

She was startled, these were not the words she had expected. She had thought of taking the Book from the world to resolve man's use of it for evil. It had never occurred to her that it was a surrender.

The man smiled. It was like spring sunlight, bright without warmth.

'The truth is in the Book, the power to save the world,' he said. His eyes did not leave her face, nor once glance at the Book in her arms.

'I know. But they still have the knowledge from within it. No one can take that away,' she answered.

'Ah, but they can!' he argued. 'Without the Book, what is only copied from it can be twisted, altered, and in time no one will know any more what it truly said. Had you not thought of that?'

She stood still. For the first time her mind was confused. What he said was true. It could be lost, changed. It was happening already.

'They have abused it.' She looked at his beautiful face that tugged at her memory with such terrible longing and ache of passion. 'They use it as a symbol of power, to get dominion over each other.'

'There will always be someone who misuses it,' he said gently. 'Is that a cause to rob the rest? If you struggled with them, laboured to bring them understanding, would that not be a far nobler thing to do?'

He was right. She was running away. Was this, after all, the final test of love?

He was standing very close to her now, almost at her elbow. 'With that Book, and the knowledge that is in it, used with wisdom, guarded against the unrighteous, you could be the saviour of the world! Every man and woman who lives, or has yet to live, could be freed from sin, guided away from error and false belief. Generations to come would bless your name!' He was watching her face. 'No one ever born would be loved as you would be.'

'All . . .' she repeated in slow wonder. 'I could save them all?'

'Yes, you could! Not a single soul need be lost . . .'

Then at last she knew him. She saw the darkness in the soul behind his eyes, and understood that she looked upon the face of Asmodeus himself. He was not horror, bestiality, decay, but the holiest of all truths distorted. It was the corruption of what had once been sublime. The path to hell was not a violent fall but a slow descent, one subtle, shallow step at a time.

'No . . .' She held the Book closer in her arms. 'No, I cannot save the world. Another, long since, has lived and died to redeem all from the death of the body. You know that – you were there! I am not taking truth from the world, only the Book which has become a token of dominion, because they do not yet understand it. They want salvation without labour and without pain. But God will never cease to speak to the heart of everyone who listens.' She faced him with total conviction at last, her fear and doubt fled away. 'I will not keep the Book, nor will I use it to gain dominion for myself – or for you.'

He stared at her as if he could not believe defeat. Then when at last he knew it, the mask fell from him. She saw hell in his eyes, the irretrievable darkness of one who has looked upon God and has denied Him.

She knew him and understood his life. He had no more power over her.

He threw back his head and let out a roar, a huge, bellowing rage of sound that reached up to the stars.

From between the trunks wraiths took form, like smoke rising from the ground. They separated one from the other until they had the semblance of men, but misbegotten, with limbs and organs that melted and altered from one moment to the next. The only thing that never changed was the hunger in their faces, the devouring appetite that consumed them. They came forward slowly, eyes questing in the light.

One snatched a squirrel and stuffed it into his mouth, his features twisted with glee as if he had attained an eternal prize.

A fallow deer appeared and another wraith seized it, forced open its jaws and stretched his arm inside the beast, his own body fluid, shape-shifting to crawl inside its body and become one with it, devouring it from within.

Every formless creature of hell strove to consume, to possess, to eat and make some small creature part of it, or to slide and penetrate and enter the larger beasts and possess them.

The mortal creatures strove to rescue each other whatever the risk or cost to themselves. One after another they laid down their lives, a song thrush for a badger, a bear for a weasel, a horse for a fox. Even the trees and the flowers and grasses tangled the feet of the formless, snared their arms and were trampled and torn up.

361

The hideous battle swayed back and forth as the legions of heaven and hell met for the victory of life. The eyes of hell were avid with hope. The souls of the shapeless who had followed Asmodeus fought the unborn of the earth for the bodies they should have.

The air was shivering dark, splintered like ice. As one beast after another gave itself in sacrifice, another damned soul felt the body slip from its grasp, and the gates of eternity close for ever against it. Hope vanished like the last glimmer of a sun which shall never rise again as a night begins from which there is no daybreak and no dawn, no spark or sliver of light for ever after.

One by one, with a terrible desolation, they melted away, knowing at last their master's payment and tasting the dregs of its despair.

In the silence Asmodeus looked at Tathea once, with freezing, endless hatred, then turned on his heel and strode away into the trees, leaving an iciness in the air so savage the leaves in his path withered and fell. Even the bark of the trees was petrified instantly to stone, as though the hand of death had touched them all.

Tathea travelled on in a daze. Darkness came slowly, green and perfumed, without fear. When she could no longer see the path before her feet, she climbed into the broad arms of a tree and slept.

She walked all the following day also, deeper and deeper into Hirioth, and at sunrise of the day after, she came at last to the shore of a mere. It was surrounded by trees so vast and so ancient they must have stood since the birth of the land. Boughs were dense and twisted with age. Moss like an elfin forest carpeted the earth between the roots, and lace-like ferns descended from hollows and cups in the wood.

The water was smooth as stretched silk, and the first rays of the sun lay upon its face as if the night sky had been caught and pinned to the earth in all its splendour of light and shadow.

Then she saw a man on the shore, coming towards her slowly, smiling. He was like Asmodeus, slender and dark with a face of marvellous beauty; and yet he was also utterly different. In him was the knowledge of pain and glory, and his eyes shone with the light in his soul.

She knew him! Now at last memory returned: the skiff on the shore beyond Orimiasse, Parfyrion in its golden decay, Bal-Eeya and its storms, the lovely and barren Malgard, and Sardonaris, light on the water, and love, and death – and the palace above the sea, the Man of Holiness.

'Ishrafeli!'

He came to her and stood a moment in front of her. He lifted his hand and touched her cheek with his fingers, then her brow, then the hollow of her throat.

'It was a heavy burden,' he said gently. 'But you have done well.'

Slowly, with hesitant hands, she lifted the great Book and let the cloak fall from it. It gleamed warm in the gold of the rising sun.

She held it out to him.

His mouth was more tender than the sky, and in his eyes held such love as beggars dreams.

'No,' he answered her. 'I cannot. You took the fire of truth from heaven. You must guard it until there comes again one who is pure enough in heart to open the seal and read what is written. It may be a hundred years, it may be a thousand, but God will preserve you until that time and the end of all things. In that day I shall come again, and we shall fight the last battle of the world, you and I together.'

She opened her lips to argue, to plead, and the words were silent even in her heart. It was the law of God, and it must be so.

He leaned and kissed her once, then turned and walked away towards the water and the broadening sun, leaving her motionless on the shore, the golden Book in her arms and the fire and the light of God in her soul.

The Book

Child of God, if your hands have unloosed the hasp of this Book, then the intent of your heart is at last unmarred by cloud of vanity or deceit.

Know this, that in the beginning, through the dark reaches of infinity, was the law by which every intelligence has its being and fulfils the measure of its creation.

When God was yet a man like yourself, with all your frailties, your needs and your ignorance, walking a perilous land as you do, even then was the law irrevocable.

By obedience you may overcome all things, even the darkness within, which is the Great Enemy. The heart may be softened by pain and by yearning until love turns towards all creatures and nothing is cast away, nothing defiled by cruelty or indifference. The mind may be enlightened by understanding gained little by little through trial and labour, and much hunger, to perform great works. Courage will lift the fallen, make bearable the ache of many wounds, and guide your feet on the path when your eyes no longer see the light.

When your spirit is harrowed by despair and all else fails you, compassion will magnify your soul until no glory is impossible.

By such a path did God ascend unto holiness.

But the law is unalterable, and unto all, though the tears of heaven wash away the fixed and the moving stars for you, though God has shed His blood to lave you clean; each act without love, each indifference, each betrayal robs you of that which you might have been. Eternity looks on while you climb the ladder towards the light, but neither God nor devil takes you a step up or down, only your own act.

If it were not so, where would be your greatness at the last? Would God rob you of your soul's joy? Of that day when you stand before Him in eternal life and say not as a stranger but as a citizen, 'I have walked the long path, I have conquered all things, thou has opened the door for me and I have come home.'

The conversation between Man of Holiness and Asmodeus, the Great Enemy:

Asmodeus: I have seen the plan and it will fail, because your commandments are impossible. You ask perfection, and it is beyond man even to dream of it. The void echoes with laughter that you mock him, and his arrogance that he could believe you. He cannot do it. From the beginning he will fail. He is blind, and his journey is futile.

Man of Holiness: To be perfect is to do your best, without shadow of deceit or cowardice, without self-justification or dissembling. It is to strive with an honest mind and a pure heart, and an eye single to the love of good. It is not to climb without falling, but each time you fall, to rise again, and continue the journey, no matter how hard it may be, discounting the bruises and the pain, the grief and the hope deferred. It is to face the light with courage, and never to deny it. It requires all that a man has, to the height and breadth and depth of his soul, but it does not require more. I give no commandments, rather I make a way that they may be accomplished.

Asmodeus: Man will not believe that! He is short-sighted and full of fears. He will drown in the enormity of it. If you were just, you would ask for less. You would make the path easier.

Man of Holiness: Then he would not grow to the measure of his fullness, but be stunted, and forever less than his spirit's dream, a bird without wings, a song unsung. I know the joy and the pain of every step, as I know the scars of My own feet. He can do it, if he will.

Asmodeus: That you did it is to him a sound without meaning, a burnt paper in the wind. That journey is not for him. He will burn his soul in the fire of it, and then wander lost in the dark.

Man of Holiness: He is My child. Where I have gone, he can follow, and My glory may become his. It is My purpose and My joy that in time beyond thought he may become even as I am, and together we shall walk the stars, and there shall be no end.

Asmodeus: He is weak, and will despair at the first discouragement. But if you were to set lanterns to his path of rewards and punishments, then he would see the good from the evil, and his choices would be just.

Man of Holiness: They would also be without virtue because he would do good for the reward it would bring him, not for the love of good, and eschew evil because it would hurt him, not because he understood its ugliness and his soul was sickened by it. The path of life would divide only the foolish from the clever, not the righteous from the wicked. At the end, when judgement dawns white in the everlasting day, we would see what a man has done, but not what he is. And before I give him his place in the houses of eternity it is not his acts in the noonday, nor in the secrecy of the night, that I must prove, but the desires of his soul, because that is what he will fulfil when he holds My power in his hands, to create worlds and dominions and peoples without end.

Asmodeus: He will never do that! The dream is a travesty! Give him knowledge, a sure path. He will never be god, but he will be saved from the darkness within him.

Man of Holiness: If I save him from the darkness, then I also make the light impossible. An unknown path will test his faith. If he will begin, I shall be a guide to his feet. My arm will protect him and My spirit will go before him. As he seeks, I will give him a gift, a portion at a time. I shall bless him, and cause miracles in the bright wake of his belief in My word.

Asmodeus: After! Cause them before, and you will create his belief!

Man of Holiness: Miracles to the unbelieving create awe, and sometimes obedience, for a little space, then they are forgotten. They are reasoned away, and man forgets Me, or else he becomes superstitious and seeks after signs to prove and to test Me. That is not faith, nor is it honour, nor yet love. It is not the courage to walk the untrodden path and face the terrors of the night, because his heart has heard My voice, and will follow it forever. If he will show that trust in Me, and live by every word of My mouth, then nothing within the law of heaven is impossible. No lovely or joyous thing is beyond My power or will to give him.

Asmodeus: And beyond the laws of heaven? What then is outside your gift?

Man of Holiness: Man of holiness is My name. I am the Beginning and the End. I am God, not for My power or dominion, but because I have walked the long path and I have kept the law which is from everlasting to everlasting. Were I to break it, creation would rise up in anger and dismay, and I should cease to be God. You think it is power. You have walked and talked with Me, watched My work, seen My face, as I have seen yours, and still you do not understand. It is love . . . it has always been love.

I will not rob man of his agency to choose for himself, as I have chosen in eternities past, what he will do, and who he will become. Wickedness can never be joy. Even I cannot make it so.

Asmodeus: He will not understand that, and if you tell him, he will not believe it. He is frail, selfish, racked with terrors and delusion, easily discouraged, deceived and diverted by the moment. He cannot see further than a few days, a few years. He will always sacrifice the future for the present, the bliss of eternity for a little pleasure today. He is brief of remembrance and fragile of understanding. The weaknesses of the flesh afflict him, disease and weariness, appetites that ruin and make dark.

You have given him a body in your own image, but he will defile it! If you give him no hunger then he will wither and die. Give him desire and he will indulge it until it governs him. It will consume all other good in him. That which should sustain his life or heal his ills will become his master. He will coarsen and become gross, devouring for sensation, consuming without need. He will misuse herbs to give himself illusion so that he may escape the realities you have put there to teach him patience, endurance and compassion. He will use them to deny the pain you have put in his path so that he may learn truth and understanding.

Man of Holiness: It is part of the soul of man to hunger, as it is the greatest of his lessons to master himself. If he would become as I am, and know My joy which has no boundary in time or space, then the first and greatest step upon that journey is to harness the passions within himself and use their force for good. Without that he has no life but only a semblance of it, a fire-shadow in the darkness.

Asmodeus: Life? The power to beget life he will abuse above all the other powers you give him. He will make of that desire a dark and twisted thing to ruin and torture, to feed his hunger of the flesh and the lust for dominion which corrodes his mind. He will corrupt and pervert, distort its very nature until it grows hideous. He will call dependence, pity, even the exercise of tyranny, by the name of love. Torture of mind and body, destruction and despotism will be justified by that one word alone. More abominations will be committed in your name than in any other.

Man of Holiness: I know it, and My soul weeps. But it must be. The more sublime the good, the deeper the evil that is possible from its debasement. The corruption of love will lose more souls than any other force, and the realisation of it will redeem more, even that which had seemed lost into darkness beyond recall.

Asmodeus: It will not be. Man is riddled with doubt and ingratitude. In his ignorance and impatience he destroys what he holds. Despair walks beside him and whispers to him in the hollows of the night.

Man of Holiness: I give him weakness that he might learn humility, and out of his own failures might find gentleness and pity for others who also stumble. And in that pity he will help, and find a greater love. In his frailties, if he will look to Me, I will make him a giant, and My grace shall be sufficient for all things. I shall consecrate his griefs and his trials to him, that at the last he will know even the depth of the abyss and the heights of heaven which have no end. He will love all the workmanship of My hands, because he has walked beside it, laboured with it, laughed and wept with it, and he will cherish it, that his joy may be full, even as Mine is full.

Asmodeus: But what you give is arbitrary and unjust! You favour one above another. For some there is happiness, health of body, an abundance of treasures; for others only misery, affliction and the burden of loneliness. How can an unjust God command respect, far less love? I have heard the prayers, even of the righteous, echo unanswered in the empty caverns of the night.

Man of Holiness: No prayers are unanswered, but many answers are unheard, because man's spirit listens only to its own voice and has not learned to hear Mine. And sometimes the answer is 'no' or 'not yet', because what is asked for will not bring the happiness he imagines. I know him better than he knows himself. I give to every soul that which is necessary for it to reach the fullness of its nature, to know the bitter from the sweet, which is the purpose of this separation from Me of his mortal life. It is a brief span for an eternal need, for some too brief for happiness also. But to each is given the opportunity to learn what is needful for that soul, to strengthen what is weak, to hallow and make beautiful that which is ugly, to give time to winnow out the chaff of doubt and impatience, and fire to burn away the dross of selfishness. The chances come in many forms, and ofttimes more than once.

Asmodeus: He will see it as capricious and unfair, that you love one and hate another.

Man of Holiness: Too often he sees but a short space, and cries in the night, because he is a child. He does not see as I see, who understand him, and love him, and know the end from the beginning. It has been decreed from the birth of all things that I cannot and would not withhold any blessing when a man has fitted himself to receive it by obedience to the law upon which it rests. If I give it to him too soon he will not understand, and he will break it, or let it slip from his grasp at the moment of earning, and virtue will be swallowed up in self-interest, and the treasure will not bless, but corrupt.

Without waiting, and cost, there would no longer be the sublime gift of sacrifice, which is the greatest love. There would be only payment, the certainty of an even more precious return. It would end not in holiness, but in destitution of heart.

Asmodeus: Will you tell him of this promise? If you do, he may not believe you. If he does, he will still give, in hope of gain. And if you do not tell him, then you lie, by withholding.

Man of Holiness: I will tell him, as I tell him all things pertaining to his joy. Some will believe, and some will not. Some will give with cold hearts, conscious of their own rectitude, and with an eye to reward, and their payment is dust. But some will give because they themselves know need and have felt hunger and what it is to walk alone, and they would spare another. They understand ways of love, and I shall keep them in the hollow of My hands forever. Their names shall be upon My lips.

And others will not believe that I am, but in love they have walked My path and I have been beside them though they knew Me not. Their deeds have spoken My name, and when they see My face they shall know Me, and I shall bless them with a great blessing.

Asmodeus: You see man as you wish him to be, not as he is. Give him a religion and he will become a fanatic, a rule-keeper, a guardian of his own soul who preserves the letter of the law, and waits for the reward with open hands and a closed heart. He will persecute others in the name of the law, and understand nothing, and your name will be an excuse for lies and corruption and torture. Hypocrites will whisper it with a smile, and murder faith and hope as they do it.

Man of Holiness: I know. And if they do not repent, and learn to understand what it is they do, and if they will not then change, their path will lead to the last aloneness where I cannot follow, and the gulf between us will become everlasting. But if there is not the choice to take the downward road, then the road upward has no meaning.

Asmodeus: You know all that he needs, better than he knows himself. Why do you compel him to ask you daily?

Man of Holiness: I teach a step at a time because that is how he learns. There is a season for all things. If I gave him the greater knowledge at once he could not grasp it. Like you and like Me, he must hunger for it, and seek it, and learn by experience, in order to understand not only the nature of its beauty, but also its price. What he gains too easily he will not value, and too often he cannot hold. Time and ease seep it away from him, the first bitter wind freezes his fingers and his treasure is let go and he cannot call it back.

I do not seek gratitude for My sake, but for his. It enlarges his soul who feels it. It is a thing of joy, unclouded by arrogance or triumph. It is a bond between the giver and the given. Its sweetness lingers in the heart long after the gift is forgotten.

Asmodeus: His words are dead leaves in the wind. Gratitude writes nothing on his heart.

Man of Holiness: There are gifts which are laboured for and earned, and those which are given of grace. All men are responsible for the burden to magnify them, with wisdom and humility, and to share their fruits with all, both the loved and the unloved.

The greatest gifts of the spirit are the hardest to bear well, the gift of knowledge, of healing, of prophecy, the power to lead others and share the light. Such gifts define the path for him and he must pick them up, or lay them down. There is no middle way. Once offered, there is no choice but to accept, with all the weight he can bear; or to refuse, and close the door upon the journey forward, and sit alone in the night, having set aside forever what he might have been. All knowledge places upon him the right and the responsibility of choice. Then he must walk the path to its final step.

Asmodeus: You speak as if knowledge were there for all. It is not! Some have intelligence, keenness of mind and swiftness of understanding. Others are slow and muddled in thought. Some are tormented by unreason. Millions, like the sands of the sea, labour all their days merely to survive. Philosophy is not in their world. Again you are unjust, a respecter of persons.

Man in Holiness: Each man takes with him into life what he has chosen and laboured for here, in the creation before life. Some have already learned much and need only take the flesh upon them, and stay but briefly, even an instant, and return to Me. Some have limitations upon them, disorders of the mortal flesh which dull and confuse the mind. Others call them simple, or deranged. They need no more learning, and they are not answerable for their weakness. They, too, need no probation, but they live in order to test the patience and the compassion of others. But it is each man's choice whether he will grow or wither, take up My burden, or pass it by.

He will teach others, but before he teaches he must learn. If he lives worthily and seeks My way, I will give him words for the questioner, and answers for those who seek. He will tell in response more than he knows, even hidden things, and both will be touched by the light.

Asmodeus: You place an intolerable burden upon those to whom you answer with truth! What if it is too great for them and they cannot bear it? What if they turn aside and seek a softer path?

Man of Holiness: Those who have sought My face and to whom I have spoken as one man speaks to another, and have then turned from Me, will follow their road to its end, which is the eternal darkness, because it is where they wish to be. My heart yearns within Me, My soul grieves, the angels water heaven with their tears, but it is not in My gift to change it, even as I cannot change you. If I were to, I should cease to be God, and chaos would consume the stars. It would be the end of all things.

Asmodeus: Then when you spoke of mercy and love, it was mockery, a hideous farce of pretended light. You knew before he began that he would fail! Over and over he would fail. Sin and error will flow from him like the rivers of the firmament. You begat him for damnation!

Man of Holiness: I know he will sin, and make mistakes. He is yet learning. His life in the flesh is a journey, not an arriving. For this reason has My best beloved offered Himself to face all frailty, all pain and all darkness and loss, that the creation which surrounds us, and has kept its holy estate without strain, may grant Him the wish of His heart, which is the eternal life of all the children of My spirit and the workmanship of My hands. Thus even until the last day of judgement before Me, there may be repentance.

But repentance is more than words, and more than sorrow. It is understanding the bitter from the sweet, the light from the darkness, casting aside all sin because it is vile to the soul, and loving the light above cost or price. To repent is to change, no longer to desire that which separates from Me, which injures and cramps and withers the soul. When hunger for that change fills the heart of man, then will I give the grace and the power to accomplish it. And when it is done, I will wash the sin from all remembrance, and it will exist no more.

Asmodeus: Repentance takes time, and experience. What of those, countless as the leaves of the forest, who will have no time? What of the legions of those lost in wars and famines and pestilence?

Man of Holiness: For them I have decreed a space between the death of the flesh and the last judgement. In that time will be the teaching and the repentance of the dead. No spirit of man ever conceived shall be without knowledge and time to choose all that he will be.

Asmodeus: You ask man to live in hope, and faith in that which he cannot see. You give him nothing but words in the air!

Man of Holiness: I will never leave him alone. The night and the day are filled with the spirits of those who love him, who will speak to him in the language of his friend, and in the voice of the stranger who passes his door, whose hands will bless him and whose arms will bear him up when he is weary and broken. Hope is the gift of angels.

Asmodeus: Another gift! You have promised him all manner of gifts and powers if he obeys. If you then withhold them, you break your word. Yet if you keep it, and give him power to perform miracles, then he himself will remove the need for faith, and for the growth you hold to prize above all. The righteous will walk the earth healing the suffering. They will calm the tumult of the elements, create bread out of the dust, command war to cease, and it will do so. And you will be defeated by your own gifts.

Man of Holiness: I will give power to man only as he learns wisdom to use it, and as he understands the purpose of life. And if he misuses it, I shall take it from him again. There is no swift or easy path. The power to feed the hungry, clothe the naked, heal the sick, even to raise the dead, does not bring one soul a step closer to the fire of courage, the purity of honour or the love which is the light of the universe. If it did, then I would do it myself. Man in his frailty and his hope, his blindness and his compassion, already has all he needs to teach the truth, to heal the heart and to lead the way upward.

Asmodeus: The seeds of contradiction are in your words. If you do not give him power, he will never learn its use; if you do, then soon he will abuse it, because he will forget who gave it to him, and in the imagination of his mind he will think it is his own. He will tyrannise and oppress, because it is his nature.

Man of Holiness: Real power is to understand the difference between good and evil, to know who he is, and what he desires to be, and then to have such a passion, a hunger, that he can govern himself until he becomes what he wishes, until he has the courage, the integrity and the compassion he has glimpsed in vision. When he has strength, and can stay his hand from using it, when he trespasses on no man's agency, when he can let go of an injury and forgive, when he loves Me with a whole heart and there is no division in him, then he has real power. And in suffering oppression he will learn the fragility of freedom, and its cost. He will learn to treasure it for others as deeply as he does for himself, knowing that in the end it is the same thing.

Through pain and knowledge of what it is to sin, he will learn to forgive others, as he himself longs to be forgiven. Love is the beginning of all redemption, and no one can love with the infinite passion and tenderness, the laughter and the patience and joy that is My way, unless they first forgive.

Asmodeus: Man may forgive when he is weak, and knows his own need of mercy, but he will not see another's offence with the same eyes as he sees his own. Wait until he is strong, then it will be far different. Power is the ultimate corrosion of the soul. It is the worm in the night, grown monstrous on its own blood. In the end it will devour all else. Yet without power, he cannot go where you have gone, nor become as you are.

Man of Holiness: The probation of the flesh has many purposes, but none greater than learning to use power righteously, and none more difficult, or more dangerous or beset with as many traps and snares for the soul. He must learn to stay his hand, never to trespass on another's agency to choose, no matter how much wiser he may believe his vision to be, or how much greater his own light. He may see the path far ahead, and every precipice that hovers on the lip of the abyss, every morass that would suck a man into its bowels and consume him utterly. He may plead and teach, exhort and implore, yet he must not rob another of his right to choose for himself, good or ill.

Love does not excuse. Even I must watch and wait, because to do otherwise would begin the chain of ruin which would in the end destroy heaven itself. There must be opposition in all things; without the darkness, there is no light.

Asmodeus: Man will never understand that! He will not accept loss! It is beyond his concept of morality with its urgency, its blindness to all but the individual, and the moment. His small, finite mind cannot imagine so far! The strong will abuse the weak, most of all when they believe they love them. They will protect them unwisely, because they glory in their own strength. They will trust their own wisdom above yours. Their pride will not allow admission of error in themselves or in those of their blood or their race.

They will foster dependence, because to be needed is the ultimate dominion. They will demand obedience, because in it is the illusion of glory. Thus the weak will lean upon the strong, and both will be damned.

Man of Holiness: It is the test of the strong that they should help the weak for as long as that need exists, that their patience should never tire or grow short. They should nourish the young, the tender, the frightened and the weak until they, too, become strong, and no longer need them. To love is to desire growth, that every soul may reach the greatness of all its possibilities.

373

Asmodeus: But what of the impaired of body or mind? What of those who are not whole?

Man of Holiness: The impairment is temporary. The limping step of the cripple is to see if the swift will stay his speed and bend to lift him up, if need be forfeit victory of the racer to carry him who is maimed and weary, to guide him who is lost, and bear his burden for him. To all I will visit some weakness, in the full tide of life or in the limitations of age. I will test his humility to accept the help of others, with grace, and without anger or envy, self-pity or despair.

Asmodeus: He will rail against you when his strength fails him. Man is born to ingratitude. He will let nothing go, except you force him. You will break his fingers before he will lose his grip on what he deludes himself is his. Allow him authority over another, and then take it from him, and he will hate his successor, and he will hate you also for his pride's sake. He will imagine that to magnify another diminishes him, and that service is a lesser call.

Man of Holiness: I give him earthly power not to exercise dominion, but to minister to his fellows, and in ministering to learn those skills which he does not yet possess, each in its turn, until he has them all. And as he gains each, he must step back, and with the patience of love, and his greater skill, sustain his fellow while he too learns, and forgive him his errors.

Asmodeus: And is the earth also to forgive? Man in his arrogance will imagine himself its master. He will defile it, corrupt it in his greed and his stupidity, desecrate its beauty for his pretty gain, pollute its very life, murder and torture its creatures. Is that, too, merely experience?

Man of Holiness: The creatures of the earth are Mine also, the workmanship of My hands. In beauty have I formed them, in infinite complexity, each perfect in its sphere, and their innocence is blameless before the judgement of eternity. They have kept their order and have no sin for which to answer, and on the last day it will be well with them. Every bird that flies, every fish that inhabits the oceans and creature that runs or creeps upon the land, every flower and herb or tree of the forest from the smallest to the greatest, whether the span of its life be an hour or a millennium, not one of them is hurt without My knowledge, and My grief. I know all things, and they shall not perish from My sight.

For a space the earth is lent to man, to be under his stewardship, not in his possession, and he will answer to Me for every stick and stone of it, every leaf, every living thing upon its face, for good or ill.

Just as there are those who will ruin and destroy, so there are those who will cherish and make beautiful, those who will love and who will heal, those who will praise, and see My hand in all things.

All gifts, all wealth, whether it be of goods or of talents, of health or of intelligence, of wit or laughter or the art to create or to build, or of time itself, are a trust, to see whether they be used with generosity of heart or with meanness, with love or without it, with joy and gratitude, and humility, that he return it to Me, rich with the harvest of sharing. And I will magnify it to him into time and eternity without end.

Asmodeus: Then you have to command him in all things, because he will do nothing that does not repay his own need. He thinks only of the day, or the hour.

Man of Holiness: Man who loves, whether he seeks My face or not, will do much without command. He will always be engaged upon searching for good. The joy of others will become as dear to him as his own. He will not look upon any man's sorrow without seeking to heal it. I will instruct him in the first thing, and he will find the hundredth for himself. He will rejoice with those who win, and his heart will ache with those who lose and who mourn. Every man will be his brother.

Asmodeus: As long as all is well for him, why should he do otherwise? But what when the earth fails him? What of his care for the weak then, the burdensome, the profitless mouth when there is famine, the sick when there is plague? And there will be, because you have not removed either their foolishness or their greed from them, nor their ability to destroy. Neither have you taken My power from the world. I can still spread rumour with My word and My breath. I can sow hatred and whisper lies, and I can reap the last grain of destruction. I can cover the face of the earth with war until the armies of humanity have drowned the soil with blood, or with disease and deformity in the noonday, and madness in the night, until a man knows not the face of his brother, and the flesh rots from his bones. I can corrupt nations in the light of the sun, and lead them open-eyed to the grave. And I will! My promise is as sure as yours!

Man of Holiness: I have known you from the birth of time. You too are My son, and I will not take the right to choose even from you. You will be what you wish to be, and the everlasting recompense for that will be yours, as it will be all men's, and has been from the beginning.

Asmodeus: You have not answered Me! What of man then, in the day of My power, when his world has crashed about his ears and there is death and despair on every side?

Man of Holiness: In tribulation he will find his greatest strength and his utmost nobility. When he is persecuted there will be those who will bear it with patience, and without hatred, self-pity or vengeance. There will be those in flight from a monstrous foe, who will still return to the very jaws of destruction to rescue the weaker and the slower, though they know him not, who will comfort the terrified and the grieving without thought of self. When there is starvation there will be those who will give their last morsel to feed the stranger, or nurse the dying, though the plague afflict them also. Where there is tyranny and war there will be those who will offer their own lives for their fellows, and who will look even upon your face rather than deny the good they believe. They will sacrifice all they possess for love of the light they have seen. And those are they who in eternity I shall take to My heart and all things shall be theirs, even My glory. They shall see the light of the worlds like the risen sun upon the dew of the grass. The heavens shall be before them and they shall understand and be filled with that shining peace which has no end, and the joy which is the everlasting laughter of the stars.

Asmodeus: And what of the others, those lost millions who do not seek the heights of courage and sacrifice? Have you no pity, no love for them?

Man of Holiness: For each one there shall be the glory he can abide, the kingdom and the dominion whose laws he is able and wills to keep. In any more, or less, he would find no peace. It can be no other way. When a man leaves his tabernacle of clay for a space, and then at the last is made complete again with a perfect flesh, never more to be divided, he carries with him nothing but the wisdom he has gained, and the nature and desires of his heart. Experience shall make him whole, for good or ill, and that is his treasure, the sum of what he is, which shall never be taken from him.

Asmodeus: Where is the proof for him? You have left in the world no evidence that cannot be disputed a hundred ways. You ask him to walk an unknown path, with belief rooted in no more than hunger and hope, a shred of meaning, the cry in the night of a watchman on a tower he cannot see. No echo is left from the time before the veil was drawn over his soul. He will not do it.

Man of Holiness: No man can give to another his faith. It is learned little by little, by accepting the small things, putting to the test one principle at a time. Nourish it with courage, and hope, and it will grow until it has the power to divide oceans, or create bread out of ashes, or any other thing that is wisdom in Me. I shall never fall short, nor give less, until faith shall become knowledge.

But more blessed is he who trusts Me when he has not yet seen, but walks by faith, and with courage. From the first stumbling beginning until that day when he walks upright beside Me and needs no command because he sees all things, I shall ask of him nothing whatsoever, except it be for his eternal good. But he must have the white fire of courage, which defies even the darkness of the pit. It is that virtue without which all others, even love itself, may in the end be lost.

Asmodeus: So much is wasted in your economy. Man is proud, rebellious, and full of doubts, like shadows in the wind, and disobedient to the core. Everywhere he will see waste, and pain, futile effort, hope destroyed and trust betrayed. Weariness and disillusion is the common path. Your prize is for the few. Mine would have been for all!

You are bound by the very laws which make you God to allow man his choice! Then let him choose between My plan and yours! See if he will not take mine, with the lesser reward – and the lesser risk! Not one will perish or lose that which should be his. And the hosts which follow Me shall be mine forever!

Man of Holiness: No good or lovely thing will be lost to those who keep My law and who have loved Me with a whole heart. To no one is My glory impossible. Every man is My child, with My image graven upon his soul. But many will not choose Me, and if they choose you, then they are yours to have and to hold forever. The morning that he was born of My spirit, I gave him his freedom.

Asmodeus: That was your first and great mistake. On that rests all the others. He is a flawed creature and will never be what you want him to be. He will always betray you in the end.

Man of Holiness: He is My child, even as you are, and I have taken all into reckoning. My purpose cannot be frustrated. I am God, and from the beginning have I known the end.

Asmodeus: The end will be war, and the abomination of destruction! Ruin will cover the face of the earth as the waters cover the sea. When that time comes there will be no more middle ground, no safety for the heart or mind or body, and in terror and despair man will choose Me!

Man of Holiness: There never was middle ground, only for a space of sunlight was there the illusion of it, while the thunder of guns was far away. But out of that desolation I will create a new earth, and those who have chosen Me I will welcome home, and they shall be before My face forever. They shall never again taste fear nor stand alone, and they shall know Me as a man knows his father, and together we shall dance to the music of eternity.

Asmodeus: But why? Why all these aeons of labour and pain, all this waiting and yearning, the making and toiling of worlds, the hope and the failure, the disappointment and the agony of pity, all for a creature who is worthy of nothing? A firefly on the winds of darkness.

Man of Holiness: You do not understand. It is because I love him.

Asmodeus: Is that all?

Man of Holiness: That is all. It is the light which cannot fade, the life which is endless. I am God, and Love is the name of My soul.